OF BLOOD AND IRON

JAMIE BRINDLE

Edited by
DEVON STRAYER

Jamie Brindle

To Wolf People, whose music I listened to incessantly while writing much of the first draft of this story.

CONTENTS

ACKNOWLEDGMENTS

Many thanks are due to Devon Strayer for sterling editorial work. Several arcs and sub-stories were not included in the first draft, and only came into being after suggestions from Devon. Any faults that remain are, of course, my own.

Thanks are also due to the table which broke my back by being lifted awkwardly, and to the weeks of post-surgical recovery which allowed me the time to write this novel. What a painful way to win the time to write.

FREE NOVELLA!

For news, updates, offers and FREE stories, be sure to sign up
to my newsletter at
www.jamiebrindle.com
You will also receive a FREE copy of my novella, 'All Quiet In
The Western Fold', which is a prequel - of sorts - to this novel.

❧ I ❧

THE DEEP DARKNESS

~

There is a deep darkness in a place under the earth, and the village above it is cursed.

The crops are poor, and what does grow is stunted. The well holds bad water, thick and cloudy and sour; and in time, the people become cloudy and sour, too.

"It wasn't always like this," Old Nan tells the children, ever so many children, with their big eyes and thin faces, arms like sticks and feet covered in dust.

The children do not believe her, but they are here to hear tales, so they wait for her to go on.

Outside, the rain is coming down. How can it always be raining, and yet the fields are full of dust? No one knows the answer, not even Old Nan, so it's best not to ask the question.

"Once, this was not a bad place," she says at last, her three remaining teeth glinting yellow in the flickering firelight. "This was a good village, a happy-on-the-hill village, a sunshine and apples and laughter village. Do you know, you little heathens, that this very village, in this very hut, in *this very room*, was where the very first falling into love happened?"

Back and forth the children glance, but not one makes a sound.

"I thought not," says Old Nan at length, and settling back in her chair she lays them out the story, and lays it out like this:

❦ 2 ❧

THE GREATEST REUNION

~

"Once upon a time," (says Old Nan) is a very fine way to
start a story, but that is *not* the way this story starts,
because this story starts back before they had time.
In those days, everything happened all at once or not at all, which
sounds confusing, but the people who lived there were used to it, and
so they managed very nicely.

There were no days and no nights, no Spring before Summer, no
Autumn to sweep the falling leaves to Winter. It was never too cold or
too hot, there was always enough to eat, and no one ever got old, and
no one ever died.

Now.

Back then, in this very village, in this very hut, *in this very room*,
there lived a girl. And it was right here that there was once the site of
the greatest reunion that ever was. It's a long story, I warn you, so you
must be patient.

No, David, she was not a *young* girl, and do you know why? That's
right: because there was no time. How can a girl be young when there
isn't any time passing to take the measure of?

She was not young, and she was not old.

She was just a girl, and she had straight hair and a crooked nature and she made her home right here.

Now this girl, she lived a sorry sort of life, let me tell you.

Why? I'm coming to that.

First of all, she had no friends. Oh, people knew her, alright; they knew enough to stay away...until they couldn't stay away. But you'll see why soon enough.

Second of all, she had no face. Oh, I don't mean she was ugly: ugly isn't the word. I mean she had no face at all, just pale skin where her face should be, with thin skin over the hollows of her eyes, and red skin over the hole of her mouth, and two little flaps of skin where her nostrils should be.

And third of all, she had the curse of utter understanding, and that was what was worst.

Now let me be quite clear, because I see some puzzled looks here about me.

Understanding can be a terrible thing, do not doubt it for a moment. This girl had the curse of understanding, and she never was wrong. She just had to glance, and she would know.

And *do* you think that would be such a fine thing now little Lucy, with your hair so gold and your head full of dreams? I'll tell you now, it was *not*.

People would come from far and wide to speak to our girl, and she didn't turn a one away.

They would shuffle in and sit before her, and our girl would glance at them, and understand them in an instant, understand them utterly, understand them so much better than they would ever understand themselves.

She never wanted to tell them, but they always wanted to know.

They insisted.

Because even back then, back before days and nights and death and hunger, back when the world was so young that it did not know what time was for or how to make use of it, even back then the one thing that people yearned for was to understand themselves.

Our girl would tell them, and no one ever left satisfied.

And so, of course, she never had any friends.

Oh, how she wanted a friend!

Now it came to pass that there was a man. And this man was a prince, only his kingdom was lost. It was an island kingdom, and it had been washed all away when there was a very great storm. This prince had been visiting some very princely friends of his far off and away and further far again. So when this prince came to return to his kingdom, it was nowhere at all to be found.

What was his name?

This was before names, child, didn't I tell you that? No? Well, it was before names.

But I'll give you a name for him, as you asked so kind. People think that names are free, but they're not. Names have value, and that's why you should value it when someone gives you theirs, and why you shouldn't give your true name out for free to just anyone.

This prince, his name was Valiben.

Stop interrupting, I'll come to what he looked like!

Valiben could not understand what had happened to him or why. He could not understand where his kingdom had gone, or what he was supposed to do to find it again. All in all, he was lost, and he wanted very much to be found.

On his wandering way, although he never found any word nor rumour of his kingdom, he *did* begin to hear murmurings of a certain girl who had inherited from somewhere the curse of utter understanding. And so it was that he made up his mind to seek her out.

Valiben came to our girl. Do you know where he found her?

That's right: in this very village, in this very hut, in *this very room*.

And our girl understood at once exactly what he looked like. Of course she did. How could it be otherwise?

He had been tall, but the road had been long, and his back had bent with every step.

He had been fair, but the wind had been rough, and his skin had chapped with every gust.

And his eyes had been as pale blue as crystal, and blue as crystal they still were, for some things are not worn away.

"Who are you?" whispered our girl, though she understood who Valiben was oh so very well.

I'll tell you how she spoke when her mouth was covered over with skin, John: she spoke very softly, and the red skin that covered her mouth fluttered like a broken butterfly, and you had to strain to hear her. Would that have filled you with disgust young Daisy, with your straight-standing ways and your pretty face? Don't lie to me child: it would have disgusted you, I know. It would have disgusted you, and it disgusted Valiben, too.

But he was no craven, not our Valiben. He had come this far, why not a little further?

"I am Prince Valiben of the Lost Kingdom," declared the prince. "And if you are the girl I've been looking for, you know why I have come."

Our girl nodded at him.

She knew, oh she knew.

Valiben sighed, and tears sprang up in his eyes.

"Then will you tell me?" he asked her. "Tell me what I have come all this way to understand?"

Our girl cocked her head at him, and her teeth moved under the skin that shouldn't have been there, and Valiben realised that the girl was smiling at him.

"There is a price," she whispered, and Valiben felt cold.

But he squared his shoulders and, "Name it!" he said, because that is the sort of thing princes are supposed to say, even lost ones, and no one ever found a kingdom by being coy.

Our girl stretched her jaw and the skin over her mouth pulsed very fast, like a breaking heart, and Valiben realised the girl was laughing at him.

"I never shared my understanding with any but the common folk before now," our girl breathed at him, and he strained hard to hear her whispers. "And they paid but one price, and that price was the truths I told them. But you are a prince, and princes should pay more than the common folk.

"You will start with the first price, the price of truth, which I have already mentioned, and which you will pay the same as any other.

"You will add to that a single true smile, which you must win for my face, and that is a wondrous rare thing.

"And if you manage that, then you must pay the final price, which you will not like at all, and which you will never agree to pay, so you may as well leave now."

But Valiben would not turn back, because when you are as lost as he was you may as well keep going forward as back, and any one direction is exactly as promising as any other.

"If you are cursed with understanding as I have heard, then you know already that that is not true, because I will never give up, and I will pay any price to find my home again," said Valiben.

And our girl, she nodded at him, slow and solemn.

"You are very stubborn, I understand *that*," she declared. "But you shouldn't be so quick to say you will pay *any price* without first understanding the terms."

Valiben scoffed at that.

"I am a prince!" he told her. "And no price is beyond my means. Do you want your weight in silver and sapphires? Just say so, and it will be yours! Would you prefer a little island somewhere to call your home, far away from all this dust and drizzle? Tell me, for there is no lack of small, beautiful islands in my kingdom. Or maybe you want servants, one hundred long-limbed servants to wait on you hand and foot, and tend to your every need? My people would all die for me, and they number in the hundreds of thousands. If it's servants you want, all you have to do is ask."

But the wind blew outside and our girl was quiet, and the prince felt very alone in the silence.

Finally, she shook her head at him.

"Oh, my dear," she told him sadly. "My price is none of those fine and fancy things. What would I do with silver, or an island, or a servant, or one hundred servants? I would still be rich and alone, or isolated and alone, or well-tended, but alone."

Yes, Susan, the prince was growing tired of our girl, too, and he said so!

"Well, if none of these things will do, will you not tell me your price?" asked the prince, and his voice was growing raw.

Our girl was silent. Still as stone. Then slowly, very slowly, she tilted her hole-less head to one side.

"Come closer," she whispered.

The prince came forward, hesitated, then stopped.

He could see the pale orbs of her lightless eyes moving under her skin.

"Closer," she said.

He came closer still, and now he could see the little purple veins that criss-crossed the red skin that grew over the space where her mouth should have been.

"Just a little closer," he fancied he heard her say, though he could not be sure, the words were so quiet.

But closer he came, and now he could see the little flaps of skin that covered her nose and her ears, and he wondered how she heard, and he wondered how she breathed.

"Close enough," she said, and she leaned forward, nearer and nearer still, until their foreheads were touching, and the prince could feel the damp warmth of her burning like a fever in his flesh.

"This is the price you will pay," she told him, and the words were so quiet he would have been certain he was imagining them, except that he could feel the vibration of the sounds through the touching of their skulls. "I understand you. I understand everything you were, everything you are, everything you may yet become. I understand your heart and I understand your mind. You cannot take a breath without me understanding the meaning that has to every fibre of your body, and you cannot take a step without me understanding every step you have already taken, and every step you may yet take. Now you must understand this about me: I am lonely.

"I am lonely, so lonely.

"I have no friends. I have no one.

"So my price is this: I will share with you my understanding of where your kingdom is, and I'll even let you understand *why* you lost it. But in return you must find me a companion. In return you must cure me of my solitude."

And oh my, how our prince sighed a sigh of relief! Such a great sigh it was, if you go to stand on the brow of the hill overlooking the mill, Jason, you can still hear the echo of that sigh, even to this very day!

A price of this sort means nothing to a prince as charming as Valiben, let me tell you.

So the prince flashed his most princely smile, and he said:

"My lady, your plight moves me! But let me pledge to you now, *I* will be your friend! *I* will talk to you, and *I* will share your life, and *I* will make sure you are never lonely again!"

And our girl, she said, "No."

Are you so disappointed there, little Geoffrey? Why? Oh, you didn't think that *they* would fall in love, did you? Things don't work out so neat as they do in the stories. Yes, I know very well that *this* is a story, too, Jessica; but this is *my* story, and I am the one telling it, and if you don't like it, maybe you can tell it different when you are old and withered as a an oak-root, sitting round a fire with a gaggle of ungrateful little heathens!

Shall we go on?

You all promise to be *quite* quiet?

Very well then.

So, "No," said our girl, and the prince looked like he might cry.

"No?" he asked, in a very small voice.

"No," repeated our girl.

Now you have to understand, my little beloveds, that 'no' is not a word that princes are used to hearing. They almost don't know what it means. And add to that the fact that what the prince was offering was himself, and I'm sure you will realise that what the prince was feeling was:

"I'm not good enough, you mean."

He said it flatly, and it looked as if all the fizz and flavour had gone out of him.

Now our girl was a lot of things, and she caused a lot of people a lot of hurt.

But she was not cruel, and you must never think that of her.

"You are a very good prince, and no one could understand that better than I," she told him, and he looked up at her earnestly, as if he could read the truth of her words in the unbroken smoothness of her skin. "But I could never find friendship with someone who I understand as well as you. For friendship there must be equality, and you could never understand me as well as I understand you, not if I talked for the rest of forever and you were here to listen. No. The friend I need is...one who I cannot understand. *That* is the person you must find for me; and when you bring them here, and present them to me, and when I have my friend, that is when you shall understand where your kingdom is, and why it was lost to you."

And Valiben understood.

He kissed her hand – for this is something princes do to ladies, even faceless ones – and he bowed to her, which is also something princes do, and he left this very room, this very hut, this very *village*, and he went upon his way. But now his wanderings had a meaning. Now he had a purpose.

He must find a friend for our girl: a friend that she was incapable of understanding; that was what she had asked for. That was what he would find her.

Now it came to pass that after travelling for so long that he had worn out three pairs of shoes and six pairs of socks and twelve pairs of laces, that Valiben came to a...

Hush!

No, listen, you heathens, *listen*!

Can't you hear it? It's the bell!

Oh, I suppose it means the men are back from their hunting.

Yes, Heather, you can go and see what they caught, and get in their way, and miss the end of the story...or you can not be a rude little girl, and wait here, and listen patiently, and not be a nuisance.

You'll go, will you? Fine. It's all the same to me.

Anyway, the prince came to a river, and by the river was a tree on a little hillock, and the day was so hot, and the shade under the tree seemed so cool, and the moss down there looked so soft and inviting, that Valiben decided to sit down and rest. He undid his twelfth pair of laces and slipped off his third pair of shoes, and he took off his heavy pack that was filled with cured meats and travel-cheeses and all sorts of other good things to eat. Then he leant back with one arm over his eyes and tried to get some sleep.

He was just drifting off, when he fancied he heard a little voice, calling out for help.

He started up and looked all around, but he could see very far from the hillock, and there was no-one at all to be seen.

"Strange," he said to himself. "Well, I must have been dreaming."

So he laid back down, and squirmed about until he was comfortable, and he was just starting to doze again when...

"Help!"

This time Valiben jumped up very quick and smart, and peered all around in every direction; and when that was no good, he looked suspiciously at the tree, and even climbed a little way up the big, broad branches. But there was certainly no one there.

"Harrumph!" he snorted to himself. "This is no good! My mind is playing tricks on me!"

And he plucked up some strands of grass and shoved them in his ears to keep the worrisome world at bay, and *no* young Robert, I *do not* think that is something you should take to doing, thank you so very much. No, not *even* if your brother snores.

Anyway, he lay back down and tried once more to go to sleep, and he had almost managed it too, when this time there was a great big

SPLASH

and a splattering of cold water landed on his face, and, "Help!" cried the voice again, so loud and real that it was impossible to ignore.

Valiben shot to his feet and tugged the grass out of his ears, and he went to the side of the river, and *there* was the creature that had been making all this noise.

Now the river down below him flowed very fast and strong, and it was very blue, and it was *very* deep. But a little way from the main river, separated by a narrow strand of sandy mud and muddy sand, a tiny, temporary pond had formed, where a small amount of river water had become trapped and was slowly leeching back into the main flow. And in this little pond, looking rather desperate and afraid, there was a single fish, bright blue as a clear sky, and as big as a sheep.

"Help me!" gurgled the fish, and it jumped out of the water again, and landed with a splash.

And even as he watched, a little more of the water drained away from the pond and back into the river, and now the head of the fish was barely covered.

"Hello there," said Valiben. "My name is Valiben -well, *Prince* Valiben, actually – I'm on a bit of a quest, you might say, I'm trying to find..."

"Yes, yes, very good," glugged the fish. "I am so charmed to meet you, and I'm sure we can exchange pleasantries and titles later. But the problem is, you see, that I am in rather a pickle..."

And even as the fish spoke, another gush of water broke away from the pond, and ran back into the river, and now the head of the fish was poking into the air, and his gills were getting dry.

"Oh! Right!" said Valiben. "Yes, of course! Rather stupid of me, sorry."

But the fish shook its big fishy head and smacked its pouting blue lips and said, "Tush! Please don't mention it! The last thing in the world I'd want is to make you feel bad. You look like a decent sort, and I'm sure you wouldn't leave me here to drown on dry land. In fact, I must say you remind me rather..."

But at that moment a chunk of sandy mud – or maybe it was muddy sand, I never can remember – broke away from the bank, and with a great gush, the last of the water rushed out of the pond, and back into the river.

"..." gasped the fish, choking and bubbling in the air.

Valiben dashed forward and grabbed the fish, and hauled with all his might. If the fish had kept still, it may be he would have managed it quite easily, because he was very strong, after all.

But a poor fish has a terrible time trying keep still when it's out of the water, and what with the flapping and the writhing, the flipping and the squirming, it seemed to Valiben that he would never manage to reach the river.

At last, however, he gave a great *heave,* and with a splash that sent water flying into the sky, they were suddenly both in the deep of the river.

The current grabbed hold of Valiben. It was strong as a herd of horses, and tipped him end over end, and rushed him onwards, faster, faster, faster, until he couldn't tell up from down, and he was far underwater, and the air in his lungs was running out.

Suddenly, he came up sharp against a great solid something, with the water breaking against him in a rushing torrent; and after a moment he got his bearings, and heaving upwards, he broke the surface.

The big blue fish had thrust its body in front of him, and was holding them steady against the wondrous strong surge of the river.

"There we go!" gurgled the fish happily. "Well done and thank you! You helped me out there and no mistake!"

"Please, think nothing of it," gasped Valiben humbly (he was a strong believer in the humbleness of princes, you see) "Anyone would have done the same."

"Now that's where you're wrong!" the fish told him. "You're the third traveller to pass this way. The first man was the monk who got me stranded in the first place, trying to poach me for his dinner. The second was a drunk who ignored me. You were the one who thought to help. My name is Maxwell, by the way."

Valiben shook the fish by his tail, and they exchanged full names and family histories, and presently discovered that their ancestors had once met and been friends back in the days before Valiben's kingdom had been lost, and after that they realised that they were both going in the same direction, and so why not go together?

So go together they did, Maxwell swimming down the river and Valiben clinging on his side, and the banks gliding by faster than ever feet could have carried him.

"Now as I was saying earlier, you rather remind me of someone," said the fish. "And that someone was me. It was back when I was only a young fishling, far off and away and further far again..."

And with that he settled into telling Valiben about

3

THE NOBLE VAGABOND

～

W hen I was a young fishling, I was immensely rich. That wealth came from my mother, of course, though how she got it is quite another story. Anyway, I was set on travelling the world, and because I wanted to see more than the underside of lakes, I commissioned a special clockwork engine that would allow me to travel on land.

Oh, you should have seen it! It was a wonderful thing! It consisted of three large tanks (one filled with freshwater, one with seawater, and one with mud, because I was used to the finer things in life, and only low-born minnows can stand the tedium of existing in one type of water), all mounted on a most complicated arrangement of belts and pulleys and heavy clunking wheels. And the best thing was, all I had to do was turn a little handle with my mouth, and that would keep the clockwork wound nice and tight, and then I could go exploring all over the land, however I saw fit.

I travelled far and wide, and after not too long I began to get a bit of a reputation. The Noble Vagabond, they called me, on account of my high birth and wandering ways, and young ladies of rank used to be falling over one another for the honour of hosting me at their castles.

Now it came to pass that one evening I had set out from here and not quite made it to there, as it were, and the night was creeping in and the road was getting dark, and all of a sudden I found my way blocked by three very large and very ugly bandit-women, all covered in filth and armed to the teeth.

"Give us your gold!" they demanded. "Or we'll smash that pretty tank of yours, and we'll see how you like breathing our clean, fresh air!"

Now I gladly would have given them anything they desired, but the problem was I simply didn't have any gold on me. Not a nugget. I had loaned all my travelling-monies to a friend of mine who I had helped out of a sticky spot, though that is also another story.

When I said as much to the women, the first snarled like a hippo and struck the freshwater tank a terrible blow. The glass shattered, and the water poured away, and I was only just in time in darting into the second chamber.

"Very well," the next said. "Give us your sapphires, for we know how fond you fishlings are of your jewels!"

"My dear ladies," said I (though they were anything but dear, and not ladies by any stretch of the imagination). "My dear ladies, I would of course give you all the jewels I possess, but as I'm sure you will have heard, sapphires are the most beloved stones of my mother, the Queen of the Fish, and none of us are permitted to take a single one from the fishy kingdom. It is simply not done."

All this was true, but not at all to the liking of these three fearsome women, as I'm sure you can understand. This second bandit-woman shrieked like an eagle and swung her boot into the saltwater tank, and it shattered into a million pieces. Once again, I was only just in time getting away.

Now I was in the final tank, the tank filled with mud, and I sensed that things really were getting rather desperate.

"Wait!" I cried, "I haven't any gold or jewels, I swear it! But there must be something I can give you – just give me a moment to think, won't you?"

It was the third bandit-woman who answered me, and she really was a horror.

She was big as bear, with shaggy red hair and a hair lip and a lisp.

"You mith noth hath gold or jewlth, my fithy friendth," she said, "but you hath thomething far morth valublth: your handth in marrigth!"

And with that they plucked my mud tank off the top of my clockwork engine, and made off with me across the moors to a secret place hidden in the dankness and moss, a run-down town populated by thieves and broken creatures, and quite, quite awful.

They took me to their priest – all towns have priests, priests of half a thousand gods, as many gods as there are towns, though broken towns have broken priests – and paid him in stolen coins, and asked him to perform the service.

Now as was the way in those parts, the ceremony was to be performed at dawn, as the first light of the new sun broke above the swamp, and melted away the thickest strands of the stinking mist.

The bride-to-be shuffled away to get ready, and this left me with a good two hours before dawn with which to work on the makeshift priest.

I tried promising him all sorts of things if only he would help spirit me away, but he was a bitter little fellow, and he didn't trust me. He wouldn't speak to me, at first. He whistled a dire tune under his breath, and kept his eyes hooded. After an hour, I had talked almost non-stop, and was still none the closer to securing my escape. I was running out of things to offer, and was beginning to feel that my cause was rather lost. Pretty soon, I had nothing left to say, and I grew quiet.

The town was very still and sleepy by now. It was the hour before dawn, and it seemed as if the whole world was holding its breath.

"Have you quite finished your whining?" asked the priest at last.

I was so shocked that he was actually talking to me at last that I couldn't even reply.

"Oh, you think you're in such a terrible tight spot, don't you?" he sneered at me. "But listen! You've lived a good life. You've been lucky. You've had money, you've been loved, you've travelled all around these parts, and seen much of the world. And even when this morning is done and you're a married fish, you think things will be so bad? Of course they won't! You'll still have money (though maybe less of it) and you'll still be loved (though maybe your pride will take a knock), and you'll still be able to do whatever you want. Me, on the other hand? Well, it hardly bears talking about..."

"What on earth do you mean by that?" I asked the priest, eager to keep him talking.

"Oh, my story's a sad one, make no mistake!" he told me, and spat into the shadows.

I hardly saw how it could be any more desperate than mine, and told him as much.

"Listen, your story is sun and roses compared to mine!" said the priest, and his words were darkness and thorns. "Humph. Seeing as how we have a little time before your wedding, I'll tell you. Maybe then you'll understand how lucky you are."

And he leant forward, and set about telling me of

❊ 4 ❊

THE BANISHMENT

~

I wasn't always a broken priest. Once I was respected and renowned. I lived in a village far off away and further far again. My father had been the priest before me, and his father before him, and so on back and back and back as far as anyone could remember. Now, when I was a young man, the village had flourished and done well for itself, and the people were happy and sound. But it came to pass, as I grew older, that something had gone awry, and something had gone sour, and things in the village began to turn. No one knew why this had happened. The common people didn't understand it, and when their crops failed they looked to the chief. The chief was a good man in his way, but he was a leader of men, and what did he understand of curses? So when the villagers looked to him, the chief looked to me.

Oh, I had ideas, alright. I tried everything I could think of. I prayed, and I burnt pyres; I went to the sacred well and tended the sacred tree with sacred water; I even cut myself and offered up my blood, as I had heard was the custom amongst priests who lived in the lands beyond the sunset. But the curse ran deep, and nothing I tried seemed to work.

I even tried to use my whistle, the whistle my dead wife had taught me. That was a beautiful thing, my wife's whistle; and it worked every time I used it, it worked to help people and heal people and blow the dark things away. But it did not help me this time. Oh no, there was something black at work, and my whistle would not touch it.

The people grew restless and hateful. Who is this priest of ours, they asked one another, who cannot help us in our need? Perhaps he is no kind of priest at all. Perhaps we had better find another.

And at about this time, as if by magic or devilry or something in between, a woman appeared in the village. She came from somewhere and told us she was on her way to somewhere else, but the days passed and she never seemed to show any sign of leaving. She was tall and thin and very beautiful. The women did not trust her, but the men, she had them under her spell, and they would not hear a word against her.

There began to be whisperings that she was a kind of priest, too; only sharper, more cruel, hard and powerful and suited to the darkness that the village found itself in. It was said that she had the power to undo the curse, if only we were willing to pay the price.

But what was the price? Even those who whispered were reluctant to say. I knew, though. A few of the old ones, they knew too, and they took to keeping the children safe, to locking them away, especially at night, and especially when the thin woman took to walking amongst the men, speaking of things of which she had no right, and bending their minds under hers.

I opposed her while I could, but all things fail at last.

The crops failed, the well failed, the goodness in our hearts and our smiles and the scents of summer, they all failed. At last, all we had left to us was the hunt, but the animals of the forest had grown scarce and flighty, and soon the hunt began to fail, too.

Starving people are desperate people. None are easier to control.

I told them that if we could but hang on a little longer, soon the tide would turn. The hunt would begin to flourish again, and then all our lost luck would come back.

But I was wrong.

I thought the children were safe when the hunt returned, under lock and key and the spell of stories; but when the bells sounded to let us know another expedition had failed, one child was *not* content to wait, and out she came running.

Heather, my own sweet girl-child, with red cheeks and hair that smelt of newly cut grass, she heard the bells, and she would not be halted.

The thin woman was waiting, gaunt as a carrion-bird, and she swept down in all her awful beauty, and grasped my Heather, and danced her round the green, while all the while the men-folk clapped their hands and made wild noises, and laid a pyre very high.

"Where are your friends?" the thin woman asked Heather. "Bring out your friends, and we shall all dance together!"

But Heather shook her head and cried and didn't say a word. She reached for me, but a hundred hands held me back. She screamed for me, but a hundred hands smothered my mouth, and I could not scream for her.

The other children did not come. Stories held them still, held them steeped and safe, though they could not hold *my* girl, and for this reason I hate stories more than I hate any man, more than I hate this thin woman, even. I tell you this story out of hate. If I could break all the stories that ever were, that is what I would do.

They took her to the pyre. She looked so small against the vastness of the flames and the endless black of the smoke.

I tried to close my eyes, but they made me watch.

Dawn came, and rain came with it, and the people rejoiced to drink the water, though all it tasted of was the ceaseless grey ash that rose from the pyre. It covered the village until it looked as if winter had come early, as if all the land was coated in dirty snow.

Then the thin woman had me brought before her and she saw that my heart was broken, and *this* was what she wanted. She reached a claw into my chest and she tore my heart in half. Then she took half for herself, and grew stronger. She left me the other half, but half-hearts are poisoned. They want for balance. Leaving a man half his heart is crueler than taking the whole thing.

I was turned out of the village. The thin woman laughed; and even as I walked away, I could hear the villagers muttering that perhaps one child was not enough, and what would they do if it turned out the whole of the curse was not broken, after all?

But I no longer had the heart to care.

The world is wide, and full of sorrow.

My heart had no room for sorrows, anymore. All my heart had room for now was hate.

Stories had failed to protect my Heather. Stories would pay for my loss.

One day I met an old man on the road. He liked stories. He tried to tell me about

5

THE WHISPERING FOUNTAIN

⁓

Wʜen I was a boy, there was nothing I liked better than going for long walks in the ancient forest that marked the border of our little village. Sometimes one or other of my friends would come with me, but more often I would go alone. The trees were tall and broad, and the air there was still and warm. Little paths sprang up out of nowhere and disappeared while you were half way through using them. Now, it came to pass that one day arghh! Arghh! *Arghh!*

🪷 6 🪷

THE BANISHMENT (REPRISE)

⁓

That old man quickly learnt that I was not so fond of stories, and I never had to hear what happened in that one. His death was exceedingly noisy, but his screams were much more soothing to my ears than his stories. I hope no one else alive knows his story. I hope that it died with him. You cannot trust stories.

In any case.

I began to make it my business to hunt down and destroy stories. After all, it was the stories that the thin woman had spun that had made the villagers burn my Heather. And the stories of our own had done nothing to save her, even though they kept all the other children safe. It was apparent to me that stories were the enemies of my bloodline. Just as some families have a natural antipathy for dogs, say, or the feline species, so my blood is by nature set in opposition to story.

Many fewer stories now walk the earth than when I started; fewer still will be abroad when I am done.

Now after some long span of wanderings and going about my works, it struck me that although I was to some degree achieving my aim, it was in a most disordered and haphazard way. There was no organisation to my technique, no systematisation, and very little in the way of tactics.

So I decided that if I were to defeat my enemy, the best way I could achieve this was by *knowing* my enemy. To this end, I made it my business to study the great stories of the last four ages of the world. For a time, I toyed with going further back, but when you go as far back as five ages ago, the stories begin to become strange and unworkable. They do not hang together in the way latter creatures such as you or I would understand. Perhaps the people then were very different to the type we have today. In any case, I decided four ages was as far back as I needed to go.

I made one exception to this rule, and that was when I found a horrible little stump of a woman, who was able to tell me

7

THE OLDEST STORY

~

This is the story of the beginning (she began), and so you shouldn't go looking for endings here.

In the beginning there was. Was what? Just was.

There was and there was and there was, all sorts of was, all kinds and colours and kins of was.

So much was there was, that the whole was was terribly confused.

(This was before wasn't, you understand, and every possible thing was).

There was so much was, that something had to be done about it, and so it came to pass that ninety-nine was out of every hundred decided, all at once and forever, to become a wasn't.

Things were much more comfortable after this, but there was still too much was, far too much.

So again, ninety-nine was out of every hundred remaining was flipped over inside itself and became a wasn't.

I don't know where they went. Maybe they started being wasn'ts here the moment they became wases somewhere else. In any case, it wasn't our problem anymore, and that's the important thing.

Now. If you can imagine, we're still at the beginning, just a little bit further in, and now there's enough space to make sense of what there actually *was* there, without things getting too crowded.

In the almost-beginning, there was a flatness, and on the flatness lived The People.

I don't know where they came from. I suppose they were just one type of *was* that didn't become a *wasn't*. Just chance, I suppose. If the whole thing was run again, maybe it would be different.

The People were alone in the darkness. The nights were cold and vast. Their bodies were small and delicate and finite. The rest of everything was endless.

Can you imagine their terror? To awake from the dark of nothing to the utter awareness of being? To the sudden awful aloneness?

How do you think they coped? They told one another stories.

"We are the seeds of a giant egg," they told one another.

"This great flatness is the back of a huge turtle," they said (turtles were one of the things that had stayed being a *was*).

"We are the imagination of the Universe," they whispered, as they sat around their flickering fires, and fought to keep the darkness at bay.

Did they believe their own stories? Maybe not at first. But the more they told them, the more likely they seemed. Before very long, it was *obvious* that the Sun was the amorous Flaming Man who chased the chaste Pale Lady endlessly around the Egg of the World. It was *obvious* that the oceans were the great mass of amniotic fluid that sprawled out when the Earth was delivered. It was *obvious* that the mountains were the facial stubble of the great Father who slept under the earth.

So many things were simply *obvious*. They must be true. Everybody said so.

Now it came to pass that one day there was a boy who simply did not find the stories good enough. His name was Sate.

"Yes, but how do you *know* the sun is actually a flaming man?" he would ask. "*Why* do you think the oceans are the birthing fluids?"

"They just *are*!" sniffed the elders. "Now stop worrying, and get on with things!"

But things would not be got on with, at least as far as Sate was concerned.

In fact, they got worse.

"How do I know that I'm really real, even?" Sate asked himself. "Maybe I'm not really anything at all. I only think I'm real because people have told me I'm real, because people treat me as if I'm real. Maybe I'm nothing. Maybe I'm just a story too, a story being told by an old woman to pass the time and help make sense of it all."

As soon as this thought occurred to him, Sate began to doubt everything. When he thought something, he couldn't tell if he had *really* thought it, or if he had just *thought* he'd thought it, because that was the way someone had told his tale.

Before long, Sate realised he didn't know anything.

He didn't know where the world came from, or what had been there before.

He didn't know if he was real, or for that matter, if anyone else was, either.

He didn't know if it was actually worth getting up in the morning, or saying hello to anyone, or eating, drinking, or feeling sad or happy or anything at all.

He wondered about killing himself, but then he wasn't at all sure that death was real, either, and anyway, he doubted that would solve his problems even if it was.

One day, he found he could not go on.

He collapsed in a heap in a field just outside the flatness where The People lived, and he broke apart.

He didn't cry, because he wasn't sad.

What he did instead was gibber.

He gibbered and jabbered and yammered and yowled. He shrieked every word of every truth he thought he had ever known, and none of it made sense anymore.

The sun and moon and the stars wheeled overhead, but to Sate they were no longer these things; instead, they were a chaos of unknowable light and darkness, a broken dappling of *other* that was awful in its intensity and unbearable in its strangeness. That's what happens when all the stories come apart.

That was how the monk and his friend found him.

"Now, now, my boy," the monk said kindly. "What ever is the problem with you?"

Sate sniffed and took some deep breaths.

"I'm lost," he said at last. "I don't know my ups from my downs, my ins from my outs, my gods from my dogs. I don't know where the world ends and I begin, and even if I did know these things, I wouldn't believe a word of it."

The monk nodded. He stroked his beard ponderously.

"Would you like," he said at length, "to have some pie?"

Sate rolled his eyes.

"I *don't know*!" he moaned in exasperation. "That's what I'm trying to tell you!"

The monk nodded, and pulled out of his pack a most delicious, crumbly, and altogether flavoursome pie. I think it had blackcurrants in it.

He tore a piece off. As the crust broke, a wave of steam poured out.

"Here," he said, and handed the chunk of pie to Sate.

"I told you, I don't know if I *want* a...ow! Ow!" Sate yelped as the hot blackcurrants slithered out of the pie and burnt the back of his hand.

"Oh, so you agree the pie is real, then," said the monk amicably. He shared a meaningful glance with his friend, a gaunt, bright-eyed man.

"No, not at all," whined Sate, sucking his hand and trying not to look at the pie, which he suddenly realised did smell rather delicious, even if it was too hot. He looked from the monk to his friend and back again. "Maybe you've just tricked me into thinking there's a hot pie there. Maybe you used magic or you hypnotised me. Then again, maybe *you're* not real. Maybe I'm just dreaming you or imagining you. Or maybe you're real, but *I'm* not, and you're just imagining me."

The monk shrugged, and his friend shook his head.

"Maybe," he said, and took a bite of his pie. "However, I believe this to be a delicious slice of pie, nevertheless."

Sate found that he was eyeing his own slice hungrily. His mouth was watering (or at least, he thought it was).

"I'll eat it," he said at last, "but that doesn't mean it's real."

"Of course not," agreed the monk amiably. "Personally, I tend not to worry about that sort of thing."

"Wa' sora thin?" asked Sate.

"Don't speak with you mouth full," said the monk.

"Sorry," said Sate, swallowing. "What sort of thing don't you worry about?"

"Why, about what's real and what's not. About what gods to believe in or where the world came from or why we're here. I don't tend to worry about any of that."

Sate snorted disdainfully, but he reached for the pie, and broke himself off another chunk.

"Well, then we're not so different, are we?" he said, "Neither of us believe in anything. We're both lost."

The monk's friend snorted at that, and shifted restlessly.

"We don't have time for this," said the bright-eyed man. "Where have we come, anyway? This doesn't feel like the right direction."

The monk gave Sate an apologetic smile, and turned to his friend.

"If we are where I think, Tobias, then time is not a problem; at least, not here" said the monk. "You remember what the others said? Something's gone funny with time. It's broken, somehow. I think we've wandered into somewhere very early on. Or some*when*. No, I think we can spare the time to help this poor young man."

The man called Tobias looked intently at Sate, as if he could measure every ounce of his soul at a glance. Sate wondered if he might catch fire from the sheer force of the man's glare.

But Tobias seemed satisfied with whatever he found there, for after a moment he relented, and said, "I'm sorry, boy. This cruel world can make monsters of us all."

Sate shrugged, though he felt himself warming to the two strangers (even if they turned out not to really exist).

"I was saying we're not really so different," said Sate again.

"Not at all," said the monk. He bit, chewed, swallowed. "You don't believe in *anything*. I, on the other hand, am perfectly happy to believe in *everything*. For example, I know that I was born and that one day I will die. After that, I'm going to live for ever. Also, I'm going to be in absolute darkness and absolute nothing, for all eternity. I'm also going to spend some time – well, forever, too, actually – feasting and fighting in a big hall with all my ancestors. Then again, in all probability I'll be reborn, as a worm or a king or both. Or I might just live this life again. I know all this with *absolute* certainty, by the way."

There was silence for a moment.

"But...but, those are just *stories*," spluttered Sate at last. "They're not *real*. No one knows what *really* happens! No one knows why we're *really* here!"

"Stories are important," said the monk, quietly. "Don't you see? Stories are all we have."

By his side, Tobias closed his eyes and bowed his head.

The monk hesitated.

"Well, stories and pie," he allowed grudgingly, and broke the remainder in three. Tobias waved his piece away, so the monk ate it, too.

Sate took his third. He stayed silent, but looked thoughtful.

The sun began to sink behind the mountains.

It did look a little, just a *little*, like a fiery man bedding down behind a spiny protrusion of facial hair.

Sate smiled. The pie *was* good.

"Take myself and my friend, here," said the monk. "We would be lost without our stories. They seem to have run together somewhat. Now we share it; and it is a dark story. Dark as dark gets. And yet, I wouldn't trade being a part of it for every pie there ever was. And that's saying something."

"I'm sick of stories," said Sate. "And I've no time for dark ones."

"Me too," whispered Tobias. "Sick to death." But the monk ignored him.

"Oh, the dark ones are the most important," said the monk. "It's the dark ones that tell us most about the world; and about ourselves, of course. No, I'm thankful for this dark story I find myself in. Without it, what meaning would I have? And with it...well, we might just save the Universe."

He smiled, as if he had made a good joke; but Tobias looked up, and there was no hope left in his eyes.

"What?" said the monk. "We might just, at that."

"We should get on," said Tobias. "We won't find what we look for here. Time *is* short, whatever part of it we've wandered into. Bad things are in motion."

The monk gave Tobias a bland look, but Sate caught something sharp deep in those eyes, and he thought suddenly that the man might be much more clever than he looked.

"Oh, I know, I know," said the monk. "But we have time for a little story, surely? Besides," he added quietly, "I've always thought we chance upon people for a reason. Perhaps this young man can help."

"I've told you, I don't want to hear any dark stories," said Sate, though halfheartedly. The pie had been very good. A story might be just the thing to wash it down.

The monk pondered this information for a while,

"Do you want to hear about how we got this pie?" asked the monk, at length. "It's quite an interesting story. And not too dark at all. At least, not to start with."

Sate shrugged, then nodded.

"Very well," said the monk. He darted a sly look at Tobias. "I'll tell you the story then. It's called

8

HOW THE MONK GOT THE PIE

~

I am a humble monk, and all I own are the clothes on my back. It's all I'm allowed. I cannot hold deeds or titles or lands. I cannot carry gold or silver or jewels. I cannot even own a horse, so these two legs are my only steeds, and they have carried me far indeed.

Now this lack of wealth means that I must rely on charity or wit for my meals. I cannot buy food. It is forbidden. Usually, this does not present a problem.

People are kind. On the whole, they are kind. I believe in the goodness of people, and I rarely go hungry.

Nevertheless, there are days when I do not do so well as I might hope, and yesterday was one of those days.

I had left a land of peace and was travelling to a land of plenty. The problem was, the land *between* these places was neither. It was very rough and unfriendly, with unhelpful types and very bare, empty roads.

I was exactly halfway between the one good land and the other, when I came across an old beggar, down on his luck and covered in dirt. He hadn't had a thing to eat for as long as he could remember. He was so hungry, he couldn't even remember his name, or the colour of his eyes, or the face of his mother.

Now as soon as he saw me, I knew I was in trouble. There's a look a truly hungry man gets in his eyes, just a moment before he pounces. I've travelled my share and I've seen that look more than once.

As soon as I saw that look come over him, I made a run for it. I dashed off down the road as fast as I could, and the beggar, he came chasing after.

It soon became apparent that my cause was lost. This man was skin and bones, but the fire that burns in the hearts of the truly hungry is fierce indeed. Desperate people are the most dangerous sort.

He was just about upon me, when I spied a little hole in the ground. It was just big enough for me to fit in, so I made a dive for it, and not a moment too soon! I heard his hands *snap* together where my feet had been, and then I was scrambling down the tunnel while the beggar tried to scrabble to his feet and get after me again.

I made my way deep into the hole, as fast as ever I could.

It narrowed down at first, then opened out again into a sort of cave. Perhaps some sort of creature used to live there, I don't know.

Anyway, I just had room to turn around, and I could see the beggar's eyes, huge and white and full of madness, screaming down the tunnel after me. There was a big stone there in the cave with me. I gave it a heave, and it shifted just enough that most of the entrance was blocked off.

I could still see the wild white of his eyes glaring at me. I could hear the horrible hoarse panting of his breath. But he couldn't squeeze through the gap to get at me. It just wasn't quite wide enough.

So there we were. I was stuck in the hole – safe, but with no way of getting out. And the beggar, he wasn't going anywhere, either. Not while he could smell me. I eat rather well as a rule, and I'm sure I smell like a wonderful meal to wolves and ne'er-do-wells and other such hungry things.

Time passed. I have no idea how much of it, but I imagine there was an awful lot ticking by, while I sat petrified, watching those ravenous eyes watch me back.

At last, I decided things had gone on long enough. It was clear we were at a stalemate. I couldn't get out unless he let me pass, and he couldn't get to me unless I moved the rock.

I decided the only lucid option was negotiation.

"Now look here," I told him reasonably, "it seems we're both in a bit of a pickle."

He growled at me. I took this as the closest thing to assent I was going to get.

"Listen: I have a proposal!" I went on. "I can see that you're desperately hungry, and I sympathise, believe me, I do! But I am rather fond of my own meat and juices, and would rather not be dinner myself if I can help it. So here's what I suggest we do. You promise not to eat me, and let me out of this horrible little cave, and in return, I'll find you the most sumptuous, delicious, and all in all, most mouthwateringly incredible meal you ever heard of!"

He narrowed his eyes at me suspiciously, and muttered something obscene. It was clear he didn't trust me to return if he let me go.

"Well then, I'll give you some insurance, to be sure I'll keep my side of the bargain," I told him reasonably, and so saying, I plucked out six of my sweetest ribs, tender and juicy and terribly rare, of course.

"Here," I told him, waving my ribs in front of his eyes, which had gone as big and wide as saucers once again. "Just you let me out, and you can hold onto these, and if I'm not back within the hour, you can eat them, and that way at least you won't be so hungry, and I'll be free of this dreadful cave."

He pondered my offer carefully, but at last he accepted. He backed out of the tunnel, and I came up cautiously after him, waving my ribs in front of me like a shield.

As soon as we were out in the fresh air again, he snatched my ribs out of my hand, and sniffed them good and deep. He shuddered, and for one horrible moment I thought he was going to wolf them down right then and there, and have the rest of me for dessert.

But beggars are often decent folk deep down, and this one was as good as his word.

He grudgingly shoved my ribs in his pocked to keep them warm, and, "one hour," he told me sternly.

So off I ran in a frightful panic.

"I must get him some food!" I told myself. "Something most especially wonderful, to be sure, or it's certain I'll never see those ribs again!"

It is, I must note, a rather unpleasant sensation to be forced to run very fast while missing six ribs. It makes for a disturbingly wobbly experience.

Before long I found myself by a river. And what should I see basking in the sunlight, but the most spectacular and scrumptious-looking fish.

"Now, maybe this will do the trick!" I thought, and made to climb down the bank. But I hadn't got half way before my foot slipped, and all at once I was neck-deep in the water, splashing about and trying not to choke!

I managed to get a good hold of that fish, but it was a slippery little devil, let me tell you!

"Help! Let me go!" it bubbled at me, and I must say I felt for its plight, having been in pretty much the same situation not so long ago.

"I'm terribly sorry," I panted, as I tried to subdue the huge creature. "It's nothing personal, I assure you. Way of the world, I'm afraid."

"Is that supposed to make me feel better?" shouted the fish, giving a flip of its massive tail, and sliding out of my hands. I admit it had a point.

Eventually, I had managed to hold onto the blighter for just long enough to get half way out onto dry land, when it gave a huge *shake*! It went sailing up into the air, and came down on the other side of the water, in a little pool just off the main river.

This was too tiring for me. I decided to cut my losses and move on.

After not very long, I came to a tall pine tree. And peering up into the branches, what did I see but – wonder of wonders – a very fresh, fat, and wholly delicious-looking pig. It was lodged in a most unlikely position, high up amongst the very furthest branches.

"Aha!" said I to myself. "This could be the ticket!"

But I am rather a large man, as I'm sure you have noticed, and I hadn't got very far up the tree before the branches started snapping under me, and I was forced to retreat.

"I say, Pig!" I called up. "You look to be in rather a dire situation up there. That being the case, would you mind very much electing to fall down here and become dinner for a most hungry gentleman? I assure you, it would be in the noblest of noble causes."

"Bugger off, sunshine!" snorted the pig. "I got myself into this mess, and I'll get myself out, have no fear!"

It was rather a rude pig, I must say, and it was clear I wasn't going to get anywhere with such an ill-mannered swine.

So, not wanting to waste any time, off I dashed again.

I hadn't gone far, before I came to a clearing amongst the trees. In the middle of a clearing was a rabbit hole, running steep and dark deep into the earth. When I went over and peered inside, what do you think I saw? There was a nice fat pheasant, plump and tender, sitting just a little way down the hole.

"This is it!" I thought to myself. "My skin is saved for sure!"

Now this pheasant, he was quite the most peaceful looking bird you ever did see. He regarded me with big, trusting eyes. I stuck my hand down the hole to drag it out, and the poor little thing gave a cheerful *squawk!* And it hopped out onto my wrist.

It wobbled up my arm until it was looking me right in the eye. Then it rubbed its head affectionately against my cheek.

Squawk! It warbled again, then made a little cooing noise.

I carefully felt around with my other hand. After a couple of gropes, I came up with a nice hard rock. It was perfectly fitted for my hand, that rock. It was smooth on one side, so I could hold it without so much as scraping my palm. But the other side was sharp and jagged as a knife, very hard and cruel.

I took two deep breaths, and tried to wind my nerve up.

I gently cupped the bird's head in one hand, and lifted the rock high with the other.

Coo, said the pheasant again, and I felt his little pulse fluttering in his neck.

I made to bring the rock down.

I couldn't do it.

How could I kill the poor thing? Not so long ago, someone was trying to turn me into dinner, too. I hadn't liked that, not one bit. No, I had been going about this all wrong, I decided. How could I catch and kill anything? After what I'd been through that day, I simply couldn't. No, what I'd do was rustle up the most amazing selection of fruits and nuts and other such dainties. That would do for the beggar, and no animal need come to harm.

Slowly, almost tenderly, I lowered the pheasant back to the ground.

It regarded me for a moment with those big, friendly eyes. Then with one final *coo*, the big bird tipped me a wink and scurried back to the rabbit hole.

I felt very good and peaceful after that...at least, for a little while...

Time was getting on now, and my hour was running out. I thought of the beggar, of the saliva filling his mouth, and all his sharp, dirty teeth, and of my poor tender ribs, succulent and tasty, and completely helpless in his pocket.

But everywhere I looked, there was simply nothing else to find. No apples or pears or peaches. No grapes or gooseberries, roots or herbs, no edible plants of any description whatsoever.

By now the sun was beginning to set, and a washed out, hopeless, red sort of light was starting to fill up the world. The shadows were getting long, and darkness wasn't far off.

"Well," I said to myself, "I've tried, and I've failed. But I'm a man of my word, and what sort of a man would I be if I didn't return to the beggar, and present myself to him as his dinner, just as I have promised?"

So I turned around and marched back to where I'd left him.

I walked past the clearing where I'd let the pheasant go, and found that it was no longer in the rabbit hole. In fact, the rabbit hole was completely filled in, and who could say what happened to that pheasant? Not me.

I walked back past the tree where I'd failed to catch the pig, and found that he was no longer lodged in the tree. In fact, the top half of the tree was completely scorched to cinder, and who can say what happened to the pig? Certainly not me.

I walked back past the river where I'd failed to grab the fish, and found that he was no longer stuck in the little pool of water. In fact, the pool of water had completely drained away, and who can say what happened to the fish? I'm sure someone could, but I can't.

But just when I was about to walk on, I saw something glinting in the first silver light of the newly-risen moon. It was on the far side of the river. I splashed across, and my, that river was wondrous strong! At last I made it to the other side, and what do you think I found?

It was a pack, as which a traveller might carry along with him. By the pack was a pair of well worn shoes, laced with sturdy well-worn laces.

A most inviting smell was coming from the pack. I was so excited that my hands were trembling. I undid the string, hardly daring to hope...and I was saved! Inside the pack there was all sorts of delicious things. Meats and cheeses and pickles and jams and sauces and three different flavours of sausage and a big loaf of freshly baked bread and...oh, all sorts of other things!

I slung the pack on my back, and scuttled back to the beggar as fast my legs would carry me. I was only just in time. When I got there, the hour had just run out, and the beggar had raised the first of my poor, tender ribs to his mouth. I could see those horrible yellow teeth glinting in the darkness.

"Wait!" I shouted, "Don't eat me! Give me those ribs back, and I'll give you this feast, just as I promised!"

I must say, the look of surprise and amazement on the beggar's face when I heaved the pack down in front of him and opened it wide was almost worth all the worry I had been through!

His face lit up. He dropped my ribs (which I caught before they could hit the ground, and replaced gingerly back inside my person) and fell upon the feast as if he hadn't eaten for a hundred years.

After a while, the sounds of munching and crunching and tearing and chewing began to slacken, and I dared to venture forward and wonder aloud if I might have a taste of something or other.

"Why, my dear sir!" the beggar exclaimed. "Of course, you simply must sit down and join me! I do confess, I have been rather an awful beast. I feel simply terrible. I know it is a lot to ask for, but if you could find it in your heart to forgive me, you would show yourself to be twice the gentleman I already know you are, that is to say, twice someone of the highest respectability and moral standing."

A tremendous change really had come across the man. He looked ten years younger, not to mention twenty years kinder, thirty years more civilised, and forty years more gentlemanly, and I began to wonder if one hundred years of hunger really had been washed from him.

His eyes had lost their wide, staring quality, and his teeth no longer looked so terribly sharp.

So we sat and broke bread together, and when we were quite, quite stuffed we decided to share out what was left of the food, so that we'd each have something to fortify us when we went our separate ways.

"And here, you take this pie," he said to me, once we'd shared everything else out. "It smells of blackcurrants, and I find them quite abhorrent."

So I took the pie, and we lit our pipes as the stars slowly spun above us, and we told one another stories.

"You know, monk," the beggar said softly, and there was a certain sadness in his voice, "I wasn't always a beggar. I'm actually descended from a very great and noble house. Things have gone very strangely for me. My name is Tobias. Tobias Khazrick.

"Let me tell you the story of how I came to be wandering, lost and desperate. It's called

9

AN INTELLECTUAL TREATISE ON THE INTERESTING PROPERTIES OF IRON

~

Now as a young man growing up at court, it was naturally expected of me that I would devote the greater part of my time to the cultivation of those characteristics most valued in high society. It was understood that I would be proficient at such things as dancing, fencing, and holding civil conversation. My time was supposed to be spent in honing such practices, and in learning my place in the great society I found myself at the heart of, with the aim of one day playing a leading role therein.

It surprised and upset my family immeasurably, therefore, when I announced my intention to forsake all these pursuits, and applied instead to attend the Academy.

But my will was iron, and having anticipated their opposition to the direction I wished my life to follow, I had applied in secret, and it was only when I had been accepted and all the necessary steps completed that I informed them of where I would soon be heading, presenting them with a *fait accompli*.

I had always been interested in the world – both the heavy, solid material world around us, and that other, ephemeral, obtuse world that lies unseen beyond the range of our senses or our reason, but which we all know, deep in our hearts, to be as true and powerful as the other. For this reason, I knew the Academy was the only possible place I could go. It was the only place where I might fit in, and where I could ask the questions I was never permitted to ask in my old life at court.

As a young boy I had developed what my mother called an *unnatural infatuation* with stories. Oh, I listened to all sorts of stories, and read all sorts of stories, too. Histories, biographies, stories about warfare and hunting and so on. But what I really loved, and what my mother found most hateful, were those stories you might call *faery* stories; that is, stories of magic and distant lands, stories of enchanted swords and strange curses and mysterious, beautiful princesses that lived for thousands of years and were something other than human.

Now my reading in this regard had led, indirectly, to the theoretical paper I had submitted along with my application to the Academy, which was on certain conjectured properties of that most stolid and reliable of metals, iron.

I had long been fascinated by the role this material had to play in the stories I loved so much. Time and again, iron was implied to be anathema to the world of faerie, and to the mysterious denizens that dwelt therein. Iron horseshoes hung on doors protected those within from enchantment; it was iron swords that slew the folk of the forest; and was it not the iron march of our own civilisation, our great iron machines, our contraptions of steel and steam and slaughter, that formed the cement of out own modern age? We have spent the last two centuries dragging all the iron we could find from the depths of the earth. We have covered our cities and our countries with iron. Could it not be, I wondered, that it is with iron that we have forced the ancient, hidden world to heel?

These are not new thoughts, of course, and the letters I received back from the Academy noted as much. But they indulged my naïveté, and indeed, they must have found something promising in my papers, for though the reply they sent made sure to mention the unoriginality of my ideas, it was, after all, accompanied by a certificate of acceptance.

It was with delirious happiness that I arrived at the Academy, and I threw myself into my studies with a dedication and vigour that impressed all the Masters. All? No, not quite. There was one Master, a grim man by the name of Amos, who did not like the direction of my work at all.

Now I must backtrack here a moment and tell you that although the first two years at the Academy are spent for the most part in a generalised learning of all sorts of arts and sciences, both ancient and modern, yet all students must elect an area of special interest in which to carry out some work of their own, under the supervision, of course, of a named Master.

I had decided to take my interest in the properties of iron further. To put it simply, I had not only proposed to carry out a series of investigations into the anti-magical properties of iron; but I had also conjectured the existence of the polar opposite of this metal, and was devoting my time to the discovery or synthesis of this proposed substance.

And what was more, my work was going well. In the first place, I had demonstrated empirically that iron radiates a field of a sort that could be termed anti-magical. Any creature or substance of magical origin that comes within the sphere of influence of this field is disrupted by it. In the end, of course, I demonstrated that if the field is strong enough, it is disrupted quite fatally. But now I am getting ahead of myself...

I also noted that, as with the gravitetic and magnetic fields, the strength of this anti-magical field is inversely proportional to the distance from the iron source being considered.

I demonstrated this numerous times with those resources available to me. For example, a fellow student of mine who was carrying out his own research into parapsychic powers found that his subjects consistently performed more poorly when exposed to the iron samples I had gathered for my experiments. I took my samples to sites of famous hauntings throughout the city – all, I might add, places where iron was notably absent from the rooms and immediate surround. As I had expected, there were no apparitions whilst I carried iron; though when I returned unencumbered by the metal, I observed more than one such manifestation.

All this was enough to convince me that I was not wasting my time; and though my masters were not as enthusiastic as I, this evidence persuaded them to let me continue.

Now as I mentioned, there was one master who did not warm to me at all. Amos was not from these parts, having travelled from some far-off country that no one had heard of or was very interested in. He was tall and rather thin and never smiled. He kept his own work deadly secret, which was quite unusual – most of the Masters liked nothing better than talking about their own projects – and I knew at once that he had taken a dislike to me.

He cornered me one day after giving a lecture – all Masters were required to do this, though Amos seemed to regard it as a complete waste of his time – and demanded to know the nature of my work.

"Pah!" he exclaimed, when I had outlined my experiments. "Is that how we allow our students to squander their time? Nonsense and fairy dust? You should give it up and work on something worthwhile!"

I invited him – rather stiffly – to come to my apartments and see a demonstration of my work, but he didn't even reply. He just spun on his heel and strode away.

Of course, I didn't let him put me off, though I must say I was rather upset. I resolved to work twice as hard, just for the joy of seeing the look on his face when I published my findings, and proved my theories correct.

Time passed, and to my chagrin, my progress slowed. What I had demonstrated already was all very well, but my experiments were all rather circumstantial. What I really needed was to find some way of proving beyond doubt that iron interfered with magic; and this was rather difficult, given the fact that most of my contemporaries, and nearly all of the Masters, were of the opinion that the existence of magic was ambiguous; or, if it once had existed, that it had now been driven from the world. Worse still, I was no closer to finding any hint of my proposed polar-opposite of iron.

I had attempted all sorts of experiments to identify this substance. At first, I wondered if gold might not be the metal I sought. After all, it seemed in many ways to encompass every other opposite of iron – it was soft, while iron hard; it was fair where iron was dour; it was the rarest of metals, while iron was profligate, scattered throughout the bones of the earth. But it was also expensive and difficult to obtain, and the small amounts I was able to possess proved in no discernible way to achieve my goal. Later, I considered a whole sequence of other metals and substances, ranging from the superficially promising to the frankly bizarre...but all with no success.

I began to lose hope. After some months with little or no progress, I found I had small appetite for my work. My mind seemed to become clouded, and no thoughts would come easily. But my work had been my life; and without it, I found that in truth I only half-lived. Food lost its savour, water no longer tasted sweet. The very colours of the world around me seemed to fade and shine less brightly.

It was at this time that Sebastian, a fellow student of mine and the closest thing I had at the Academy to a friend, recognised that my health was beginning to suffer as a result of my work.

"I'm going back to my parents' estates for the summer," he told me one day. "Tobias, why don't you come, too? It would do you good to get away from things for a while. The country air will do you right."

At first, I was having none of it. But Sebastian was a good man, and he did not give up on me. Eventually I relented.

"After all," I told myself, "it need only be for a month or so. And if I find I really cannot stand to be away from my work, then I can always charter a coach of my own and leave early."

So five days later, we left for Sebastian's home in the country.

~

AT FIRST, WE TRAVELLED BY TRAIN, FOR THE ACADEMY IS SITUATED in the very heart of the realm, and the railway extends in every direction from our city towards the more distant reaches of the Empire. But before very long, the rails ran out, and we were obliged to change to coach. A day further, and the road rotted away to little more than a dirt track, and we were forced to load our most essential bags onto horses, and leave the remainder for servants to collect.

I had always been a fair rider, and had never been fearful of travelling narrow passes or close forests. Yet the ride we took that day was nothing short of alarming. The trees pulled in nearer and nearer, until it seemed every second that one had to duck or dodge to avoid getting struck by a bough in the face. The sun sunk, and the only light was from a narrow sliver of moon that poked down through the waving branches a thousand miles above our heads. And all the while, the road climbed, higher, higher, until with a jolt I suddenly realised that the trees to my left had fallen away completely, and had been replaced by a terrible, vertiginous drop down a steep gorge lined with rocks that glittered like wet teeth, to a churning strip of river far below.

I took a deep breath and gripped my knees tight around my horse. But I did not say a thing, and on we went.

At last, we rounded a corner, and all at once a thousand lights seemed to blaze out at us from a formidable manor house nestled on the very crook of the mountain we had been climbing.

"Welcome to my home!" Sebastian smiled, his eyes shining in the darkness. I could not help but smile, too.

His family were wonderful beyond what one could expect of the people of this world. They welcomed me like one of their own, with smiles and handshakes, and a warm embrace from Margaret, his mother. They showed me to my room and provided me with garments so that I might change out of my travel-worn clothes.

But it was at dinner that I lost myself to them. We had been seated at the long table, and had already started laying in to the delicious spread of warm breads and tart cheeses – the family did not wait on formality – when I noticed my hosts were coming up to their feet. I looked to the doorway – and there she was.

I had never before seen a girl so beautiful.

She was slender and quite short, with a delicacy to her movements and in the line of her jaw, an unbearable lightness to her step, in the faintest upturning of her lip as it shimmered in the warm glow of the candlelight. Her golden hair slipped around her shoulders, and the colour of her eyes was...unknowable.

Her name was Sebille.

I was quite overcome; and how I got through the rest of that meal without burning up in embarrassment or fainting dead away, I simply do not know.

Yet I managed. Not only that, but we talked.

We *talked*.

It seemed the most natural thing in the world. I made jokes – I, who had not thought of anything but the deadly serious nature of my work for the last two years and more – I made jokes. And she laughed! In fact, we all laughed; never had I had such a kind, jolly time. Certainly not with my own family back at court. There was no starch in these people. They laughed from somewhere deep inside their stomachs, it seemed to me, and the laughter had the most rich, wonderful, *honest* quality.

When I went to bed, I wondered how I would ever sleep, for my head was full of Sebille, her laugh and her eyes and her endless golden hair.

But sleep I did, the most nurturing, deep, and natural sleep in the world; and when I awoke, I felt more refreshed than...well, I do not think I had ever felt so young, so new and awake and ready for the world. And for once, my work was the furthest thing from my mind.

So the days passed. The weather there was a wonder, for the sun always seemed to be shining, yet the grass was always damp and fresh underfoot, and I never saw a flower wilting. By day we explored the forests and dells nearby, or went riding about the little villages, Sebastian and Sebille and I. When night came, we would return to the house, and eat and tell stories or read to one another from the books in the library, for they had the most astounding collection.

Sebille and I grew very close. After a while, it seemed that Sebastian would often find one reason or another that meant he could not join us on our walks. We smiled at him and said, Oh, what a shame.

But we all knew it was no shame.

I first kissed her by a little pool in the green deepness of the forest. Her lips tasted like honey and spring, and the warmth of her skin and the incredible softness of her hair overcame me...and all at once it was too much.

"I love you," I told her. And, "I love you, too," she told me back.

We held each other, and the world had never been more full of rightness. If we could have frozen the world right then, if we could have stopped time itself...

But that is not how the world works.

The days continued to pass; they continued to be wonderful, of course. Only now, with every day I awoke with a hint of sadness in my chest.

Summer was running out. Already, the days were getting shorter again. Midsummer had come and gone. The fruit on the trees were hanging huge and ripe; and when I examined the leaves, the faintest tinge of red was starting to creep in.

Soon I would have to return to the Academy. Soon I would have to leave her.

The prospect of returning to my work had never before filled me with anything but excitement. Now, I thought of it with dread.

"We'll come back again!" Sebastian told me, trying to cheer me up. "I always return to my family in the winter. You should see this place, when frost covers the land, and the waterfalls themselves freeze in mid-air! And who knows," he added, giving me a wink, "perhaps one day we shall be more than friends – maybe one day we might be brothers!"

I laughed and punched him on the arm and we said no more of leaving that day. But he was only saying what we had all thought, Sebastian and Sebille and I. One day…

At last, we could put off leaving no longer. The rain had begun to fall, and we knew autumn had arrived. A clear day came, and we had to make a break for it, or else be trapped at that wonderful house for a month or more. Oh, what a sweet confinement! But no…the Academy was waiting for us. We had to go.

Sebille rode with us a short way. When we came to the little pool where we had first kissed, her brother held her and bid her farewell. Then he went on ahead, and we were alone.

I held her and touched her hair with my lips and…and I wept.

She pulled me tight and we made promises then, one to the other, the kind that men and women make, and which should never be made idly or broken thereafter. A ring I gave her; and she gave one to me.

Of pale gold it was, and a tiny shard of emerald nestled there, too, as green as the summer grass.

"While you wear this, we shall never be apart in truth," she told me.

I kissed her again, and promised never to take it off.

And then there was nothing more to say.

I left her.

Setting out on that return journey was a dark time for me, and I remember little of the first part of it, except my unforgivable surliness, and Sebastian's unrelenting attempts to cheer me up.

At first, he tried to lift my spirits with jokes and fooling. When that failed, he spoke of his research, and attempted to pique my interest into talking about my own. It is a measure of how much a moping, lovesick fool I had become that he could not provoke me to fall into long discourse on this subject.

It was not until we were on the train once more, and heading back to the comforts of civilisation that he was able to engage me, to bring me out of myself a little.

"When I was a lad, I used to hate travelling," he told me.

I grunted.

"I used to make a horrible fuss about it," he said. "And there was only one thing my mother could do to cheer me up."

"What was that?" I asked, barely managing to keep the disinterest from my voice.

"Stories," he said. "She knew ever so many. They were mostly nonsense, of course. But they held my attention. She told some of them so many times, I know them off by heart."

He paused, giving me a chance to ask for one.

I stared out at the trees, and wondered how I would get through the months to come without a single sight of the girl I loved. I gritted my teeth and waited for him to start speaking anyway.

Sebastian opened his mouth, paused, shut it again.

"Well, I'm sure you don't want to know, anyway," he said, settling back and appearing to close his eyes.

I frowned. I knew he was aching to tell me. It was not in Sebastian's nature to stay quiet for very long. What game was he playing?

"After all, it was only her favourite story when she was very young," he said, giving a big yawn and stretching out his feet. "I'm sure you don't want to know about the things that used to enchant her."

I bit my lip. I knew what he was trying to do. Still, I was like a fish with a hook in its mouth. Sebastian was pulling me to the surface without even having to lift a finger.

"Wake me up in good time for dinner, there's a good chap," he said.

I tried to force myself not to ask, but it was no good.

"What?" I asked. The word felt like it had been dragged out of me.

Sebastian blinked open his eyes and stared at me innocently.

"Yes?" he asked. "How can I help?"

I sighed, turning to face him. I could see a smile twitching at the corner of his mouth. All at once, it made me want to smile, too.

"You know damn well how you can help," I told him. "Stop blathering around and tell me. What was this story she was so fond of?"

"Oh, you want the *story*," said Sebastian. "Here I was, thinking all you wanted to do was stare out of the window and look romantic."

I leant forward and punched him on the shoulder. For a moment he stared at me, horrified. Then we both burst into laughter. It felt like I hadn't laughed in a hundred years. It felt good.

"Very well," he said. "I'll give you her favourite story. It's been in the family for years. It's called

10

A SMALL PORTION OF A GREAT DARKNESS

∼

There are all sorts of kings in the world. Some are good, some are bad. A few might even be remembered. But of all the kings there ever were or ever might be, the King of Night was most proud.

He sat on a throne made of empty space and ruled over a kingdom of endless time. That is what things are like in the deep night, you see: endless and empty. Night is the deep breath. Night is the place between, and the only things that can exist there are figments and wonderings, the half-formed, the shadowed.

Now it came to pass that King Night had a daughter, though he had no queen. Why was there no queen? Sebille always wanted to know that, too. But that is not part of this story.

The Darkling Princess was the daughter of King Night; she was beautiful, as only a princess can be beautiful. Yet she was sorrowful, as only a motherless daughter can be sorrowful, and she came but rarely to the court of King Night.

King Night did not care. He was not cruel - though he could be strange and savage - but his heart was cloaked in darkness, and he was blind to the suffering of his only daughter. This made her more sorrowful than ever.

When the Darkling Princess was old enough to realise that her father was blind to her suffering, she wept.

"He has no heart!" she complained to her cat, Midnight. "He couldn't care if I lived or died!"

Midnight had white fur and green eyes, and she was the only bright thing in King Night's realm.

"That is not true, my lady," purred Midnight. "Your father cares much for you, in his own way."

"If he cares for me, why does he not comfort me?" she asked. "I have no mother to dance with me, no mother to kiss my brow, no mother to hold me and tell me things will be well."

Midnight was sorrowful then, too, for it was true. All daughters deserve to be held.

"It is not in King Night's nature to comprehend sorrow," said Midnight, weaving against her mistress's legs. "His heart is thick with darkness, and strange tides move him."

"I know he is not a bad man," said the Darkling Princess, and it was true. "He gives comfort to strangers. Many pilgrims seek his realm to rest awhile. The darkness gives them solace. Why not me?"

"I do not know," said Midnight.

And if the cat was silent after that, she thought hard, and kept her counsel.

At last, she walked away, for her head was clearest when she was alone.

"The problem is the darkness," Midnight said to herself. "King Night's heart is thick with the stuff. Perhaps I could steal some?"

And Midnight thought on how she might sneak in, not just within King Night's throne room, but into his very heart. It might be possible. She was a most lithe and subtle creature.

"But then, my coat is so very white," she reflected. "King Night would never miss me. His eyes are sharp as shadows, and he would be wrath. And then, even were I to manage it, wherever could the darkness be hidden?"

For King Night knew his darkness, knew every inch of it, and wherever it went, he went also. His realm was wide and passed through many worlds.

"No, it cannot be done!" Midnight decided sadly. "Why, King Night hasn't lost an ounce of his darkness in an age. Not since..."

And then she cut off, because an idea had just occurred to her.

Her eyes glowed like emeralds and she played with the idea as if she were frisking a mouse. She turned and tumbled it, looked it over every which way, pondered on how it might run, let it scuttle and scurry and then, with a sly grin, she pounced. "Yes," she said. "Yes, that might do. It just might." So off Midnight went, choosing her path with care. She walked by crook and hollow, taking many turns which others would not see, and came through at last to that secret place which others do not know.

"Who goes there?" challenged Aubrey, the keeper of the gate. "And what is your business?"

"Midnight," said Midnight. "My business is my own."

Aubrey nodded, for this is the correct answer, as all true cats know.

"Enter then," he said, and stepped aside.

Midnight strolled in, a spring in her step, for the Court of Cats knows no king and knows no queen, and all cats are lords there.

She looked about, passing from haunt to haunt, but she could not find the one she sought.

"He must be here, though," she told herself, and kept looking.

The Court of Cats is a strange place. It was made by cats for cats in an earlier time, and the rules there are different. No rooms are too hot and no rooms are too cold - and certainly no rooms are wet - and there are always mice to catch, but beyond that it cannot be understood. Cats, after all, keep their own counsel.

But no matter how far into the Court of Cats she passed, Midnight could not find the one she sought.

She walked under the earth and over the earth and fell through air and landed soft and splendid. The hunting was good, and she had blood on her teeth and on her paws.

And then Midnight sat on her haunches and licked her paws and waited - for cats, more than any other creatures, understand patience -

and *then* a certain door opened and a wind blew, and in walked the one she sought.

"Hello my freshling," said the big black cat, padding softly over to crouch by her side.

Midnight inclined her head the slightest degree.

"Hello, Torquemada," said Midnight lazily. "How is your Mistress?"

"Oh, as hungry as ever," said Torquemada, for he was in the employ of a most infamous and most feared Mistress, which Midnight knew well. "And how is yours?"

"My mistress is as beautiful as ever," said Midnight. "And her father still mourns for the secrecy of your Mistress. Will they ever be friends again, do you think?"

Torquemada's Mistress and King Night had once been intimate, though not for many years and many again.

"Oh, I think not," said Torquemada. "After all, my Mistress loves her portion of darkness; and King Night is jealous of any darkness he cannot see."

It was true: Torquemada's Mistress kept a steep darkness tight around her - as all the storytellers know - and no-one was ever the same, if once they stepped inside - if they ever came out at all - not even King Night.

"What a shame," said Midnight. She made a show of licking the blood from her paw.

Torquemada chuckled to himself.

"What a pretty red paw," mocked Torquemada. "How very well it suits you."

Midnight let her head hang.

"It's this cursed white fur of mine," she mewed. "All colours stick to it! How I wish I had a lovely black coat, like yours! It is *so* beautiful."

Torquemada preened.

"Do you like it?" he said. "Yes, it is rather wonderful, isn't it? One of my best features, my Mistress is always telling me so."

"Oh, I love it," said Midnight. "In fact...no, you wouldn't be interested..."

And she turned her head away and seemed shy.

"What?" demanded Torquemada. "What wouldn't interest me?"

"Well...I was just thinking," said Midnight. "You wouldn't want to sell it, would you?"

Torquemada went very still.

"What," he said coldly, "could you possibly offer me of equal value?"

Midnight met his eye for a moment, then looked away.

"No, you're right," she said. "A most stupid idea. I know you wouldn't possibly."

"No I would not!" said Torquemada.

"A very silly idea," went on Midnight.

"Most silly," agreed Torquemada, somewhat mollified.

"After all," said Midnight carefully, "without that beautiful black coat, how would you possibly ever get up to any works of slyness?"

There was a long, heavy pause.

"What do you mean?" asked Torquemada.

"Oh, you know," said Midnight, "we all know you're a most subtle mover, a clever-creeper; that you slip about wherever you want, and no one ever stops you. But then, most of that is surely down to that dark coat of yours. No one can see you in it. If *I* had your coat, I'm sure I'd be just as sneaksome as you."

At that, Torquemada was sitting up straight.

"Fiddlesticks!" he hissed. "My subtleties are mine alone, and not the work of this coat, as beautiful as it is. I'm twice as sly as you."

Midnight stretched and yawned.

"Prove it," she said.

Torquemada opened and closed his mouth.

"Prove it?" he said. "Of course I shall! I can beat you at any act of subtlety. Name the challenge: you will lose."

"Pah," said Midnight. "What challenge would be fair? With that dark coat of yours, you'll always win."

"Hah!" said Torquemada. "Then we will go to the one place where darkness is no help."

"Wherever might that be?" asked Midnight innocently.

"Why, the realm of your mistress, of course!" said Torquemada. "King Night sees inside every darkness. To him, darkness is lightness. In his realm, my coat will give me no advantage."

Midnight pretended to think on this.

"Hmm," she said doubtfully, "I suppose you *might* be right. Very well, if that is what you wish, we will have the contest there, in King Night's realm."

And so off they went, passing out of the Court of Cats, and back by breeze and by moonlight, they came to King Night's realm. And Midnight led them to his very throne room, and watched him from afar.

"There is the master," said Midnight. "Now watch, for I will show you how sneaking is done!"

And off she crept, padding on silent feet. She weaved and tickled her way across the throne room, past winds made of shadows, a stealthy, brightening thing. And delicate and beautiful she shimmied up to King Night himself - and though he looked outwards, she felt his awareness on her, none the less. Then she leant forward and - placing one paw on his chest - she nuzzled in to his flesh and licked the darkness that ringed his heart.

"What are you doing, little cat?" King Night asked.

"Master," Midnight whispered so only King Night could hear. "I have brought with me Torquemada, an embassy of the Mistress of the Wagon, who you must well remember."

"Remember her I do," said King Night, and the air was cold.

"Master, this boastful cat has been telling of how his Mistress has the finest darkness that was ever known," said Midnight.

"It is not so," said King Night. "I remember her darkness. It is deep; mine is deeper."

"True," said Midnight. "Thus have I brought him, to see with his own eyes. Only permit him to walk as close to you as I am now, and he will skulk back to his Mistress and tell her true, and boast no longer."

"Bring him then," said King Night.

"Master, I will," said Midnight. "But hear me, if it please you: he is a most timid and cowardly cat. If you even look at him, if you only speak one word - he will surely flee. And then the matter will never be rightly settled."

"I hear you, little cat," said King Night. "I will not look on him. I will not speak to him. Bring him."

Midnight sauntered back to Torquemada, her eyes blazing green.

"You see?" she said, showing off the freckling of tiny shadows that coated her whiskers. "I went to the very borders of his heart and tasted the shadows that spin there! You cannot do better; I have surely won."

"Pah!" said Torquemada. "You think that is subtle? You say that is sly? Watch me, then."

And off he trotted, across the room of dancing shadows, into the deep swirls of night that hung around the King. King Night felt the cat come close, but he did not look, and he did not speak, and he was still and all around the shadows raged.

Then Torquemada leant forward, closer, closer, until his face was next to the very heart of King Night. King Night felt the whiskers tickle his heart, but he had loved the Mistress, once, and he was proud, and he would not have it said that her shadows were deeper than his.

Midnight watched on, and if she was caught on the very tip of concern that her plan would fail, she did not show it, for cats - as has been said - keep their own counsel.

Then Torquemada leant just a little closer, and nuzzled just a little deeper...and inhaled.

King Night's eyes snapped open, for it was as if a cold, clear wind had blown into his soul, and a little of the shadow there was shifted. He shook, and his great dark arms trembled, and his hands reached for the cat on his chest; but Torquemada was gone.

"See?" said Torquemada triumphantly. His dark coat was covered now in a thicker darkness, for he had done just what Midnight had determined must be done, and which she herself could never do: he had stolen a portion of King Night's darkness. "I snuck the closer! I am the better at padding and plotting! I am the most subtle."

King Night was coming to his feet. His eyes were cold as diamonds, for if the night sometimes gives refuge, it does so without granting forgiveness.

"Alas, it is true," sighed Midnight. "You are the most skilled. Well, you win. Why don't you give King Night back his darkness and be on your way?"

Torquemada looked at King Night, drifting across the throne room towards them, face as black as thunderclouds. The cat's smile faltered.

"He will...understand, won't he?" Torquemada asked. "I mean, he must see it was a game...a type of bet..."

Midnight looked thoughtful.

"He isn't fond of games," she said. "Perhaps it would be better if you just go. Quickly."

"But...but I will never get this wretched stuff off in time!" said Torquemada, plucking at the shadows. They clung to his fur. They would not shift.

"That's a shame," said Midnight. "King Night owns every shadow. You'll never escape him with those stuck to you."

For an instant, Torquemada looked panicked. Then relief washed over him.

"You forget who I am," he said. "And who my Mistress is. No, I know just where to take this darkness. I will add it to *her* darkness, and King Night will never find me. Yes, that is what I will do."

King Night was very close now. The bulk of him seemed to fill the whole world.

"Be quick then, my friend," said Midnight. "You run! Don't worry. I will take the blame. I will keep him busy."

Torquemada smiled, a sly, sneaky smile.

"I told you I was the more subtle," he said. Then he was gone.

"Indeed you did," said Midnight, and she smiled too.

At that moment, King Night stepped close and his voice was empty and awful.

"I have been tricked," he said. "My darkness has been stolen. Even now, it is being taken where I cannot follow. You brought him here. It is your fault."

"That is true," said Midnight. "Your heart has lost a darkness. I am to blame."

"Little cat, then you must die," said King Night.

He reached out a hand, as thick as the shadow of mountains. He wrapped it around Midnight, and then he began to crush.

Midnight felt the life squeezing out of her. There was no pain, just a stifling of breath, a slowing, a fading. The world wavered, and Midnight prepared to sleep.

But at that moment there was a cry.

"Oh, stop!" came the voice of the Darkling Princess. "Father, stop, please!"

The hand loosened a little but did not let Midnight go.

"My daughter," said King Night. "I cannot let go. Your pet has betrayed me. She has let shadows be stolen from my heart. Justice must be done."

And with that the fist started to tighten once more.

Then came the sound of weeping - terrible, disconsolate weeping, for the Darkling Princess loved Midnight very dearly...and once again the fist stopped its squeezing.

There was a long, long pause.

"Do...do not cry," came a voice, so thick with grief and strange that it took Midnight a moment to realise it was King Night. His words came shakily; his hand shook too.

"Do not punish Midnight," pleaded the Darkling Princess. "She was only trying to help me: and look! Is it possible it has worked?"

Then the fist loosened some more, and all at once Midnight was dropping gently to the floor. Above her, King Night stooped, and his shoulders sagged, and great black tears rolled down his face; for his heart was full of shadow no longer, and he could see the misery of his daughter, and his heart was broken.

"I am sorry," said King Night. "For all of it. I have been blind. I am so, so sorry."

Then they embraced, father and daughter, and Midnight was warm, because she knew that if daughters need to be held, fathers need it too.

The Darkling Princess looked at Midnight over her father's shoulder, and, "Thank you," she said.

Midnight purred and looked at her mistress with her emerald eyes. Then she turned away,

"A job well done," she told herself, as off she slinked. And though she had done what she set out to, still there was a sadness on her. For now that King Night had room in his heart for his daughter, the Darkling Princess would need Midnight less keenly. Which was as things should be; still, the way things should be is not always the happiest way.

She went once more by crook and moonlight, sliding through darkness and secret paths. In time she came again to the one who kept watch.

"Who goes there?" challenged Aubrey, the keeper of the gate. "And what is your business?"

"Midnight," said Midnight, and she said no more.

Aubrey regarded her with sharp eyes.

"And of your business?" he asked again.

Midnight sighed.

"I have done myself out of it," she said. "Though if I had it still, it would be mine alone," she added after a pause, and Aubrey relaxed.

They stood together in companionable silence.

"To lose one's business is a strange lightness," said Aubrey at length.

Midnight gave him a slow look.

"Indeed," she said.

"We fight and we struggle and sacrifice," he went on. "And after all that - if we win - our stories go on without us, and we are left behind."

"I would not be so crass," Midnight said at length, "to ask what business brought *you* here, O keeper of the gate."

Aubrey twitched a whisker. It was nowhere near a smile; still, a warmth settled over the two of them. They drew a little closer.

"I would not be so crass as to tell a story to one who did not wish to hear it," said Aubrey.

"Oh, I always like to hear a good story," said Midnight. "I always have time for that."

Aubrey stretched his paws.

"Listen, then, to my story. It is called

❧ II ❧

THE PLACE WHERE MY FRIENDS
WERE TAKEN

~

T his world is fresh. It is full of life, and time, and potential. It
is easy to forget what a wonderful thing that is. Not all
worlds are so.

Worlds wind down. That is the truth of it. They spin and spin, and
it seems they will go on forever. Then they start to unravel. Before you
know where you are, they are lost. I should know. I have been places. I
understand.

In another place, I fled.

I knew no other life, for I was born into flight, the last remnant of
a dying world. Things were different then. I was different. It was
before I learnt, before I changed...

I am getting ahead of myself. It is so long since I thought of these
things.

The world I was born into was...it was a kind of carriage. It is difficult to describe. Imagine a huge carriage. Vast, it was vast. There were
rooms, ever so many rooms, and many floors, even. People were there,
lots of them, lots of humans and nearly-humans. I was the only cat,

though I did not understand what that meant. I was so young; it was before understanding.

And my world moved. It rolled forward, endless, unstopping; the road stretched on into the West, broad and twisting. We always moved along that road. We had to, for death followed behind.

I had never known a world that wasn't dying. From my earliest memories, we always fled; the fires always followed.

The fires. A great wall of fire, as wide as the horizon, so high the very sky was scorched. When it drew close, the scent of cinder filled the air, and the forest around us was full of the crashing of terrified beasts. If it overtook us, we would die.

So we fled. So we pushed onwards, staying ahead of the fires. And I was happy. By and large, I was happy, if only I had known it. Often we do not realise we are happy until that happiness is taken away.

I watched the plains roll by, and mountains in the distance, and trees dancing on the plains. Their shadows were long and their bark looked soft - the very thing for sharp claws! - and I thought, *I would stop now, and play in those trees, and roll on that soft grass.*

So I went to Kye, the old man who kept the carriage rolling. I rolled about his legs, and told him to stop the carriage, for I wanted to play.

"What's that, Puss?" he asked, for I could not make the speech of men, though I did not then know it. "You want to eat?"

And he gave me dry meat.

I went to Unity, she who brought them all together, she who told them to flee, when it was flee or meet the flames. I bumped my head against her hand and asked her to stop, for I wanted to play.

"Not now, Puss," said Unity. "Things are going grim. A darkness comes; I cannot see clearly."

And she stroked my head, and pushed me off.

I went to the back of the carriage, and watched the plains roll away behind us, and the glorious trees with their soft trunks were passing away, too; and far behind them, blazing against the darkness, the great wall of fire rushed after us, snapping at our heels. I was too angry to care about the flames, though.

"They never listen to me!" I complained to myself. "I might as well be invisible. I never get what I want!"

"To get what you want, one must take it," came a voice, and I jumped straight up in the air and stared about wildly, for I had thought I was alone.

"Who's there?" I asked, for I could still see no one.

"Down here, brave one," came the voice again. It was a strange voice, thin and hungry, but with something hard in it, something hard and hungry and toothsome.

I peered down into the shadows beneath the carriage. There, in the lee of the great wheels, I saw something flapping, keeping pace just above the ground.

"I can't see you," I complained. "Come into the light."

"As you wish," answered the voice, and up it swooped: a strange bird, huge and ugly - though afterwards, of course, I would understand what *huge* really meant. Yes, and *ugly*, too.

Its beak was of stone and its eyes were red fire; but its body was a cage of bones, hollow bones, and it flew on wings of tattered leather; and these were hung on white bones, too.

"Who are you?" I gasped, and drew back, for the thing looked evil and smelt worse.

"I am Claw," said the bone-bird. "I am of the Nest. And I am smallest, too, just like you. I know what it is to be ignored and unlistened-to."

I knew I should run, oh I knew it deep down. But the creature had read me well, and could see how to use me.

"They never do what I want," I said uncertainly. "They never listen.

"And what is it you want, brave one?" Claw asked me. His words clack-clack-clacked like bones falling down a mountain.

"I want to play on the plains and on those big, soft trees," I said; and even then, my voice sounded like a whine to me, and I knew I should leave, I knew I should say no more.

"Then play you shall," Claw told me. "It would be a very simple thing to arrange."

"But already we are leaving the plains," I said. And it was true. The plains were being lost behind us; the road was entering a broad, cruel desert, and we were following it, and the world behind was becoming lost to the flames, as I have said.

"Come, you are not a fool," Claw told me. "Now listen: I come from a great Nest. We live up in those fine mountains we have just passed, my nest-mates and I. If you only stop the carriage, I will take you back to meet my Nest. And there are many soft trees and many miles of green planes on which to play between here and there."

I laughed then, a nasty, bitter sort of laugh.

"Stop the carriage?" I said. "And how might I do that? They never listen to me."

"Then make them listen," said Claw.

"How?" I asked.

Claw tilted his head. He opened his stone beak and

12

CEASE YOUR TELLING

⌐∾

The command whipped through the air, cutting the narrative field like butter.

The little story screeched to a halt, its characters and settings tumbling over one another as the Telling was abruptly cut short. Then it just stood there, panting, a look of profound surprise running through every plot twist and story arc.

"Easy, easy now," came the voice again, and Indigo Shuttlecock stepped out of the shadows. She had been watching the little story for some time, and she had known something was amiss. It was her job to know such things. She was a Sheriff of the Order, after all. If she didn't spot problems with the Storystream, who would?

"What...er...what seems to be the matter, Sheriff?" asked the little story. It sounded nervous, which was only natural. It was not every day that a story found itself ordered to cease mid-Telling.

"Too early to say, friend," said Indigo. She kept her voice nice enough, but put some weight there to show she would brook no argument. "Something ain't right, though. That's sure as sunrise."

Indigo walked around the little story, inspecting it from every angle. The story kept its twists and arcs spread wide, frozen open for the Sheriff to see. That was a wise move, Indigo reflected. Nothing screamed suspicion more than a story clamping up its characters the moment a Sheriff took an interest.

She reached out and inspected the main players.

"A cat, looks like," she said, talking half to herself. "And...and what's this thing?"

Indigo stared at the simulacrum, the shimmering representation of a strange hollow bone-bird which projected outwards from the reality of the story.

"Oh, that's my villain," said the little story. It was unable to keep a tiny note of pride from its voice. "Clever little fellow. Provides quite a challenge."

Indigo nodded.

"Yeah, seems like it might," she agreed. She tilted it, inspecting it closely. "Looks like it provides a fair whack of narrative engine, too," she added.

The little story was impressed.

"You're not wrong there, Sheriff," it said. "Why, there wouldn't *be* much of a story without..."

But Indigo broke in.

"What's your name, little story?" she asked, handing the villain back.

"I'm *The Place Where My Friends Were Taken*," said the little story smartly. "I'm from a way outs Charmward. Not from these parts at all."

"I guessed that, *Place*," said Indigo. "Knew it soon as I saw you. What's a little story like you doing way out here in my Fold?"

The little story opened its mouth to answer, looked puzzled, and closed it again.

"I...er...I don't rightly know, Sheriff," it said. "Truth be told, don't rightly know where *here* is..."

Indigo nodded to herself. Something about this whole affair was looking more and more wrong. She had noticed the little story wandering along the outskirts of her Fold, a strange look to the Telling which suffused it, animating the characters within. Rightly speaking, it wasn't her job to deal with every stray story that passed by - just so long as they didn't cause trouble in her patch, in the Western Fold. Still, something about this one had her hackles up...

"This here's the Western Fold," Indigo told the little story. "We don't go looking for trouble here, *Place*. But we don't run scared from it, neither. The Folds are safe-havens. Sheltered places, protected from the hurly-burly of the rest of the Storystream. You bringing me problems, *Place?*"

Indigo Shuttlecock gave the little story a long, slow stare.

"I...I don't want no trouble," it stammered.

"I'm sure you don't," said Indigo. "Looks like you might have brought it with you, all the same."

There was something worrying about the little story, something Indigo couldn't quite place. It wasn't in the characters or the setting, she was sure of that. Nothing in the internal architecture of the story seemed wrong, it was just...

"Who initiated your Telling?" Indigo asked.

"Came from some story about King Night," said the little story promptly. "Often happens that way. Got a strong lead in there. Been told that way, well, must be nigh on a hundred times..."

Indigo nodded. She titled her head as if sniffing out a scent.

"And before that?" she said. There had been a strange resonance to the Telling that had animated *Place*. You could tell a lot about a Telling by the specifics of the resonance. It bounded down sequences of stories like a waterfall rushing down a canyon. Most of the time, the bobbing of stories through the Storystream was a semi-random affair, full of push and shove and blind, joyous energy. But other times - times like this - an odd weight seemed to accrue, a purpose...

But the little story was shaking its head.

"Can't say as I remember," it said. "You now how it is, Sheriff. There's so many ways into a story - even a little story, like me...I can't say how the Telling before mine was set in motion..."

Indigo looked carefully at the little story, and decided it was telling the truth. Whatever was going on here was strange, but she had found out all she could from *Place*.

"Thank you for helping me with my enquires," Indigo told the story.

The little story relaxed.

"Why, of course Sheriff. Any time, just let me know how I can help..."

"You can help by staying still and preparing to be boarded," said Indigo.

The little story just had time to guess what was about to happen.

"But, won't it hurt?" it asked in a worried voice.

"No," said Indigo, and it was true.

Indigo plunged into the little story. She gestured, and waves of characterisation and plot parted before her hands. She contracted her body - after all, she was a Sheriff of the Order, and was granted such powers over the world of stories - pulling herself inwards, inwards, until she was a mote, a tiny atom spinning through the world of the little story. She passed from character to character, examining them one by one. She came to the cat - little more than a kitten - and traced it back, running its motions back through the multi-dimensional haze of possibility and perspective which forms the bedrock of any story.

"I see," she said.

Indigo Shuttlecock stood before the entrance, the gateway leading from the small story she had crept inside. This was where the Telling with the strange resonance had come from. She peered in. Sure enough, she could see another story. This one was hung with darkness and shadows.

"King Night," she muttered to herself. "That's for sure."

There were lots of stories about King Night. They were always popping up.

But who had Told this one? And what was it about the resonance that felt so *wrong*? That was the question.

Now Indigo was moving through King Night's story. The dimensions of this story were different, the tone was different, and the rules by which the story had unfolded were different. A less skilled Sheriff might have been confounded - might even have become lost, never to be found again, trapped inside, swallowed up by the story and made to play some minor part. But Indigo Shuttlecock was no milk-Sheriff; she was tried and tested, and she knew the way of things.

She located the Telling that had animated the story of King Night, and siphoned herself into it; and then she reeled, for she felt that she had come close now to the odd resonance that had made her suspicious in the first place. She scanned through the folds of the story, searching, trying to put her finger on what it was that made her so uneasy...

And then she saw it, and she understood.

She floated, tiny and potent, a spark in the eye of the story, imbued with all the powers of a Sheriff...and she knew she was overmatched.

"Oh dear," she said, in a very small voice.

For a moment, she was frozen, overcome by the realisation of what she had found, what she was up against.

Then she pulled herself together.

"Still, there must be something I can do," she told herself. "Something *we* can do." For there were others of course, others like her, those with powers over Story. There were many, many Sheriffs, a great many - one for every Fold, though the Folds were only a small part of the unimaginable vastness of the Storystream. And then, there were many creatures more powerful still, those that prowled the stories, Telling without being Told...

Maybe she should go to them. Maybe she should get help.

Then again, maybe she should try and understand things better, before begging for assistance?

"Still, what's stopping me from doing both?" she thought.

And as if the thought had freed her from the paralysis of fear, Indigo fished about inside herself and fetched out a tiny thing - the smallest of Tellings - an echo of herself, imbued with the task of fetching help. She flung it out into the story. It winked and vanished. No doubt it would wait for a way to send a signal, then lead help back...

Now that that was resolved, it was time to act. Indigo was suddenly thrusting herself outwards, bursting up from within skein upon skein of story. Reality shimmered and wobbled around her, re-aligned, settled...

She took a breath.

Her frame of reference had changed completely now - for the Universe was full of them, frames of reference beyond counting, and not one was any truer than any other - and she stood, a slim, tough woman, laying off in the darkness a little way from a fire.

She knew now what she must do.

Two figures sat at ease by the fire, eating the last morsels of what looked to have been a very fine meal. The first was rather stout, with a pleasant face and a peaceful air. The other looked hungry and travel-worn.

He's the one, Indigo knew. *The one who has seen it. The one who has* touched *it...*

He was in the middle of telling his tale, while the other man looked on.

Indigo slipped through the darkness, stepping suddenly into the blight blaze of the fire. The two men blinked at her.

The stout man was the first to recover himself

"Why, hello there, my dear," he said. "You do seem to have crept up on us! But please, you must be cold, and hungry. We have only a little food left, but you are welcome to share it."

Indigo nodded, and tried smiling. It was a strange thing, being incarnated in what was - relatively speaking - a normal body. She was used to existing in the odd, nebulous, many-dimensional form of a Sheriff of the Order; to be rendered in simple flesh and blood was quite a novelty.

"Sure is kind of you," she said, sitting down and helping herself to an apple.

"Warm yourself," said the stout man. "It's cold now the darkness has fallen."

"That's true," said Indigo. Then she looked at the other man, a sly, darting look from the corner of her eye, and she said, "Still, nothing warms me better than a good story. Been a while since I heard one."

The two men exchanged a look.

"Well, it's funny you should say that," said the stout man. "My friend here was just telling us a most interesting tale. I'm sure you will like it. Why don't you carry on, Tobias?"

The thin man looked up at her.

His lips were parted in a slight smile, but there was something in his eyes, something distant and sad.

Oh yes, thought Indigo. *It is him, alright. It is certainly him. Why else would he have that look, if he hadn't touched it?*

"Very well," said the man called Tobias. "I will take up my story. It is called

⚛ 13 ⚛

AN INTELLECTUAL TREATISE ON THE INTERESTING PROPERTIES OF IRON (REPRISE)

~

The Academy seemed very different to me on my return than it had when I had first arrived two years before. Instead of a fortress of knowledge and secrets it seemed...small. The stones and spires looked glum, brooding, without heart or warmth. Sebastian and I parted, and I thanked him one last time for the great kindness that he had shown me, and we went to our separate rooms to unpack, promising to meet again soon.

But when I entered my chambers, I knew at once that something was amiss. Quickly, I lit the lanterns and forced the darkness back.

My rooms had been ransacked. My papers had been rifled and left crumpled and in disarray on the floor. And my great collection of iron samples had been gone through most mercilessly, and many of them had been stolen.

It took me the best part of a week to put my rooms back in order, and to get something of a feel for the damage that had been done. On close inspection, it seemed that not many of my papers had actually been lost, though I suspected one or two were missing. The research that was most strikingly missing was regarding my latter – and wholly fruitless – attempts to synthesise the proposed anti-substance of iron.

Now it is a strange thing, but for some inexplicable reason this fact actually had the effect of sharpening my determination most remarkably. If someone thought my work had merit enough to steal...well then, did that not mean that someone thought that I had been on the right track?

I had not been able to concentrate on my work for many weeks now. First there had been the disenchantment of my failures; then had come Sebille, and all thoughts of work had been driven from my mind.

But now...

I threw myself back into my work with renewed vigour. I had lost the greater part of my tools and my iron samples – but so what? That path had led nowhere, and if I wanted to succeed, I told myself, I would do better to try a new direction.

Iron covered our cities, it was true. But did it not come from the ground? What, then, was I doing filling my rooms with iron, and looking there for answers? I perceived that the only use I should now have for this substance was in making heavy locks to bar my door, and keeping a steel knife close by in case of further intruders.

I began to stray beyond the Academy as much as I was able. At first, I took my experiments to empty shops and warehouses in the further reaches of the city. But soon even this seemed too close, and I formulated the suspicion, deep in my heart, that the substance I sought would not be found in any settlement, nor under the dirty yellow glow of the *electro* lights that now illuminated the great cities of men.

I often thought of Sebille during this period; and many were the nights that I returned exhausted from my work, and wanted nothing more than to flee the city and my failures, to run to her and leave the concrete and the dirt and the endless crushing greyness of the iron lands. When this feeling overtook me, it was to Sebastian I would turn; for who better than he could share the memories of the sweetness of Sebille?

But Sebastian, I found, was scarcely free to spend his evenings with me.

As I have said, every student at the Academy is nominated a single Master who acts as the overseer of their personal work. The Master who was overseeing Sebastian was working him very hard and cruel; and he could hardly spare one night in ten, for fear that his Master would carry out the terrible threat he had already hinted at: that of recommending Sebastian's expulsion from the Academy.

Sebastian's Master, of course, was Amos.

One night, after I had not seen Sebastian for perhaps a fortnight, I was woken in the small hours by a most insistent rapping at my door. I stumbled up and made my way to the porch. On my left hand I wore the ring Sebille had given me, for I never took it off, and the faint light from the moon outside fractured on the fragment of emerald, and cast green shadows on the pale wall. In my right hand, I grasped my knife.

"Who's there?" I asked, for ever since the ransacking of my room I had grown wary and suspicious.

"It is I, Sebastian," came the reply, and I opened the door at once.

It was my friend indeed, though at first I scarce recognised him. He looked as if all the milk and softness had been melted from his face. His clothes hung loose on him, and his smile had all but gone. He wore a thick scarf around his neck, and did not take it off when he came inside, as if he was troubled by a chill that could not be chased off.

His eyes had not changed, though, and there was still something of his old lightness in them.

"Why, Amos wants to make a skeleton of you!" I joked, and we both laughed as I fetched out the whisky and poured us each a drink.

"He wants to make something of me, that's certain," Sebastian said darkly, and a chill entered his voice.

"Tobias, did he ever talk to you of your work?" he asked me suddenly.

I shrugged, and told him of the words we had exchanged the year before after that Master's lecture, for truly that was the only occasion on which we had spoken.

"It seems to me that the man is...well, I wonder if he's trying to steal your work!" Sebastian tossed back his drink, and went on. "He keeps asking me to accompany him, help him with his own research.

Oh, he tells me it has a bearing on my own, and implies that if I help him, things will go easier when he talks to the board about my progress. But I'm not blind, you know! My work has nothing to do with metals or chemicals or *electro*, nothing of that kind. And yet there I am, hour after hour, shifting and examining and recording things in his workshop. And what do you think it involves? Why, iron, of course! Between you and me, the whole thing is wearing me quite ragged!"

I thought of my ransacked rooms, of the stolen iron samples and my missing papers. Was it possible that this man who had been so hostile towards my work was secretly involved in similar research?

"Well, what do you think he's trying to do?" I asked.

"I couldn't say, but I thought you ought to know," Sebastian shrugged and made his way to the door, stifling a yawn. "But whatever he is trying to do, he's quite prepared to sacrifice me to do it!"

He laughed wryly. I thanked him for the information, and made my way back to bed.

After that, I did not see Sebastian for some days. But to my shame, I had once more become so absorbed in my work that I did not concern myself with my friend's absence as perhaps I should have. I have often wondered since if things may have come out differently, were it not for this utter selfish obsession of mine.

A selfish obsession...the fires of which were fed by a sudden moment of truth.

I must pause now to ensure you know a little of the background necessary to understand the paths my thoughts were taking. It has long been thought by the alchemists and their more modern descendants that iron can exist not only as an element in its own right, but in two forms of chemical compound, that is to say the *ferrous* state and the *ferric* state. The form taken by the metal is dependent on the nature of the second element to which the iron is bound, and the resulting compounds have various different properties.

It was twilight on an autumn evening, and I was coming to the end of another set of fruitless experiments on the banks of a little river some miles from the hustle of the city.

Now the fancy had come into my head that, as the worlds of story and faery were so bound to the natural world, that perhaps the element I had been searching for, this anti-iron, was as obvious a thing as the very earth itself. A foolish idea it seems now, but at the time I had been quite hopeful, and had subjected simple riverside earth to every conceivable treatment I could think of, with the design that in this way I might synthesise some of this proposed element.

On this day, I had spent no less than seven hours constantly in this pursuit; and as dusk drew in and I perceived that my every endeavour had failed, I grew wroth. Picking up a sod of earth that I had been treating with various chemicals, I let out a cry of frustration, and hurled the thing away from me, up into the sky.

I watched the dark mass as it sailed into the air, glinting in the pale moonlight and the deep reflected green of Sebille's ring. The earth reached the zenith of its arc, and fell. It dropped towards the silver shimmer of the river, where it met its clouded reflection in that glittering surface...and passed through into the deep water below.

It is not a separate element.

The thought echoed in my mind, sonorous and clear as the deep truth of a dream, as complete and perfect as if it had been dropped there by a greater being than I.

I thought again of the earth hurtling towards that silver sheen of water, striking it, being transformed as it passed through and sank into the depths.

It is simply iron in another form. It is the same metal, just differently bound.

At that moment, I swear I heard Sebille laugh, her voice soft and joyous like the riffling of the river. I spun around, and there, for one golden moment, I was sure I saw her standing amongst the trees, pale and beautiful and full of fey life. I stumbled towards her...and the illusion broke, shadows shifting in the moonlight, until only empty darkness remained.

But if Sebille was not there, the revelation held fast in my mind.

I knew, somehow I *knew* that I was right.

I gathered up my equipment and stumbled home in a daze.

After that, I redoubled my efforts, and focused once more on iron itself. I knew there must be a way to change its form. I felt like a man who has stumbled upon the door he has sought for so long, but on trying the handle, finds to his dismay that it remains locked.

No art I tried could open that door.

I employed every likely chemical technique my research had uncovered, and my rooms were stained deep with traces of charcoal and scarred from acidic fumes. I had even approached the problem using the mysterious and burgeoning science of *electro*, and though I did show this strange force to interact with iron in novel ways, yet my hoped-for aim was not realised in this manner, either.

Then one day, something tremendous happened.

Autumn was coming to a close, and the chill of winter was not far off. The nights had begun to draw in, and it had grown dark in my chambers without my noticing it, so entranced was I with my work, when of a sudden there was an unexpected knocking.

It was Sebastian. If he had looked tired before, he looked positively unwell now. All traces of his previous health and happiness had gone, and there was a sullen wildness in his eyes. His skin was thin and bruised, with many grazes on his hands. I welcomed him in, stopping my work at once, and quickly built up a fire to chase the chill from the room. Sebastian helped me fetch the logs, and soon we had a blaze going, and we got to talking.

I spoke with some excitement of the recent breakthrough I had made in my theories, and showed him the equipment I was using to perform my experiments. He tried to take an interest, picking up a few bowls and burners half-heartedly, nodding and attempting to smile, but I could see that something was wrong, and soon he crept close to the fire again. It was as if he tried to chase some deep, utter chill from his flesh; but no matter how he held his hands to the flames, he never seemed to find warmth. His scarf was wrapped tight around his neck, and his head hung heavy on his shoulders.

At length I could take it no more.

"Damn it, Sebastian, won't you tell me what is wrong with you?" I asked him.

But he shook his head.

"I am simply being worked too long and too hard," he told me, though he looked like a man haunted by more than simple exhaustion. "Amos will now permit me no time for studies of my own. All I seem to do is sleep, eat, and perform the tasks he sets for me. All of which seem to involve that ghastly metal you're so fond of," he added, and for the first time a ghost of a smile tickled his lips. "I must say, I've grown to loathe the horrid stuff."

We talked some more, but in truth I was anxious for my friend, and did not wish to keep him from rest. He looked as if he could sleep for a thousand years, like someone in a tale.

"Not much longer now, anyway," he said, trying to force another smile as I saw him to the door. "The holidays will be here soon. And then I will return to my blessed family for a time. And you, Tobias, you will come, too!"

He clasped my hand suddenly. It was a gesture of fierce affection, and I was quite touched by it. I noticed a small cut on his hand, a scab opened by the rough logs as we had built up the fire.

His finger moved over the ring Sebille had given me, and as the flickering shadows cast by the blaze danced over his face, I could see much of her likeness there.

"How I wish she was here now," he said wistfully. "As, I am sure, do you."

I clasped his hand in return.

"We shall both see her soon," I said, trying to sound hopeful.

He nodded, but I could not help but notice the sadness in his eyes. Then he was gone.

I closed the door after him, and a sense of utter foreboding swept me up. But I could not face it, not that darkness in the dark of night...and so I returned to my work.

The ingot of iron was as hot as the burner could make it; in beaker nearby, the acid of sulphur boiled happily away.

It was only at the very last moment, as the ingot rattled and slid towards the spluttering liquid below, that I caught the faint glinting of colour on the dark metal.

A splash of red.

Blood.

Then the metal hit the liquid, and the mixture started to seethe.

A flash of light filled the room, so bright that for a moment I was blinded. There was an awful *crack*, and a spray of liquid on my hand: the beaker had shattered, sending a mist of acid up.

My hand screamed pain, and in the panic of the moment I forgot everything but trying to locate my ammonium, lest the acid burn me to the very bone.

It was not until I had soaked my wound and neutralised the acid that I was able to think clearly.

I thought of the speck of blood, the unearthly flash, the crash that had seemed to fill the whole world.

My heart was pumping very fast.

I staggered to the worktop. It was covered with a thousand shards of broken glass...and there amongst them, tiny and ugly, and quite, quite perfect, was the substance I had been seeking all this time.

It was smaller than the ingot from which it had been formed, and only a faint, reddish sheen to the metal distinguished it from the substance it had been before.

But there was a hush and stillness in the room, and I did not doubt for a moment.

I had succeeded. I had synthesised an entirely new compound. I had created the state of bound iron which I had proposed, and for which I had searched so long: faerrous sulphate.

Faery iron.

~

I RESOLVED TO TEST MY DISCOVERY. I CRAFTED THE SMALL ARTEFACT I had created into a chain I wore around my neck, and I took myself off to the famously haunted sites of the city that I had visited when I was beginning my studies, what felt like a thousand years ago. I thoroughly divested myself of all traces of iron first, and kept my hand firmly clasped around the precious object I had forged.

Things came.

Sometimes there was nothing more than a sudden, unnatural coldness to the room, a prickling in my spine, and a sureness of *other*. But more than once I perceived pale lights and figures form up in the darkness, and one time a child I could not see began to weep quietly, and tugged insistently at my fingers, though his hand was as chill as water at midnight, and it passed through mine again and again.

The child followed me when I left, and it was not until I removed the faery iron from my skin for a day that the crying faded and eventually vanished.

I was delirious with excitement. All my striving, all my hard work had been vindicated. And although my further attempts to replicate my first success by mixing my own blood with various other ingots of iron and acidic compounds had thus far been in vein, nevertheless I felt that the back of the problem had been broken. It would only be a matter of time. I had succeeded! I had been right!

Then one day a Master came knocking at my door. When I let him in, he told me that my friend Sebastian had collapsed and had been rushed to the infirmary, where he was laid up feverish and weak, and grievously ill.

～

I RUSHED TO SEE MY FRIEND, AND WHEN I ARRIVED, FOR ONE horrible moment I thought I was too late. Sebastian was thin and pale, looking impossibly shrunken in the sturdy infirmary bed. He was so still and sallow that I hung back, fearing to break the peace of death. But then his eyes flickered and opened, and he turned his face towards mine.

A thin light crept in through a window high above, and the shadow of recognition flitted across his brow. He reached out a hand, and I grasped it in both of mine.

"Alas, I have been used most wrongly," he whispered, and I had to strain to hear him.

His fingers squeezed my hand, and he brushed the ring Sebille had given me.

"I am glad you are here," he said. "I would not choose to die alone."

"Die? No, you shall not die!" I told him, and there was a horrible false heartiness in my voice. "Why would you die? I see nothing wrong with you but a thinness and a few scrapes and cuts on your arms. Nothing that time and care will not heal."

But I was wrong, as we both knew.

He smiled then, a sad smile, as if indulging one final foolishness of a slow pupil.

"You mean you have not guessed it, at last?" he said.

"Guessed what?" I asked, feeling foolish.

"My family," he began, and then broke off, coughing.

He gestured for the water, and I poured him a glass.

He took a small sip. "Enough," he said, and I took it back.

"You have met my family," he went on. "They have met you, and they love you...as I know you love them. From the first time I met you, I knew this would be the case.

"My family..." he tried again, pausing. "There is a...certain wildness in our blood. I trace it from my father, and him from his mother, and so on back and back until...until you come to a wedding in the forest, under strange stars that you do not know.

"We all carry this tint within us, all my family. It is our heritage, however faded and faint. Sometimes, as in me, it is weaker, and we can travel deep into the great cities of men, without fear of the sickness that now haunts our kind. In others, the blood runs strong, and to come under the terrible sway of your metal cities would spell doom...and such a one is my sister, for she is a true throwback, and the blood of the forest-folk runs almost pure in her."

He spoke these words, and I knew that it was true.

I thought of the single ingot of faery iron I had made. I thought of all the drops of my blood I had sacrificed in vain thereafter, and suddenly I knew why not one attempt save the first had worked.

"You helped me succeed," I whispered to him. "You knew what I was trying to do, and you knew how to achieve it. You spilt your blood on purpose! Faery blood. To help me find my precious substance."

He nodded, and then a strange fierceness welled up in him, a last surge of will animating his features. He leaned towards me and his teeth pulled back in a snarl.

"If *he* was going to have some, then so must you!" he bit off each word, hissed it in my face.

"'He'?" I said. "You mean Amos?"

Sebastian nodded and slumped back into the bed.

"At first, he only suspected," he sounded tired now, and his eyes were half closed. "He could sense something in me; and of course, he came sniffing around your work as soon as he realised what you studied. But when we departed for the summer, yours were not the only apartments he broke into. He found enough in yours to start experiments of his own...and he found enough in mine to be sure of who...of *what* I was."

I wanted to scream at my friend; but I held my frustration in check.

"But *why* did you help him?" I said, keeping my voice as steady as I could.

"Because he knew all too well how to bind me," he replied, and reaching his unsteady fingers to his neck, he unclasped the scarf that was wrapped there.

A thin band of dark metal was locked cruel and tight around his throat. The skin where the metal touched was blistered, red and weeping. There was a lock in one segment of the device; a black emptiness marked the keyhole

Iron.

I reached out to touch the collar; but Sebastian flinched, and I let my hand fall.

"This is beyond forgiveness," I said. "I will go to Amos, and I will..."

But Sebastian leant forward suddenly, and, "No!" he said.

"No," he said again, more softly. "You must not do anything to anger him. You do not know him, you do not know what he is capable of. He is not...he is not someone to be taken lightly. He is...strange, in his own way. He has taken from me what he wanted, and soon he will be gone, and then he will leave us in peace. But if we confront him, if we challenge him...I fear he will strike quickly, and strike hard. I have already sent word to my family. They will soon be sending what help they can. Until then, it is safer to play things meekly, and to be discrete. In any case, he has promised to...leave me the key when he departs."

"Ah, yes," said I, shaking my head in disbelief, "and when will that be, pray? Surely he has not gone to all this trouble, done all these vile things just to leave once he has succeeded! Go? Why should he go?"

Sebastian actually laughed.

"Oh my dear, not everyone is so besotted with knowledge for its own sake as you are!" he chuckled, but it caught in his throat and turned into a cough. "No," he went on, "Amos does not care for our kind, or the wisdom he might learn from us...he simply wishes to use us for his own ends. And whatever they are, I do not think they will involve staying in this part of the world. Or *any* part of this world, for that matter."

I had gone quite red at this point, for of course I had still been worrying that one of the worst things that would come of all this was the theft of my academic research. That my friend had seen through me was an embarrassment only mollified by the good-natured way that, even now, he could find enough heart to laugh at my foolishness.

"Not in any part of this world?" I said. "And what on earth do you mean by that?"

Sebastian took a deep breath. For a moment his eyes closed. The skin there looked red and his face seemed very tired.

He was just about to speak, when a creak from behind me announced the door was opening. I turned, for a horrible moment half-expecting to see Amos there. But it was only a little girl, thin and tough-looking. She had big eyes that seemed to drink in the whole room.

"Blue, is that you?" asked Sebastian, trying to crane around me.

"Yes, sir," said the little girl. Her voice was meek enough, though there was something bold in those big eyes of hers.

"Tell me, my friend," he said softly, "what is it you imagined your precious faery-iron would achieve?"

I couldn't believe he would speak so freely before any newcomer, small child or otherwise.

But he waved my concern away.

"Oh, don't worry yourself, Tobias," he told me, and I noticed a sad smile now danced on his face. "Blue is another patient here. Her mother has had to go somewhere, so there is no one to look after her. She is keeping me company. And I," he said to the little girl, "have been telling you all sorts of silly stories, haven't I?"

"Yes, sir," the girl said again. I frowned. It seemed wrong to talk of this matter with anyone else present, whether they thought it nonsense stories or solid truth. Still, she had gained the trust of my friend; she was making him smile, too.

I shook myself, replayed his question in my head.

"Well, it would have the opposite effect to normal iron, obviously," I said after a moment. "Where iron repels faery-kind, faery-iron is attractive."

"It can do more than that," he told me. "In its simplest form, the substance provides protection for those of the blood, allows us to move freely from the forests and into the iron lands unmolested. Yet the story does not stop there, for just as normal iron can exist in differing forms, so faery-iron can be forged into differing substances with different properties. Amos does not seek to make trinkets to bring faeries to the iron cities. Amos seeks passage out of this world, and into the green lands beyond."

As Sebastian spoke, I felt something stirring in me. Memories of all the stories I had loved so much as a child raced through my mind.

Passage to the faery lands, I thought.

Oh, the days and weeks I had spent in summers past, wrapped in blankets, curled by fires and head lodged firmly in books, filled with dreams surpassing sweet...how I had longed for just this! To *travel* to the faery lands! To *escape*!

By my side, the little girl slipped to the floor and started playing with a doll. Still, her eyes kept darting up. I had the sense that she was following the conversation closely.

"Different forms, you say?" I asked Sebastian. "And he has done this, then? Amos has created this other form, this second form of faery-iron?"

But Sebastian shook his head. For a single moment, an expression of such pain crossed his face that it seemed to transform him entirely, to break him into something less, something fallen. In an instant, it was gone, so quick that I almost believed I had imagined it.

"No, not yet," he said. "He has not yet learnt how. Though I fear he has his suspicions."

I let out a sigh.

"And what would he do, then, if he could pass freely into those other worlds?"

Sebastian shrugged.

"Who knows?" he said. "Perhaps he would vanish into the green forests and deep places, and never be heard from again. But I fear that he would set to work on some mischief. There is much of cunning and pain in that one. And something else, something unbalanced...broken..."

His voice trailed off, and his eyes fluttered closed.

I cursed myself for a fool. In my excitement I had forgotten the delicate condition of my friend. If I was not careful, I thought, I would tire him beyond his meagre reserves of strength.

"I should go," I told him, and rose to my feet.

He opened his eyes again, and regarded me fondly, a half-smile on his lips.

"I am glad that you came," he said softly. "But you must promise me. Promise me that you will not seek to talk to Amos. Promise me that you will not try to reason with him or plead for me."

At first, I protested; it seemed unthinkable that I should leave my friend to the hideously cruel use Amos was making of him.

But at last, he prevailed, and I made my promise.

"Remember," Sebastian said, "you are at court no longer. If you think to treat Amos as you would a roguish courtier to be shamed by your words or chivvied into behaving with honour, then you had best think again. He would turn on you with the same utter ruthlessness with which he has bound me to his will. I say again: he is not a man to be taken lightly! Leave him be, and presently we will find ourselves in a stronger position. I have sent word. And...you do not think you have met *all* my family already, do you?"

His eyes sparkled then, and I felt an answering gleam of hope in my heart.

I laid my hand on his, and at his request helped him replace his scarf around the iron shackle that bound his neck. Then I made to bid my friend farewell.

But at that moment the little girl spoke.

"Wait," said Blue. "Won't you wait for the story, before you go?"

I looked at her for a moment, nonplussed.

"A...story?" I asked her. "Now?"

"Yes," she said. "Sebastian always tells a story at this time. To warm us off to sleep."

I must confess, her request seemed like the most natural thing in the world at the time. Though looking back on it now, the whole business of the little girl seems odd, as if it ought not to have happened. Still, I can see her sitting there now, as vivid in my mind as all the rest of it.

"Very well," I told her, though listening to a story then was the last thing I wanted.

"I will try and make it something jolly," said Sebastian. "I've had enough of sad stories. We need something hopeful."

"Yes, tell it," said the little girl. "Tell it now. But make it short. Make it short and make it a swift story, fast moving."

And once more, it seemed quite right that she should make such a demand.

"I'll tell this story then," said Sebastian. "Though I can't remember now just where I heard it. It is called

🏵 14 🏵

THE CRY FOR HELP

~

Once, there was a waterfall, high up at the very roof of the world. On top of the waterfall, there stood a little girl, slim and tough. She looked about with her big, silent eyes. But she could not see the one she was looking for, so she sat down and told the story of

15

THE CRY FOR HELP

~

Once, there was a green hill, high up above the plains and with a view over everything. On top of the hill stood a girl, slim and tough. She looked about with her big, watchful eyes. But there was still no sign of the one she looked for. So she thought and she frowned and she told the story of

❧ 16 ❧

THE CRY FOR HELP

~

Once, there was a bird, flying so high that the whole of creation was nothing more than a bluegreen smear of life below. On the bird rode a little girl, slim and tough. She looked about her carefully, studying everything with eyes that were huge and subtle. And then there *was* a sign of the one she looked for. She could see him, far below, sat at table with many others, looking bored and grumpy and rather stupid.

"Still, it is to him I must go," said the girl to herself.

She squeezed her knees together, and the bird dove downwards.

Faster, faster, faster it plunged, until it was a streak of white cutting through the blue sky.

Below her, the one she had been looking for turned from a speck to spot, then to a figure, and then to a great, hulking man with drooping jowls and thick whiskers.

A moment before the bird would have plunged them into the ground, the man looked up, and if he had looked stupid at first glance, at second glance you saw he was much sharper; and at the third and forth glance you understood he was much more clever than he had been letting on.

By the fifth glance - which was all the little girl had time to manage - she understood that the man had seen her coming all along, but had waited for her to get close before saying in a bored, lazy drawl

17

CEASE YOUR TELLING

≈

There was a tearing noise as the tiny carrier-story slammed full-speed into the command. For an instant, it was suspended there, a streak of pale gold, translucent against the sky. Then it was ripped apart, smashed into a thousand smoking portions of plot and characterisation.

Not that there was much of either there, by the look of things, thought High Sheriff Grok. At first glance, the tiny story had been nothing more than an envelope, a sort of parcel by which someone had been trying to reach him.

He stood, a broad, rather fat and dour-looking story, wearing a pair of heavy-duty similes across his chest like gun-belts, and regarded the other members of the committee.

"Sorry 'bout that," he drawled. "Didn't mean to startle ya."

In fact, he had been rather gratified by the looks of panic and dismay which had shone on those pale, pen-pushing faces. Not one of them had ever worked on the ground; not one of them knew the real difficulties faced by a Sheriff on a daily basis. They never had to deal with stories that had got sick; with villains who refused to play the part of villains anymore; with new-fangled working-time directives which meant any sub-plots over a certain size were entitled to holidays every ten narrative cycles. No, these...these *bureaucrats* (truthfully, he could not think of a more damning word) knew nothing about the challenges he and his Sheriffs had to put up with. It had felt good to startle them with a little blast of it.

"What...what was it?" asked one of them, a small, anaemic-looking man who didn't look like he could handle a badly-Told nursery rhyme.

That was a good question. Grok pushed his chair back and prowled over to where the largest remnant of the tiny story sat. It was a twist of smoking, shaking narrative potential. Evidently, this part was made of something tougher and more real than the rest of the story. He had to admit, he hadn't expected the thing to shatter like that. His command had been peremptory, but still: any half-decent story should have just been slammed to a standstill, sprung open for inspection, not broken to pieces. The whole thing was rather strange.

"Up you get, you lily-livered excuse for a character," Grok said, poking the remnant with a boot. "What do you mean by screaming down on me like...oh!"

And he cut off, because at that moment the little twisted remnant of story shook itself and sprang upwards, unfolding into the shape of...

"Indigo Shuttlecock," High Sheriff Grok muttered to himself. "I might have known."

The slim, tough-looking girl was only a simulacrum - an echo of the actual Indigo Shuttlecock - Grok could tell that at a glance. She had been much more solid than the story she had rode in on, but she was nowhere near being real, not in the way Grok thought of things as real.

"High Sheriff Grok," came the nasal, high-pitched voice of another of the Council, "please be so good as to enlighten us as to..."

Grok felt the skin on the back of his neck start to crawl. The voice belonged to Councillor Maria Flunk. If there was ever an individual who was able to make Grok angry just by the mere act of existing, it was Maria Flunk.

"Sheriff business," Grok growled over his shoulder without turning round.

"But really Sheriff, we insist that you..."

"You ain't got no authority to insist on nothin'," spat Grok. "Just you go on with your numbers and rules and such. I'll deal with this."

And so saying, he grasped Indigo Shuttlecock and marched her away from the gathering, not caring at all what shouts came after him, and not stopping until they were far away and out of earshot.

Indigo waited until Grok had brought them to a stop before saying, "Don't worry, boss, no need to thank me."

"Thank you? Why the hell should I thank you?" demanded Grok.

Indigo shrugged.

"Ain't you always sayin' how you hate them council meetings?" she said. "Got you a good reason to leave early."

"Yeah? And what's that?" said Grok. "For that matter, where's the rest of you at? Looks like no more'n seven or eight percent of you there. Which usually I wouldn't say is such a bad thing, given how much trouble you invariably seem to be in."

"I'm five actually," said the echo of Indigo Shuttlecock. "Didn't figure I could spare much more of myself, what with what's goin' down."

Grok raised a thick gnarl of eyebrow and waited for her to go on.

"I mean, I don't like to bother you, but I thought you should know."

"Know what?" asked Grok.

Indigo sucked her lip.

"Don't know for sure," she admitted. "Found a strange story, wandering, far away from home. Not one of ours, didn't belong to my Fold. Something didn't seem right, so I investigated. The resonances were all wrong. The way the story was being Told...well, someone doing the Telling had been in contact with something...something special. Something *dangerous*."

Grok felt a tingle of dread creep through him. Indigo was no flighty fool, however hard a time he gave her. He gave all his Sheriffs a hard time; but of them all, Indigo was far and away the most solid. If she was asking for help, he knew he had to take her seriously.

"Dangerous? Dangerous how?"

The sending of Indigo Shuttlecock hesitated for a moment, then told him.

When she was done, Grok gave a whistle.

"Faery iron, is it?" he said. "You did the right thing, sending for me. Ain't had to deal with a problem like that since..."

And he trailed off, because he couldn't remember *ever* having to deal with a problem like that before, though he had heard about it many, many cycles ago, mentioned as a theoretical possibility.

"What do we do?" asked Indigo. She looked calm, but Grok was good at reading his Sheriffs, and he saw worry there, deep down and locked up well.

"You got this story all looked into, I assume?" he asked her.

She nodded.

"Sure," she told him. "Looked it up and down, seen how it turns out."

"And?" he prompted.

Indigo shook her head and looked away.

"I see," said Grok. "Well, better see it for myself, then. Got to work out what there is to do. Lead on, Sheriff."

Indigo made an awkward whistling noise.

"Might be as there's a problem there," she said. "I mean, correct me if I'm wrong, but from where I was standing it looked like the story I rode in on was blown to pieces."

"Damn," said Grok, who had forgotten this in all the excitement. "Didn't mean to do that. Frail little thing that it was, couldn't have hit it with more'n a grade six order to cease. Couldn't you have caught yourself something more robust to ride?"

Indigo rolled her eyes.

"Seein' as how speed was of the essence and all..." she said.

"Yeah, yeah," said Grok, waving her into silence. He understood the logic well enough. If he had wanted to track another Sheriff down, he would have used the lightest, flimsiest carrier-story he could fashion. The greater the intrinsic narrative weight of the story, the more difficult it would be to steer. It would have its own places to go, its own resolutions to reach.

"Well, can't we just follow the trail backwards? How many stories did you hitch a ride on to find me?"

"Might work," allowed Indigo. "Came through the Flashways, about three cycles. Tiny things. It's just…"

And she gave the stout Grok a meaningful look, taking in his fat rolls of excess characterisation, his massive limbs made of layer upon layer of ancient, antique sub-plots.

Grok shot her an indignant look.

"Sheriff Indigo, are you tryin' to say I'm too *fat* to ride the Flashways?"

"Not sayin' anything boss," said Indigo, keeping her face carefully neutral. "Those Flash stories is awful delicate, that's all."

"Too fat, indeed," said Grok. "I was riding the Flashways before you was even a Sheriff! Hell, I was doing it back when you were a teething little story yourself, without even a dream of one day going to the Academy!"

"Right you are, boss," said Indigo. "So you want me to lead the way?"

"That's exactly what I want, and hop to!" he snapped. Then, as she was leading them away, "Insolent pup," he added, under his breath.

If she heard it, the echo of Indigo Shuttlecock chose not to respond. She was looking around now, searching close to the ground, picking up the few smoking remnants of the tiny story she had rode in on. After a few minutes, she seemed satisfied.

"Think I've found enough," she said. "Should be able to reverse the Telling with this."

"Make it so," said Grok.

Indigo moved her arm up in a wide arc, sprinkling the remnants of the story as she did so.

Just then, Grok became aware of footsteps. He turned just as a thin, wiry hand was planted on his shoulder.

"Sheriff Grok," said Maria Flunk, omitting the 'High' and instantly enraging Grok a few degrees more than he would have thought possible, "would you *kindly* tell us what is going on? You can't just walk away from the Committee like that, however little use you think we are."

In the background, Grok was dimly aware of Indigo Shuttlecock reaching upwards on tiptoes, trying to call back the sparks of story she had let fly.

"Er, boss..." she said, but Grok ignored her.

"No, *you* listen to *me*, Miss-so-high-and-mighty," he snarled, turning to face Maria Flunk. "I don't think you're completely useless, only useless in every way that matters."

Maria Flunk shook with indignation.

"How *dare* you?" she demanded. "You grunts think that you're the only ones who know what hard work is! Just because I'm not down on the factory floor working directly with stories..."

"Boss!" said Indigo, waving her arms frantically now.

"Hard work?" echoed Grok. "Ain't only hard work you don't know about, it's any kind of useful work! When was the last time you even *saw* a story? You just sit up here legislatin' an' pontificatin' an'..."

"*Boss!*" screamed Indigo.

"What?" shouted Grok and Maria Flunk together.

But by then it was obvious.

The sparkling fragments of story had formed up into a brightening arc of pure narrative. What Indigo had thrown together as a quick weave, a small loop of story meant to shuttle them back to the Flash-ways, had now mutated and swollen terribly: the fate of all stories which are not adequately kept in check during their Telling.

"Now, damn it Sheriff, Tell it now!" ordered Grok.

He felt Maria's claw-like hand tighten on his shoulder, and realised too late what that would mean.

His eyes widened.

But Indigo was already speaking.

"Gotta tell you my story now," Indigo yelled, competing with the rising hurricane of narration. "It's a funny old tale. Its called

❧ 18 ❧

CRY THE RETURN

~

There was a pendulum. It was big as bridges and weighed as much as the whole world. It swung from the darkness on one side of the Universe to the lightness on the other, and it could take you from somewhere to anywhere else.

The pendulum reached the apex of its swing, and from the shadows jumped the figures: a small, tough girl with big eyes, and next to her a huge, grizzled man with grey whiskers and...

...And next to the man, holding on to him with one wiry, talon-like claw, a scowling, rake-thin woman emerged from the darkness, too (despite the spirited attempts of the man to dislodge her) and as the pendulum began to swing down, cutting the huge space like a scream, everything began to shake and shudder and dust rained from the emptiness above because the weight was too much and the weight was too much and the weight was

❦ 19 ❦

TOO MUCH

~

High Sheriff Grok roared, no longer able to tell if the words that echoed over him were his own or Indigo's or the last scream of the breaking story. There was a terrible bone-deep tearing noise, a moment of weightlessness, and then everything went horribly still.

It was all silent. Grok was still crouching on the cold, smooth surface of the huge pendulum. Only now it wasn't moving. Not an inch.

He looked up, and a wave of vertigo washed through him, because there in the distance - a few feet and a mile and a whole Universe away - the pendulum also stood. A sheet of darkness separated the two instances of the pendulum, shifting and twirling like severed pieces of an enormous bunting.

On the far pendulum, he could make out a tiny figure. It was looking around, trying to get its bearings.

Grok swallowed. Dread tickled at his belly. Indigo had been right. He had been too heavy.

He took a deep breath, steadied himself. He had got himself out of worse fixes than this.

"Indigo," Grok called out. "Indigo! You okay?"

His words seemed to die as they shot out over the endless blank expanse of ruptured story.

"Boss?" Indigo's voice came back frail and thin. "Is that you?"

"I think so," said Grok. Then he sighed and patted his ample belly. "Guess you were right, Sheriff."

"You think you can make it across?" called Indigo.

Grok looked at the inky black expanse separating the two pieces of the severed story.

"Not a chance," he called out. "Where does your end lead out?"

There was a pause, as Indigo examined the far end of the tattered story they were riding in.

"This end comes out on the Flashways," said Indigo. "Pretty sure I can see the rest of me. Sitting round some camp-fire. Listening to the story we're trying to get to."

Grok cursed under his breath. They had been pretty close to making it, he guessed. If only he had weighed a little less...

Then he froze.

His eyes swivelled down to where a thin, furious woman was clinging on to the surface of the pendulum as if scared it would suddenly start bucking like a wild horse.

"Maria Flunk," he growled.

He hadn't been too fat. It was her fault. The story could have taken his weight. They would have made it, if only that accursed...that accursed *bureaucrat* hadn't insisted on clinging on.

"This...is...most...irregular," Maria Flunk hissed. "When I get back, I will be submitting a very *strongly* worded report to the Committee, let me tell you, and this sort of frankly *unsafe* story will be outlawed!"

Her words were passionate and full of venom, and would perhaps have been chilling were they not spoken by someone who was so completely terrified of being shaken off an utterly stationary object.

As things stood, the sight of the pen-pushing Maria Flunk absolutely removed from her safe, sterile world of numbers and charts and regulations was enough to bring a smile to his lips.

He opened his mouth to ask her how she liked seeing a story close up for once and how she meant to be getting home, when it dawned on him that she certainly wouldn't be getting home. Not at all. Not without his help.

And however much he despised Maria Flunk, he couldn't just abandon her here. Couldn't leave her to sway forever on a tiny fragment of a broken story. It would be worse than death, to leave her here. Whatever else he was, Grok was a High Sheriff. Dealing with things like this was his responsibility.

But then, if he had to babysit Counsellor Flunk, how would he ever get to Indigo's emergency in time to help?

Grok squeezed his eyes shut and pinched his nose.

What to do, what to do...

"...I think you might be able to reach it!" Indigo's voice broke through at last. He realised she had been trying to get his attention.

"What's that?" Grok demanded, looking up.

"I said, I think I recognise that little wisp of story up away yonder," repeated Indigo. She was pointing to a flap of narration that hung down from the darkness some way above Grok's head.

He peered up, trying to make sense of what it was he was seeing.

It looked like a small stone arch, though what was beyond it he couldn't tell.

"How's that, Indigo?" he shouted back. On the floor, Maria Flunk carried out a whispered diatribe invoking a multitude of evil-sounding clauses and promising retribution of an unheard-of scale against any story that wasn't iron-clad in unbreakable plotting ten feet thick.

"Saw it on my way back last time," she called. "Matter of fact, looks like it might even be the little fellow that caught my attention in the first place."

Grok eyed the small triangle of story uncertainly.

"You think she'd do?" he asked.

Indigo shrugged.

"Might just," she said. "You got many other options you ain't telling me about?"

That was true enough.

Grok thought about it.

He was pretty confident he could leap up and work his way into the tatter of narration Indigo had pointed out to him. Once there, getting onwards shouldn't be too difficult - he wasn't just a Sheriff, after all, but *High* Sheriff, and when he said, 'Jump,' most stories said, 'How high, and what's the arc?' Then again, he would be pulling Maria Flunk along after. She would make things a hundred times more difficult, he was sure of that...

"But I don't have a choice," he said to himself.

"Boss?" called Indigo.

"It'll have to do," Grok called out. "Get away with you, Sheriff. Go whatever way you can, get back to the rest of you and wait for me there. I'll be along as soon as I can."

Indigo nodded and whipped off a loose salute.

"Sure thing, boss," she said. "See you on the other side."

She jumped, scrambled for a shimmer of story in the far distance that Grok could only just make out...then she was gone.

Grok stood, staring after her for a moment, impressed by the agility with which she had leapt out of the broken story.

If only I could still do that, he thought. *Oh, to be young again...*

The sound of Maria Flunk tentatively getting to her feet brought him back to himself. He wasn't young any more. Hadn't been for a very long time.

"What now Sheriff?" asked Maria stiffly. It looked as if she had passed through the denial-and-gibbering stage to the just-holding-on-to-sanity-by-a-thread stage. He had seen such things before. Bureaucrats, who thought they understood the system so very well, suddenly confronted with the terrifying reality of the Storystream. It was the difference between reading about carnivores and being eaten by one.

"Now we get gone, too," he told her.

"What?" she demanded. "How?"

Grok wasn't looking at her. Instead he was eyeing the little triangular flap of story way above, and wondering how to reach it.

"Oh, easy," he said, with a hint of irony in his voice. "We just gotta leap up there and persuade that funny little story to let us in. Then it'll be a simple matter of working out where the hell we are, and how to get on to Indigo while we still have time to do any good..."

"I see," said Maria. Her voice sounded surprisingly calm, all of a sudden. "Well, don't let me keep you."

Grok turned round to see that Maria Flunk had quite composed herself and was staring at him with cold, indifferent eyes.

"Huh?" he said.

"You get on," she told him. "I'll just wait here. I'm sure the rest of the Committee will have organised a rescue party by now."

Grok was frowning at her. She couldn't be that stupid.

Could she?

"This here story's broken down," he told her slowly, trying to get the information through to her. "It ain't going nowhere. That means we have to leave. And fast."

"I see," she nodded briskly. "You and your sweaty little friend quite clearly have no patience for these things. Addicted to adrenaline. I, on the other hand, am a paragon of calm and patience."

He stared at her, not quite believing. Didn't she know what would happen to the story, now that it had finished being told?

"Stop being silly now," he said. "Ain't just me as has to leave. You stay here, you won't last long."

Hesitantly, not quite believing what he was forcing himself to do, Grok held out his hand.

Maria Flunk stared at it as if it were made of animal excrement.

"I - am - staying - *here*," she said, biting off each word as if they were pieces of a bitter apple.

Grok found that his temper was fraying. Here he was, trying to help a fool - help a fool that would end up being *dead* if she wasn't careful - and all he was getting was grief.

"No - you - are - not," he replied. He reached out for her, and she slapped his hand away.

"Stay away from me!" she shouted. "If you come any closer, I'll..."

But her words were swallowed up. A huge noise echoed around them. It was horrible, full of teeth and grease and hunger.

The pendulum swayed under them.

For a moment, Maria Flunk stared at him with huge, horrified eyes.

"What was...?" she started to ask, but there was no time.

Grok reached out and wrapped her in one big, meaty arm. She

tensed, as if being touched by him was the most objectionable thing she could possibly imagine. Grok wished he could tell her he felt the same way.

Instead, he focused all his attention on the triangle of story above them.

The roar came again. Closer now, hungrier...

It's getting near, he thought.

Grok licked his lips.

"What are you doing?" Maria demanded. She sounded frantic, unhinged. "Get us out of here! Get us out of here! Get us..."

Grok leapt.

Not a moment too soon. There was another rending crash, and the pendulum below them was suddenly dashed away. Grok had a vague sense of sharp white teeth buzzing into the stone of the pendulum, gnawing it away to nothing.

The triangle of story above them swelled.

"I need to hear a story," Grok shouted. "Any story will do. I think this one might be called

❧ 20 ❧

IN THE ORBIT OF A STORY

∾

A nd then the darkness and the pendulum were gone, and Grok was suspended in light. He floated, one arm around the tense Maria Flunk, deep in the cloying substances of the story he had leapt into.

Well. That had been close. Another few moments and...

"What was that, Sheriff?" demanded Maria Flunk.

"Something hungry," he told her. "I'll explain later."

He glanced around. They were enmeshed in translucent folds of story. They billowed slowly, giving half-seen glimpses of characters and events, settings, plot points. It all seemed rather strange and out of focus.

"Must have come at her from an odd angle," Grok mused to himself. "No wonder she looks strange."

Grok was well-versed in the many frames of reference it was necessary to swim through when one dealt with stories. In moving between them, a Sheriff soon came to understand something of the fundamentally, well *gloopy* nature of reality. A story looked very different when viewed from the outside as it did from the inside. For that matter, *he* himself would look very different in different contexts. Inside a story, the story might bend him into whatever shape best fit its needs...

"Where are we?" asked Maria. "More importantly, how are you going to get me home?"

Grok shook his head in irritation. Her words pecked at him like a swarm of tiny, carnivorous birds.

"In a story," he told her. "Well, I think we're more or less underneath a story, as it goes. That's what comes of hitching a ride. Don't worry. I'll get us out soon enough."

Maria Flunk sighed, as if she were the most put-upon creature in the whole of creation.

"If we *must* travel together, is it really necessary for you to...to touch me like that?"

She glared down at where his hand rested on her forearm, her lip twisted in disdain.

I could just let go, Grok thought. *Just let go and get the hell out of here.*

It would be much quicker that way. Pulling Maria along after him would make things much more tricky. And would it be so bad, so very bad if she were to become...lost? Maybe not make it back to the Committee for a few cycles?

For a single golden moment, Grok basked in the glory of a world without Maria Flunk. Then he realised how much paperwork her disappearance would entail, and scowled.

"Better hold on tight," he said, sounding surly. "If you ain't holding on, I might lose you."

"I see," muttered Maria. For a moment, she looked as if she were seriously considering letting go.

Then she sighed.

"Very well," she told him. "Let's get going, then."

Grok nodded. No point spending any more time here than necessary. If they were lucky, it would just be a simple matter of jumping out of this story and then getting directions to where Indigo had headed. She had sounded pretty confident that the story they were now in would provide a way back to her.

Keeping one hand on Maria, Grok lifted his other and concentrated.

"Time to let us go," he commanded the story. "Spit us out."

Nothing happened.

Grok blinked.

That wasn't right. The stories *always* did what they were told. He was High Sheriff, after all!

He scowled, and repeated the command.

The story gave a faint, a very faint grunt. The ether around them shifted slightly, then thumped back into place.

"Does something seem to be the problem?" demanded Maria Flunk.

"Can't understand it," Grok started to say. "Should only take a nudge to send us spinning out..."

But Maria chose that moment to pull her forearm out of his grasp; and as soon their touch broke, the story was swooshing about him, shrinking (or perhaps he was getting bigger), every mote of characterisation folding inwards and letting him leave.

Understanding flooded through him.

It was her. It was that damned...that damned *bureaucrat*!

It made sense, in a horrible sort of a way. She was everything that a Sheriff was not. She did not care about stories, she couldn't feel them pulsing in her veins, as real and vibrant and true as life itself.

She was rejecting stories; could Grok really blame the story for rejecting her?

Once again, the temptation shot through him: he should just leave her here. It wouldn't be cruel - she would find her way out eventually, he was sure; and after all, he had a mission to attend to, a most urgent one. He *had* to get out. That was clearly important...

Grok sighed.

He couldn't do it. However much he wanted to, he couldn't just leave her.

He had to bring her out. However difficult that made things...

He shook his head, and made an impatient gesture. At once, the story was streaming round him again, rolling backwards. Now he was a tiny speck once more, a mote falling through the layers upon layers of narrative energy. Then he was back, standing next to Maria again.

"Oh, so you've decided not to leave me to die here, after all," said

Maria acidly.

Grok glared at her.

"Don't push it," he said. "I can just as easy change my mind a second time."

She snorted.

"I doubt that," she said. "You know quite well just what trouble you'll be in if you don't get me home."

"It'd be worth it," he muttered under his breath.

"What?" she said sharply.

"Shh," he told her. "I'm trying to think."

He couldn't swim out of the story with her. That much was apparent. The story wasn't letting him issue it the usual commands, not while he was touching Maria Flunk, at least. What option did that leave them...?

Grok nodded to himself.

"Have to do it manually, then," he decided.

Luckily, a Sheriff made it his business to always be prepared for just such an eventuality.

Grok reached inside his shirt, and pulled out a glimmering red-golden thing. It gave off little puffs of sparks.

"What is *that*?" asked Maria, wrinkling her nose.

"It's a plot device," Grok told her. "Multi-purpose. Custom-built, very useful."

"And what do you intend to do with it?"

Grok made a few final adjustments. The plot device gave a satisfying little *clunk* noise and changed shape. Suddenly it was a bent, spiky object trailing a rope of pure causality.

"This," said Grok.

He spun the plot device twice around his head, then hurled it upwards. It shot away, leaving a trail of glimmering sparks. The rope unwound behind it. Grok tied it around his waist.

There was a distant *thump* from above them and the rope went taut. Grok tested it a few times. It seemed to hold.

He held out a hand for Maria.

"You're going to climb out?" she asked doubtfully. "On *that*?"

"You got a better plan?" he asked.

Maria didn't.

After a long, difficult journey, Grok gave a final heave and pushed his head up out through the topmost layer of narration. He turned and pulled Maria up after him. Then they lay gasping on the very roof of the story.

It looked huge from up here, spread below them in rippling swirls of plot.

That's just because the story's not letting me go back to my proper size, Grok told himself. *If I didn't have to carry this dead-weight with me, the story would look so, so small...*

He shut that train of thought off. It wouldn't do him any good.

"Okay," he said, pulling himself to his feet. "On we go."

They set off across the roof of the story. Most of the time, the clouds of narrative energy were so thick and cloying that they couldn't see at all down into the story proper. At other moments though, the folds and billows shifted, blown away in a wind Grok could half-sense. Then they could gaze straight down, down into the very centre of the story, where they could see the characters and events play themselves out, an endless dance of plotting and causality, rolling through the same sequences again and again.

"You know," observed Maria in a voice rather different from her usual hectoring tone, "I must say there are times it looks almost...almost..."

She paused, as if searching for a word she didn't quite understand.

The story below them had blown especially clear, and the many, many miles of swirling plot drifted and danced vividly beneath their feet.

"Almost beautiful," she said at last. She looked up at him, doing something strange with her face. It took Grok a few seconds to realise she was smiling.

He opened his mouth to reply, and the world collapsed.

He just had time to think, *it's given way!* and he was falling, spinning end over end, down, down, down into the chaos of the story. As he plunged down, he felt the strands of the story plucking at him, probing him, testing his intrinsic narrative field.

It's looking for a way in, he realised. Which was so laughable, a big grin burst out on his face. Then he felt the tendrils of story burrowing deeper into his substances. He thought about Maria - whose hand he still clutched - and about the waves of fear washing off of her. He thought about how powerless he seemed to be, as long as that contact remained. He thought about the needs of the story, a great hulking torrent of narrative inevitability, and he understood what was happening. It was trying to pluck them, like flies out of a hurricane, to pluck them out of the maelstrom and shoe-horn them into whatever roles it needed. The smile died on his lips.

Just let go of her, he screamed at himself. If he let go, the story would be his to command. He could escape. He could be gone in the time it took to say, *once upon a time...*

...and yet he didn't want to. And it wasn't - he realised to his profound disgust - simply because of the paperwork he would have to complete if Maria Flunk failed to return. No.

He thought of the way she had looked a moment before the fall. He thought of her mouth, as it quirked to form the word, 'beautiful'.

The story screamed about them, and they were held suspended now, two tiny centres of characterisation, held powerless, at the mercy of the story, ready to be slotted into place.

But Grok was too horrified to feel afraid. It was so obvious, of course, now that he thought of it. He had spent his existence dealing with stories. He should have known where things were heading with Maria from the moment they got thrust together, an odd-couple pairing who couldn't stand one another...

He opened his mouth to scream, but no sound came out. The story around them roared too loudly for anything else to be heard.

It sang to them, telling itself to them, again and again until they were steeped in it, lost, utterly lost, and all that remained in the way of memory of a time that existed before was the feeling of their hands, gripping tight, holding on to one another and to a distant, shared past...

It went on for an eternity and an age and an infinite loop of tellings. But even before a single narrative cycle had passed, Grok felt his awareness shrinking down, the knowledge of who he was and what he had been doing shrivelling inside himself, being packed away, and all that was left was the story he was now a part of, telling itself again and again, and which was called

~

The Place Where My Friends Were Taken (Reprise)

~

So I sat there, a prisoner, trapped inside the cage of bones, and knew it was all my fault.

I begged Claw, I screamed at him. But he wouldn't listen to me. He wouldn't even hear me. His hard, cold bones enmeshed me - a tiny, foolish cat within a trap I had walked right into - and though I could see the world beyond, sounds came to me as if creeping through syrup.

I watched as the cavern filled up. Oh, it was awful.

One by one the huge bone-birds flapped up to their nest, their eyre high in these forsaken mountains. The floor was filthy with decayed scraps of old meals, and with the stinking, white excrement of the creatures, for they were not clean. And inside of each bird, trapped inside the cage of ribs, one of my friends now sat. I saw their wide eyes, I saw their miserable faces. One by one the bone-birds had captured them. I thought of our carriage, our magnificent rolling carriage, abandoned on the planes below; and the wall of fire sweeping towards us even now, sweeping from the East.

When the last of them had returned, the bone birds set up a great clamouring. They were full of life; exultant, full to the brim - quite different from the sickly creatures that had first swept down on us. Those creatures would never have captured my friends, not without my treachery, not without the herb Claw had talked me into spilling in their food. No, their bones then had been thin as sticks, and the mad fire in their eyes had been dim, sickly.

Now they were splendid. They shone; they strutted, preening, prideful, hideous things. I wondered at the change that had come over them.

Then my eyes met Unity's, and in one awful moment I understood.

Her gaze was hollow, broken. The power had gone from her eyes. Her jaw was slack, her cheeks were drawn.

"No," I muttered to myself. "No, not that."

And I looked again at my friends, examining them closely, desperately hoping I would not see the same thing.

But with all of them it was the same. Kye, Thom, Layn...

All of them.

They were being sucked dry. They were being used up.

Even as I watched, I fancied Unity's face grew a little more hollow. My friends were food.

If I could have ended my life then, I would have. My disgrace was complete. But I could do no such thing. The cage in which I was trapped was tiny, bones pressed tight against my fur. I could not escape, and I had no means of hurting myself, even.

So I covered my eyes with my paws and wept. I tried to shut it all out, the triumphant screams of the bone-birds, the shrieks of my friends...and most of all, the constant voice from deep inside that told me again and again: *your fault.*

I must have slept then - or passed out - for the next thing I knew a voice was at my ear, low and urgent. I blinked, stretching as much as I was able.

The cavern was dark now - the sun had set, and only faint moonlight filtered in from the cavern mouth above us.

All else was still. Around me were many gaunt white shapes. It took me a moment to realise it was our captors, still as statues, arrayed on perches.

Sleeping, I thought, and a hope jumped up in my chest and just as quickly collapsed. I thought at first I might escape; but then, how would that be possible? It was not a cage of metal or wood, but of bone itself that held me. I was *within* my captor; if I tried to escape, Claw would know in an instant.

"Aubrey," the words came again; a rough, hissing voice. I tilted my head.

It was Kye. The bone-bird in which he was captive stood close to mine, and I was able to see my friend clearly

[*And it seems now, in telling it, that Kye was rather different than he should have been; stouter; with whiskers - which he never had before - and some kind of weapon strung across his back...which is strange...*]

When I saw my friend, I burst into tears.

"It's my fault!" I told him. "All mine. I was tricked. I was selfish. I brought us to this. I..."

But another voice cut me off.

"Don't blame yourself," said Unity.

[*Though it seems to me that her voice was never as high and nasal as I tell it now. Something very odd is going on here...*]

I saw that Unity was trapped just beyond Kye, in a bone-bird of her own. But whatever walls of force held us prisoners in check, they seemed to be weakened while the birds slept. I could hear their words clearly.

[*And the two of them were even holding hands, though I am sure that never happened...*]

"But I did this!" I told her.

"Hush," said Kye. "We don't have time for blame. Or for self pity, either. Not now."

"What difference does it make?" I asked. "Before long the fire will come and take us all. We will never get back to our carriage."

"There is still hope," said Unity. She spoke with certainty; still, their was a something troubled in her eyes that I did not like.

"They will leave this place at sunrise," Kye said. "They sleep now to prepare for the long flight ahead. You have slept deep, Aubrey. The night is nearly done, then they will awake. They don't mean to be caught by the flames any more than we did."

I knew that. Claw had hinted as much: they had been too weak to fly, not without food. I hadn't realised that the food would be us.

"So?" I asked. "What good does that do us? We could have all the time in the world and still never escape these wretched prisons."

My voice sounded petulant even to me.

"Perhaps that would be true," said Unity, "if we were alone."

I opened my mouth to ask what she meant, but at that moment there was a low scraping noise, and a strange shape shuffled into the moonlight.

It was a bone-bird, but unlike all the others. It was small - smaller than all of them save only Claw, the hatchling in which I was trapped; smaller than all my friends - and yet there was something weighty and potent about the thing. Something different...

"The bones are joined," I said, realising what it was that gave the impression of solidity.

"Yes," said the creature, and its voice was as dry as dust on rainless mountains.

"What...what are you?" I asked.

"He is a friend," said Unity.

But I was sick of making new friends. I had thought I had made one in Claw, and look where that had got me.

"A friend? A friend of whose? Of theirs maybe. Not of ours."

My words were more spiteful than I had intended. They shamed me, because I knew I was only spilling out the anger at another that in truth I felt against myself.

"That," said the strange bone-bird, "is up to you. For my part, I would help you now, because it is what is best for my people. For what they have become."

"Who *are* you?" I asked.

The creature gave me slow, silent stare.

"I am First," said First. "I am the keeper of the gate."

But I was in no mood for riddles.

"First?" I laughed. "First what? First of these tricksome devils? Are they your fault, then?"

I did not expect an answer, but First looked at me sadly, and said, "Yes."

That took me back. He spoke into my silence.

"I was made, long ago, from the earth and the bones of the mountain. These you see before me are my children - my great, great, grand-children - and their time has passed."

"You are old, then?" asked Unity.

First nodded.

"Older and sadder than it is possible to know," he said. He turned his black eyes on me. "I was preserved, you see. I was changed, so that I might last. Last a long, long time. And protect them. Protect them all. Not just from death, no; but protect them from what they might become. From the stain they might become on the world, for there was always mischief in our blood."

And First shifted so that the moonlight shone on his bones, and I understood suddenly that they were no longer bones, that he had been consecrated in stone. His form was of stone, and a flesh of stone was on him, and black stones were his eyes.

"Who did this to you?" I asked. "Why?"

"That," he said slowly, "is another story."

"And one there is no time for," put in Kye.

Unity was nodding.

"There is a way," she said. "I have seen it. But..."

And she looked troubled and said no more.

"It must be so," said First. "Either that, or you all die. Slow, rotting deaths, digested in the bone bellies of my children."

"What are you talking about?" I demanded.

"Escape," said First. "You must escape."

"Must? Must?" I spat. "Yes, I agree! But *must* and *can* are very different things!"

And I hissed my frustration.

A shudder passed through Claw and I froze.

The vile hatchling stirred uneasily in his sleep.

We sat in tense silence while we waited for him to awake.

After a moment, he settled back. I allowed myself to breathe.

"You must escape," said First again. His voice was implacable as stone. "And you can. If I help you."

Something stirred in me then, a faint glimmer of hope. But I would not let myself believe it might be possible.

"Oh, it's that simple, is it?" I muttered.

"Not quite that simple," said First, and again his voice was sad. "Nothing like this ever is."

I thought I understood him then. I wondered what he wanted from us, in exchange for our freedom.

"There's a price, then?" I said.

"There always is," he told me. "But if you don't take my offer, you must all pay a price; and a steep one."

I peered closely at him, trying to make out the expression on his face of beak and stone. But the moonlight was fading. Night was wearing on.

"What price was worse than the slow rotting death you mentioned?" I asked.

"For the others, it is the price of losing a friend," he told me, and it took me a moment to realise what he was saying, though I still had no idea as to how it might come to pass.

There was a long, heavy silence.

"You don't have to do it," said Unity softly.

But I did. It was my fault we were there. Of course I had to do it. Whatever *it* was...

I closed my eyes.

"Tell me," I said.

First shuffled closer, his dark eyes black as the space between stars.

"I am of stone," he told me. "I was made to guard my people, to guard their way. But...but they have lost their way. They have become bitter and twisted things, these children of mine. The world is changing now. Much is being unmade. Their time should be done, too."

"And what is stopping you from unmaking them?" I asked. First's body looked old and slow...but the stone was cold and strong. I imagined it slamming into those twists of bone, imagined the bone crashing and crumbling to dust.

First shook his head.

"They are my children," he said. "I cannot hurt them. It is not permitted. Old forces govern

these things; they will not be cheated."

At that I threw back my head and chuckled low in my throat.

"So there we have it," I said. "You cannot hurt them, though you have the strength. I lack the strength, but I would hurt them in a heartbeat. If only I had your strength, then perhaps all would be well."

But First only smiled at me.

"Yes," he said.

He lifted a limb, holding it before me, heavy and cold.

And the stone began to flow.

Slowly at first, leeching and rippling, then quickening, moving like a living thing, it drifted like smoke through the air towards me.

It stopped, quivering, an inch from my whiskers.

"This is the price," First told me. "To take up my mantle. To become stone. You will have the strength of stone, the strength of mountains. You can kill my children, as they should have been killed long ago. You can set free your friends. There is still time. But..."

"But?" I repeated.

"But you will be of stone," First went on. "You will be the keeper of the way, and I will be gone.

"You will not be able to leave the mountain."

The words sunk in.

I could set my friends free, I could right my stupid wrong. But I would have to watch, watch as they left, watch as they scrambled back down the mountain, watch as they fled into the West...and watch as the fire came upon me from the East.

I looked at Unity. I looked at Kye. They were my friends. They did not hate me, not after all the wrong I had done them.

And I knew if I refused this offer, if I refused this curse, this last chance...then they would not hate me either.

And we would die slow deaths by endless inches.

I knew what I had to do.

"I will do it," I said softly. "Of course I will."

First regarded me with those black, black eyes.

"Will it hurt?" I asked; but before he could reply, a lilac glimmering shone suddenly in the cavern mouth.

The sun. The sun was rising. The first rays were peeking into the cave.

The bone-birds began to stir.

First looked at me again. There was a question in his eyes.

"Now," I told him urgently. "Do it now."

"Be brave, little cat," he told me.

Then his arm was touching me. And the stone was flowing, scalding my fur, burning me, freezing me so deep I felt I would never be warm again. I opened my mouth to scream, and stone was in it, forcing down my throat, a gush, a torrent, unstoppable, unbearable...

Beneath me, I was dimly aware of the floor shaking as Claw shook himself, realising that something was wrong.

And then the pain was gone. I stood, as still as a statue - for no breath moved me now - and gazed about through onyx eyes fired in the heart of the mountain.

The cavern was spread before me. It felt like I was seeing it for the first time.

The bone-birds looked so small, so frail. And vile. They looked such petty, twisted things. And in them, trapped still, wits wandering once again now the birds stirred out of sleep, my friends, jailed, listless. And, below me now - for Claw had flapped up to a higher perch - I saw First, frozen and still...but of stone no longer. Now he was of bone, pure bone, white as fresh snow, shimmering in the sunlight pouring into the cave.

For a single frozen moment he held his shape. Then a gust of wind blew in, and the old bones shattered.

As if waking them from a dream, the bone-birds stirred, full of life, full of malice...and full of fear.

They had seen me.

"What...what have you been doing, little food?" screeched Claw. He was turning his head, straining to peer in at me, trapped within his own ribcage.

Trapped?

No longer.

"I have been growing cold, little hatchling," I purred at him. "Cold and strong...and terrible."

I reached out an arm, my paw heavy and massive and full of power. I knew what I was now. I had been a cat pretending to be a human.

Now I had become what I was always meant to be.

A predator.

My claws flew down, scratching wide gouges of bone, tearing my captor to pieces.

The scream that escaped him is something I will never forget, for it gathered around me, swirling around my body where I was imprisoned inside him. It was gaunt and awful, so loud that all other sounds were lost. Then it was released, shattering outward with his shattering ribcage, and dying to a sigh even as Claw himself died.

I glared about me, measuring, accounting my prey. None would escape me. Not one.

"Flock him!" they screamed, and they came.

It was hard, vicious work.

They fell. One by one they fell, torn, broken, severed.

Bone is strong...but the stone bones of mountains are stronger.

And then it was done, more swiftly than I would have thought possible. Bones filled the cavern, and dust shimmered in the air, dancing in the sunlight pouring from above. Not a one of them lived, for I had slain the whole nest.

Scattered about the floor, my friends were waking up. They looked about with wide eyes.

"Where...where am I?" asked Thom. "I dreamt..." and he trailed off, lip curled at some disgust he could not name.

My gaze fell on Unity, and her eyes were not clouded.

"You made your choice," she said, and there was both pride there and sadness.

I bowed my head.

"I did."

"We must go," said Kye. "If we go now, we may be in time."

And it was true: when we came to the lip of the cavern and gazed out, we saw. The fire blazed, as bright and as terrible as the sun. Unity led my friends around the peak of the mountain, and all the green, endless lands were spread that way; and the twin shadows of the mountain - one cast by the sun, the other by the encroaching fire - reached down; and between those twin arms, our carriage.

Our carriage?

No longer.

Their carriage, for I was of stone now, and could never leave the mountain.

Unity looked at me, and she was full of grief.

She came on and hugged me, fierce and warm, and her breath was soft on my cheek.

"Remember that we love you," she whispered.

"Always," I said.

Then she closed her eyes, and I felt her marshaling her tears.

When she opened them, they had become contained again, strong. As they needed to be.

"Go," I told her.

And they went.

I watched them, my friends, my only friends, who I had known since I was a tiny kitten. They slipped and slid down the mountain. I watched them until they were minuscule specks crawling across the plain, and I did not cry. I watched them, and I felt the heat mounting at my back. The fire was drawing very near.

There was no movement on the plain below, and I thought that perhaps they were too late after all. Perhaps the carriage was broken, perhaps whatever magic moved it had failed, and my friends would die. I did not care that *I* would die, if only my friends might escape.

Then with a shudder, the carriage began to roll. Slowly at first, then faster, faster, faster, until plumes of dust were spreading upwards in its wake; and then it rolled into the desert, and it was lost in the sparkling wide sea of sand, and my friends were gone.

Only then did the tears come, warm and heavy, and they were of relief as much as sadness, for I knew the fires would not claim them that day. So I turned my back on them, and looked into the East, for I had decided that if I must die, I would face my death full-on.

The wall of fire was very close now, closer than I had ever seen it during our endless flight out of the dying world. It filled half the sky.

Even as I watched, it reached the foothills of the mountain, incinerating them in an instant.

"Well, if this is how I go, then at least I did some good before the end," I told myself. And the fires rolled up the mountain, engulfing trees and streams and rocks. Water hissed instantly to steam, earth fell away into a vast half-glimpsed blackness opening behind the flames.

I leaned forward. A wind picked up, a hot wind, blowing from out the flames. It was huge and hungry, and burnt my eyes. But I forced my eyes open. I would see it all. Even to the end.

Then the flames were leaping and surging up the rim, passing the cavern mouth, coming towards me in a terrible flood.

And something shifted in the air beside me, and a cracked voice said, "It is a most interesting thing to see, the death of a world."

I turned and there beside me stood the hugest and most ancient cat I had ever seen.

"Who are you?" I asked, and if my voice betrayed no shock, it was shock I felt, deep in my flesh of stone.

"I am Ish," said the ancient cat.

The fire took the cavern mouth. On the ground around us, shrubs and grass withered and burst to flame.

"Why have you come, Ish?" I asked.

Ish yawned.

"I have never seen the death of a world," he told me. "I have seen everything else, but not that."

Then his pale eyes looked on me, and a smile touched him.

"And I have come because I am tired," he said. "But the gate must always be kept. I cannot abandon it. Not unless..."

The fire was almost upon us. Beneath my feet, the rock itself was growing red and soft.

I understood. He needed to tell me no more. For all my kind know of the Court of Cats, where we learn to travel before we are even conceived.

"I cannot leave the mountain," I told him. "The stone of my flesh will not allow that."

Ish shrugged.

"Take a little of the mountain with you, then."

So I made my second pact. We looked at one another, his pale eyes on my dark, and he smiled and I smiled. I lowered my mouth and clasped a small rock between my teeth. I swallowed.

Then the flames took him, and I walked away.

I turned slantways. I crept past hollows and through the thin spaces and came, by twist and by shadow, to where I have been ever since.

To where we are now.

To the gate of the Court of Cats, where I have been the keeper for so long that time has lost its meaning; and now my story is done...

[...*apart from one thing*]

I need to tell these invaders to

🦎 21 🦎

STOP SPOILING THINGS

∾

A huge paw – huge as mountains – dropped from the sky. It scooped them up and withdrew, and all at once the chaos was leeching from the world, and Grok remembered who he was and who he wasn't and what had happened to him.

He stared up at a starry sky, and waited for the world to start making sense.

After a little while, he realised it wasn't going to do that on its own, so he decided he would have to work things out as he went along. He staggered to his feet.

"Ow!" said a high, nasal voice at his elbow.

Grok looked down at his hand, to where it gripped tightly onto a smaller, slighter hand.

"Oh," he said to Maria Flunk. "Sorry."

But he didn't let go, and she didn't ask him to.

"Where are..." she started to say, but there was a loud, warm snort from above them, and whatever she had been going to say changed into a strangled scream.

Grok looked up. He didn't scream, but that was only because he had spent a lifetime meeting mysterious monsters in distant stories and occasionally having to stop them eating him. On the whole, a huge, stone cat was not the worst thing he had faced. On the other hand, as long as he was holding on to Maria, he was effectively powerless. And he would not be letting go of Maria, not under any circumstances. He hated himself for it, and he hated the laws of narrative inevitability which had led them here, the echoes of characterisation which had washed off of the story they had been sucked inside; but that was the fact: he would not leave her here.

"I will be asking the questions," said the cat. Grok was inclined to agree.

The cat was huge. It stood at least a thousand feet high, and was regarding them with dark, unreadable eyes.

"What were you doing in my story," demanded the cat. "You were quite spoiling it."

"Didn't mean no disrespect," said Grok slowly. "Matter of fact, we were just passin' through and..."

"I have a good mind to eat you," said the cat. Now it sounded bored.

"Now just you wait a moment," said Grok. "I'll have you know I'm High Sheriff, and you're just..."

"I am the keeper of the gate," said the cat. "What business do you have in the court of cats?"

Grok frowned. Was it possible? Had he made it all the way here? They must have been pulled further off course than he realised. He opened his mouth to explain, when he felt Maria move.

"Our business is our own!" she said. She was shaking and looked completely terrified. Still, she forced the words out despite the terror, and Grok appreciated that. He thought the cat did, too, because something shifted in its stance and amusement shone in its eyes.

"Very good," said the cat. It yawned. "Still, perhaps it would be best if I eat you, all the same. It is messy having...creatures like you here."

"Oh, stop playing with them, Aubrey," came a second voice. Suddenly another cat was coming into view. This one was pure white, and very beautiful. "Leave them alone. You've finished your story, and I for one do not think they spoilt it."

The cat called Aubrey yawned again, then settled down on his huge front paws.

"Very well, Midnight," said Aubrey. "Then I really must let you be going. I'm sure the Darkling Princess is missing you most terribly..."

A flash of understanding shot through Grok.

"Wait," he said, turning towards the huge white cat. "Are you...that is to say, are you part of a story about King Night?"

Midnight regarded him coolly from out her emerald eyes.

Then she gave a slow nod.

"Oh, yes," she told him. "Yes, that is one thing that I am."

Grok felt himself sag with relief. He was close then, after all. All he had to do to reach Indigo was follow the big white cat back out into her own story, and he was sure he would be able to find her trail.

"That's a stroke of luck," said Grok. "Listen: we need to get back to a friend of mine, one of my Sheriffs. Something pretty shady is amiss, and, well...the truth is I can't issue orders here, not like I'm used to. So I'm asking you. Please, we need your help. It's important," he added, feebly.

Midnight watched him for a moment, then slowly blinked her eyes.

"Of course," she said.

Grok sighed with relief.

"Great," he started to say. "If you can just point us the way back to..."

But he cut off, because the huge white cat was moving, dipping her head faster than he would have thought possible, so fast he didn't even have time to scream.

The mouth yawned wide, the teeth glinted, the gullet glistened wetly.

Then the mouth snapped shut.

"...your own story," Grok finished lamely. He hung suspended from the cat's mouth. Beside him, Maria stared at him and clutched his hand so tight he thought it might break.

But they were already moving, space and time sliding around them, squirrelling through the dark folds between the worlds as only cats know how. Shadows moved about them, dark and cloying, so thick it could only mean one thing.

"King Night," thought Grok – but then Midnight *leapt* upwards, and Grok felt the nested bubbles of narrative energy shift in ways that even he, a High Sheriff of great skill and high renown, would find hard to equal.

The world twisted crazily, colours and shapes merging in a hallucinatory kaleidoscope until, until, until...

Grok sat on a dry clump of earth, beneath a starry sky. Next to him, Maria was breathing hard. Of Midnight, there was no sign.

Grok took a deep breath too. The air smelt wonderful. Fresh and clean and without – he was happy to note – even a hint of cat.

Then he saw the fire flickering in the distance; and silhouetted against the flames, the slight, wiry figure of Indigo Shuttlecock.

Grok sagged with relief.

"Where...where are we?" asked Maria.

"I think," said Grok cautiously, "that we are just where we need to be."

He led them towards the fire. When Indigo caught sight of them she jumped to her feet, and strolled over to meet them. Behind her, the figures of three men stared blankly into the flames. They were still, enchanted, baffled by loops of forgetting that Grok could half-sense trailing from Indigo.

"Boss!" she shouted, giving him a grin. "You made it!"

Grok looked away from the three men and back to Indigo.

"'Course I made it," said Grok, making his voice as gruff and unconcerned as he could manage. "Triflin' little thing, really. We just got delayed by..."

He saw Indigo's eyes dart from his face to his hand. To Maria's hand. He had the overwhelming urge to let her go.

He did not.

"There were complications," Grok finished. "But we got through them. Together."

And he gave Indigo a pointed look.

Indigo's eyebrows went up. She looked on the verge of making a comment. Then she shrugged.

"Hey there, Councillor Flunk," she said.

Maria nodded. She looked like someone who was determined to make every effort not to let the oddness get to her.

"Sheriff Indigo," she said. "I understand there's a problem."

Indigo nodded.

"I think things are really bad," she said. "I've seen the way things are headed. Bad. Real bad."

Grok nodded. He had only got the faintest glimpse of the story, the quickest tour as Midnight had shot through it and deposited them here. But for him, it had been enough to get a sense of what was wrong. Indigo had been right.

"What you think we need to do, Sheriff?" asked Grok.

Indigo looked troubled.

"Sorry to say it, boss, but I think this is above us," she said. She sighed. "I think we need to tell someone."

"Tell someone? Tell who?" asked Maria, who seemed to be winning the war against oddness.

Indigo spread her arms.

"Well, I was thinking about that," she said. "How about we go downstairs? Go to Rosewater?"

Grok wrinkled his nose.

"That effete, preening little..." he trailed off.

"But if we tell him, he might be able to tell..." Indigo stared to say, but Grok cut her off.

"No way," he said. "Rosewater doesn't like to get involved. We need someone else. Someone who..."

Maria Flunk gave a little cough. The others looked at her.

"I know who we could ask," she said in a small voice.

Grok frowned.

"Who?" he said.

"It would be most irregular," said Maria. "Quite against regulations. I don't know *what* the rest of the Council will say..."

She trailed off, and looked at the ground.

"Who?" asked Grok again.

Maria looked up.

She told them.

Grok felt his guts tie themselves up in knots.

"Not her," he heard himself saying. "There must be someone else."

But Indigo was looking at Maria with an admiring light in her eyes.

"She's right, boss," said Indigo softly. "It has to be her. She is the strongest, the most powerful..."

"...The hungriest," put in Grok, and they all went silent.

But it was true. There was no one else he could think of. No one else that he could imagine persuading to get involved...

"Damn it," said Grok. "We'll hear the rest of their tale. And we'll think about it, long and hard. We won't rush into this. If we tap her, there's no going back..."

To his relief, both Indigo and Maria nodded.

"Come on then," said Indigo. "Better come and meet them."

Indigo led them over to the fire, where the two men sat, still staring blankly at the flames. As Indigo approached, they shook themselves and blinked, as if waking from a dream.

"These are my friends I was telling you about," said Indigo. "Don't worry. They love stories just as much as I do. So why not get on with yours?"

Grok noted with approval that Indigo had put just the faintest glimmering of narrative energy into her command. Just enough to spur things along, not enough to contaminate the tale.

One of the men was thin and drawn. He had sad, clever eyes; Grok knew at once he was the one. He could smell it on him.

Faery iron.

"Yes," said Grok, keeping his voice light, "tell us the rest of your tale."

The storyteller nodded slowly.

"I will," he said. "I will finish my tale now. There is not so much left to tell. Only the rags of it. Only the sorry end. It is called

22

AN INTELLECTUAL TREATISE ON THE INTERESTING PROPERTIES OF IRON (SECOND REPRISE)

~

T he hour was by now late, and the streets were all but empty. My boots echoed on the damp cobblestones, but my mind was full of the whirl and wonder of what I had learnt that night, and I scarce took note of where my feet led me.

My friend was of the blood...and my love, too! All the time I had spent dreaming of magic, searching for a way to reconcile the rational world of science and reason with the deep truths I felt in my heart...and I had met a family of faery blood, and not even known it!

And Amos...every time my thoughts turned to that monster, I felt my blood turn to molten metal in my veins. I wanted to search him out, to scream at him that I knew the awful truth of how he had used my dear friend; and no courtly words would I use, let me tell you! I felt my hand tighten on my knife. No, I did not even wish to speak *any* words with him, high or low. I wanted vengeance. More than that, I felt that his presence was something truly malign, profoundly disturbing and unpleasant. A creature that could act the way Amos had towards Sebastian was too dangerous to be left free, to be let have the run of the world. As soon as we had the support of Sebastian's family, we would have to act to ensure Amos could not similarly molest any other free creature again...

I stopped sharp. Without realising it, my aimless wandering had brought me to the grand street where the Masters kept their quarters. All around me the stout buildings reared into the sky, several stories higher than most of the surrounding city. I surveyed the windows before me, and found my eyes resting on the house that belonged to that monster. I imagined Amos there, curled up tight and safe like some vast, vile spider, snug in his web.

How I longed to storm the steps to his rooms, burst open the door and bring my knife to his sour throat.

"But I have made my promises..." I muttered under my breath.

And a voice – very softly by my ear – replied, "You haven't promised away all your options."

I was too shocked to cry out.

The voice was known to me. It was Sebille's.

I whirled around, and for a moment there she was. Sebille – my Sebille! - slender and kind and wondrous beautiful, with eyes that twinkled like stars.

It was Sebille, and yet it was something else.

The shadows cast by the moon and the stars, by the burning of lanterns in windows, and yes, even by the strange *electro* lamps, all these shadows conspired together, rubbing one against the other, until rising out of the night, she stood there before me: flesh and bone of darkness, and white hair wound from silvered lunar dew, with the shadow of her smile upon her shadowed face.

"Sebille," I said, and made as if to touch her.

But my hand passed straight through her faery-flesh; and she laughed at me then, fey and wonderful, and she said, "Nay, I am not her! At least, I am not *all* of her. Just a shadow; just *her* shadow."

"She has sent you to me, then?" I asked her.

"Not *to* you," she replied, "*with* you." And with one dark arm she gestured to my left hand, where a certain ring leaked pale emerald light into the night.

She laughed at my astonishment.

"And to think, all the effort of trying to make faery-iron, and you were carrying a chunk of it with you on your finger all the time!"

I shook my head. I could not believe it was true.

"But...why?" I managed at last.

"To keep one eye on you, and help keep you from harm. The world is wide and my mistress would have no harm come to the one she loved. At first, I thought my only challenge would be to keep you from starving yourself while you obsessed over your little experiments."

I smiled at her; and the shadow smiled back at me, something feral and wild and wonderful in her face.

"But now," she went on, "now it seems that there really is some danger here. This...Amos," she rolled the name on her tongue, as if she were inspecting something venomous and unsightly, "he has been interfering where he would better have left well alone. He has done grave wrong to my brother; he has done great wrong to my family."

At the mention of the monster's name, I felt my blood begin to sing once more.

"He is a villain," I said shortly. "Had I not made my vows, I would be beside him now, and my knife would be at his throat."

The shadow smiled wickedly at me. She leant in close, so close I could see the tracings of the cobblestones gleaming thinly through her shadowed flesh.

"And what promise was that, pray?" she asked me. "I heard you make several promises. You promised you would not talk with him, or reason with him, or plead for my brother. I heard you promise all these things. But I did *not* hear you promise not to, for example, stalk the man and perform some subtle act of mischief. Nor, for that matter, did I hear you promise not enter his chambers and obtain a certain key."

She spoke the word softly, but it seemed to knell like a bell, and hung in the air between us.

I searched her dark eyes, but there was no hint of a joke there. She was serious.

I paused.

"Yes," I said.

THE STREET WAS NEAR-DESERTED, AND A SOFT MIST HAD BLOWN UP from somewhere. I moved in shadows, and a shadow moved by my side.

The great building where Amos made his home was squat and vast and would have been ugly were it not for the sheer daunting grandeur of rearing stone and baroque masonry from which it was formed.

I do not know the name for the manner of enchantment she used to spirit us past the doorman; but a great tiredness and dizziness came upon the poor man, and he sat down quite suddenly in the porch, saying, "Oh!" and blinking stupidly up at us as we flitted in. We moved through the high halls and up switchback wooden stairs, our feet whispering on soft carpets, and carrying us past many thick oaken doors until, at last, the Shadow paused by one, and waited for me to reach her side.

"This is it?" I asked, and she inclined her dark brow.

The door was locked. I made as if to force it, but, "No!" she commanded.

She held out one hand towards me. For a moment I stared, uncomprehending, at the shifting ebony shades of her skin. Then, hesitating, I slowly let my own hand fall towards her.

Her teeth shone bright moonlight as she smiled, and when her hand enclosed mine, it felt like a cool velvet glove had clasped me. She turned and drifted towards the door; as she moved, she pulled me with her, as gently as a cloud; and when I glanced down again, I saw that shadows were creeping further up my arm – to the elbow, the shoulder, then my neck, and then…

In a matter of two breaths, I was encased in shadow, and I slid with her, balancing inwards until we were no thicker than…well, than the thickness of a shadow. I felt the crisp roughness of the oak against my skin as I slid between the frame and the door. It felt like nothing. It felt like taking a deep breath, and there was no pain.

As simply as that, we were inside, and her shadows were slipping away from me, and I stood as real as life once more, and her dark form beside me.

We had come to the lair of Amos, and the room was deathly still.

There was not a sound to be heard, and it was very dark.

We passed silently through the passageway linking the door to the greeting chamber. The room was sparse and ill-kept; it did not look as if the man ever entertained guests.

Beyond this, three doors led off in different directions. One was closed; when the Shadow gestured towards it, I strained my ears, and at last I heard it — the faint, quiet sound of breath being drawn in sleep. His bedroom, then.

The Shadow drifted like smoke into the one of the other rooms, and I followed after, making as little noise as I could.

An old-fashioned oil lamp had been left burning at the lowest ebb, and I gently turned up the illumination, until I could make sense of the room; and when I did, I felt very much at home.

This was the room where Amos carried out his research, and so like my own (only larger, more full, and infinitely grander) that I felt something almost akin to a stab of jealousy. Burners and beakers crowded for room amongst the benches, with papers piled high, and all sorts of interesting looking compounds and samples in various state of investigation were scattered around seemingly at random. On one bench, I noted with sudden bitterness, a selection of iron samples of various sizes stared back at me, squat and dour, and I recognised them *at once* as being, one and all, the pieces of metal that had been stolen from my quarters a few months before.

I ground my teeth at that, and would have risked saying something, however grave the need to remain undiscovered...had not my eyes then fallen on the selection of metals on the further bench.

A similar selection of iron samples of various sizes...only, *no*, said my eyes, *that is* not *mere iron...*

It is difficult now to explain how I knew. Was there some subtlety of tone or colour? Some glimmering mark that I recognised as being somehow grander than a base metal could claim? Or perhaps it was a smell, a tang in the air, an *electro* current rising from the faery-iron and finding in me a path through which to earth those ephemeral charges...Or maybe it was none of these things.

In any case, I knew what I saw.

Seven samples I counted there in front of me, ranging in size from that of a peanut to that of an apple. They were all faery-iron. Every last one.

The seven samples were arrayed out in a ragged double-line around a stretch of fine silk. It looked as if perhaps there should have been an eighth sample there, surrounded by the others, longer by far and much larger; though of this proposed sample, there was clearly no sign.

Without so much as glancing at the Shadow, I unslung my shoulder bag and moved towards the samples. There was no doubt in my mind that the right thing to do was to liberate the faery-iron. For one – well, these artefacts were themselves the product of theft! Amos had stolen more than once – iron from me, and something infinitely more valuable from my friend. How could it be stealing, then, to take back what was never his?

Then again, it seemed to me that I ought to take the metal, not just as a balancing of ownership, but as a defensive act; that is, to remove objects of remarkable power from the grasp of a man so clearly unfit to use them.

My hand was a fraction of an inch from the first tablet of faery-iron, when the faintest whispered voice said, "Wait!"

I paused. Sebille's shadow shimmered against the wall as the oil lamp burnt away the darkness.

"What?" I asked, as quietly as I could.

She gestured, pointing behind me. I turned, and glanced at the mantelpiece above the fireplace which she was indicating. It was lined with seemingly uninteresting objects: a small clock, a little tray filled with half-burnt fragments of pipe-tobacco, a plain, dirty, black metal key...

My eyes drifted past the key, paused, shot back to it.

It was the key to the collar my friend had been forced to wear, I was certain.

"If you take the key, the hold this man has over us vanishes," she whispered to me.

I nodded.

With Sebastian released from the collar, we could flee the city. We could await help from his family, and return only then to crush Amos, ensure his plans never reached fulfilment.

Forgetting about the samples on the bench top, I moved to the mantelpiece. I picked it up – it was lighter than it looked, and very unbecoming after the spectral sheen of the faery-iron – and shoved it firmly in my pocket.

I smiled at the Shadow. My heart was thumping in my chest, but I felt as if I were lighter than the air itself. We had done it! And without any broken promises...

I made for the door. We could head for the infirmary again as soon as we were outside – I was sure we could plead our way in somehow, despite the late hour – and before dawn was breaking, my friend would be free and we would be well on our way, away from Amos, away from the brooding dirt and darkness of the city...

The Shadow made a small noise. I turned to her.

She was staring at the collection of faery-iron objects, running one shadowed hand forlornly along the oily darkness of the metal.

"Something is wrong," she said. Her voice was soft, but I caught some chill in it that froze the smile on my face, and halted my steps. "These four samples, they are true faery-iron. Made from blood I know well, I can feel the echo of it in the metal. But these..." her hands drifted near the other nuggets of metal, but did not touch them. "These are something else. Sebastian's blood is here, I can feel it...and yet, it is not...pure..." she trailed off.

I came closer again, and peering at the metal in the flickering orange light, I perceived that, yes, she was right. What it seemed had happened here was the attempted welding of two metals together – a failed attempt. What had appeared on casual inspection to be discrete chunks of metal were, in fact, various fragmentary pairs, laid close by but scarcely touching, and with definite cleaving lines between. In each pairing, one half held that secret red-tang glint that I had come to associate with faerrous iron. Each other half did not.

Sebille's Shadow was shaking her head, dark traceries of doubt forming up on her brow.

"If he is attempting this," she whispered, as if speaking to herself, "then he is working towards something darker than I had feared."

A floorboard creaked behind me.

"My plans have deeper and darker orbits than any of your kind could guess."

Amos stood behind the doorway, thick-necked and imposing, a dim blackness to his eyes, a hunched readiness to his stance. His arms were spread to the sides, blocking the door. His hands were hidden behind the walls on either side of the door.

"We have guessed enough," the Shadow said, and the warm strength of her voice – so like her mistress – filled my heart with hope. "Guessed enough to know that you cannot be trusted. Seen enough to know that your designs are crooked and unkind."

Amos snorted.

"And what do you know of crookedness, little shadow?" he laughed at her. "The world is a crooked place – or rather, it is *lots* of crooked places. Believe it or not, you might say that what I seek is the end of crookedness. I want things to be straight and simple, with no gleam or glamour."

I moved forward then, but as I did so, Amos drew out of the darkness of the doorway...and in his hand he held a sword.

The blade was not long; it was slender and narrow, and as it turned in the orange lamp-light, I noted the way the illumination pooled like dark oil on one aspect of the metal, and the breath caught in my throat.

"Yes," he said watching my eyes dance back and forth along the blade. "It took some time, but I finally found a way of uniting the metals. Faery-iron and its poorer cousin, smelted together in the heat of...blood, of course."

Here he held up his other arm, and I saw all at once the great number of cuts and welts that covered his pallid skin.

"Blood calls to metal," he said musingly, eyes fixed on me all the while, cold and cruel and careful. "Did you know that, Tobias? It is *their* blood that can sing iron to its other states. But human blood will suffice for the joining. This blade is quite deadly to any creature, natural or otherwise. Still, one last anointment remains, and I am quite certain of my calculations this time. I had not hoped to finish my forging quite yet, but it seems I have been lucky..."

His voice rose to a crescendo, and suddenly he was sweeping out with the blade, moving faster than I would have thought possible. The metal sang through the air. I jerked backwards, more out of reflex than thought, and the sword darted through the air the merest fraction away form my face. I stumbled away, desperately trying to keep the table, chairs, anything between myself and the grim shape that stalked me.

Amos advanced, a cold smile on his face. I pulled my knife out with a shaking hand, though in truth it looked a feeble small thing next to that spectral glinting blade of his.

"Why do you fret, boy?" he asked me, his eye flicking again and again to my hand. "I will not hurt you. Not much at least. Just stay still and let me take what I want, and soon I will be gone from here forever."

I shook my head, and circled further round the room. My mouth was very dry, and words would not come.

"Do you know," he said, his voice strangely muted and low, "do you know that once upon a time, I had a whistle that would have made all this much more simple?" He sighed, and tilted his head. "It does not work so very well here, though. There is too much iron in the earth. Too much in the towns and in our pockets. I don't miss it, though. If the price for what I want is the loss of my whistle, then so be it."

Without warning, Amos suddenly stormed forward and flipped a chair towards me with a foot. I ducked to one side, but this was just what he wanted, and before I could do anything that dreadful blade was whistling down towards me. I desperately tried to force my knife up in time, but I knew that it was hopeless. I gritted my teeth, tried to ready myself for the cold bite of metal in my flesh.

Something flickered in the corner of my vision.

Sebille's shadow surged suddenly from the far corner of the room. Her darkness darted across my assailants face, and I had the fleeting impression of her hands outstretched like talons. Then she slammed into his shadow, grappled with it, pulled it to the floor.

Amos cried out, and all at once he was reeling backwards, following his own shadow as it was torn backwards. He tried to shrug his shoulders away, but they were sealed to the dark pool on the floor cast by the orange oil-lamp.

He hissed at her then, a venomous light in his eyes; but Sebille's shadow only laughed, throaty and fey. Then he was rolling on the floor, struggling to bring his sword around to bear on the shadow.

Her dark eyes met mine across the tumult of the room.

"Get out!" she hissed at me. "Take the key and go!"

I nodded my understanding and dashed past the grappling shapes on the floor.

I reached the door, and began struggling with the locks and bolts. They were thick and grim, and when finally I had discerned their working, still it took me some seconds more to overcome their ponderous weight and awkwardness. At last, I had the trick of it, and the lock began to turn.

There was a roar from behind me, and I whipped around in time to see Amos sweep his sword in a brutal arc towards where Sebille's shadow tussled with his own against the stone wall. The shadow gave a cry and leapt to one side, releasing her prey only a moment before the blade sang past her. A single lock of her shadowed hair fell to the floor and dissolved into the darkness.

Amos staggered to his feet, crashing backwards into a brace of chairs, reeling upright and struggling to keep his hand on the sword hilt.

I turned back to the door, gave the lock one last turn, and heaved it open. It groaned and swung open, and I took one step across the threshold into the passageway beyond. I glanced backwards. Amos was on his feet now, and already racing across the floor towards us. On the wall to my side Sebille's shadow was gliding towards the door, one hand outstretched towards mine. My eye flicked back to Amos. His sword was raised. It was looping through the air, awful, unstoppable.

It was sliding towards her back. I could see it happening. I could see where that cold faery-steel would intersect with her beautiful shadowed neck.

There was no thought to the action. Before I could command my body, I was moving forward. My own knife was moving upwards to meet the sword, trying to impose itself between that deadly blade and the slender shadow it struck for.

For one horrible moment, I met his eye; there was triumph there.

His sword hand flickered. The trajectory of his blade altered – just a fraction, but that was all he needed.

The glinting metal tore through the air, missed my own blade by the breadth of a hair...and sliced into the emerald ring I wore on my finger.

Pain exploded in my hand. Against that pain, the world receded to background. I had the faintest impression of Amos' sword rebounding backwards, fragments of my ring exploding outwards around the room. I was reeling backwards, too, my knife dropping from my grasp, my hand trailing an arc of blood from the ruined finger which had been mangled by the blade and the bursting of the ring.

I fell to the floor in the doorway, cracking my head so hard that stars danced in my vision. But for one awful moment I saw her: Sebille's shadow, her eyes meeting mine in horror, her dark mouth twisted in terror and pain.

Then the wind came.

It swept into the room from nowhere into nowhere, tearing at my clothes and hair and chilling me to the depths of my worthless heart.

The wind took her. It swept her up, her ring of binding broken, her rock uprooted. She cried out for me. I clutched for her with my hands, but I could not stay her. Away she went, clawing and screaming and crying for safety.

She was torn from me, and my heart was broken.

The wind faded. I was alone with Amos.

I tried to pull myself to my feet. Blood seeped from my wounded hand; the floor was slick with it, and my feet would not obey me.

He towered over me, a strange fire in his eyes

Slowly, a grim smile swept over his face.

"I told you, boy, that I did not mean to hurt you," he muttered the words, as if he almost could not be bothered to speak them, as if I were so far beneath his attention now that it pained him to condescend to me. "And to think," he went on, "I had assumed I would have to use that poor friend of yours..."

"You...you killed her!" I tried to fill my words with the venom I felt, but they sounded thin and weak in my ears.

He shook his head, as if dismissing the mistake of a foolish pupil.

"No, not quite," he said, "but it seems it was enough."

Then I noticed what he was looking at.

The sword in his hand had changed, though truly I am unsure if I can describe how.

The sheen was still there, that subtle shimmering oil-haze of faery-iron, exotic and weightless and strange. But the tone of it had shifted, somehow. The reddish glimmer had shifted to a deep purple, a fire like stars at midnight, distant and awful...fantastic, deadly.

"This crime will not go unpunished," I promised him.

He snorted, and then one final time he looked into my eyes; and I wondered then, for truly I have never seen such pain, and I realised all at once that I pitied him as much as I hated him.

"In stories, crimes are avenged, the wicked are punished," he said. "The stories have lied to us, boy. Our world does not work like that."

For a single moment he held my gaze.

"Stories are pretty lies, no more," he smiled thinly. "It is time for the unmaking of lies, for the breaking of glamours."

Then he turned and swept out his sword in a lazy arc. A great light shone out where the blade sliced through the air, and...there was a space, an absence, a hole leading from this world to somewhere else. It hung there, carved out of nothing, exactly where he had torn it. Strange green light leaked through and dappled the dour room.

"Put your faith in iron, boy," he told me. "Trust me. I used to be a godly man; but no god helped me when I called. The old stories will soon be shattered. This iron world will be the only one left."

Then he stepped through into the pale light beyond, and the hole he had carved closed behind him after he had gone.

I curled into a ball, weeping. By the time the darkness took me, I could not tell if the wetness on my face was blood or tears.

23

SILENCE AROUND THE FIRE

~

Indigo Shuttlecock waited for Tobias to continue, but he remained silent. She thought about waving him along - she was a Sheriff of the Council, and such things were easy for her - but she had learnt some time back that stories were best left to unravel in their own way.

Instead, she turned to Grok. The High Sheriff had a grim look on his face. His brows were knotted, his eyes were very dark.

"You were right to call me, Indigo," said Grok. "This here's a mess you've found. A *big* mess. Might be it's the *last* mess, if someone doesn't do something about it."

Indigo began to answer, but the monk cut in.

"Who *are* you, anyway, if you don't mind me asking?" said the old man. His voice was friendly, but there was something keen in his eyes. Indigo liked him. A man of spirit. It was a shame to have to glam him again, but rules were rules.

"Sorry, boss," said Indigo, flashing Grok an apologetic smile. "Nearly forgot what I was about, there."

She raised one arm, meaning to suspend the narrative energies infusing Tobias and the monk.

"Rules be damned," came a small voice from her elbow.

Indigo blinked. She had never heard *any* of the senior Committee members speak disparagingly about the rules before. Especially not Maria Flunk.

Indigo looked speechlessly from Grok to Maria and back again.

"Boss?" she asked, uncertainly.

Grok nodded slowly.

"She's right, Indigo," said Grok. "Ain't no time to be fussin' on the rules. Specially not in this case. Think these here gents have a right to know. Might be they can help."

"That's most kind of you," said the monk.

"To know what?" asked Tobias, straining to reach out of the darkness of his story. His voice was distant, clouded.

Indigo let out a breath.

"Difficult to explain," she said. "Thing is...well, think of it like this. That man of yours. That Amos. He's dangerous, like you said. Much more dangerous than you can imagine. And with what he's armed... well, we have to stop him."

"He's no man of mine," said Tobias.

"True enough, true enough," said Indigo. "But that don't change the facts. He's dangerous. Very dangerous. Not just to you or me, not just to where you've come form and where you're going. He's dangerous to everyone and everything. To the whole Storystream."

"The Storystream?" asked the monk.

Grok snorted.

"Damn it, Indigo, you do have a way with words, doncha'?"

"Sorry, boss," said Indigo.

"Look, here's what you fellows need to know," said Grok. "This Amos is set on destroying the...the Universe. Call it the Universe." He darted a meaningful look at Indigo. "And us three, well....we're guardians. Protectors. We ain't like...bound to things, not in the way you might think normal."

The monk nodded wisely.

"Ah," he said. "You are spiritual people, like me."

"Yes," said Grok, at the exact moment that Indigo said, "No."

They stared at one another for a moment.

"Yes," said Indigo. "Very spiritual, me."

"Very," said Grok. "Anyway, the important thing is: we're here to make sure things don't get any more squiffy than they've got already."

Indigo frowned at that. A thought had just occurred to her. She turned to Grok.

"Do you think this has anything to do with the Tuesdays?" she asked.

"What's that, Indigo?" said Grok.

"Well, seems as we've been havin' an awful lot of them recently," she said. "Tuesdays, I mean. Had at least three yesterday, and that's not counting the one that was meant to be there."

Grok nodded thoughtfully.

"Could be right, Indigo," he said. "Seems as if somethin's up with time. It's decomposing, fragmentin'. Been hoping it was just some minor glitch that would sort itself out, but now that we know what's on the loose out in the Storyst...in the *Universe*, I mean...well, wouldn't surprise me if someone had only gone and done something damn stupid with the Wheel..."

He trailed off and a thoughtful silence fell.

"We need to tell her," said Maria Flunk. "There isn't another way."

Grok looked pained.

"But surely, if we went to the Committee, if we told them, if *you* told them..." Grok started to say, but Maria cut him off.

"No," she said. "We can go to the Committee, and we should. But you know what they're like. What *we're* like..."

"She's right, boss," said Indigo. "I don't want to ask the Mistress any more than you do. But..."

"Who's the Mistress?" asked the Monk.

Indigo turned to him with a half smile.

"Oh, no-one to concern you, sir," she said. "Just someone I'm goin' to have to have a little word with, after we're done."

Grok raised an eyebrow. He looked surprised. And perhaps a little relieved.

"You sure you up to that, Indigo?" asked Grok. "I could go. Maybe it should be me..."

"No, it's better if I do it, boss. We all know there's bad blood 'tween you and the Mistress. Besides," she added. "I think I might be able to sell it to her. Might be she'll even count it as a favour owed, if I give her fair warning..."

"I will come, too," said Tobias. His dark eyes glittered. "If she can help me find Amos..."

"And me," said the monk.

Indigo shook her head. The last thing she needed was untidy story elements bobbing around while she parlayed with one of the most dangerous entities in the entire Storystream.

"Thanks, but no," she said firmly. "You got your own path to walk. Ain't I seen something you lost? Might be you could do the most good by finding that again."

Tobias frowned.

"Something I've lost?" he said. "But...but I haven't told that yet. How could you have *seen* it?"

Indigo opened her mouth, but no suitable lie would come. She wasn't built for lying. She never did it well.

"Oh, it's a spiritual matter, you can count on it," said the monk, coming unexpectedly to her aid. "Very spiritual people are our friends here, I can tell."

Indigo looked at him carefully. The monk smiled back. It was an entirely innocent smile. Far too innocent, she thought.

Yes, she certainly liked this one.

"That's right," she said. "I've seen it in a dream, I suppose. You've lost something. You've got to get it back. Best for all of us if that's what you put your energy to."

Tobias gave a slow, reluctant nod.

"It's settled then," said Grok. "Maria and I will get to the Committee - for all the damn good it'll do - and you get to the real work, Indigo. Get to the Mistress. Make her listen. Make her help." He thought for a moment. "And try not to get eaten."

"Right you are, boss," said Indigo, getting to her feet and dusting herself down. "And these here folks'll get looking for this amulet of theirs. Then maybe they can help, in their own way."

It was the monk's turn to look confused.

"Amulet?" he asked. "What amulet?"

Tobias looked uneasy.

"I was coming to that." he said softly.

"Don't stop on account of us leavin'," said Indigo. "Better to finish the story, then be on your way."

Tobias looked at her uncertainly.

Grok gave her a meaningful glance.

"Think it would be for the best, Indigo, if you just..."

He trailed off.

"Yes, boss," said Indigo.

She waited until Grok and Maria Flunk were standing. Then she reached out into the darkness with one hand and reached around until she found what she was looking for. She gave a tug, and the flap of an adjacent story flowed open at their feet.

"This is the way for the three of us, at least to start with," said Indigo. "I'll branch off a little way in, and make my own way. And meanwhile," she said looking back at Tobias and the Monk, as she stepped out of the story and into the wide lands beyond, "you should

✣ 24 ✣

FINISH YOUR TELLING

～

W hat more is there to tell? I weary of the telling, as my hope has grown thin of ever making a happy ending.

I awoke from the darkness of dreams to another kind, more terrible because this darkness haunted the waking world. I was taken to the infirmary, and before long Sebastian and I had reversed our positions. Now he stood over a sickened friend, the cruel iron loosed from his neck by the key his uncle – who had also been the one to discover me – had found in my bag.

Every time I thought on it, I almost lost myself to sorrow. Had I but waited...

His uncle had been close. He arrived in the city the very night I had so foolishly rushed to Amos' quarters. He had come to Sebastian as the dawn was breaking, for he had sped the last leagues with fearful speed. They had both felt it, you see. Blood calls to blood.

Sebille.

They had felt her breaking.

She had bound her shadow in the ring she had given me, to travel with me in the iron lands, to keep me safe and watched. With the breaking of the ring, her shadow had been torn free of the anchoring that bound it, both to her life here, and to this world itself.

Sebastian's uncle explained it all. He did not revile me. Perhaps that was not within his nature, though in truth he could not scorn me more than I already scorned myself. I watched his great hands - brown and rough as the bark of a tree - and could not meet the deep blackness of his eyes.

Iron has differing forms. Ferrous and ferric. Faerric and faerrous.

An energy of one form or another is required to affect the interconversion of these forms. So the folk of the blood had known for long ages. So Amos had discovered, much to their horror...much to our grief.

Amulets of faerrous iron – Traveller's Iron, an iron passport, - can be formed only from death or breaking. Forged in blood, rarified in parting.

Sebille's shadow had left our world. I did not know what this would mean for Sebille herself, and press them as I might, neither Sebastian nor his uncle would tell me.

"Who can say?" grunted the uncle, speaking deep and darkly in the coach as we hurried away from the city. "There are many books of lore, but the wise are silent on this matter. We cannot be sure what we will find."

Sebastian himself would say nothing. He said he did not blame me, but sometimes I felt his eyes roaming over my face, and when I looked up there was nothing of our old friendship in his gaze.

I had abandoned my experiments and my life at the Academy with an abruptness, a finality which left no room for return. I had, in fact, fled the law as well as my past life, for the matter of Amos' vanishing was far from settled as far as the men of the watch were concerned; and the greatest fear that beset me as our carriage rolled further into the wild was that we would hear the galloping of horses, the cry of, "Halt!", the command to return to the dead world we were fleeing.

But when the path faded again, and we mounted our horses for the final stage – treacherous and deathly cold in the grim grip of winter – I knew that we had passed beyond the sphere of the legal devices of my world. The stars blazed impossibly bright; no mere law-man could arrest our progress here.

The house was in mourning. I asked for her as soon as we arrived. I could not stop myself.

Her father looked grim; but he took us each by a hand, Sebastian and I, and there was neither hate nor blame in him.

Her room was empty, and and a terrible stillness was on the air. What had been left of her when her shadow vanished had fled, also.

"She was parted from herself," her father told us. "She is fled, far off and away, and further far again. Neither part that remained is the Sebille we know. The light needs the shadow, just as the shadow needs the light; the risks she took in dividing her nature have been realised in full. Neither half will find rest until they are united once more, though I fear that great mischief will come of this splitting before that happens"

It was clear then what I must do.

Sebastian argued that it should be him, that it was his duty, his *right* to set out in search of her.

But I knew this was not true.

He had told me himself: the blood was weak in him, as it had been strong in his sister. His family needed him; they had lost a daughter.

Let me go, I said.

I had never belonged in this world. The farther shore always called me.

And his family agreed.

A certain amulet they had, rare, enchanted. Passed down through the glamoured generations from a time when our worlds – maybe all the worlds – were closer.

I took it with pride, and bidding farewell to the great cities and the endless miles of tracks and the sickening march of order that was curdling the whole of this iron world, I set out one night through the trackless forest, and did not make camp until the air smelt of summer, and the stars above were strange.

So I trekked from land to land, passing from one place to another, always searching for that far destination to which a secret, sacred part of my love had been blown away.

I do not know how long I have been searching. After a while, time seemed to lose its meaning. I lost my clothes, and had to beg for these rags you now find me in. I lost my belongings, my packs, my food, until at last all I had left was the amulet with which I was able to travel freely through the spheres. To that I clung most desperately, even when I lost all else, for I knew it was my one hope of finding her whom I sought.

But at last, I lost that, too. It was taken – tricked away from me!

And when the amulet was lost, I also lost my hope, and I wandered hungry and alone through this broad and wild world, starving, empty, hollow...broken.

At last I collapsed near here, and refused to move an inch further. I grew so hungry, but there was nothing to eat. And in truth, I welcomed the hunger, for in my hunger I lost myself.

I was desperately hungry, but I was far too weak to move.

For an age I lay there, the sun and the moon chasing one another in the sky.

Then, one day, the moon perceived my misery from her lofty mantle, for she is so high and gentle, and she sees half the world.

"Little beggar, why do you cry?" she asked me one night, when the stars had fled her brilliance and the world was pale and still.

"I cry because I am hungry," I told her, though in my deepest heart I knew it was not just for food that I hungered.

The moon smiled down at me, sadly, and a single silver tear rolled off her cheek and flashed away into the night as a shooting star.

"Little beggar," she said, "I am very high, and I see much of this sad world from up here. And I think, also, that it is not simply for food that you long. Let me tell you a tale of longing, for then you may understand that you are not alone, and you might take hope that one day your longing shall be fulfilled.

"This tale took place far away beyond the river, many miles from where you are now, though when I peer back over my shoulder, I can still see the land where it occurred. It is called

THE TEARS OF THE MESOMORPH

❀

Once there was a very beautiful young man called Paliquain. He was not from these parts, though I watched him all the same, for I see far, and my eyes are subtle and keen.

He was not a prince – they did not have princes in the land in which he lived – but you might say he was the next best thing. He wore the fairest clothes and ate the finest delicacies. He had many servants and never had to lift a finger for himself. He dressed in silks and diaphanous lace, and was carried everywhere in a splendid ornate litter hung with delicate drapes.

Now, though Paliquain was somewhat a vain and stupid man, he was by no stretch of the imagination evil. He frequently hurt those around him by acting without thought or by not caring one way or another how it might affect them. But he would never actually go out of his way to do anyone else harm, and – to the growing horror of his family who were, without exception, vile, selfish, and spectacularly greedy creatures – it gradually became apparent that Paliquain could, sometimes, be quite caring.

For example, on one occasion his mother found him trying vainly to stick the wings back onto a small bird that had been dragged in as an offering by the foul-tempered family cat.

"But it's only a *bird*!" his mother tried to explain to him. "And honestly, doesn't the silly little thing amuse you, the way it squeaks and turns around in tiny circles? It's rather funny, isn't it?"

But Paliquain did not think it was funny, and he shed big, bitter tears when his mother tore the broken little thing out of his hands and tossed it into the dusty street over the high wall.

Another time, his aunt caught him in the act of giving some of his old clothes to one of the servants.

"You little fool, you'll just give them ideas above their station!" she scolded him, and made sure to have the servant doused in vinegar after he was flogged, just for good measure.

But the final straw came when Paliquain entered one day a room he had no right to be in. Now in the house where he lived, Paliquain and his mother and his aunt and his sisters had the run of the whole of the ground floor, and of the three floors above. The only place that was absolutely out of bounds for any of them was the basement. That dark place was for Paliquain's father alone.

Paliquain's father was a skin-changer, a beast-whisperer, and a very ancient and disreputable creature he was, too. In fact, though Paliquain called him father, he was actually his great-great grandsire, and many generations of nasty, ignoble creatures he had spawned before Paliquain even drew his first breath. Now skin changers are not all bad, but some of them are most especially evil, and Paliquain's father was of this type.

To keep his skin fresh and his flesh supple he had to take regular meals of youths and maidens. He would choose only the prettiest and most tender, and after charming, cajoling, bullying, or bribing them down into his basement, he would ravage them.

No one in those parts had the power or the courage to question the disappearances: the finest flowers of that land were plucked and harvested, and though dark tales were told of the big house on the hill and the stern family that lived there, the common folk were in thrall.

Now attend.

It came to pass that one day, as I mentioned, Paliquain chanced to forget himself, and wandered down into the basement in a quest to find one of the young servants, whom he had charged with fetching him a glass of chilled pomegranate juice, and who was taking entirely too long about the task.

He pushed open a door that was meant to be locked, and stumbled upon his father, half-changed into the guise of an awful flay-backed creature, fur-covered and hunched over the serving boy. There was only a little blood, but the boy's skin was sallow yellow, and his hair had turned white as chalk.

For Paliquain's father, this was too much. He seized Paliquain and wrestled him into the very darkest corner of the basement, and then he sealed him in very tight. He waited until nightfall, and then he fetched his sister – Paliquain's aunt – who was an ancient creature herself, and well-learned in enchantments and changing-spells.

"It's clear the boy's not one of us," the old woman said. "We should kill him and be done with it."

But Paliquain's father was very proud, and would not consent to the murder of one of his own blood, however much he despised him.

"If I'd wanted the boy murdered, I would have done it myself, witch!" he told his sister. "I brought you here for your spell-craft, not your council!"

The old woman scowled; but she did not have the strength to go against her brother, not in any open fashion. So she wrought her spells in that darkness under the earth; and when they were ready, she had her brother heave Paliquain in to the room, and then she doused him in will-words and green fire; and as quick as that, the magic was done.

Paliquain's fair face flattened. His shoulders hunched and rippled, his clothes tore, his knees buckled and bent backwards, and every inch of him ripped and tore and grew huge, until at last he stood before them, awful and broken and strange.

When the spells were done, they put him out of the house, and closed the great doors on him. At first, he could not believe what had happened, and he tried to gain help from the common folk. But they saw only a terrifying, hulking monster, and despising him in their fear, they threw rocks at him, and drove him away.

Wherever he went, people met him with revulsion and fear, and no one would offer him any kindness. He took to travelling at night, wretched and alone, and above all desiring the warmth of friendship, though the shame he felt when he even saw another person rendered him completely incapable of attempting any kind of contact.

He wandered far and without purpose. He lived in the hills for many years, in a green land far from his home; and the people who lived in those parts, who occasionally glimpsed him from afar at dawn or twilight, called him the *mesomorph*, though he did not know why.

He was intrigued by the people of those parts, for they were quite unlike those of his own native land. Every person there lived a free, contemplative life; no man paid fealty to any other, and there were no great houses of the type he had grown up in. On certain, sacred nights these people would come together in gatherings, sitting around great bonfires and telling stories to one another beneath the stars, as the wood crackled and the smoke carried embers far off and away and further far again.

On these nights, the Mesomorph – for so he thought of himself now – used to creep up as close and quiet as he could, and listen to the stories. At first, he understood very little, for the language was strange, and he could never get too close for fear of becoming discovered. But in time, he learnt to understand their speech, though he never got a chance to speak it himself.

They told all kinds of stories. Some were stories of their own people, of things that had happened to themselves or their fathers or their great-great-grandsires. But at other times they spoke of strange, very distant lands, where even the sun and the moon were different, and where the world itself seemed to operate by other sets of rules entirely.

They spoke of realms ruled by goblins and creatures made of fire. They spoke of worlds in mirrors and mirrors that could take you there. They told of a whole world that did not exist except as music, where men were born as single notes and married into great chords and measured the fidelity of their ancestry in the fineness of their tones and were related to one another in great extended families of minor seventh cousins and flattened sub-dominants once removed, and who took part in great, bloody wars of disharmony, and which was ultimately destroyed by a mighty weapon that harmonised the resonant frequency of every vibration in the cosmos and dissolved the entire reality to background noise.

They also spoke of a realm, stranger still, where men had conquered the open, endless tyranny of the Universe by bending reality back on itself until the world formed a closed sphere, and queer things and questions had been pushed back, ever back, by the iron march of progress and steam until all things, nearly, now answered there to reason, and the green spaces were vanishingly rare.

In time, the Mesomorph came to learn that the land of these peaceful, contemplative people was so rich in tales because on a certain night of the year, when the stars shone on the chalk hills in just the right way, and the wind was in the West, and the last warmth of the summer was settling into the bones of the earth, on just this certain night, hidden doors would be opened; and then from this land of tale-tellers, travellers would set out. And when they returned, a year or two or ten years later, it was with strange tales of distant worlds in tow.

After looking for many years, he found at last some of these secret places, and even watched the doors open, when the air was rich with autumn and the night was heavy and ripe. But though he watched the doors with longing, he never passed through them; he would always retreat, and satisfy himself with stories.

They told a thousand other tales, and the Mesomorph listened to them all and soaked them up in his loneliness like a frozen man basking in the sunlight.

Grim tales from nearer lands they told, too; and here is one such:

❧ 26 ❧

BLACK JACK GAUNT

~

Black Jack Gaunt dances under the full moon, and all the girls dance with him.

Out they come, from the huts and from the fields, against their better judgement and despite their parents' pleadings.

"Don't go a-dancing with Jack!" warn their mothers, "He dances to one tune, and no good can come of it!"

But Jack's hips are limber and his bright eyes are cruel.

"Don't dance with Jack," say their fathers, "His feet are fleet, and he'll dance you all away!"

But Jack's slippery shape is alabaster beauty in the slanting moonlight, and all the girls do swoon.

So Black Jack Gaunt makes his dance, right there outside the village in the dusty ground, and not a man with man's-blood in his veins can come out to challenge him, for that is his magic, on this night which is his alone.

Now out comes Daisy, and all around would agree that Daisy is the fairest, the straightest-standing, so tall, so slender, so fresh and tender. Out she comes to dance with Jack, and the world holds its breath.

Jack takes her hand and spins her in the moonlight, and the plumes of dust look like dark blood at their feet.

Black Jack Gaunt, he is the very devil. He is handsome as a devil, too, for all his gauntness, for his movements pulse like life itself, and he is dressed in silken finery.

"Oh come back, girl, come back in!" calls her father, pressed up against the window of his cottage, and able to come no closer, "Jack is a stranger, and he'll make a stranger of you!"

But the roar of blood is in her ears, and Daisy does not hear.

Before long, the moon begins to fade; but Jack has made his choice, and his night is nearly done.

Away he dances, and all around him drop the girls, like puppets with slit strings, down to the ground and down into sleep, deep, deep, deep, cold and silent and still.

Away he dances, and dances Daisy with him.

When the sun comes up, Daisy's father can come out; but his girl is long away.

～

BLACK JACK GAUNT RETURNS TO HIS CAVE OF BRIGHTLY GLITTERING carvings, and Daisy is in a swoon.

There are many fine things here, oh so many fine and glittering things; and each one was once a girl, just like Daisy. Now they are merely things; oh, but aren't they pretty?

Jack leads Daisy to a place by the fire and lays her gently down. He gets out his cooking pot and all his special herbs. And now he makes a soup.

Daisy smells the simmering pot, and stirs up from her sleep.

She looks around, all wide of eye, and wonders where she is.

Black Jack Gaunt reaches a long hand out into the darkness under the earth and snaps the neck of a deep-burrowing mole. He pulls it back and smiles at her and starts squeezing it into the soup.

"My dear, my lovely," he whispers to her, "tell me, what is your true name?"

But Daisy, who is sometimes wise, shakes her head and replies, "I'll not give you that for free!" and shivers in the darkness.

Jack is patient. He has played this game for many long years.

He shades his bright eyes and runs his nails through the mud, skewering seventeen fat ripe worms and stirring them into his soup.

"My dear, my lovely," he cajoles her, "tell me, what price is your true name?"

And Daisy, who is sometimes brave, runs her slender hands down her tender thighs and replies, "The price of my name is that song you sing, the one that makes us dance!" and she licks her lips in the darkness.

Jack is slow to anger, despite the girl's pride. He needs her true name; the dance alone won't do, and neither will the soup.

So he scuttles away to a corner where a pool of putrid water festers, and fishes out a stinking fish, white of eye in the darkened cave, and lobs it into the soup.

"My dear, my lovely," he purrs to her, "this is the song I sing, though no one can sing it like me!"

And with that he sings the song for her, which no one before has remembered, because on Jack's night when the moon is full, all the important things are forgotten.

And Daisy listens to the song, and locks it into her mind, and remembers it very closely.

"There, my dear, my lovely," says Jack Gaunt, and his eyes are burning cold. "Now you have heard my song. Will you not let me have your one true name?"

And Daisy, who will sometimes risk great things on narrow chances, bites her full red lip until the blood runs, and replies, "My true name is Black Jack Gaunt, and this is my cave, and that is my broth, and you are mine alone!"

Oh, how Jack does wail!

Up jumps Daisy – and singing Jack's song, she dances Jack's dance; and what can Jack do but dance too?

Daisy writhes and sways; and Jack is hers indeed.

She picks up the broth and spits into it, once, twice, and again; and now her blood is mixed in, and the broth is hers indeed.

Then, "Drink!" she commands, and of course he does; how can he do otherwise?

Jack shakes, and he howls, and he cries, and he pleads.

But Daisy, she is very cold.

Jack shrinks as he shakes, and glows as he howls.

But Daisy, she has made her choice.

Jack is gone: in his place, a brightly gleaming carving, beautiful and thin.

And Daisy, she is Daisy no more.

~

BLACK JACK GAUNT IS GONE FROM THESE PARTS, THOUGH HIS STORY is told in the hills.

Daisy never came back; and her father, he sickened and died.

But not long after she went away, many lost girls came home. They tumbled and fumbled back from the earth, covered in mud and mildew, and not a day older than when Jack had danced them away. Some were welcomed by fathers still living. Others came home to find a hundred years had slipped by.

Now the mothers look to their sons, for Black Jack Gaunt had his dance stolen, and the woman who whispers the young men out into the moonlight is very thin and very beautiful, and no one has said 'no' to her yet.

27

THE TEARS OF THE MESOMORPH
(REPRISE)

~

S o the Mesomorph listened to stories underneath the stars; and in time, little was left of the man he had been, of Paliquain the nearly-prince of a brooding house, for not only was his body vastly different, but his spirit had also changed greatly from that which it had been before.

If he could have, perhaps he would have remained in that land forever, alone, silent, creeping at night to the edges to listen secretly and not be seen.

But the world does not work that way, and all things change. A war came to those free people who lived in the hills, and their stories were snuffed out forever. The land was smashed and ruined, the people were decimated and scattered, and one day the Mesomorph awoke and realised that he was the only living creature within a hundred miles who remembered the tales told under the stars, and that it was time for him to move on, too. He thought then of finding once more the doors that opened to other places, and of passing through them into worlds beyond. But this world itself was wide and terrible enough for him, and he misliked the brightness of those doors, preferring instead the shadows and the twilight.

Once more he took to wandering in darkness across the face of the world. He travelled for many years more, living a poor sort of a life, subsisting on scavenged things and stolen things and small, scuttling squealing things that he snatched from the mud and riverbanks and which crunched in his mouth and tasted vile.

At last, he came to a low wide country made of moors and mists and straggly trees that could never draw close enough together to be called a forest. He found a cave in the side of a small hill, and once he had cleared out the old bones and broken things that filled it, he took to sleeping there during the day, and roaming out to hunt things from the damp places in the twilight.

But it was not his cold cave nor the slithering prey in the moors that kept him there. Oh no, indeed it was not.

For near the moors, there was an old town, the shadow (one might say) of a town that had flourished there many, many turns gone by. This shadow-town was the place where people fled to when the world was done with them or when they were done with the world, and it would not reveal itself to anyone wholesome or clear-hearted. It was a place of broken creatures, a wretched place, always cold and damp and wind-bitten; and few good works were done there.

Bandits lived there, and thieves; also tricksters, liars, godless men and men with soiled gods; also drunks, devils, and dervishes, pariahs, pock-marked hangmen and hopeless runaways; and many other people who had fallen through the cracks and settled down to a slow decomposition amongst the marsh water and the stink of mud.

In such company, the Mesomorph felt able to reveal himself at last. He came into the town as the sun was setting, and red-golden light filled the stinking streets. He watched the townsfolk warily, and the townsfolk watched him back. But they did not hate him – or they hated him less than they hated themselves – and he understood that at last here was somewhere that he might find some faint echo of peace.

But that was not all. If it had just been the town to hold him, mayhap he would have been held for a day or a year or the lifetime of a lesser man.

There was a woman.

The Mesomorph saw her from afar, and that was that. He was beholden. He was undone. He was pierced through and through, and no amount of squirming of the poor thing in his chest that amounted to a heart would ever free him from the binding lines that now held him tight to that dreadful town. And *that* was why he found himself a cave nearby, and *that* was why he was drawn, night after night, back to the low town in the mud and the moors: so that he could be near this wonderful woman he had found.

The woman was not beautiful. She was big and grizzly. Her arms were broad and her hands were hoary and hairy and covered in mud. Her nose had been broken three times in anger, and once more for a bet. Her hair was red – not red like fire, or red like the setting sun, but red like an angry boil, and it was so thick and rough that it would score your hand awful raw were you to give it a stroke.

She was the leader of a small band of disreputable bandit women that operated out of that town, wild and untrustworthy and very dangerous, and the Mesomorph was quite, quite in love with her.

He paid court to her. He brought her flowers and glittering things and pleasant sweets to eat. But the flowers all wilted, and she sold the jewels and ate the sweets, and laughed at him, both in his face and behind his back, and told him she would never love him, not if all the stars fell from the heaven and all the snails took up home in the sky, so he might as well forget about her and leave her alone.

But the Mesomorph did not give up – though his heart tore a little more in his chest – and he took, instead, to writing her elaborate love poetry, the kind that begins in the soul and ends in tears, and takes in the whole wide world of loss and sorrow in between. But she was an earthy woman, this bandit-queen, and not overly fond of words. When he recited them to her, she would mock them back at him in her lisping voice; and when he wrote them down and sent them to her, she would cross them out and use the paper for writing shopping lists of all the things she wanted to steal. So his love poems did not win her, either.

Despite this, the Mesomorph kept on trying, and he never quite lost hope...until, that is, one evening he came into the town in the dead of night, and he saw figures in the broken churchyard, and in a horrible jolt of understanding, he knew that his time was running out.

"Who's that in the churchyard, getting ready for to wed?" he asked the Mistress of the Wagon, who bedded down there from time to time, and who was sitting sultry in the darkness of her carriage, stroking her cat with slender hands, and observing all with ruby luminous eyes.

"That is a visitor, a captive of our precious darling," the Mistress of the Wagon whispered in her narrow voice. "The talk is that he is very well-to-do; and at dawn, he will make a fine groom for our bandit-queen, whether he wills it or not; and then she will run him back to his kingdom, and be fabulously rich."

"So it looks like your days are numbered, sunshine," added Bartleby the pig, stirring from where he had settled down to doze on the roof of the wagon, and tipping him a fat piggy wink.

"Quiet, Bartleby!" chided the cat, yawning hugely and stretching his paws. "The only good noise a pig can make is sizzling."

But the Mesomorph heard neither the pig nor the cat; already he was striding off towards the distant churchyard, his heart rending and scraping like tortured metal.

He slowed as he drew near; and in the darkness, he heard the groom talking to the priest, begging to avoid the marriage, pleading to be set free and released unbound back into the world.

"I could set him free," muttered the Mesomorph darkly. "He doesn't sound like a big man. I could wrestle him to the ground and crush out his juices and strip down his flesh. That would put an end to this marriage!"

But the more he thought about it, the more he realised that if he followed this route, his love would never forgive him. So he bided his time, and he listened some more.

Eventually, the groom ceased his desperate begging, and for a moment silence fell; but hardly any time at all had passed when the priest laughed a nasty laugh, and made his reply.

Now the Mesomorph listened in growing astonishment as the priest told of his own bitter history, and of the raw hand that fate had dealt him; and as the priest went on to tell how and why he had come to hate stories, to hate the lights and the lies and pretty enchantments of tales, an idea began to form in his mind.

At last, the priest had explained how he was making it his goal to destroy stories, and live in a land where truth and reason ruled the world, and he fell silent. The sky was beginning to lighten in the East, and dawn was not far off; and into this silence, the Mesomorph stepped and made himself known.

"What if I told you I have heard of a world where there is no such thing as magic?" the Mesomorph said. "What if told you that there is an iron land beyond the valley of the sun where there are no hidden places, and one thing always follows on from the last, exactly and in due course?"

The priest eyed him up and down without enthusiasm.

"Then I would tell you that I hate people who tell tales, even tales of a land that functions without tales," the priest spat into the dark-ness and his hand went to his knife. "I could travel for my whole life and never find such a land."

"That's because this place has closed itself off," whispered the Mesomorph, sidling closer, speaking slow and steady. "In this world, if you walk far enough West, you'd end up returning from the East. The men there have strange beliefs and wills of iron. So strong have they wished it, that they have bent the world back on itself: they have sealed themselves off from the bitter mystery of the Universe, and they control their own fates."

The priest sneered, but he looked interested despite himself.

"If it's sealed off, then how am I to find it?" he asked; and the Mesomorph smiled inside.

"Oh, I could help you find it," he said causally. "I know where there's a door, you see."

There was a thoughtful silence.

"I say, I'm sorry to butt in," came the voice of the groom, "but I can't help but noticing that dawn is nearly here. The thing is, that I was rather hoping to have affected some kind of escape by this point. I wondered if perhaps *you* might be able to help me, whoever you are?"

The Mesomorph peered at the groom, the last gloom of night giving way to a pale, washed-out greyness, and all at once he perceived the husband-to-be. His big white eyes stared out from the large mud-filled tank in which he floated, looking up at the Meso-morph eagerly.

"Oh," he said, nonplussed. "You're a fish."

"Spot on," said the groom. "I see that you are clearly a man of perspicacity."

"I was expecting someone with more..." the Mesomorph spun one hand vaguely in the air, "well, more legs, I suppose."

"Stop blathering," cursed the priest, moving closer to the Meso-morph, and breathing hard and heavy as he peered up into his craggy face. "You're telling me that there's a door to this world? And that you know where to find it, and how to open it once you get there?"

The Mesomorph nodded.

"Yes," he said. "It only opens on certain days, and it is hidden...but with my help, you could find it and pass through."

"And what would you want in return?" asked the priest.

The Mesomorph shifted uneasily.

"I am in love," he said at last. "Refuse to marry my love to this...this fine..." he hesitated, and glanced at the groom. "This fine fellow. Marry her to me instead, and I shall show you how to find the world of which we speak."

The priest glared at him, and the Mesomorph had never felt so small, so entirely measured and seen through.

At last the priest stepped back.

"Very well," he said. "But we shall have to act quickly."

And with that they sprang into action. With a heave and a splash they pulled the groom out of the mud-filled tank in which he had been swimming. Then the Mesomorph ran as fast as he could to one of the ugly little streams that flowed away from the run-down town, and flung the fish into the putrid waters.

"My, my!" exclaimed the nearly-groom. "Escape has never smelt so stinky! Or perhaps I should say, a stink has never smelt so welcome! Thank you for your help! You'll never know how truly grateful I am, and if you ever need the help of the fish, be sure to let me know, and I'll do exactly what I can, and probably a lot more!"

Then the huge blue fish swam away through the turbid marsh-waters, making his way by swish and by splash to the great roaring oceans, and the clear kingdoms of his birth.

By the time the Mesomorph had made it back to the churchyard, the sun was just peeking over the low hills in the East.

"Here she comes," muttered the priest, and he was right.

The bandit-queen was making her way up towards the church, clothed in her finest off-white rags, looking huge and stately and – to the Mesomorph – quite stunningly lovely.

She was flanked on either side by her fellow bandit-women, both dressed in tattered pinkish scraps and leavings. The party drew towards the churchyard, steps ponderous and heavy.

Quick as a flash, the Mesomorph had leapt upon the mud-filled tank. But he was an awfully big creature, of course, and though the tank was large and splendid, it was clearly too small for him to fit inside.

"No, you idiot!" hissed the priest. "Move it over here! No, over *here*. That's right, pull it up right over this marshy bit of ground."

The Mesomorph did as he was bid.

"Now jump into the slime!" commanded the Priest. "Yes, very good. Now all we have to do is..."

And he picked up the tank, and used a rock to smash through the bottom.

"And we put it...just so..." he muttered, lowering the broken tank over the head of the Mesomorph, which now emerged from the slimy marsh-water, covered in mud and filth.

"It's a good thing your head looks so much like a fish," said the priest, and the Mesomorph glared up at him with baleful eyes.

But at that moment the bride arrived, and both the priest and the Mesomorph fell silent.

The marriage went ahead as planned, and without the slightest hitch.

When it came to the exchanging of the vows, the Mesomorph filled his mouth with mud and gargled them out, and no one suspected a thing.

When it came to the giving of rings, the Mesomorph did his best to play the part of the reluctant groom, and was actually so recalcitrant in giving up his hand, that the bandit-queen thrust her own huge arm into the tank and made to pull him out.

But this was the moment the Mesomorph chose to strike, and with a monstrous tug, he overbalanced the bandit-queen, and heaved her into the marsh. There then commenced a great splashing and struggling, and when the murky surface parted some time later, it was to reveal two vast, dreadful, mud-hung creatures dripping and steaming in the rising sun...and both with rings on their fingers.

"Man and wife," pronounced the priest, and that was that; and though the bandit queen made ever-so-much a grumbling and a to-do, she never did try *too* hard to get away from her unexpected groom.

The bridesmaids laughed and cackled and made foul, bawdy jokes, and they were happy, and the bandit-queen was happy, and the Mesomorph was happiest of all, because for the first time in as many years as he could remember – since he had been broken and remade by the magic of his aunt, in fact – he was not alone, and his longing for company had been sated.

But that night, when the great celebratory party that had swept up the whole of that desolate town was winding to a close, and the Mesomorph was making ready to carry his new bride off to bed down in his cave in the hills, the priest caught his sleeve and whispered in his ear.

"A bargain is a bargain," he said, quiet and cold. "Have your wedding night, and much joy may it bring you. But tomorrow we set out for the door you told me of, for I *will* have what you promised me."

And the Mesomorph felt a shiver of doubt rush over him then, and he wondered for an instant if he had not done a very foolish and selfish thing, for there was an awful stillness in this broken priest who hated stories.

But, "As you will," he said. For he *had* promised, after all. And what was it to him, really, if this poor man wanted to flee the wide green lands, and shut himself up in a terrified little world that bent over backwards to close its horizons?

The next day, the Mesomorph set out to lead the broken priest to the land where the doors could be found. His new bride came with him, and her bandit-ladies strode by her side, and never has a party gone in less fear through the wild lands, for they were quite certain that of all the horrible and dangerous things in those parts, they were themselves amongst the most disreputable.

At last, they came to the wild hills where the songs of autumn could still reach into the bones of the earth, and the Mesomorph showed the priest where to look – misgiving the act in his heart – and the priest thanked him grimly and without warmth; and then they parted company at twilight, with the wind beginning to rise and a certain uncanny light glimmering in the dells and hidden places.

When the Mesomorph peered back through the gloaming, the broken priest was gone.

But a wanderlust had overcome the little party by now, and rather than returning by the winding path that led back to the low, brooding town, they instead turned another way; and travelling by night, they embarked upon a great deal of adventuring and questing, not to mention a fair amount of slaying, banditry, treasure-hunting, and avenging, and eventually built up quite a reputation for themselves as doers of mostly-good deeds and almost-righters of nearly-wrongs.

One morning, after an exhausting night during which they had undone no fewer than twelve dark enchantments and rescued a captive prince from the clutches of an evil antelope, they were enjoying the hero's welcome that had greeted them on their return.

The drink was flowing freely, and stories were in the air; and of course, the Mesomorph was asked how he had met his bride, and where they hailed from, and he told them then the story that I have just told you.

"Well, my friends," said the innkeeper, "I must say that you are indeed very brave and nearly fearless. But the quality of the monsters that you young folk have to face today is on the wane, and no mistake! The creatures now are not nearly so dire or terrible as they were in my great-grandfather's time. Adventurers today, you don't know you're born! Back in the time-before-time, oh, there were monsters then that would boil your blood, and eat you whole for a pre-breakfast snack! Let me tell you about the greatest monster that ever darkened the skies. She made her nest far and away and further far again, and was known in all these lands as

28

KA'THARLON, THE GREEN DEATH

~

Not so many miles from here there used to be an ocean, though the world is changed now. That is the way of things. The years pass, and time sweeps us all to dust, and the very heart of the land is broken and remade constantly. We cannot fight these changes; mostly we cannot even remember them, for a human life is a very little thing, a narrow flame dancing for one glorious moment in the sunlight, then vanishing forever into the vast darkness, and who can say for true what the world was like when our ancestors walked here?

I am rambling. I apologise. Now please attend.

Near where we are now, the ocean once broke, for the hill on which we stand used to be an island, and was surrounded on all sides by water. We were not alone; in fact, we were part of a huge archipelago of islands that stretched in a great-reaching arc, and formed a single kingdom. A fisherman or traveller could sail from one island to the next, and always be sure of sighting land within an hour or two. If you were to turn away from the string of islands and head East, however, the ocean was huge and desolate. Young explorers with fire in their blood used to set out that way, looking for gold and adventure. The ones who returned found neither, but instead simply reported an endless expanse of blue-green waves, with no hint of land however far they sailed.

They declared the ocean was empty...but they were wrong.

There was at this time a very great but very arrogant magician. Her name was Wom Ya, and she was greedy for power. She was also jealous of the stature of the throne, for we had a prince in those days, and sorcery had, by tradition, always been sworn servant to the crown. That meant that any member of the blood royal could – in theory at least – command the services of any practitioner of the art, without notice or payment, and expect to be obeyed immediately and without question.

Sorcery flourished amongst these island kingdoms in that time, for the old magic was tied to the salt waves and sea, and every rocky outpost had its own kelp-wizard or conjurer. But of all the magicians, Wom Ya was the eldest and most potent. She had lived for ever so many years, and her blood was thick with salt and power.

Now it came to pass that the prince of the kingdom had to travel abroad, for he was visiting with princely friends in other kingdoms far away. While he was gone, he appointed his youngest brother, Prince Myst, to rule in his stead. Prince Myst was not a bad man, but he was weak; and his ascent to power was exactly what the ancient sorceress had been waiting for.

Wom Ya sought out Myst, and turned his head with fancy talk and pretty magics, until before very long it was really Wom Ya who ruled the islands, with the young prince doing whatever she told him without qualm or question.

Soon, the people began to grow restless, for they were being treated most appallingly, and they were not used to such wicked rule. But Wom Ya twisted this to her end, too.

"Your brother has been too soft on the common folk!" she told Myst. "A prince is not like the people he rules – he does not love them or listen to them, any more than a man loves or listens to the bees that he keeps in his garden! Oh, the pride of them! The wicked, shameless pride! You are above them, my prince. You must give them a show of your power, let them know once and for all that you are of an altogether better, a nobler class than they."

Myst pondered this, and though deep in his heart he had misgivings, her voice sounded so wise and her words seemed so sensible, that at last he was convinced that she was right.

"Very well," he said. "Well, maybe I could hold some kind of a tournament. If I beat everyone at swordplay, that would show them all how much better I am than them."

"No, that simply won't do," said Wom Ya firmly. "That would just make them angry and jealous, and then they would rise up and tear your royal body to pieces. No, the key is to make them afraid of something...and then to have you save them from it."

"But how on earth are we going to do that?" asked Myst, and Wom Ya smiled a foxy smile.

"There is an island, hidden far out to sea in the East," she told him. "It is not on any maps, and you could sail half your life and still never find it. But you could reach it in three nights, if you knew the trick of it, which I do."

"And on this island?" asked Myst, leaning closer.

"On this island, there is a creature," Wom Ya whispered. "Her teeth and talons are huge and sharp as razors. Her body is vast and awful, and she is swift and deadly as lightning. She is Ka'tharlon, the Green Death, and dread flies with her; if you but unleash her on the common folk, they will beg you to bind her again. And when you do, they will love you forever and remember what it means to respect and obey their betters without question."

At first, the young prince was horrified by Wom Ya's plans. But she worked her will on him, and like a worm turning an apple to rot, slowly he was corrupted. At last his resistance was undone, and he yielded.

They set out one night when the waves were still and the water was inky-black. Wom Ya called up a dark wind that filled their sails and swept them far out to sea. And when the night was coming to an end, and morning was sprinkling pink light ahead of them, the ancient magician flung an enchantment round the dawn to prevent it from breaking, and hustled darkness back from the corners of the world, and they sailed on. For three nights Wom Ya did this, and on the fourth night of sailing without the breaking of a single day, a jagged landmass rose ahead of them, rearing huge and ugly up into the sky.

Their boat snagged on the black shingle. Myst jumped ashore, and dragged the boat up onto the stones.

They had reached the island of night, where the sun never rises and the stars never shine; but though the sky was dreadful black, an unnatural illumination hung over the land, and Myst could make out the landscape almost as clear as he could back in the daylight world.

There were forests and streams and mountains here, just as there were on the archipelago; only here, the forests had dark leaves and dark boughs and were attended on by swarms of dark insects. The streams ran with black water and the mountains were composed of great slabs of black rock.

They followed a path up from the beach and deep through a forest until they reached the foot of a mountain. They climbed this until the dark island was spread below them and they could see very far out to the endless sea. Here they found a cave, yawning wide like a gaping mouth.

"Now you must go on alone," Wom Ya told the prince. "Follow the cave without turning left or right. In the heart of the mountain you will find a great cavern, and there wrapped in slumber you will find Ka'tharlon. She has been sleeping these many years, and would surely sleep until the end of the world, if no one were to disturb that which she guards."

"And what is it that she guards?" asked Myst.

"The Green Death has been set to guard a certain door," said Wom Ya. "Only lay your hand on that door, and she will awaken at once, and be wroth."

"And how will I prevent her from falling on me then, and tearing me to pieces?" Myst wanted to know.

"Take this magic potion," said Wom Ya, handing him a very beautiful bottle, worked about with tracings of red-gold. "When you are close to the door, drink this tonic. It has the power of making anyone who drinks it invisible. As soon as Ka'tharlon has been roused, simply stand still as stone, and she will never perceive you, and will instead leave this island and go to ravage the common folk of the archipelago, just as we have planned. But be careful – the effect only lasts for a short time, and if you drink it too soon, it will wear off while the monster is still near you."

For a moment Myst hesitated, for he mistrusted the old sorceress more than ever; but he was only young, and only small, and his will was all but gone. So he took the beautiful bottle and made his way into the cave.

The passageway into the heart of the mountain was long and dark. There was no seeing anything here, and Myst went with one hand before him and another to the wall, feeling his way slowly forward. There were many openings to the left and to the right, but Myst took none of them. After some time, a vile stench began to fill the air, sweet and awful like rotting things, and Myst felt he must be getting close. A little further, and a very faint tinge of light began to filter up from the cave ahead, pale green and ill-favoured; a little further still, and he sensed that the passageway was opening up around him, until all at once he realised he was standing in a vast cavern. All around the dark walls a pale greenish tinge glanced off the rocks; but overhead, there was only blackness, still and complete.

Myst stepped into the cavern, and as he did so, he perceived that there was a pit near the centre of the chamber, and it was from this pit that the ugly green light was spilling. Slowly, dragging each step, his heart hammering in his chest, Myst edged towards the pit. He drew close and peered in...and then he saw her.

The pit was filled with silt and slime, with brackish fog rising up, and so it was that Myst could only catch glimpses of her, but glimpses were enough. He saw coils of shining flesh, ripples of muscle and sinew, teeth, talons, a terrible forked tongue, a scaled coat that shone like awful cold jewels, and wrapped up tight against her body, two powerful back-swept wings, and these were not green, but black as nightmares and vast as castle walls.

Ka'tharlon, the Green Death, slumbered in her pit.

Myst drew back, and he wanted very much to run away, to be done with this horrible place, and to feel the free wind upon his cheeks. But he was bound to go further; Wom Ya had bound him most tight.

So instead of going back, he worked his way slowly around the pit, and there, sure enough, he found that there was a stout wooden door embedded in the dark rock; and it was not latched nor locked, but it was closed firmly.

Myst edged then towards the door, and for the last time he wondered if he was not making a very great mistake; but his will had been overcome by the ancient salt-magic of Wom Ya, and truly he had no choice.

He laid one hand on the door, and turned the handle, and shoved.

The hinges creaked and the door swung open, and light fell from the room within, and lit up his youthful face, and the sight that met his eyes filled him with wonder.

A deep noise like the cracking of worlds croaked from the darkness behind him; and turning back towards the cavern, Myst placed one foot beyond the threshold of the door, and kept one hand clutched tight around the red-golden bottle Wom Ya had given him.

Ka'tharlon awoke.

She stretched up out of the darkness of her pit, waves of stench and the vile secretions of her sleep sloughing off her as she unfolded her enormous body. Her legs slid into the cavern, and she shook her wings out and she yawned, her maw cracking as wide as a great chasm into oblivion, and let loose a terrible deep roar of awakening, so loud and awful that the mountain itself was shaken, and Myst fell down to his knees.

Then Ka'tharlon opened her eyes and looked for the door that she guarded...and she saw Myst.

"That door should never be opened until the remaking of the world," said the monster, and her voice was sweet as poison and deep as the roots of a mountain.

"I...I did not come here to pass through the door," stuttered Myst. "I just came to...that is to say, we wanted only to wake you..."

"And wake me you have, little creature," said Ka'tharlon. "Tell me, do you know what it is that I guard? Do you really understand so little of this insubstantial reality that you would risk it all for the glory of the forbidden?"

"I told you, I did not come to open the door..." said Myst, but the monster cut him off.

"Lies!" Ka'tharlon roared, and the air thundered and hummed. "You are facing death, boy. At least have the courage to face it with a true heart."

Then Myst remembered the little bottle he held in his hand, and decided that the time had come indeed to drink the potion down and become invisible. The tonic was sickly sweet, and so thick it stuck in his throat. But he made himself swallow every drop, and when he was done he let out a deep sigh of relief and cast the bottle aside.

He held one hand up in front of his face and waited to turn invisible.

Nothing happened.

"Very well," said the monster, and she chuckled awful and deep, "those who cannot face their death with courage, face it with drink. Give my regards to the creator, little one."

"But..." stammered Myst, confusion twisting his face.

And with that Ka'tharlon reared up into the air and smote down towards the prince, falling on him and tearing his body to pieces.

Ka'tharlon swallowed the flesh down and licked her bloody lips and laughed her deep laugh; and then she turned to curl up back in her pit.

But as she turned around, she froze, for at that moment she noticed a second figure had stepped out of the darkness of the cavern, and was walking towards her, quite unconcerned and carefree.

It was Wom Ya, who had stolen down after Myst, and who had crouched in the darkness by the cavern's edge, watching everything, waiting.

"And who is this second creature, who walks so unconcernedly to their doom?" asked Ka'tharlon, her teeth shining green in the dark of the cave.

"I am Wom Ya, of all sorceresses most potent," said Wom Ya, and she smiled. "Who am I who walks with unconcern? I am your mistress, worm! I am she who commands, and thou art she who obeys!"

Ka'tharlon started to laugh then, deep and nasty; but Wom Ya said,

"Silence!" and the laughter stopped as completely as if it had never been.

Then Wom Ya said, "Roll over!" and with a terrible crash and thunder of scales on stone, the great monster keeled to one side, and rolled the whole breadth of the cavern, and the whole breadth back.

The creature lay there, panting, terrified; for Wom Ya had been very cruel and very cunning, and the potion that she had given to Myst had no properties for invisibility, and indeed no power at all over any mortal. But that potion *did* impart a great tendency to subservience in all unnatural creatures; and since the potion was in Myst's flesh, so it had passed into the monster who had devoured him.

Then Wom Ya smiled and she said, "Go now to the archipelago and there lay about you with malice and violence, until one tenth of the people lay dying and one tenth of the buildings are ruined."

And with a great wail, Ka'tharlon flung herself unwilling into the air, beating her wings so that a hurricane filled the cavern. She surged upwards towards a secret opening that was placed in the cavern roof, and by that passed out into the eternal night beyond.

Wom Ya licked her lips and walked slowly to where the unguarded door stood half-open. She peered through, and looked upon that which lay beyond.

She was curious, but if she was greedy and evil, she was also wise, and she knew enough of hidden things and secrets to understand something of what lay within.

So she closed the door tightly, and she took out some salt dust from her robes, and she scattered it about the floor, where the blood of the prince had been spilt.

Then she said some words and light flared three times, because even someone as vile and ruthless as Wom Ya knew better than to leave *that* door unguarded while its true guardian was away making murder. And so it was that Ka'tharlon was relieved of the task for which she had been spawned, and her new master cared not.

Then she left that place, and she reclaimed her boat from the shore where she had left it, and she travelled back across the seas for three nights without breaking dawns, and came on the fourth to the islands of the archipelago.

When she reached the islands, she found that they were in uproar. The people ran hither and thither, crying and terrified. Smoke rose into the sky and blood filled the streets.

"Wom Ya! Wom Ya!" they rushed to her, calling out. "Wom Ya, you must help us! A great monster has fallen on us from the sky! It has set about us with talon and tooth, and many people have been killed! You must tell us where our prince is, for truly, this monster must be destroyed!"

Then Wom Ya frowned very deeply and contrived to look most sad.

"Oh, what terrible wickedness!" she cried. "For this sounds like the monster Ka'tharlon, the Green Death, of which I am sure you have all heard. My good people, it hurts me to tell you this, but your prince is dead, slain by this same vile creature which now despoils our fair nation!"

"What, the young prince is dead?" asked the people. "Surely this cannot be!"

"I'm afraid it is true," Wom Ya told them. "I saw it with my own eyes. I had learnt by my arts that Ka'tharlon had been released again into the world, and when I told our prince, he felt that it was his duty to slay the beast, or else to die trying. Alas, he was over-matched. He was devoured and is no more."

With that, a great wailing went up from the people.

"Then we are lost!" they shouted. "If our prince could not defend us, who shall?"

"Good people," said Wom Ya, "I am only a humble sorceress, but I would gladly give my life for the common fortune; and if you want it of me, I would be your champion, and battle this monster until the last breath of my body."

Then the people cheered and shouted that, yes, they wanted Wom Ya to be their champion.

"Very good," she told them, "but such things do not come cheaply, and we must all make sacrifices in these difficult times. Firstly, it will be necessary that every man and woman will have to pay a monster-tax, one third of their income. This will be used to set up a standing army the likes of which has not been seen for many years. As it is quite certain that the monster has spies and traitors amongst us, it is, of course, necessary that the army answers only to me, and will do exactly what I ask of it without question."

The people grumbled at the terrible expense, but they were so scared they consented immediately.

"Secondly," Wom Ya went on, "it will be required that every first son and every first daughter submit themselves to the forming of this army. Training will begin at once. It will be a difficult and dangerous life, but filled with honour, and the whole kingdom will thank our brave soldiers for the protection they offer the realm."

The sons and daughters grumbled then, thinking how much they had enjoyed living in peace, and how little they wanted to live in fear and war. But they had been so brutalised by the coming of the monster and the terrible depredations it had left in its wake that they felt they could do nothing but agree.

"Finally," concluded Wom Ya, "as we are now entering a time of war and strife, it will become necessary to re-order the education of our children, so that they are prepared for the difficult days ahead. All children older than the age of three will henceforth be obliged to attend special camps arranged by me, where they will learn their true place in the world and what is required of them."

The mothers and fathers grumbled then at the thought of losing their children, but they were so frightened they did not dare to oppose the old sorceress.

And as easily as that, Wom Ya had her way, and the kingdom came under her sway.

Time passed, and things became very bad. The army grew into a harsh and brutal body, and was used as much to keep the people themselves in check as it was to protect the realm from outside threat. Those who spoke too loudly against Wom Ya's rule disappeared without warning and were never heard from again. Children were taught almost from birth of the constant threat of the monster, and of how they owed their very lives to the benevolent rule of the ancient sorceress who looked after them all. What was more, the kingdom itself grew quarrelsome with its neighbours, and before long there was dark talk of the necessity to strike the first blow in the name of peace.

From time to time, Wom Ya thought it best to remind the common folk of the constant threat they were under; and so it was that at frequent intervals she summoned Ka'tharlon from her hidden island, and bid her harry the archipelago. When this happened, she would then make a great show of coming out and opposing the monster, and seeing her off with salt-winds and sea-storms. So the people remained under the shadow of terror, and came even more to believe that it was only Wom Ya who kept the dread monster at bay.

Now it came to pass that around this time there was a great warrior who made it her business to seek out and slay monsters wheresoever they might be. Her name was Frayn, and the blood of giants was in her veins. She stood seven feet tall and fought with a spear of charred ash that was woven through with all sorts of enchantments, and she had never been defeated in battle.

When word reached Frayn of the monster that returned ever and anon to despoil the islands of the archipelago, she determined to seek this creature out and put an end to it. But when she came at last to the islands after a long and dangerous journey, she was looked on with suspicion, and taken under escort by the guard, though not before she had cut down a great many of them.

"I will come with you," she said at last, not wanting to kill any more soldiers, "but I will not surrender my spear, and you must take me at once to your leader, as I intend to slay the monster that has been bringing such woe to your lands."

She was brought before Wom Ya, who was deep in discussions with her generals as to how best they might go about making war on a neighbouring kingdom, which – it was obvious to everybody – was clearly in league with the monster, and must be overwhelmed and conquered.

"Who is this you bring before me?" demanded Wom Ya, suspicious of the strange woman.

"My name is Frayn," said Frayn, "and I have travelled for many leagues to pit myself against the monster that plagues you and, if fate so wills it, to destroy the wicked creature."

Now this made Wom Ya fret inside, for she perceived that it was a great warrior who had come before her; but her greedy heart was also filled with desire, for she saw at once that this warrior clearly had giant's blood in her veins, and the blood of giants is a most rare and powerful tonic, from which many deep magics can be brewed.

The old sorceress was ever sly and subtle, and so she made a show of smiling and making Frayn welcome, and she said, "Could it be true? Has a warrior come at last with strength enough to slay the daemon that plagues us? For I see at once that you are both wondrous brave and formidable strong, and if ever any warrior had a chance to defeat the Green Death, it is most certainly you!"

Then she ordered the guards to let Frayn walk free and as an honoured guest, and she declared a great feast in honour of her coming and had decreed a national holiday, even for the common folk.

That night, when the feasting was done, Wom Ya took Frayn aside, and asked her where she would start her hunt for the monster.

"I have heard that Ka'tharlon makes her home on a certain dark island that can only be reached by sorcery," Frayn said. "It is my intention to sail to this island and look for her there."

Wom Ya laughed and shook her head.

"What you say is true," she said, "but the trick of reaching that dark island has long been lost to us, and no one now living knows the method of getting there."

"That may be so," said Frayn, "but my spear here is spun around with enchantments many; and when I once declare a creature my enemy, my spear will always lead me to where their heart beats."

Wom Ya forced a smile.

"Then truly we have cause to celebrate," she said. "I am quite sure that your spear will lead you to this island, and when you get there, I am quite sure that that same spear will be the death of Ka'tharlon."

Then Wom Ya bid Frayn and all her guards goodnight, and retired to her chambers. But she did not go to sleep, and instead she stayed up late into the night brooding on how she should act.

Then in the middle stillness of the night, when everyone else had long since made their way to bed and the whole world seemed cloaked in stillness and shadows, she went alone to the beach, and from there she took her boat some way out to sea. When she was far enough from land that no one could possibly see her, she filled her mouth with seawater and whistled down the wind with salt-sounds and vowels of power. Then she called out a command to Ka'tharlon, who was still under her sway, and summoned the monster to attend her.

The waters surged beneath her as the creature came, beating mightily through the air and settling with an enormous crash into the sea.

"You have called me, and I answer," growled Ka'tharlon, steam and vapour rising from her flanks.

"Of course you have, my little pet," preened Wom Ya. "Now attend! There is a certain warrior woman in these parts who would hunt you. I need you to kill her for me."

Ka'tharlon snarled and hissed, for she misliked very much being the plaything of another, and though she was fierce and terrible, she had not been made to murder for the sake of murder itself.

But, "I am bound to obey," she said, for it was true. "Only tell me who you would have destroyed, and it shall be so."

"In the royal castle on the largest island of the archipelago sleeps now the warrior known as Frayn," said Wom Ya. "You will know her by her great height and stern bearing and by the tall spear she wields. You will not strike now, but tomorrow in the full light of day; and when you come, you will not kill her outright, but carry her back to your cavern and there keep her bound and await my coming. Now begone!"

And with a great hissing and seething of waters, Ka'tharlon rose into the darkening sky and sped back across the waves to her island home.

Wom Ya made her way back to the archipelago, all the while dreaming and scheming of the many deep magics she could distil from the giant's blood, when once Frayn was captive.

When she reached the shore, she found the largest rock that she could carry, and she laid it at the spot where the waves were pounding the hardest. Then she swept her hands and called to the ocean, and a great weight of water she made to leap into the air and smash down onto the rock, sundering it into many pieces. But at the moment that the rock broke, her cunning hands darted out and she snatched up the sundering cracks as they appeared in the stone and she took those self-same cracks on with her, hiding them by her wit in the folds of her palms.

She reached the castle just as dawn was breaking; and there, in the courtyard, she found Frayn the warrior preparing to go out and hunt down the monster. Her pack was on her back, and her tall spear was in her hand.

"Oh, I see you are ready for the fight!" said Wom Ya, smiling at Frayn and looking admiringly at her spear of charred ash.

Frayn shrugged her broad shoulders. "Life is short," she said, "and there are many monsters to slay."

"Too true, too true," agreed Wom Ya, shaking her head sadly. "But before you head out, I wondered if I might first have a good look at this wondrous spear of yours, for if it is as you say, then it is a mighty weapon indeed."

Frayn frowned then; but she was a great warrior, and was not afraid of old women who smelt of salt, and anyway, her spear was wrapped around with enchantments many, and she knew it would never strike her when in the hand of another. So she consented, and handed the spear over.

"Ah, yes, a wonderful weapon!" admired Wom Ya, turning the spear around and making the metal tip glint prettily in the sun. But as she handled the shaft, she let slip the sundering cracks that she had carried cradled in her creased palm, and slid them into the hard charred ash.

She felt the wood weaken in her hands – though it did not break yet – and she smiled to herself as Frayn took it back from her.

"With such a weapon, surely you cannot help but be victorious," said Wom Ya, and Frayn nodded and said her farewells and made to depart to the ocean.

But at that moment a shadow passed over the sun, darkening the whole world, and a terrible wind sprang up from the direction of the sea.

"The monster!" cried the people, who knew all too well the signs that heralded Ka'tharlon's coming.

"The people say truly," shouted Wom Ya above the rising gale. "It seems the beast has heard tell of your prowess, and means to bring the battle to you!"

But if Frayn felt any fear, she did not show it; and placing her pack calmly on the ground, she gripped her spear tight and made ready to fight her foe. She shielded her eyes and peered up into the sky.

With a great crash, Ka'tharlon dropped from the clouds like a green thunderbolt. The air itself seemed to tear, and the world was filled with screams and terror as the people fled the courtyard.

Down, down, down plunged the monster, huge and awful, making straight for the glint of Frayn's spear amid the scattering crowd.

At the last possible moment, the warrior rolled to one side, and so it was that Ka'tharlon's talons raked the ground where she had been standing, splitting the stone to rubble and sending a great wave of earth high up into the sky. The creature shrieked and wheeled, her wings spinning in a wide arc that crushed and ruined all they touched. But Frayn was already rising up again, and even as she rose she was thrusting her enchanted spear forward, bringing it with all force into the flank of the monster.

Ka'tharlon snarled as the metal struck her scales, and Frayn cried out in triumph...but the shout died on her lips. With a deep crashing sound like endless waves breaking on stone, the shaft of the spear cracked.

The ruined spear-tip fell, glinting sadly on the ground beneath the monster's feet, and Frayn gripped the broken shaft uselessly in her hand; and it was all Wom Ya could do at that moment to keep from smiling wide and shouting out for joy.

For a single moment Ka'tharlon regarded the warrior with her huge, cold eyes. Then with snake-speed she surged forward, and snatching Frayn up in her talons, she launched herself into the air and sped across the sky.

By the time Frayn realised what was happening, it was already too late to do anything, for the ground was very far below her, and falling further with every sweep of those vast black wings. So instead of struggling, she hung limp and wondered what she might do; for though her spear was broken, she was still a very great warrior, and she had not been defeated yet. And it did cross her mind that it was a strange thing that her spear had shattered, for it had been wound about with enchantments many, and the wise had told her that it would never be broken until the very breaking of the world, too, was nigh. She pondered deeply on the old sorceress who had handled the spear, and her thoughts were brooding and dark. And still she held tight to the broken wooden shaft of charred ash, for even a broken weapon is better than none.

Before very long, the land had fallen away completely, and they were far out to sea. And before much longer, they were speeding into the darkness; and soon after that they were falling out of the sky towards a dark island scattered with dark trees and dark rivers; and when Frayn saw this, she knew that the monster was taking her back to its lair.

Ka'tharlon dropped through the secret opening in the top of the black mountain, and settled with a great shaking of the earth into the wide cavern where her pit waited. She tossed Frayn down amid the dust and silence, and turned to crawl back into her pit.

Frayn stood then, but her leg had been broken when she had been snatched up, and it was all she could do to use the broken spear-shaft to keep herself from falling. She gritted her teeth and breathed hard, for the pain was very great.

"Monster, why have you brought me here?" she called out, her voice thin in the emptiness of the cavern.

Ka'tharlon sighed a tired sigh, and half turned as she settled into her pit.

"I brought you here because I was compelled to do so," the monster said, sounding hopeless and sad. "For I was tricked into consuming Wom Ya's salt charms, and while her magic stays deep, so I shall stay her slave, bound to do whatever she asks of me."

"Then Wom Ya is indeed the true monster, as I had feared," said Frayn, and she cursed her foolishness in letting the old woman touch her enchanted spear.

"Yes, Wom Ya is a very sly creature, and not to be trusted," agreed Ka'tharlon. "Even now, she makes her way to this island, and when she arrives here, she means to use the giant's blood that runs in your veins to distil deep magics and potions."

Then Ka'tharlon settled down into her pit and slumbered; but though Frayn had been outwitted, and though both her spear and her leg were broken, she was a warrior still, and she made it her business to explore the cavern, and see if there was any hope of escape.

She found that there was no nook or cranny in the whole place – for the cave that led from the outside of the mountain had been sealed shut by Wom Ya's magic – and there was no weapon hidden anywhere that she could find. But at last she found the stout door embedded in dark rock, and wondering where it led to, she placed one hand on the rough wood.

At once a cold wind blew up from nowhere, and a thousand pinpricks of cold light coalesced out of the darkness, forming a shape which forced itself between Frayn and the door, gaunt and grim and holding a pale sword.

"Halt and stand back," commanded the spectral figure, its voice seeming to come from every corner of the cavern.

Frayn took a step backwards, but she was not afraid, for she had faced many foul and dangerous things in her time, and peering closer, though the figure was grim, it also seemed young, and somehow sad.

"Who are you?" Frayn asked.

"I am the guardian of the door," said the figure, "and none may pass this way until the breaking of the world."

Frayn peered closer, and she saw that the pale body of the guardian was criss-crossed all over with cuts and tears, as if it had been rent very greatly and fixed back together with red-golden light.

Far in the distance, there was the sound of a boat scraping across dark pebbles, and Frayn wondered if Wom Ya was drawing near.

But she did not panic at the approach of the ancient sorceress, and instead she looked the guardian in its pale eye.

"What is it that you guard so carefully?" she asked the ghostly figure.

"I guard the very centre of things," the spectral shape replied. "The hub around which the worlds turn, and the wheel that keeps the walls from falling."

From some way in the distance, there was the sound of footsteps falling on dark stone, and Frayn wondered if Wom Ya was getting close.

But she did not fret, and instead she lifted a hand and pointed to the guardian's pale face.

"And tell me," she asked, "why is your face so drawn and sad? And why is it crossed here and there with cuts and tears, shining red-golden in this dark place?"

The figure shook softly, and a single red tear rolled down its white cheek.

"I am pale and sad because I am murdered and bound to service by Wom Ya," the spectre replied. "And I am crossed with these deep cuts because Ka'tharlon tore me with her teeth and talons, ripping my body to pieces. I am the ghost of Prince Myst, beguiled and betrayed, and I shall never find rest while Wom Ya's salt magic holds sway."

Then from near at hand came the creaking of dark rocks being opened by spell-craft, and Wom Ya stepped into the cavern with a cruel seashell dagger in her hand.

"Come now and lay down, Frayn," said Wom Ya, "for you are out-tricked and beaten, and I mean to open your veins with my dagger and taste the salt of your blood."

But at that moment she saw Frayn talking to the ghost of Prince Myst, and she saw the closeness of the door that should never be opened; and Frayn looked back at the old sorceress and she smiled.

"My spear may be broken," she said, "but it was wound about with enchantments many, and not every one of them was bound to the metal tip."

Then she lifted up the charred-ash shaft, and this had been ensconced with magics that made it unbearable to the shadow-touch of ghosts and wraiths and spectral things; and the pale figure of Prince Myst drew back before it, and a smile was on his face.

"Pass then, Frayn," the ghost said. "For though I am bound to service, it is with gladness that I fail."

Frayn stepped forward and flung the door wide, and there was no one to stop her entering.

Wom Ya shrieked out a curse and ran for the door; and as she ran, she called out to Ka'tharlon, commanding her to fall on Frayn and tear her to pieces.

But neither the sorceress nor the monster were swift enough; and before either could draw near, Frayn had passed within, and shut the door behind her. When they drew close, the ghost of Prince Myst floated down from the darkness and barred their way, and neither of them were able to follow the warrior inside.

For the longest moment there was silence complete. Wom Ya stared at the ghostly prince, and Prince Myst stared back at her with triumph in his pale eyes. Ka'tharlon settled back on her huge haunches, and tilted her head to one side as if listening for something.

Then a noise came. It did not come from behind the door, but instead rose from nowhere and everywhere, a distant crashing, rending noise, dull and dreadful, and gaining slowly in volume until at last the whole world was full of it; and then the ground began to shake.

Wom Ya turned and tried to flee; but the cavern floor heaved up as if with the beat of a vast drum, and she went flying through the air and crumpled in a pile. Ka'tharlon crouched, four-square and stout, growling deep in her throat as, with a monstrous cracking, the sides of the cavern split, and slabs of rock began to rain down upon them.

Prince Myst floated there, quiet and untouched, regarding everything with his pale eyes; and then the walls of the cavern were falling away entirely, and they stood, the three of them, as if on a great plate of dark stone while all around was whipped to chaos, with colours and shapes and thousands of various objects, trees, buildings, creatures, people, all turning in a maelstrom around the central stillness, with the wooden door standing firm at the very heart of things.

Then with a deafening thunder like a hammer slamming into the anvil of the world, the spinning motion stopped. All around them, the objects, colours and shapes fell from the sky; and at the same instant, a great wash of brown earth shot up from all sides and fell in a spreading tsunami into the deep distance. There was stillness, and they were alone.

The plate of dark stone stood quiet, and all sides of the great cavern had been swept low, save for one, and that was the wall into which the wooden door was placed. Here, the wall stood a few paces high, only rising a little further than the door frame.

Stars were above them. Around the stone slab were trees. Crickets chirped in the darkness, and a peace was on the land. No-where could be heard the crash of waves on sand.

Wom Ya staggered to her feet and looked around. She seemed shrunken and frail, and her face was broken and thin.

There was a clicking noise. The wooden door opened, and Frayn stepped out onto the plate of dark rock. She shut the door behind her, and it closed with a deep snap.

"What have you done?" muttered Wom Ya, walking unsteadily towards the tall woman. "That room should not have been opened. It was not time for the unmaking. There were many, many stories still to come."

But Frayn stood proud and unafraid.

"I turned us only a quarter circle," she said, and something flashed in her eyes. "It was a re-making, not an unmaking, for the great unmaking is yet to come."

"Well, you have not unmade me, foolish woman," Wom Ya spat, and she seemed to regain something of her firmness and malice. "That was a mistake for which you will dearly pay."

Then Wom Ya gestured to Ka'tharlon who crouched huge and scaled beside them.

"You will destroy this warrior-wench, my pet," she said. "I have no patience for potion-making now."

Ka'tharlon turned her massive head towards the old woman and said, "No."

A silence stretched.

Then the great monster was swivelling her body, pivoting towards Wom Ya as the old woman backed and scrambled away, a growing panic in her face.

"I smell no salt and hear no waves," Ka'tharlon boomed. "There are no gulls nor breakers, currents nor tides, kelp or seaweed in this remade world: we are far from the ocean, and your magic has no depth here!"

And with a wordless roar, the huge monster launched herself into the air, moving so fast that her body was wreathed in a green fire that shone brighter than the stars.

"No," said Wom Ya, unbelieving; then, "No!" again, as she perceived the green speck above them start to turn, to flip over in the sky and begin to descend once more towards her.

Wom Ya began to move. At first she hobbled slowly; but as her terror began to grow, faster and faster she went, fleeing the open plate of dark stone and making for a line of trees in the far distance.

But she was not fast enough. She could never have been fast enough.

Ka'tharlon was hurtling back to earth. From a speck to a dot, then from a dot to a ball, then from a ball to a huge, roaring blur of unstoppable wrath, the monster crashed out of the sky towards the old woman who, in her arrogance, had sought to bind her to her will.

At the last possible moment, Wom Ya abandoned her flight and turned to stare up at the gargantuan creature. Frayn had a single frozen impression of the old woman crouched there, small and broken, with Ka'tharlon falling down upon her from above.

Then the monster hit the earth, and once more cacophony filled the world. When the dust had settled, a scorched and buckled area of earth lay smoking where the monster had gone to ground; nothing besides remained, and of neither old woman nor vast creature was there any sign.

The ghost of Prince Myst smiled the ghost of a smile. Frayn turned to the pale figure by her side.

"In a way," she said at length, "I am sad that the creature is dead. I would have given her such a fight as was worthy of a tale or two."

"Dead?" mused the ghost. "Yes, maybe they are dead. If they are dead, I do not see them here in my death."

"Is that the way of death then?" asked Frayn. "Do all the dead see and know one another?"

But the pale figure shrugged his shoulders.

"Who can say?" he said at last. "I certainly see more than when I lived. Everything is clearer now. Everything is...simpler, somehow."

Frayn nodded. She looked up at the stars, and to the Eastern sky, which was becoming streaked with dashes of pink and lilac.

"And amongst that which is clearer," she said, "is it included where we are now? Or which parts of the world that we knew still exist? Or was it all swept away when I passed through that door?"

Prince Myst smiled again, though it did not touch his eyes.

"Much has passed away, I think," he said softly. "Trees and creatures and folk. Much is not lost, but has been shifted. The islands are gone. The archipelago has been scattered like chaff, and no ocean rolls within a thousand leagues of here. But the lands are not all that have shifted, for the powers that abide in that room are potent, and when you turned that quarter circle, the days and seasons were shattered as neatly as the lands and seas."

Then his eyes clouded over, and he said, "My brother has been searching for an answer for ever such a long time. He wandered away from his kingdom for the sake of friendship, and it had fled far away when he returned."

"You can see your brother, then?" asked Frayn. "Is that one of the powers of the dead?"

But Prince Myst shrugged again.

"It seems to be one of *my* powers," he said. "Though much good it does me. If I were free to go to him, I would. Yet I am bound to guard the door; the force of obligation that keeps me here is the same power that holds me yet to this world. It fills my heart with loneliness to think of the endless ages to come; that I must dwell here, alone and friendless, while years fall like leaves, with no relief or company."

Then Frayn squared her broad shoulders and took a deep breath, for she found that she liked Prince Myst very much – even if he was a ghost – and she had slain a great many awful creatures, and had perhaps wandered far enough in her time.

"Then I shall wait with you," she said. "And should anyone seek to pass the door, well, it is better that two be here to stop them than one. After all," she added, with a touch of pride, "*you* were not able to stop *me*."

The ghost looked at her, long and steady; and a smile bloomed on his face.

"I would like that," he told her.

"Do you know what I would like?" she replied; and when Prince Myst told her he did not, she said, "A story."

"Very well," said the ghost, who was becoming more transparent than ever in the growing light of dawn. "I shall tell you a story of my brother. I have been observing his progress for quite some time now. In fact, he has made it something of a quest to understand what became of his island kingdom, and I do not think he will rest until he knows the answer. He is now far off and away and further far again. Anyway, he recently passed through a place called

29

THE LAND OF THE MOST LOVELY

~

There is a land far from here where the lads and lasses are the most lovely in the whole world. The area is renowned for it, and folk travel from far and wide to gape and marvel at the sheer beauty of the young people there. No one knows why this is. Maybe there's something in the water. Maybe the sunlight has a certain quality that soaks the skin and makes flesh supple and firm. Or maybe the land is simply blessed, who can say?

In any case, nearly every youth and maiden there is beautiful beyond enduring; and into this land, by the meanderings of chance, my brother Valiben came.

Now Valiben had been wandering for many days and many nights; and he had been trying to find that one special person who was quite completely beyond the power of understanding. Why? Well, because that was the price a certain lady had set, on the payment of which, she would use her curse of perfect understanding to tell him what had become of his island home.

Though Valiben had met many people and had many strange adventures, he was no closer to finding the one he sought. For of the many curious and cantankerous, obtuse and obstreperous, mysterious and mystical individuals he had come across, there had not been a single one whom, after some questioning and consideration, remained in any important way unknowable.

In fact, it had become a matter of contention between my brother and his travelling companion as to how they might, when it came to it, know they had found the person they sought.

"After all," said Max, his rich blue scales glittering spectacularly in the sunlight, "we might find someone who seems completely perplexing to the likes of you or I, and yet who your Lady might know utterly in a heartbeat!"

Prince Valiben shook his head stubbornly, and did his best to keep his head above the water (it was always difficult to have a conversation with Max while the fish was swimming full-pelt, but during their travels, the pair had learnt very well how best to discuss things while still making good speed).

"No, my friend, you are very dear to me, but you simply *must* be wrong!" he insisted, tugging on Max's gills to emphasise the point. "After all, even when you can't claim to understand someone to their bones, still you can say, 'here is a man, and I know there are wheels turning behind the eyes, even if I cannot say how fast they spin, or how the cogs are laced, or what thoughts they are going to swirl up into his mind.' And I tell you, when we meet our man, we will know him because *we will not sense those wheels at all*."

"Who is to say this person must be a man?" protested Max. "She wanted a companion, you said. She didn't specify man or woman. For that matter, she didn't specify man or fish."

Valiben stared at his friend.

"It's not you," he said flatly. "How many times…?"

"Oh, tush, I know it's not me the Lady seeks," said Max, waving a fin airily. "I am really quite simple to understand, and I wouldn't want it any other way. In any case, I do not see at all how your reasoning goes. After all, when confronted by a very stupid individual…" But suddenly Max stopped dead in the water, as if all of *his* gears and wheels had frozen at once.

"Why, maybe that's the answer!" he said suddenly, and splashed his tail in excitement.

"What are you talking about?" demanded Valiben.

"Well," explained Max, "you recall when I told you what land this is we are passing through?"

"Of course I do," replied Valiben. "This is the land of the most lovely. You told me so only this morning."

"That I did, and I told you true. Now listen," went on Max. "This land grows, as I have mentioned, the most beautiful youths and the most dazzling maids. You can take my word for it. I spent many happy days in these parts when I was a young fishling."

"I already took your word for it," complained Valiben. "I took your word for it and wondered if there might not be, amongst those most lovely of young men, one who might do for my Lady. And if you recall, I distinctly remember you telling me that these young beauties were strictly of the most simple and docile sort, and not at all likely to present any difficulty in understanding, even to the likes of us."

"This is true, good sir," admitted Max, "and yet a new thought now presents itself to me. Do listen carefully. A stupid man, it must be admitted, presents no great challenge to read. Their thoughts are as open to you or I as completely, even, as ours must be to your Lady."

Valiben nodded agreement.

"But have you not noticed that a *truly* stupid man, presenting as he does much less in the way of, ah, raw material as it were, becomes, paradoxically, something more of a riddle?"

Valiben frowned.

"I'm not sure I follow you," he said.

"Listen," went on Max, his voice becoming more excited, "if you present a stupid man with a single delicious piece of cake and a bell, and tell him that he can either eat that one piece of cake now, or else he can count out ten minutes in his head, and then when this span has passed, ring the bell, and when he does this he can have not one piece of cake, but ten, what do you think that stupid man will do?"

"Why, he will eat the cake at once, of course!" answered Valiben promptly.

"Of course he will!" agreed Max. "The other option you have given him is just too complicated for his simple brain. He will become confused before you have even finished talking. The only thing he will remember is the one slice of delicious cake in front of him; and he shall eat it!"

"What, after all, is your point?" asked Valiben.

"I'm coming to that," said Max. "Now, instead of our stupid man, let us take instead a *truly* stupid man. We give him the same option, cake, bell, and all. What do you suppose the *truly* stupid man would do?"

"Well, he might..." began Valiben, and stopped. "I suppose, he might very well do the same as the other," he managed at last, but he sounded unconvinced.

"You are absolutely right," agreed Maxwell. "He might do the same as the other. He *might*. But then again, he might be so completely stupid he doesn't even remember that cake tastes good. Maybe he won't even eat it. Or maybe he will wait ten minutes before using the bell to squish the cake to smithereens. Or perhaps he would take it into his empty head to eat the bell and ring the cake. You simply *cannot say*!"

Maxwell floated in the water grinning a big fishy grin. Slowly, Valiben began to smile, too.

"So, if what you say is true," he said slowly, "then it may be we have been going about this all wrong. We don't need to find some devious, complicated, clever, curious man. Someone like that has wheels in his head that are spectacularly fine and amazingly intricate, but they are still just wheels, and my Lady would know how they turned as soon as she looked at him. No, what we need is to find someone who is so utterly, completely, and unreservedly stupid that they don't have any cogs in their head to predict *at all*!"

"Exactly!" beamed Maxwell. "We need to find a man with a mind so empty and vacant that he makes a *truly* stupid man look like a merely stupid man."

Valiben pondered a moment.

"We might call such a man a truly *truly* stupid man, I suppose," he said. "But where are we to find such a creature?"

Maxwell's grin widened.

"I might return your attention, my friend," he said, "to the fact that we are travelling currently through the land of the most lovely. And it has been my observation when I travelled these parts before that, as a *general* rule, the lovelier the lad or lass in question, the more simple and docile that person turns out to be."

Valiben slapped his hands together.

"Then it is settled!" he shouted happily. "We must make at once for the place in this land of beauties that boasts the most beautiful beauties of all!"

Then they set about congratulating one another and remarking very much on how clever they each were, and carried on at once towards a village Maxwell had visited once before which, in all this lovely land, was famed even amongst such exalted company as boasting the most lovely lads and lasses of all.

~

NOW IT JUST SO HAPPENED THAT AT ABOUT THIS TIME AND IN THIS part of the world there was a man named Krow. Yet *was* he a man? Not really, but we are coming to that.

In any case, man or monster or something in between, Krow was the person in those parts who got the things he wanted. If he wanted meat again for dinner (and he never wanted anything else) he got meat again for his dinner. If he wanted the people who lived in the winding alleys and cramped hovels to pay him larger taxes, he would simply let his chancellor know, and it was larger taxes that he would be paid. And if he took it into his head to make most especially sure that of all the beautiful youths and maidens in that lovely land, that the *most* lovely would come and work for him, and serve him hand and foot...well, wasn't it only natural that he would get this, too?

Krow was well-haired and ill-favoured, grizzly and dark, with thick folds of hoary flesh that built up around his eye sockets in big fleshy waves; and behind these, his black eyes glimmered coldly.

His family had lived in those parts for nigh on as long as any could remember, and their house was the biggest and grandest for many miles around. In fact, they were considered something akin to royalty, and they were notoriously cruel to the common folk who served them.

So it was that, after a little asking around, Valiben and Maxwell learnt that all the most spectacularly beautiful people had gone away from the local villages and were not to be found unless one wanted to make the journey to the dusty town on top of the hill.

"But, really," complained Valiben to a young woman they had found tending her sheep by the banks of the river, "are you really telling me that only the least beautiful of your people remain here in your native village?"

"Just so, sir," replied the woman meekly, who was unused to meeting with princes, and was blushing a rather stunningly pretty shade of pink. "We that remain are those judged to be amongst the ugliest people amongst these parts."

"But my dear woman!" protested Max. "You are without a doubt one of the most enchanting examples of the human female I have ever had the good fortune to encounter. Were you a fish, I would marry you at once. As it is, I must console myself by contemplating how incomparably brighter the world is now that I know you are in it."

"Your friend is too kind," muttered the woman. "But I tell you, it is true. Why, only last week Krow sent messengers to the villages, demanding that we once again send a tithe of our most beautiful youths and maidens to his great hall. It is a terrible burden on our poor village. Not only do we lose our able bodied, our young and fit and firm, but those of us that remain are all so incredibly foul and unpleasant to look at that we spend most our time avoiding one another. We are all just too ugly."

The young woman fluttered her remarkably pretty eyelashes and sighed.

"I simply cannot believe that," said Valiben gallantly. "But tell us, if so many of these beautiful young people are being taken off to work for Krow and his family, do not others return?"

But here the young woman shuddered and glanced around as if fearful that they might be overheard.

She opened her mouth to speak//
CRACKKKKK

//but at that moment there was a horrible tearing noise, seeming to scream at them from every direction at once.

The young woman fell to her knees, and Valiben looked around desperately, sure that some terrible attack was coming.

But he could see nothing. Everything was as it had been. There was the stream they had been following, there was the gently rolling grass swaying up the hill towards the distance, there was the vague outline of a row of trees on the horizon...

And then he saw it. It was so small and subtle, at first he could not believe what was happening right in front of his eyes.

A sword was hanging in mid air a little way distant. It was protruding through a patch of blue sky, and on either side of it the air seemed to bend and fray, as if the fabric of the atmosphere itself had somehow been laid open.

"What is...?" breathed Maxwell, but his voice faltered before he could finish the question. The sword darted downwards again, firmly; and again, that awful tearing sound rolled out to meet them from the ripping sky.

The sword sliced down, ending its arc by passing through a chunk of green grass, which it cut through as easily as if the resistance offered by both air and earth had been exactly nothing.

Valiben gazed at the blade. There was something terrible about it, terrible and strange, something he could not quite place. The air seemed to shimmer around it, as if it burnt as hot as molten metal in a blacksmith's forge, and light skittered awkwardly in its presence.

Valiben made to step forward, towards the blade and the hole it was forcing open, but, "Wait," said Max, and there was something in his friend's voice, some note of warning he had never heard there before, and he halted.

A hand thrust through the hole, grasped at what appeared to be no more than a patch of sky, and *heaved*...and suddenly the hand was shown to be on the end of an arm, and the arm was attached to a man, heavyset and tall with a small dark beard and a grim look in his eyes. The man was clambering through the hole his sword had cut in the sky; and through that hole, Valiben fancied he could catch a faint glimpse of a strange room he did not recognise, lit by lamps of fire; and on the floor there, a young man with blood on his hand, and a look of horror in his eyes.

But even as he watched, the tall man pulled himself entirely through the hole and planted his feet firmly on the grass; and when he did that, the hole began to close up behind him.

The tall man looked around him; and there was a joy in his face, though it was savage, and Valiben disliked it at once.

The man's eyes danced from hill to river to maiden…then settled on Valiben.

He turned decisively, and started marching towards the prince.

"I…know him. Or else, he reminds me of someone…" said Max in a whisper. He paused, then shook himself. "In any case, this man is not to be trusted, or I am a kestrel. If you jump back into the river and hold tight to my side, I can have us all away from here at a moment's notice."

Valiben nodded, and he pushed the maid behind him, so that she stood on the very lip of the river, and was quite ready to jump.

"My friend," replied Valiben, "I think you may be right. But this is surpassing strange, and I fear we must find out more about this man, if indeed we can."

So he licked his lips and made his legs limber, though he stood his ground for now.

The tall man came closer. When he was no more than a few paces from the stream he stopped. He looked at Valiben, and he scowled.

"How deep in have I come?" he demanded, fixing the prince with a cold glare.

But Valiben frowned, for the question made no sense.

"How deep?" he replied. "As far as I can see, you're still standing on dry land, and so you're not in any depth at all."

"Of course," the man muttered to himself. "You don't know do you, you poor fool? I have grown used to having enlightened enemies…"

He trailed off. Valiben took a deep breath. He was beginning to wonder if there was not something wrong in the head with this strange man who had appeared from nowhere and had a wild look in his eyes.

"This is the land of the most lovely," said Valiben, watching the man warily. "I am Prince Valiben, and these are my friends. Who are you?"

The man regarded him coolly for a moment.

"I have gone by many names," he said. "But none of them matter any more. I am the undoing. I am the end of lies. I am the death of glamours."

Valiben shook his head.

"I am afraid I do not understand you," said Valiben slowly.

The tall man smiled at him, a thin, nasty up-curling of his lips.

"Oh, you should be afraid," he told Valiben. "And you are right: you most certainly do *not* understand me."

Then he edged a little closer. He raised his sword - his strange, awful sword - a fraction. Only a fraction, but Valiben noticed it, and he shifted slightly, and got ready to jump.

"I am going deeper in, do you hear me?" the man said, and his voice was so sharp and so quiet, it was almost a hiss. "It is just like following the pull of a magnet, so there's no use trying to stop me. Every slice will bring me closer." He tilted his head slightly and sniffed the air, like a hunting dog trying to catch an elusive scent. "And I am not so far away now, I know. Otherwise...why would I have come here?"

Then his smile turned into a snarl, and all at once Valiben realised that the man was about to strike, was *already* striking in fact, and he was so fast, *so* fast, and even as he began to push backwards and launch himself into the river, he wondered if he had not left things too late...

That awful burnished blade swept through the air towards him, and

❦ 30 ❦

PAUSE TO DRAW BREATH (MYST HALTS HIS STORY

~

"Why did you stop?" asked Frayn, frowning.

"I..." said the ghost of Prince Myst. "I...do not know."

"How did your brother survive?" she pressed, her hand gripping tight to the shaft of her spear. (It had been wound about with enchantments many, and when she was anxious she always drew comfort from the feel of that solid wood).

"He...that is to say...that never happened," Prince Myst was frowning a ghostly frown.

"What?" demanded Frayn. "But you just told me that a man came from nowhere. That he cut away the very air, that he climbed out of the sky, that he said...many strange things. What do you mean, that never happened?"

The ghost was holding his pale head in his pale hands. Frayn could see the faintest glimmerings of pink through his translucent body, as a pink dawn began to break in the East.

"I watched my brother and his friend make their travels across the world," said Myst slowly, his eyes down, a look of concentration on his face. "I meant to tell you of all I saw. How they came to the land of the most lovely, how they decided that of these lovely people, the very most lovely might be the one that they sought, how they found then that the land was ruled over by a very grim man named Krow, who had taken all the most lovely men and women to be his servants, and how these same servants seemed to be disappearing. How my brother and his friend went to the court of this man, and were welcomed in, but found it less easy to leave. And how they met there someone who might well be just as evil and dangerous as Krow, maybe more so...but who had been wronged in the past by that man, and who wanted revenge. I was planning on telling you all of these things, and other things besides. But not once in the story was I planning on telling you of this...this tall man and his strange sword." He shook his head. "It did not happen like that. I am sure it did not happen like that..."

Frayn waited. Something about this made her uneasy.

She found her eyes wandering to the door. It stood as firm as ever, planted squarely in the single slab of black rock which was all that was left of Ka'tharlon's cavern. She shifted her weight.

"Why did you stop your story when you did?" she asked suddenly.

"Because I did not want..." began Myst, then he halted.

"You did not want what?" pressed Frayn.

"I did not want to hear myself telling another story..." Myst spoke hesitantly. "One in which something...something bad happened to my brother."

"Do you think you could tell it from the beginning again, only this time tell it how it...how it *really* happened?" asked Frayn.

"I don't know," said Myst simply.

But he tried.

He tried...and the same thing happened again.

Frayn stopped him when he was describing how the tall man had walked towards Valiben.

"You've done it again," she said, and Myst stopped speaking.

Dawn had truly broken by now, and the birds were starting to sing.

"I think I can tell it from a bit further on," Myst's ghost said at last.

"What do you mean?" asked Frayn.

"When I try and remember how the story goes, it all seems...confused, for a while," he told her slowly. "It's the strangest thing, but I think...I *know* that they are confused by it, too. My brother and his friend. They can feel that something is not right, they can almost remember what happened when I tried to tell their story. It's as if there are echoes of how things could have gone differently, washing against them. They are like people newly awoken and still dragging sleep around with them. The whole story is like that, for a while. But then, I think it gets to a point where it starts, well, feeling *right* again."

Frayn settled down, and looked up at the ghost eagerly.

"It goes like this," he said, trying to sound confident. "I was telling you of a place that was far off and away, and further far again. It was called

THE LAND OF THE MOST LOVELY
(REPRISE)

~

S
o it was that they made their way to the dusty town at the top
of the hill, which was where Krow was said to make his home.
They followed their river into a canal, and they followed their
canal up a series of locks, and when they got to the top lock near the
middle of the town, Valiben climbed out onto dry landed and he
shouted:

"Hear me! Hear me, O good folk that are most lovely! I am Valiben,
Prince of the Archipelago; <u>and</u> this is my friend and companion,
Maxwell, Prince-In-Waiting of All Fish of the Upper Depths, and
Duke of the Northern Seas! We have come in friendship, and would
greatly desire an audience with the lordly man known as Krow. Will
any here carry him a message and speed us on our way?"

Now Valiben managed this little speech in a very princely way, for
he was a very princely man; and it was a good thing he was *such* a
princely man, for the very moment he started speaking, every man
and women in that place turned their eyes upon him, and my word!
Never had Valiben seen such beauty, not on earth or in his wildest
dreams or in his most fevered imagination. It took all his princely

dignity to stop himself from burning up right then and there in a shame of embarrassment at his own daring to have addressed such perfect-looking people.

But, as I have said, Valiben was a prince, and he gritted his teeth and he forced his mouth to smile, and he managed to hide his shaking, and presently his heart began to slow a little, and by then the people (who were all rather dull-witted despite their fantastically noble appearances) had worked out what it was that Valiben was asking for, and some had gone running to take the news to Krow, and others had hurried forward to help, and they fetched a great glass tank for Maxwell to swim in, and mounted it on the back of a stout wagon pulled by a big horse, and before they knew what was happening, the two travellers were being ushered through the dusty streets of the town towards the huge, splendid house where Krow lived. And if Valiben and Max failed to notice the ruby-pale eyes that watched them carefully out of the cracked door of a certain wagon parked in a cramped, out-of-the-way corner, can we blame them? They were in the centre of a whirlwind, and if they did not note The Mistress of the Wagon, then you can be sure that *she* noted *them*. She watched the commotion pass and she//

//*would* have smiled to herself in the darkness, had she not felt that certain *CRACKKKKK* that had split the fabric of the worlds but a short time before, and which *she* could remember (for she was a creature who understood the way things were woven) even if princes and fish could not//

//smiled to herself in the darkness.

"In any case," (said Prince Myst, shaking his head and trying to clear it, while Frayn frowned hard and felt a chill creep up her spine), "Valiben and Maxwell were led through the streets, and soon they stood before the grandest mansion they had seen since coming to this part of the world. It was built all of pink marble and ornate glass, and reared up into the sky high above all the other buildings. Balconies and buttresses sprang up from every side, and they had to pass through a great high wall of dour stone before they were able to approach the entrance. And when they did approach the entrance, why, there was Krow waiting for them.

He stood on his steps with legs planted squarely and he smiled at them with his mouth and measured them with his eyes.

"Prince Valiben!" he greeted them heartily. "I am most honoured by your visit. As I am by yours, O Prince of the Waves," he added, inclining his head to include Maxwell in his tank.

"My lord," said Valiben, giving the most princely of princish bows. "We apologise for arriving at your great hall unannounced. But we are, in fact, engaged upon a most urgent quest, and I am sure you understand our predicament."

Krow bowed most deeply - though his eyes never left them - and he waved his hand through the air as if brushing away such foolish notions as propriety or presumption.

"Tush, my dear prince, tush and nonsense!" he said. "It is no inconvenience whatsoever, and I am quite sure that when we learn of the nature of this most noble quest of yours we shall do everything in our power to speed you on it."

Valiben opened his mouth to reply, but Maxwell - who had seen quite enough of such aristocratic exchanges in his time, and who was, in fact, getting rather hungry, bobbed up in his tank and spoke quickly.

"We're here, my good man, because we have heard that you have gathered yourself quite the finest selection of beautiful lads and maidens that are to be found in these parts," said he. "We are on a quest to find the least understandable person the world has ever known, and we have developed a theory that we might find such a person here. We simply wish to conduct a few interviews with some of your most dazzling young lovelies, and then we shall be on our way. I might add, if we could trouble you for a solid bell and a rather large cake, that would also help us tremendously."

Krow smiled thinly at the big blue fish.

"And if you happen to find among my courtiers this one that you look for?" he asked, and though his voice was soft there was something cold as winter there.

"Then we would seek to offer them, ah, alternative employment," said Valiben. "Though of course, we would be *very* grateful for all your help."

Krow stared at Valiben flatly for the longest time; and our young prince began to feel beads of sweat bursting on his brow.

Then his face broke into a cold smile.

"Of course," he said, and swung his arm round, inviting them to enter his mansion. "My servants will show you to a suitable suite of rooms in which you can conduct your interviews. I shall have my chamberlain compile a list of the twenty most beautiful servants in my employ, and see that they are sent to you directly."

Valiben and Maxwell thanked him profusely, and assured him of their undying gratitude//

//but at that moment there was a terrible sparking and screaming noise. It was coming from the thick oaken gate which led through the stone walls into the grounds of the mansion. Every head in the courtyard turned at that sound; and Krow arose with a terrible look of anger and - yes - of fear, for he knew very well what creature was trying to make her way into his domain, and she was indeed to be feared.

The hinges on those thick oak gates squealed and screamed. For a moment there was silence, and it seemed as if the tough wood had prevailed. But then came an awful blow, and the doors were defeated. The wood crumpled and sagged inwards, the thick copper hinges flying off into the courtyard. And behind the gate stood a wagon, made of simple dark wood. There was no beast of burden to be seen pulling it, and no driver mounted on top; yet the wheels rolled forward all the same.

Valiben looked from the wagon to Krow, and back to the wagon again. Their host was breathing hard, and he seemed ready to run. The wagon rolled forward a quarter-turn of the wheel...but as it rolled over the invisible threshold marked out by the place where the oaken gate had been, a wave of sparks screamed up from either wheel, and the wagon could come no closer.

Krow let out a ragged breath.

"It holds," he said to himself. "I knew it would, and yet...the curse holds, and we are safe."

Then without saying another word, without even sparing a glance for Valiben or Max or any of his beautiful servants, he stormed towards where the wagon had been stopped by whatever strange enchantment was laid there.

"How do you like that, you sour mistress, damn you!" Krow was shouting as he approached the wagon. "You tried that before, did I not learn you well enough then? What we won was won fair, and you will never get it back! Best you remember that, then slink off away with you!"

The wagon stood still and silent while Krow finished his tirade. When he had stopped speaking, he stood there panting, sweat forming on his brow and trickling down his neck.

The wind blew softly, and not a sound was there to be heard.

"Well?" Krow called at last. "Have you nothing to say, O mistress of a small world?"

Silence began to stretch again, and then with a grim creaking

✳ 32 ✳

MYST HALTS ONCE MORE

~

Myst shook his head, and stopped his tale.

"What happened?" asked Frayn, leaning forward. "Did the door to the wagon open?"

Prince Myst gave her a frown.

"No," he said. "I mean, I don't know. I mean, that wasn't the way it happened, either."

He sounded perplexed.

The wind blew, and little birds called from the distant line of trees.

"You mean, that...that wagon never came to Krow's mansion?" asked Frayn, at last.

"Oh, yes, yes, of course it did," said Myst, sounding distracted. "But it wasn't meant to get there for quite a while yet. You see, Krow and his sister had cheated her, years ago. That was how they got their powers. That was how they had come to dominate that little land..."

"Cheated who?" asked Frayn. Now she was the one who was frowning.

"Oh, the Mistress of the Wagon, of course," he said. "She is...she is, well, *dangerous*." He pondered the word, tasting it on his tongue.

"But the wagon didn't come to the mansion *then*," he went on, looking worried. "I mean, of course it didn't! What would be the point? Krow's sister had laid a line of her spit and moon blood around the whole place - Krow's sister was well-versed in enchantments and changing-spells. And the Mistress of the Wagon knew very well she could never break that line, not without some help. That was why she waited until she could talk to Maxwell. Once she convinced Maxwell that they could work together, all Valiben had to do was break the circle that protected the mansion, and she could roll right in." He faltered again. "Only..." he muttered.

"Only in the version you were telling me a moment ago, the Mistress of the Wagon *did* try to get in," said Frayn. "Even though she knew it would never work." She rubbed her chin with her hand. "I wonder..."

Frayn felt uneasy in her bones. Something was wrong here. Something tasted...sour.

And for no reason she could put her finger on, she found herself once more looking over to the door they guarded. It looked safe enough under this bright sunshine, with the wind sighing through the air and the birds singing nearby. And yet...

Myst was shaking his head.

"Perhaps it is best if you tell a story, instead," he told her. "I'm not sure I like my story anymore."

But Frayn shook her head.

"No!" she said, more sharply than she had intended. Then, "No. Please, I think your story is important. I think maybe...maybe this version is even more important than the way it should go. So please...tell me how it ends?"

Prince Myst licked his lips. He hesitated for a moment, then, "Oh, very well," he sighed.

Frayn smiled slightly, and relaxed.

"So, to continue this story (which I am no longer sure is mine), the door of the wagon creaked open, and

❧ 33 ❧

THE MISTRESS OF THE WAGON
SPOKE

∿

"I have not come here to trade insults with you, Krow," she said. Her voice was quiet, but it carried and all those in the court-yard heard it as clear as if she was standing at their shoulder.

"I see you very well, O master of meat and bones," she went on. "I see you very clearly indeed, you and your sister, and I know all your little magics. I am an old thing, and I can out-wait you. I know that I will not gain entrance while this circle holds. But something...unfore-seen has occurred."

Valiben moved forward to see her...but though the door of the black wagon had creaked open, the Lady had not emerged. All that could be seen was a deep darkness within the wagon...and shining out from the depths, two ruby-pale eyes and a flash of sharp white teeth below.

Krow was silent for a moment, and Valiben could feel the suspicion rolling off him in waves.

"Then why have you come here?" he asked at last.

The wagon shifted slightly, and those dreadful eyes moved closer, though the darkness still clung to them, thick as treacle.

"I have come here because I am old and I understand the way the worlds hang together," she told him. "I have come because I see clearly where others do not see at all. I have come because the old feuds must be laid aside for a time, in the cause of facing a common enemy.

"I have come because someone now walks abroad who wields a sword of faery-iron. And he must be stopped, or everything turns sour."

Her words came to an end, but her eyes continued to stare out at them, measuring, urgent.

As she spoke these words, a muttering went up from the crowd. But Valiben did not hear it, because inside him, something was shifting.

Yes, he thought to himself. *He was tall, and the sword was strange.*

He could not say where these thoughts had come from, but they troubled him. He glanced to where Maxwell was swimming in his tank, and the big blue fish looked back at him. Something passed between them.

Valiben opened his mouth to speak, but the words would not come. His mind was seething, full of confused impressions and half-remembered images.

He stalked forward, and his words were strange and grim.

It was so frustrating, like trying to grasp the fragments of a melting dream.

And then*, he struck me. He struck at me, and I would have died...*

Valiben blinked, and saw that Max was still looking at him. There was understanding in his eyes. His friend had seen him too, this tall man, this common enemy the woman with ruby-pale eyes spoke of. It was so strange, somewhere between a true memory and a flickering thought, a might-have-been...

Maybe somewhere it did *happen...*

Krow leaned forward and spat into the dust. Valiben blinked, coming back to the world around him.

"That's what I think of your tricksy words, Mistress," he told her. "I bested you once before, and you believe me a fool if you think I will fall into your little patterns so simply."

Then he turned on his heel and strode back towards his mansion.

"Wait!" came a voice, and Valiben looked almost as surprised as Krow when he realised he had spoken.

Krow paused and looked him up and down. All the false smiles and pretty manners had melted from him, and now he looked what he was: a thick-set dangerous brute of a man, with little patience for the wishes of others.

"Yes, my prince?" he asked, but there was a sneer in his voice.

"This...this lady," said Valiben slowly, licking his lips. "What she says..."

"She is no lady, boy," growled Krow. "You would do well to remember that."

"Whoever she is," went on Valiben, shaking himself and regaining something of his princely demeanour. "I...am not sure I quite understand what she is talking about, but something feels, well *right* about it. Or rather, everything she's saying sounds wrong, but it...it *feels* true."

Krow looked him up and down, and Valiben had never felt less like a prince and more like a boy in all the endless days and nights that he had spent wandering, homeless and friendless and looking for his lost land.

Krow leaned closer. Valiben could smell the meat-smell of his breath, could taste the sour sweat and see every speck of dirt on his thick hair.

"That's how she gets to you boy," Krow whispered. Then he lifted one thick arm and tapped Valiben hard on the side of his head with one finger. "She gets to you right here; and if you let her do that, you are lost."

Then Krow was striding away, heading back up the veranda and into the marble arches of his mansion. There was a rustle of silk and lace, and all his servants shook themselves and scurried after.

"You'd do well to choose wisely, boy," Krow called to them over his shoulder without looking back. "You may come with me, or go to her, but I fancy you won't do both."

Then he was gone, and the courtyard was deserted except for Valiben and Maxwell.

The wind blew desolately, and the broken gates creaked. Beyond the gates, the door to the wagon was still open; and in the darkness that hung there, those awful ruby-pale eyes watched them slyly.

Valiben felt very cold. He moved closer to Max.

He opened his mouth to speak, but that strange, low voice came again, as if its owner was standing just behind his shoulder.

"I fear the master of meat and bones is right, young prince," the Mistress of the Wagon said. "Maybe it was meant that you should go with him, and that we were not to meet today. And yet it seems the stories are coming apart; if we poor creatures are to survive, we must make new stories. The old ones are in peril."

Valiben glanced at Max, then took a step closer to the wagon.

"What do you mean?" he asked her. "What stories are coming apart?"

The eyes moved within the wagon, yet still Valiben could see no more of the Lady that dwelt there.

"I think you know in the deep and quick what I mean," she told him, and she made a sound like laughter, though there was nothing pleasant in it.

And Valiben frowned then very deeply, because something in him *did* know what the Mistress of the Wagon was telling them, though he misliked it indeed.

"The tall man," he said softly; and when he looked back and caught Maxwell's eye, the fish bobbed at him solemnly. "I have not met him and yet...maybe I *do* know him, after all."

"He is grim, and tall, and the sword he carries is strange," the Lady said, and Valiben and Max both nodded, because this was true, though they could not say how they knew it.

"I was...I was going to swim away from him," said Max. "I was getting ready to beat my tail, I was just waiting for you, my friend..." he looked at Valiben, and his eyes were large and puzzled. "And then there was darkness," he went on. "And then it had never happened...only now, I wonder if maybe it did..."

"It did happen, and it did not," came that strange voice again. "It almost happened, then the story threw him out. It fought back. Stories are like that. They know what shape they are meant to be, and they do not like being cut or stretched."

"Why do you keep speaking of stories?" asked Valiben.

But if the Mistress of the Wagon answered *that* question, neither Max nor Valiben heard her.

At length, her voice came again.

"You should come with me now," she told them. "Come with me now, both of you. He is abroad in the land, and sooner or later he will find you. He is...drawn to you, somehow," and here Valiben fancied her gaze shifted and was meant just for him. "If you follow your story, he will find you. And when he finds you...then, I fear, your story may end. Maybe all the stories will end."

Valiben shivered despite himself. Those pale eyes were filled with such awful secrets...and yet her voice was so soft and low, and he found his foot had moved a pace without him willing it to.

"Come with you?" Valiben repeated, trying to force disbelief into his voice. "How...how could we abandon our search and come with you? We are here for an important reason, we are here to find..."

"I know what you have come here to find," her voice cut him off. "Just as surely as I know you will not find it here. I know the shape of this story, so I'll save you both the bother: the master of meat and bones keeps many pretty pets and does great harm to them. But there is none here that would prove at all difficult in the way of understanding. Yes, you would do some good here, that's how the story goes. You might uncover an evil and put an end to it - and I might have helped you, don't think for one second I resist the caress of any story that cares to touch *me*, for I dance my part as willing as any other - but *your* quest was never destined to end here. Come with me now, and you may yet find your happy ending. Stay in this poisoned story, and I am sure yours will not be the only tale that ends here."

"But...but just one moment, my good lady," complained Max. "You just told us in one breath that stories do not like being poked or prodded, and then in the next you warn us not to follow ours. Now I may just be a very simple fish, but if we come with you, well, won't our story be upset with us?"

In the darkness of the wagon, a set of white teeth opened into a wide grin.

"But you see, my friend," came her voice, a thread of dark silk twisting through the courtyard, "I am the Mistress of the Wagon, and *my* story is the story of she who understands stories. Do not fear for *your* story, O prince of the Northern Seas. I will whisper her such a sweet melody, she will forget herself in my music and come a-dancing with me. That is *my* magic, and I know some tricks this tall stranger has yet to learn."

Once more, Valiben felt his foot stir forward before he had properly willed it; once more he stopped himself and looked back at his friend.

"What do you say, my good fish?" Valiben asked Maxwell, trying to sound light, but his voice was strained.

Maxwell thought for a moment.

"Well if you decide to go, I hardly see as I have much of a choice," Maxwell said. "And besides," he added, more brightly, "I've always wanted to meet a woman who could sing to stories. It's one of only three types of woman I am yet to meet, and I would like to get them all ticked off before the end."

The big blue fish smiled roguishly. Valiben grinned back, and led forward the horse that pulled the cart on which Maxwell's tank was perched.

As they approached the breeched doorway, the black wagon rolled backwards and gave them room to pass out onto the road. Valiben peered in, but even close up, there was no more of the Mistress to be seen that her two bright eyes, and the space inside the wagon looked impossibly big and empty. He did not want to go in there.

But I must, he thought.

He had just raised one foot to enter, when a voice called from above.

"I wouldn't go in there if I was you, sunshine," said the voice.

Valiben froze. He flicked his eyes up. A fat little pig sat on top of the wagon, and stared down at him curiously.

"I mean, I've seen lots of people get in," the pig went on. "And I've seen lots of people get out, too. Thing is, they don't often come out in the same frame of mind. Or the same world, for that matter. Nah, you're much better up here with me."

"Oh!" said Valiben. He peered back into the darkness of the wagon.

The eyes within tilted, as if the lady who dwelt there was turning her head and regarding him curiously, wondering what he might do. "I see," he went on. "Thank you for the advice."

"Hey, don't mention it," said the pig cheerily. "Just let that horse go, and you can tie your friend's wagon on to the back of ours. That's it. Then jump on up top, next to me. Plenty of room, you'll see."

But when Valiben had done as he was instructed and clambered on top of the black wagon, he found there was not so much room after all.

There was an outraged hiss, and Valiben gasped as something warm and furry was yanked out from under his foot. A big black cat shot to the other side of the roof in a dark flash.

"Don't mind Torquemada," said the pig, indicating the affronted cat, "he's always trying to find something to moan about. Me, I like to take things easy. I'm Bartleby, by the way."

"Ah, pleased to meet you," said Valiben to Bartleby, and then, because he felt he was in a strange enough situation that he wanted to avoid making enemies if at all possible, "I'm sorry about your tail," he added, addressing the big cat.

"Pray do not mention it," said the cat coolly, but Valiben sensed it relax somewhat.

"What now?" called Max, from his tank tied behind them.

But it was the Mistress of the Wagon who answered him.

"Now we leave this dangerous story, and get as far away from it as possible," came her soft voice from the depths of the wagon. "Torquemada, if you please..."

And no sooner had she spoke than the black cat was up on his hind legs, and fastening Bartleby into a strange contraption worked into the top of the wagon. It was made of cogs linked to a treadmill, and Valiben had not noticed it until he had clambered up onto the roof.

"Ouch!" complained the pig. "Not so tight! You're just being cruel!"

"Stop moaning," said Torquemada crisply. "These are desperate times, you know."

Then the big black cat leapt onto Bartleby's back and pulled out a small leather whip, which he cracked theatrically in the air.

"Onward, Bartleby!" he exclaimed, and with a tugging and a creaking and a grinding of gears, the pig surged forward on the treadmill, and the wagon began to roll off down the hill and away from Krow's mansion.

At first, they moved only slowly, and the dusty hovels and stone walls rolled past at little more than walking pace. But before long they began to pick up speed, and soon Valiben was holding on very tight to the edges of the wagon, and wondering desperately what he would do if he fell off.

"You do not need to worry," said Torquemada without looking at him. "The wagon knows that you are riding it. You can let go. It will not let you fall."

Valiben licked his lips, and cautiously tried letting go with one hand.

To his surprise, he found that the cat was right. No matter how fast they went, no matter how many or how violent the sways and bumps, the wagon always seemed to tip back at just the right moment; Valiben was quite safe. He let go with his other hand and looked back at Max.

Max's wagon was still attached, and flying along behind them with the same great speed. Occasionally one of the wheels would hit a dip in the road, and when this happened the big blue fish would jump up out of his tank, survey the scenery with interest, and then fall back into the water with a great splash.

"How interesting!" Maxwell called to him. "Have you noticed what's happening to the people out there?"

Valiben frowned. He had not noticed anything happening to the people they were passing. That was probably because he had been far too concerned with what had been happening to him. Now Valiben took in the men and women who were whizzing past them on either side - really at a tremendous rate by now - and what do you think he saw?

"They are slowing down!" Valiben shouted to Maxwell, and it was true. The people they were passing seemed almost frozen. They were stilled in the act of turning a head, lifting a foot, making a gesture. Valiben even saw an apple tumbling through the air between two children, moving so slowly it almost seemed to have stopped entirely.

"Nearly there, Bartleby," muttered the cat. "Just keep it up a little longer...."

"That's...easy...for you...to say," panted the pig.

"Nearly where?" asked Valiben and Maxwell together.

"Never you mind!" snapped Torquemada, sounding outraged. "Can you not see that we are concentrating? Honestly, some people..."

Bartleby rolled his eyes and tipped Valiben a wink, but he did not say anything else. He seemed far too out of breath.

"Sorry," muttered Valiben, meekly, but no one heard. They were going so fast now that the wind whipped the word away as soon as it was spoken, and Valiben had to squint against the rush of air.

The wagon shuddered, then for a moment it was suddenly rolling as smoothly as if the wheels were spinning on butter, and all the jerking stopped. It only lasted a second, and then with a crash and a bump, they were clattering along again.

What was that? thought Valiben, but before he could ask, he noticed that all the hair on Torquemada's back was sticking straight up, as if he had been struck by lightning.

"That's it!" shouted the cat. "Now Bartleby! The last push, now!"

The pig said nothing, but all at once he was redoubling his efforts, straining in his harness and rushing forward on the treadmill so fast his little legs became thick pink blurs.

The wagon tipped, shuddered...and settled once more into that impossibly smooth roll it had tasted a moment before - only this time, it did not stop.

Valiben looked up. The landscape around them *blurred.*

The green of the trees melted into the blue of a stream swam into the gold of the sunset mingled with the dusky limbs and faces of the frozen people, faster and faster and faster, until...

...they were riding through nothing.

White. Everywhere was white. There was no sky, no ground, nothing to be seen in any direction. Just nothing. Just white.

Valiben looked down, and suddenly realised they were no longer moving.

Of course we're not moving, he thought. *There's nothing here to move* against.

Bartleby was still running, though; and Valiben realised that the cat had snagged a lever as soon as they had come through to this strange white land.

Torquemada saw him staring at the lever, and fixed him with a glare.

"That is why it is *so* important that you do not interrupt us," he said coldly. "Can you imagine what would have happened to our poor piggy friend if I had not thrown this lever at *exactly* the right time?"

The cat lifted one eyebrow austerely, and Valiben gave a little embarrassed shrug.

"The mechanism would have remained in gear, and our Bartleby here would have been catapulted over our heads into that wide white yonder." Torquemada glared at him for a moment, then seemed to soften. "Not that *I* would be overly affected by such a turn of events, of course. But our mistress is unaccountably fond of him, and it would not do to upset her."

"Oh, I see," said Valiben, feeling rather chastised. He turned to Bartleby, who was slowing down to a brisk trot. "I'm very sorry, my friend," he told the pig earnestly. "I did not realise you were in such danger."

"Ah, don't listen to this old twonk!" laughed Bartleby, coming to a walk, then stopping altogether. "He just likes to feel important. If he hadn't flipped the lever, I'm sure I would have landed somewhere soft. *Everywhere* 'round here's soft!"

"And where is 'here', exactly, my fine pig?" asked Maxwell, rising up out of the water.

But it was not Bartleby who answered him. There was a low creak, and the door of the black wagon swung open.

"We are in the place between stories," came the voice of the Mistress of the Wagon, clear and cold. "It is one way to travel between stories...or maybe it would be more accurate to say that this is one way to travel beyond *the* story, for really there is only one story, and we all share it. It is not the only way. But it is also a place where we should be able to bide a little time."

"So we can stay safe from the tall man?" asked Valiben. "The one with the sword?"

"That is right, my prince," said the Mistress, and Valiben could hear the sour treacle with which she uttered the word 'prince', and knew that this was one lady whom titles would *not* impress. "We should be safe from him for..." she paused. "Well, for a little time at least. Though time, of course, is not what it once was."

"Was it ever?" agreed Max vaguely. "Do you know, when I was a young fishling..."

"The place between stories?" repeated Valiben, talking over Max. "I've never heard of such a land. How did we get here, exactly?" *And can we get out again?* he wondered, but did not ask, perhaps because he worried what the answer would be.

"You have never heard of it because you have been prince of only a very small world," said the Mistress of the Wagon. "You have never heard of it because the deeper truths are hard to find, and difficult to believe when you find them. *I* know the truth of things - something of the truth of things - because I am old, and because it is my business to know them. It is my nature."

The voice paused. The silence here was so intense that Valiben could hear ringing in his ears.

"Good," said the voice at last. "I am glad that you are listening. Be still, and perhaps you will become a little wiser.

"The world is like..." the voice hovered on the word, stretched it nice and thin. "The world is like a river. It is one thing, one enormous long entity...and yet it is made up of many individual drops of water. Ever so many, a *great* many. So many thousands upon thousands that no one could ever count them all. And how does that river look, to the people that dwell within? Well, it looks very different to the people who live in a small backwater stream, cut off from the main flow, than it does to those who live in the raging torrent of the middle stream. And though every drop of water is distinct, is different, is flowing in its own direction and at its own speed, on its own course and from its own starting point...yet every drop is influenced, in some subtle way, by every other drop in the whole river. Their destinies cross time and time again.

"When two drops are close to one another, and are packed in tight as they are at the centre of the stream, then it is easy for the people who live there to move between them. Sometimes they do not even know they are doing it. Sometimes, a hundred drops of water, a *thousand,* will roll together for so long that the people who live there stop thinking about them as being separate worlds. In fact, many people do not even know the borders of their world, or think of the world as having any. To them, the world goes on forever and ever, just like our river flowing on from nowhere into nowhere.

"On the other hand, those drops of water that are furthest out from the central current, from the constant roar and pressure...these tend to drift further apart from one another. Sometimes they do this to such an extent that they become isolated. They cut themselves off from the river, bend over backwards into themselves; and the people who live there tell themselves that they are alone."

Suddenly, the Mistress of the Wagon burst into laughter. It was so genuine, and so unexpected, that Valiben gave a little jump and nearly fell off into the drifting clouds of white nothing that swayed gently below him.

"Can you imagine?" asked the Mistress. "One world amongst so many countless thousands upon thousands...laying so close to the next that they are, in a manner of speaking, touching. And they think they are *alone*. But then a single life is such a small thing, and wisdom comes to those who wait. To those who have the *time* to wait..."

The Mistress trailed off again. Valiben waited for her to go on, but the silence continued to stretch.

At last he could bear it no longer.

"And is that where we are now?" he asked. "We are in one of those small worlds, those inward-facing worlds?"

Bartleby and Torquemada looked at one another for a moment, then burst out laughing.

"This?" choked the pig. "This, one of those little closed-in spherical worlds? Don't be daft, sunshine."

"I told you already, we are in the place between stories," said the Mistress of the Wagon, rather more sharply than before. "We are not in one of the sad little backwaters of limp, fetid story any more than we are at the raging torrent at the heart of all stories. My prince, you must learn to listen more carefully. Think of this place as...as the sand on the riverbed. Or the air that flows above the water. When we left the land of the most lovely, we left your story behind. When we did that, we came here, to the place between stories."

"It's a kind of emptiness," said Bartleby helpfully. "Sort of a place where nothing has happened yet. We had to escape your story to get here, though. That's what all the sweat and speed was for! Had to build up our own narrative field so that it was strong enough to snap away from the pull of your story."

"Yes," added Torquemada, not wanting the pig to get one up on him, "and the beauty of this place is that it is exactly as close to one story as it is to the next. So it is one means of navigating your way through the river, as it were."

The black cat looked smug for a moment, then remembered that this did not become him, and went back to examining his claws nonchalantly.

"That is one advantage, my pet, it is true," came the Mistresses' voice again, low and sweet this time. "Though it is not the only one."

"But I still don't understand," said Max, bobbing up and down in his tank. "What has all of this got to do with that tall man? And with us? Who is he exactly? And why have we gone to all this trouble just to get away from him?"

"The tall man is an agent of undoing," said the Mistress, and now all the warmth had dropped away, and her voice was very hard. "That is all you need to know for now. He is no friend of stories, and he would end the whole world - would end the exact extent of each and every world - if only he were given half the chance. And it is not *us* that he has very much to do with, at least not directly...only you, my prince. Only you."

Fish, pig, and cat all turned to regard Valiben.

"Me?" exclaimed Valiben. "He is after *me*? Why? Whatever did I do to him?"

But the Mistress of the Wagon only laughed again.

"Dear me, you did nothing *to* him, my young prince," came her voice. "No, you were simply the pathway that called to him. That called to his *sword*. He was seeking the centre, you see. He was seeking the centre, and the secret heart that beats there."

"Are you trying to tell me that *I* am the centre of the...of the...world?" Valiben looked horrified.

"Of course not!" put in Bartleby. "No one's the centre of the *world*, you prat! No, what it is - and pardon the interruption, Mistress, but I think I know where this one's not getting it - what it is, right, is that, well, not to put too fine a point on it, you are a *story*."

Valiben frowned.

"What do you mean, I'm a story?" he said slowly. "I don't *feel* like a story."

"No, not only you," said Torquemada, not unkindly. "You, me, your friend the fish over there. We're all stories. Or rather, we're all *in* stories, which is more or less the same thing."

"It's a, a watchamacallit, a *philosophy*," added Bartleby. "I mean, think about it, right? We tell each other the story of how our day went, of where we came from, of what we want to do. We make up stories to explain who we are, what the world is, and where we'll go when the world is done with us. And what's left of our little lives even a few years after we're gone, or a few miles away from where we live? Nothing, really. Just memories and tales. Just stories. When you get right down to it, *everything* is just a story."

Sudden understanding dawned on Valiben's face.

"Oh, you mean we're *philosophically* all stories," he said, relaxing somewhat. "According to you, we are *metaphorically* stories."

"Yes," agreed Bartleby affably, "except that as well as being *philosophically* a story, I meant that you *actually* are, as well."

Valiben sagged. Perhaps he did not understand this, after all.

"Oh, you can worry about it later, my little princeling," came the voice of the Mistress. "Or forget about it later, if you prefer. But for now, we need you to *listen*. You are not the centre of this - or any other - world. You were the centre of a *story*, a story being told by your brother. And the reason you were singled out by the tall man, is that he desperately wants to get to the place where your brother *is*."

"And where is my brother, exactly?" asked Valiben wearily.

"Why, at the centre, of course!" exclaimed the Mistress. "He is at the very raging centre. He is there right now. And you, my fine friend, are a means by which this tall man can find his way there. So if we want to lead this man away from the centre of Story, you are the one who can do it."

Valiben took a deep breath. He looked at Bartleby and at Torquemada. They looked back at him, but said nothing. He did not know what to do.

But none of it made any sense. Rivers and stories, stories and rivers...Was it possible? Could it be possible...?

He glanced over to Maxwell, and the big blue fish bobbed out of the water and shrugged.

"But...but how do you *know* all of this?" asked Valiben.

"I know many things, my sweet," soothed the Mistress. "Many things. Many mouths come to whisper in my ears, for they all know that I am one of the few with power or wits enough to stand against what we face."

There was a chuckle from the roof the wagon.

"I thought that Sheriff was going to faint when she came to ask your help," said Bartleby. "It's good to see one of them Sheriffs come a-begging."

"They are so very proud of their little Folds," added Torquemada. "Their little bastions of Order. Silly little creatures. They know so much less than they think they do..."

"And yet she asked me, all the same," said the Mistress, and there was a cold steel in her voice that made Valiben shiver. Bartleby and Torquemada were suddenly very still.

"The Sheriffs are fools, little fools guarding little worlds," she went on, in a softer voice. "But they play their part. They are more important than either of you know. They are more important than they know themselves. And this one...Indigo..." The ruby-pale eyes sparkled in the darkness. "Yes, Indigo Shuttlecock. She was scared, but she held her ground. She may yet go far."

A chastened silence settled on the wagon.

Valiben shook himself. This talk of Sheriffs and Folds meant nothing to him. But he thought back to the strange glint of the metal sword, to the *wrongness* of it. He thought of the man's narrow smile and the coldness he had seen in his eyes.

He thought back to the way the landscape had writhed and torn beneath that awful blade, and all at once he knew.

"What do you need me to do?" asked Valiben.

In the darkness of the wagon, the ruby-pale eyes glowed bright, and the smile drew very wide.

"I want you to tell us a story," said the Mistress of the Wagon.

"A story?" repeated Valiben, wanting to laugh. "Is that all? Just tell a story?"

He looked from Bartleby to Torquemada and back again. Neither were smiling.

"Tell us a story, Valiben," said the Mistress of the Wagon. "But you should know that when you tell a story in the place between stories, it is like blowing drops of water into the river. That is the other reason we have come here. The land between stories is fertile."

"But...but what sort of story should I tell?" asked Valiben.

"One about you and your brother," the Mistress answered at once. "And there is one other thing you must do when you tell it..."

Valiben listened as the Mistress spoke, and he listened very carefully, and he heard her very well.

When she had finished speaking, he nodded his understanding, and stood silent for a while, lost in thought.

Then he asked one question, and received the answer he expected.

He pondered a little longer.

Then he looked around at his strange companions.

"You know, I *have* thought of a story I would like to tell you all. It is called

34

THE TRICK

ONE

~

There were once two boys, and not only were they brothers, but also they were princes.

Prince Myst was the younger, and Prince Valiben was the elder, and their father was busy, and their mother was dead.

So.

One day, they decided that as they were getting older, and as they had never even left their native kingdom before, it was high time they went on a quest. That's what young princes do, you see. They go questing.

The question was, what could they go questing for?

They simply did not know. So they began asking everyone they could think of, hoping that someone would come up with a worthy idea for a quest.

But no one they asked came up with a very satisfying idea.

"Find a new type of meat," suggested the cook.

"Quest me out a stronger metal," said the armorer.

"If you can only find the land where they make more time and bring me some, I'd be a happy man," complained their father. "Now get you gone! Can't you see I'm busy?"

But then, "I know!" said Prince Myst. "Let's go and ask one of the salt-witches! I'm sure any one of them would know at least a hundred interesting quests we could do!"

Now Prince Valiben hesitated at this suggestion, because he knew that his father misliked the sea-sorcerers, and would never let them go to visit one if they asked.

"But we haven't asked," Myst pointed out. And since Valiben could not argue with this, they went to see Wom Ya, who was the oldest and most salty of all the sea-witches.

They found her in her kelp-lined cave down on the beach, where the waves crashed and the gulls cawed.

"What's this?" said Wom Ya slyly. "You want a quest, is it? Very well, I'll give you one."

And with that she unrolled a great parchment. The two boys saw at once that it was a huge map.

"Is this all the lands?" asked Valiben.

Wom Ya laughed, and it was not very nice a sound.

"All?" she echoed. "Stab me, boy, no! Not all the lands, not by a long way. No map can show *all* the lands. *All* goes on forever. No, this is just a map to the centre. And that's all of the world you have to worry about for the moment."

"What quest have you got for us?" asked Myst, who was really too young to understand much about maps.

"I'll show you," said Wom Ya, and pointed to the edge of the map. "This is the island kingdoms, see?"

The boys nodded. They knew their own lands, every rock and grain.

"And this," went on Wom Ya, pointing now to the very middle of the map, "is the heart of things."

Valiben frowned.

"We are supposed to go all the way there?" he asked doubtfully. "It seems an awfully long way."

"Tush and nonsense!" spat Wom Ya. "It only looks that way because you do not know the trick of getting there. But do not worry: I will show you."

With that, she pulled a crusty old seashell out from one of the little nooks in her cave, and looked at it very closely.

"Good," she said when she was satisfied, "this one is old, but it will still work."

"Work to do what?" asked Myst.

"Why, to take you to the place between stories, of course!" said Wom Ya, as if this was obvious. "Listen to me my little princelings, and understand me very well. Two points on a map are as far apart as the distance between them, but each of those points are no further than the thickness of a shadow from the emptiness that exists between the worlds. That's what this seashell is for. Just blow into it, and you'll blow that thin shadow away, and find yourself in the emptiness."

"What then?" asked Valiben suspiciously.

Wom Ya shrugged her bony shoulders.

"Just you up and blow into it again, of course!" she said. "Only this time you hold an image in your head while you do your blowing. Just imagine the place on the map you want to get to, and you'll be blown there as quick as you can puff."

Wom Ya handed the seashell to Myst.

"I can keep this?" asked Myst, his eyes huge and unbelieving.

"Of course you can, my Prince," said Wom Ya and again that sly twist was in her voice. "Just you remember who it was who helped you, when no-one else would listen. One day, it may be that you can do something for me in return..."

"But wait," said Valiben, who had been frowning in concentration. "What exactly is it we are supposed to find at the centre?"

Wom Ya leaned close in, and the two boys could smell the sour salt of her, very near and unpleasant in their nostrils.

"Could be it's the beginning," said the old woman. "Or maybe it's the end. Some say it's the source, others the point where things drain to. In any case, people have been going on quests to find the centre for as long as I have been alive, so there must be something strange and dreadful there. In fact..."

Wom Ya opened her mouth to say more, but at that moment//

//but at that moment, something *tore* in the air, and a strange thrumming nose suddenly seemed to fill the whole cave.

"What is that?" screeched Wom Ya, gazing in horror at where a hole had been ripped in the side of her cave, and from which a dreadful-looking blade of tinted metal was protruding.

Valiben and Myst looked at one another; and though they said nothing, the corners of Valiben's lips twitched.

The strange sword hacked downwards again, and more of the wall of the cave ripped apart as if it was no more than butter. Then a man, tall and grim, waded in through the widening tear. He fixed Valiben with cold eyes.

"The hunt draws to a close," he said, breathing hard. "Come to me, little story. Come to me, and take me closer in..."

The tall man was standing in the cave now, and Wom Ya looked very small and old next to him. She scuttled into the darkening depths and tried very hard to be forgotten.

Valiben held his ground. He glanced once at his brother, who held the seashell to his lips, ready.

The tall man strode forward, one hand outstretched.

Valiben waited as the man drew closer.

Waited, waited, waited...

"Now!" he shouted.

Myst blew into the shell.

~

THERE WAS NOTHING, ENDLESS, COLOURLESS, SCENTLESS, SOUNDLESS nothing. It stretched on for ever and ever and ever and...

And it suddenly contained two boys and a tall man holding a strange sword.

For a single moment, there was a fleeting impression that the nothing may, in fact, have included a cave, and the smell of salt, and the pounding of the waves on a distant beach...but as the sound of breath blowing through the twirl of seashell faded, the ghosts of the cave and the salt and the waves faded, too. All that was left once that dream was burst were the two boys, and the tall man.

The tall man reeled backwards, jarred by the sound of the seashell, and by the wind that had blown them all to this...this *empty* place.

The two boys had *not* been surprised, however.

"Now!" shouted Valiben again, and while the tall man was still looking on in bewilderment, Myst hurled the seashell as hard as he could.

It struck the tall man straight on the chin, and shattered into a thousand pearly pieces.

The man screamed in pain, and clutched at his face; and while he was distracted, Valiben grasped Myst by the hand, and hurried off with him, darting with astonishing speed away across the vast endless nothingness of the land between stories.

By the time the tall man had recovered, the boys had a long head start. And he was so enraged at having been escaped, and even more enraged at having had a seashell shattered on his face, that when he dashed off after the two boys, he did not even take the time to have a look around at the nothingness that hemmed him in on every side.

This was a shame, because if he had looked very carefully, he might have noticed a pink pig that was hiding itself rather well under a large, shifting pile of nothingness.

"Ha!" laughed the pig to himself, as the tall man ran off after the boys. "That's the way, sunshine! That's the way..."

$\approx$

"Now...what?" panted Myst, as Valiben pulled on his arm, stopping him in his tracks.

The nothingness was around them as far as they could see, but Valiben was certain the tall man was not too far behind.

"Tell me...tell me the story," Valiben panted back.

Myst nodded, trying to get his breath back.

He took three more deep breaths. On the fourth, he opened his mouth and told Valiben about

THE TRICK

TWO

~

Once there were two brothers, and they were princes and they were bored. They wanted a quest and no one would give it to them, so they went to see the witch.

"I'll give you a quest," said the witch, and she gave it to them, along with a magic seashell to take them to the place between stories, and a map showing them where to go from there.

They were just getting ready to go when///

///the tall man sliced through from a different reality, and he came after them, but at the last moment they blew the seashell, and this melted them away to the place between stories. And the tall man was stunned, and one of the boys broke the seashell on his face, which stunned him more, and they ran away.

And when one of they boys said, "Now what?" the other said, "Tell me the story."

And the first boy settled down and he told the story of

❧ 36 ❧

THE TRICK

THREE

~

W hich is a story that folds into itself for ever, and traps the tall man inside, and the story is called

✸ 37 ✸

THE TRICK

FOUR

~

Which goes round and round and squeezes tighter and tighter and this is the story of

38

THE TRICK

FIVE

The Trick
The Trick
The Trick
The Trick
The Trick
The Trick
...

AFTER THE TRICK

~

Bartleby wriggled out of the little mound of nothingness he had been hiding in, and gazed with satisfaction at the diminishing twist of story that was boiling away, smaller, and smaller, and smaller still, until in very little time, it was far too small to be seen with the naked eye.

"It's alright, guys!" he shouted. "You can come out now!"

There was a rustling noise, and some more of the nothing shifted, disgorging Valiben and Torquemada, who at once got to work in cleaning away the rest of the drifts of emptiness that had hidden the creaky black wagon, and the smaller one behind which Maxwell's tank had been placed.

"Did it work?" asked Valiben anxiously.

Bartleby beamed at him.

"Of course it worked!" said the pig. "A very nice job you did of it, too. That should hold that tall bugger for a while."

"But wait," complained Maxwell, frowning, "I'm note sure I quite understand. Aren't Valiben and Myst trapped in the story with him?"

He sounded anxious.

Bartleby opened his mouth to answer, but the black wagon gave a groan, and the door creaked slowly open.

"No, my sweet fish, they most certainly are not," came the low voice of the Mistress of the Wagon. "Prince Myst is back where he should be, guarding a certain door. And Prince Valiben, as you see, is right here. Your friend simply told a story. He made it up. In this empty place, words are apt to inflate with substance quickly."

"But...but what will happen now that Valiben has stopped telling the story?" said Max. "Won't it all just fall apart?"

The ruby-pale eyes of the Mistress regarded him from the depths of the wagon. They were cold, but there was something of a smile in them, too.

"That is the beauty of it, my friend," she whispered at last. "Without someone to tell the story, it will degrade slowly. It will shrink with every cycle, become more small and strained and meaningless. It is like a bubble which is slowly leaking air. But however small it gets, the walls of the bubble remain; the tall man will be held there for a while, at least. Which may give us enough time..."

Her voice trailed off.

"Enough time to do what?" asked Valiben.

"Enough time to prepare for when he works his way loose, perhaps?" mused the Mistress. "Or who knows - perhaps he is smaller, weaker than he looks. Perhaps he will remain trapped in your little story for an age. Perhaps he will never come out." She leaned forward suddenly, the darkness clinging to her face, her bright eyes and her smile shining sharply out at Valiben. "I must say, my Prince, that was a very fine piece of trickery. You could certainly be useful. Or at the very least, interesting."

There was a soft, wet noise, like the sound of hungry teeth being whetted in the darkness.

"Are you quite sure you would not like to ride with me, here in this lovely darkness?" the Mistress of the Wagon asked him.

Valiben swallowed. On the roof, Torquemada raised one eyebrow, and Bartleby shook his head meaningfully.

"My lady is too kind," said Valiben, trying to keep his voice from cracking. "But I really think I would be more comfortable on the roof."

Her eyes flashed one last time in the darkness, and a moment of perfect silence seemed to stretch on forever.

"As you wish," came her whispering voice at length. "I trust we shall meet again before it is all done."

And with that her eyes faded back into the depths of the wagon, and the door swung slowly shut.

"Right," said Bartleby briskly, hopping back onto the roof of the wagon and stretching his little piggy limbs, "so, looks like we're all done here, job's a good one. I suppose the only question is, where do you fellers want dropping off?"

Valiben and Maxwell looked at him blankly.

"I mean, we're in the place between stories, right?" the pig went on. "So technically, we're as close to one place as to another. Anywhere you want to go in particular?"

Valiben was completely nonplussed. He had been so taken with the need to lead the tall man out of his story, that he had quite forgotten that he had been set on any other purpose at all. He could not say why, exactly, but he suddenly felt rather empty.

"But, well, don't you think…" Valiben began weakly, then trailed off.

Bartleby looked at him expectantly.

"That is to say, I had rather assumed that…" he hesitated again. He was a prince, after all, and not used to begging.

Maxwell, on the other hand, had no such compunctions.

"What my friend is trying to say," the big blue fish enunciated, "is that after all the fuss and bother we've been put through, don't you think we deserve to be kept in the loop, as it were?"

Understanding suddenly lit up Bartleby's face.

"Oh!" he said. "You mean, you want to know how this all turns out! Don't you worry sunshine, these things have a way of sucking you back in, whether you like it or not. In fact, that rather reminds me of the time…"

But Bartleby was interrupted by a long, ostentatious yawn. Torquemada stretched his claws theatrically, then regarded them one after the other with his sharp catty eyes.

"Yes, yes, all very interesting, I'm sure," he said, sounding as if he had found more interesting things floating in his breakfast that morning. "Now I know it would be just splendid if we could sit around telling each other our life stories, but as I'm sure you have noticed, *some* of us have rather important engagements to keep. So if you would be so good as to let us know your preferred destination, we shall endeavour to ensure you are not late for whatever, ah *fascinating* engagement awaits your good selves."

Bartleby opened his mouth to protest, but Torquemada forestalled him with a single raised paw, and pointed mutely to his harness. Then he spared Valiben and Max a final, freezing stare, and proceeded to turn his back on them.

Grumbling under his breath, Bartleby struggled into his uncomfortable harness and made a few exploratory stretches.

"Don't mind sourpuss," he mumbled. "Unfortunately, he does have a point. We really should be getting going. Wouldn't do to keep the mistress waiting. So, have you decided where it is we'll drop you?"

Valiben started to speak, but Maxwell got there first.

"Yes," he said. "You'd better take us back to where we came from."

Valiben looked at him. He was frowning.

"Max," he said, "she told us. The Mistress of the Wagon said it very clearly. The man we seek is not to be found in the land of the most lovely. What is the point of us going back there?"

"Because that's *our* story," Maxwell replied. "And who are we to shirk it? Just because we know we won't get what we want out of it, does that mean no one will benefit? We need to finish the story we started, even if we know it's not going to win you back your kingdom, even if we know it will only lead to another story." He shrugged. "It's what we have to do."

Valiben was frowning; but he was nodding slowly, too.

Bartleby looked back and forth between the two friends, then grinned.

"Very well," he said. "Back to that prat, Krow's place it is. Glad I'm not stopping there though. Oh, if you want to wind him up, tell him congratulations on his son's wedding."

"What?" asked Valiben.

"He'll tell you he hasn't got a son, but just you look in his eyes," Bartleby chuckled. "You'll have scored a point there, count on it!"

Valiben nodded. Maxwell looked thoughtful for a moment, opened his mouth as if to say something, then thought better of it.

Torquemada made a few final adjustments to Bartleby's harness, made sure the lever was in the correct position, then snapped his paws together imperiously.

"Quick step now, Bartleby," said the cat. "Get her up to speed, and we shall be on our way!"

Bartleby began to run. Faster, faster, faster he went, until his legs were once more a blur, though surrounded as they now were by nothing, there was no sense of the carriage moving.

Torquemada looked searchingly at Bartleby's pumping legs, then he consulted a little pocket watch, then back to the legs.

"Almost," he muttered to himself. "Almost...almost...now!"

And with that, he threw the lever, and with a great bumping and jolting, the nothing around them was suddenly melting back into colour and form once more. Valiben reeled back, and for one terrifying moment he forgot that the wagon would not allow him to fall. Then he regained his balance, and marveled as the landscape of the most lovely flashed by them on either side.

It was the same scene they had passed before on the way here, trees and roads and people, all seeming frozen as they whizzed past. Only now, as the wagon slowed down, the people they passed in the landscape around them began to speed back up to normal.

Before very long, the wagon was trotting along not much faster than a horse could gallop, and by this time life around them seemed to be proceeding at something approaching a normal tempo.

Bartleby slowed to a trot, then to a fast walk, then he stopped entirely, breathing hard and with sweat gleaming on his pink face.

The wagon creaked to a halt, and Bartleby indicated the high stone walls they had reached.

"This is your stop, gents, I believe," he said. "Give my regards to Krow." Then he leaned closer. "And don't worry," he added. "I'm sure we'll meet again before the end."

Valiben hopped down, and unbuckled the wagon that Maxwell's

tank was balanced on. Then he reached up and shook Bartleby by one of his piggy feet.

"It has been most educational," Valiben told him, and the pig laughed. "Goodbye, Torquemada," he called over to the cat. But if Torquemada heard him, he gave no sign of it.

Valiben frowned, then leaned closer.

"You know," he whispered, "no offence intended, but I do wonder what it is that our fine furry friend there brings to your little company."

Bartleby rolled his eyes.

"Well, to be honest, sometimes I wonder the same thing," he replied. "Apart from his charming people skills, of course, I would say that the only really useful thing he does is work out when to throw that lever."

The cat must have overhead them, but he evidently thought the conversation beneath his dignity. He sniffed once, but kept his back well turned.

"Throw the lever?" repeated Valiben, disbelievingly. "Why, that doesn't seem a very hard thing to have to do! I'm sure any of us could do that - or even, why not you?"

A stillness settled over the air. Valiben noticed that even though Torquemada still had his back to them, now it was rigid as oak. The cat had stopped breathing.

Bartleby looked embarrassed.

"Ah, well, I must say that there you would be wrong, unlikely as it sounds," he said, and Torquemada relaxed slightly. "You see, I used to be of much the same opinion. And as much as it pains me to tell you, I made rather a fool of myself."

He glanced furtively over at Torquemada, licked his lips, then went on.

"We're in a rush, but it won't take a minute to tell you. It's only a little story. It's called

❦ 40 ❧

WHY PIGS SHOULDN'T FLY

~

Me and the cat, we've worked together for a long time. Not quite forever, you understand; but it certainly feels that way sometimes.

Anyway, we didn't always get on so well as we do now. Not at all. No, for the first three hundred years we were pretty much sworn enemies. For the next three hundred years, we were merely unfriendly colleagues. And for the three hundred years after that, we were antagonistic rivals. And in a way, that was the worst time.

Before then, you see, we had more or less ignored each other - well, as much as is possible when you are sharing the roof of a small wagon. But those last three hundred years - blimey, we didn't half try to show each other who was boss, ain't that right, puss?

Don't mind him. He's just worried I won't give him his due.

Hush yourself, Torquemada, can't you see I'm being humble here?

Well.

Our labour wasn't always divided the way it is now. Oh, no. It used to be arranged so that when we rode during the day, I was up in the harness and kitty here worked the lever; but when we rode at night, well, we swapped our roles, and it was me who lazed about and watched the clock.

No, no, don't complain! I'm being *sarcastic*, right? That means you can't get upset.

Sorry about him.

Now back then, we were both very proud of our positions, like I said. And we both wanted more than anything to be the big cheese in front of our mistress, and show her that it was really only one of us that she needed.

We took all kinds of dangerous risks to try and show off. For instance, I once managed to go so fast that we tore right through the place between stories, and ended up in the place *below* stories, and I'm sure you don't need me to tell you how worrying that was!

Another time, Torquemada here took it into his head that our mistress didn't have enough darkness to wrap herself up in and keep cosy, so he went off and stole a whole ream of dark from the King of Night. Now *that* was a lot of bother to set right, and no mistake!

No, I know she didn't give it back, Torquemada; but that's hardly the point, is it? It was dangerous and foolish, and if our mistress has the smile and the deft touch to keep the King of Night at bay, well, that does not make it any less foolish, now does it?

No, I know that wasn't the biggest piece of foolishness, didn't I start this story to tell them about that? No, I'm *not* just trying to show you up.

Fine. Get the wheels ready. This won't take long to tell, anyway.

(Damn sulky cat. No, no, don't worry, I'm used to it.)

Anyway.

So you can see that we were both fond of showing off, and neither of us had much more sense than a carp - begging your pardon, Master Maxwell, but they are notoriously stupid.

Now it came to pass that Once Upon A Time or In A Land Far Away - I forget which, exactly - there was a certain especially succulent person that our Mistress had charmed and cajoled into joining her in her darkness. That is her nature, and I won't say a word against it, though it is our policy to give fair warning. This soul was fresh-plucked and juicy, and perfect, just perfect, I was given to understand, for transportation to the place where my Mistress delivers her goods.

The problem with the best goods is this: they go off all too quickly, and if you are not careful, what is ripe at harvest is rotten when you take it home. So time was of the essence, as it were.

And where do you think our fine friend Torquemada was when this delicious morsel was snapped up into the darkness and ready for shipping? Well, if you can tell me, then you'll be telling me something new, because to this day I do not know; and if he can give a good account, I am yet to hear it! The point is, he wasn't there! He was not on the wagon nor underneath it; he was not to one side or the other; and he was certainly not within range of my Mistress's voice, of that you can be sure.

Oh, how she *howled*!

I had heard her shout before, but the noise she made then...

Well, let me just tell you that all the green things within two miles of our wagon withered and turned bitter on the spot. *That* is how upset she was.

Aha, I thought to myself. *Now's my chance! Bartleby, your day has come!*

So I jumped up, smart as anything.

"Don't you worry, mistress!" I told her. "That lazy cat's probably off napping somewhere. Not a problem: I'll do the job of two, you won't know the difference!"

With that, I started jogging away on the treadmill; and to make extra sure I impressed my Mistress, I doubled the pace that I would usually go along at, then tripled that again for good measure.

My, we were *flying* along!

This is it, I told myself happily, *you're really doing a good job here, Bart, no two ways about it!*

I was so pleased with myself, that when I reached for the lever...well, do you know what I did?

I only went and threw it the wrong bloody way!

SCREECH!!!

That was the noise the gearbox made, and

TEARRRRR!!!

That was the noise the harness made, and

WHOOOSH!!!

That was the noise that *I* made, as I went flying off of the wagon, and zoomed away!

Can you imagine it? All the momentum of this wagon, all the force that was coursing through my Mistress and her new pet and everything else in that huge darkness, not to mention the actual physical mass of the wagon itself, everything was transferred directly to this lithe piggy body you see before you.

I went sailing away.

I was moving so fast, I missed the first seventeen stories I broke through before I had even realised that I had left the wagon.

Zip, zip, zip.

Away they went. Now you have to understand, trans-narrative travel can be a tricky piece of navigation at the best of times. To the un-initiated, it's very easy to end up making a mistake and smashing head-first into someone else's narrative magnetism. It happens so fast - suddenly, you've forgotten who you are and where you came from, and before you can blink you are completely convinced that you're an evil stepmother or a scheming magician, or whatever other role that person's story demands of you.

It's dangerous even if you're experienced, and even if you're moving besides someone with the intrinsic narrative balance of my Mistress.

But to a single, frightened pig, desperate and alone and hurtling between stories at a rate that was fast enough to melt down the weaker, smaller tales in a single flash? It wasn't just dangerous, it was suicidal.

I twisted and squirmed like a dying worm.

SWISH! Went the stories, one after another. Lover, fool, monster, angel, madman, princess: I was each of them, one after the other, and as completely as I am me, now. I don't know what it looked like to the people whose stories I smashed through. Maybe they didn't even notice, I was moving so fast.

After that, I slowed down a bit. Huge ripples of story built up like a shockwave around me, and I don't doubt that I changed a thing or two as I passed. But what could I do? I had already made my mistake. All I could do now was hope and pray, and try desperately not to get splatted by each successive storywall I smashed through.

Eventually, I began to slow down. Presently, I tore through one final skein of narration, and found myself sailing through thin air, rather high up off the ground.

Oh well, I told myself, trying to look on the bright side, *at least I only have height to deal with now, and not trans-narration; maybe things are looking up.*

But they were not looking up at all, they were looking down.

Down, down, down I fell.

It's a funny thing, but the higher you are, the softer and more forgiving the ground looks. Forests look green and springy, water looks blue and bouncy.

As you get closer, you start to see the spikes on metal railings, the horns on bull's heads, even the thorns on rosebushes.

I glanced behind me, hoping vaguely for some form of inspiration. But there was nothing to be seen, except a faint purplish rippling in the storywall I had just smashed through, and a few trailing dots of debris scattering in the wake of my passage. I couldn't see what they were, but I was sure they couldn't help me, so I dismissed them from my mind.

I knew I should try and think of something, but really, what could I do?

Nothing, that's what!

Only close my eyes and brace myself.

Only hope against hope.

Only fall.

A forest rose up to meet me, and suddenly I was smashing through the upper branches, being slapped in the face by leaves, and tumbling end over end through an endless landscape of bark and green.

And then, with a jerk, it was over.

I lay as still as if I were dead. Above me, the blue sky was framed by many waving branches; and I was supported below by branches more.

Gently, ever so gently, I turned myself over.

Was it possible, I wondered that I had survived this, after all?

That my fall had been cushioned by the successive branches of these wonderful trees, that had passed me, as if from hand to hand, to finally lay me battered but unbroken, on the soft forest floor?

No.

Of course not.

When I looked down, I realised I was still very, very high up.

I gave a start, and promptly fell a further dozen feet before I managed to snag another branch and stop my descent.

I stayed stock still, trying desperately to think of a way out of my current predicament.

A cracking noise came from below. For one horrible moment, I thought my tree was breaking. But when I looked down, what do you think I saw? The tree was fine, but standing at the base of the trunk next to a whole pile of broken branches was a rather fat monk.

It was evident that the branches had snapped off under his weight when he was trying to climb the tree.

"I say, Pig!" the fat man shouted. "You look to be in rather a dire situation up there. That being the case, would you mind very much electing to fall down here and become dinner for a most hungry gentleman? I assure you, it would be in the noblest of noble causes."

The cheek of some people!

"Bugger off, sunshine!" I shouted down. "I got myself into this mess, and I'll get myself out, have no fear!"

For a moment I thought he was going to wait there on the off chance that I might fall anyway, but before long I saw his shoulders sag and off he went.

Phew! I thought to myself. *Now that fat so-and-so's cleared off, maybe I can get some decent thinking done, and work out how to put things right again, starting with getting out of this tree!*

But no sooner had I lain back as carefully as I could, and set my mind to thinking, than I noticed something odd in the sky.

Or rather, several odd things.

In the direction from which I had made my entry into this little reality, I could still see the purplish rippling where I had torn the storywall.

How strange, I thought. *That should have closed by now.*

But even as I watched, a few more little dots hurtled through the gap and made straight for my position. I had thought those bits that trailed me were simply debris, the random flotsam and jetsam torn from various stories by my passage.

What if I had been wrong?

I narrowed my eyes. A shiver ran down my spine. I turned my head as quick as I dared, so that I was looking straight up.

The blue sky overhead was blotted out by a great many figures.

They were closer now, much closer than they had been when I noticed them following me into this story and mistook them for debris, and much closer also than those newer dots, which still appeared indistinct because they were so small.

There were hundreds of them.

The worst thing was, I knew exactly who they were and why they had come.

They had taken a variety of forms, though thankfully mostly of roughly normal shape and proportion, and not too many of them had more than three or four extra limbs. They all had too many teeth, though. Far, far too many teeth.

I tried to burrow deeper into the tree, whilst simultaneously attempting not to fall out. It quickly became evident that this was an endeavour that was doomed to failure, so I contented myself with falling another six feet and trying to look nonchalant.

The figures were forming up in rows a little way above my tree, floating there as easily as if they could do it all day, which, of course, they could. They hovered around lazily, regarding me with cold eyes and showing me those awful snappers.

One of them was bigger and more nasty-looking than the rest. It detached itself from the others and floated closer to me, taking great care not to touch even a single twig or leaf.

It stopped a few inches from my nose. I tried to look it in the eyes - my Mistress had warned me about these fellows, of course, and had always told us not to get hypnotised by those horrible sharp teeth - but it was difficult. My eyes kept blurring over, and before I knew it I was back looking at those sharp snappers again.

"Ah, hello there," I said, trying not to let my fear show.

The figure dipped its head slightly to one side. Then it opened its mouth and spoke.

"Are you the...ah...creature known as Bartleby?" it asked me solemnly.

For a second, I considered telling them I was the cat, but it was evident the question was a formality. They had watched me break through, and swarmed in after me. They knew I was the pig they were looking for.

"Yes. Yep. That's me," I gave a little nervous giggle. "Guilty as charged, your honour."

"Why does it give me honour to charge you?" the figure sounded genuinely perplexed.

"No, I mean..." I stuttered. "I was just saying, yes, I'm Bartleby."

The figure nodded.

"Bartleby of the Wagon," he went on, "do you know who we are?"

I nodded wearily.

"Yes," I said. "You're Epitaphs. What's more, it looks like there's rather a lot of you."

"There are," the Epitaph replied, "exactly as many of us here as should be here. One has come for every story you have stolen from."

I put my trotters up placatingly.

"Hey, come on now," I pleaded. "'Stolen' is such a strong word, isn't it?"

The cold eyes continued to stare at me. Those ghastly teeth continued to shine.

"How you come to or leave our stories or where you go thereafter is none of our concern," the Epitaph replied. "What you take with you when you leave, however is not only our concern, but also our due."

I licked my lips. These guys could be real buggers. If I wasn't careful, my bacon was well and truly sizzled.

"True, true," I allowed, "but what exactly is it you think I've left with?"

I was just trying to buy time now. I was stranded and alone in a strange story, and I didn't have any plan of attack.

"The list is a long one," the Epitaph replied. "You have passed through many of our stories uninvited, and did not return all that you played with when you left. From one of us, you have taken the heart of a fair maiden. From another, the innocence of a crippled child. You wrapped yourself in three slivers of moonlight when you passed through a third, and you took them with you when you shot into the land where the ducks rule all, from which you also claimed the first flight of a duckling prince. The list is extensive, and we have no time to enumerate all the items now."

Unfortunately for me, the Epitaph had me bang to rights.

Not that I'd *wanted* to pick up all that bloody narrative ephemera, but I'd been shooting between stories pretty quick, and I hadn't really had much of a choice.

I sighed.

Bloody Epitaphs and their bloody *hunger*.

You get to understand a bit about stories in my line of work. Understand about how they hang together, understand what makes them tick.

Stories serve their purpose, you see; the tale is told, and the people in them move on, to other tales or other worlds, or into death and nothing, sometimes, for all I know. But when the stories are done with and the people they housed move on, the stories themselves begin to degrade. The substances they are made of are broken up into smaller and smaller bits. And who do you think does this degrading? Our friends the Epitaphs, of course! They spring into being the moment the story is first told, and they calculate their due very exactly, every grain of sand and spark of light. It'll all go to them in the end, once the story is done and told. The only items that are left out are the people who can move on, and the rare indigestibles which are ignored, and which eventually filter down to the place below stories, with all the other miscellaneous left over things.

Everything else belongs to the Epitaphs. And they will not be cheated of *any* of it.

Right now, I had about three hundred hungry Epitaphs eyeing me up and down, and looking to extract from me those bits of their stories that had accidentally stuck to me when I passed through them.

I was quite happy for the Epitaphs to have those bits and pieces back, of course. The only problem was, I couldn't for the life of me think of a way of separating those bits of stories from my body. And as I looked at those sharp teeth, I realised it might actually *be* for the life of me.

"Fine, fine," I said, trying to sound like someone who was totally in control of things. "Well, I'm quite willing to give you those bits and pieces back. They mean nothing to me, obviously. All just a bit of a mistake, you see. So perhaps if you would be so good as to escort me back through your stories, I will do my best to extract the appropriate items to their respective homes."

"There is an easier way," the Epitaph said darkly.

"Really?" I said, a bit too quickly. "It's a funny thing, though, I always find easier ways are less fun. Why don't we just try my way?"

"Our way is fun, too," said the Epitaph.

It grinned at me. All the other Epitaphs arranged behind the spokesperson did the same.

Somewhere in the region of three million teeth glistened down.

"The items from our stories have become completely mixed into your body," continued the Epitaph. "The simplest thing might be to divide you up evenly, and each get a bit of the mixture back."

"It is such hungry business, waiting for a story to die," another Epitaph chipped in, and all the other Epitaphs suddenly crowded in a pace closer. "We thought we could do with an appetiser."

"But...but...I've been through a lot of *bad* stories," I tried desperately. "Most of them were nowhere near as delicious and succulent as your own..."

The Epitaphs were no longer listening to me. They floated there, utterly still and tense, readying themselves to spring. I didn't have a chance.

I took a deep breath, and fell out of the tree.

Well, if I was going to be munched up, I was going to make damn sure that it was as difficult for them as possible.

I fell, and they sprang after me.

But I never hit the ground, and the Epitaphs never touched me.

There was a blinding, blurring light. I felt the story ripple around me, and then...

...and then my Mistress was coming for me.

The air ripped and blurred, and the wagon suddenly shot into being. It appeared above me, in the midst of the branches and among the Epitaphs. There was a wailing *whoosh*, and all at once the upper half of the tree was wreathed in flames, and the Epitaphs were reeling backwards from the blast. You must understand, this was all happening in a split second. I took it all in as I fell; and ever as I fell, I saw the wagon wheel round, moving impossibly fast and sliding in below me...and with a thump I landed on the roof.

Next to me, old sourpuss here was strapped into the harness and panting like I had never seen him pant before.

He did not look happy. Oh no, he looked as if he had been dragged backwards through a pond.

The door of the wagon was open. Darkness was leaking out from within; and next to us, right there on the roof of the wagon next to us, and in full view...

The Mistress of the Wagon was holding the lever. She had forsaken her darkness, and we could all see her. We could see her very well.

Some things are better left hidden. I knew her by her eyes, those ruby-pale eyes. But the rest of her...the rest of her awful self was there before me, and I was *very* glad indeed that I had never chosen to ride in the darkness of the wagon with her.

The Epitaphs were regrouping. They ignored the few glowing embers that still rained from the blasted tree, and viewed my Mistress uncertainly.

"This...creature...is our due," the leader declared at last. "He has stolen from all of us. We shall reclaim what is ours."

It showed its teeth, glittering like daggers, keen and deadly.

But our Mistress, she had a sharper smile. Her teeth were long, too, and oh how many she had!

"I am the Mistress of the Wagon," she told them, and there was a general stirring among the Epitaphs. "I come as I please and go where I will, and all things are my fodder."

The Epitaphs faltered and swayed in the air. They had heard her name, oh yes. For she was the greatest of them, was she not? She belongs very much to her story, she pampers it like a mother pampers her child, feeding it with morsels and sweetmeats, a maiden from here, a hero from there, until her story is fat and bulging...only this mother knows that when the story is done and dust, the baby will be *hers* to devour.

Oh, hush you scaredy cat! Of course she hears me - but do you think she minds? She knows her nature, and isn't ashamed. There, now you've gone and interrupted me, and I was nearly finished, too...

As I was saying.

They knew her. All the Epitaphs who ever were had heard of the Mistress. And they would not cross teeth with the likes of her, not if they wanted to avoid being swallowed up by that darkening wagon, not unless they wanted to be torn away, and their stories torn with them.

They hissed and they wailed...but they backed away.

Or rather, all but one of them backed away.

The first Epitaph, the one who had led the others, still hung in the air. Perhaps this was *its* story. Maybe that's why it felt it had the right to stand its ground and oppose my Mistress.

"Is that the story you tell us, Mistress?" asked the Epitaph. "That you are so fierce and hungry, and everything you want is yours to take?"

"That is not the story I would tell *you*," said the Mistress. "But I have a story for you all the same. Why not come here and hear it?"

The Epitaph grinned its horrible toothy grin. It rushed towards her.

It came so close I could feel the damp heat of its huge mouth beating against us. But our Mistress, she rose to meet it, as cold and calm as ever she is.

She leaned in and she whispered something.

The Epitaph made a sound then, a horrible sound, like the choking of the biggest throat you ever heard. It stuck there, absolutely still though there was nothing there to hold it that I could see. And my mistress leaned forward and starting whispering in its ear...

...And then *pop*!

The Epitaph was deflating, just like a burst balloon. It swished and rattled and its eyes were disconnected and staring. And then it was like an empty sack, all loose and flapping, like the face of an old woman that's suddenly had all the bones sucked out.

There was a final slurping noise, and the empty sack snapped into itself, and all that was left was a small bottle of clouded glass. It was suffused with a faint golden glow, and on the side was written a single letter, D. The Mistress, she scooped up that little bottle, calm as anything, and she ushered it inside the darkness of the wagon, and it was hers.

That did it for the rest of them. The Epitaphs were off.

The air rippled again as they crossed out through the storywall, making their beaten ways back to their own tales. And good riddance to them! That was what I thought as I lay there panting on the roof of the wagon.

I turned to smile my relief at my Mistress.

Her own smile was waiting for me when I turned, and my relief just boiled away.

She leaned toward me, slowly, so slowly; but I couldn't move.

She stopped a fraction from my face. I could see the etchings on her teeth, feel her cold breath.

"You did a foolish thing today," she told me softly, and that was all.

That was all she needed to say. I am hers. I did not stray or falter again.

I am hers.

She regarded me a little longer with those ruby-pale eyes of her. Then the darkness leaking out of the wagon *shifted*...

...and suddenly she was gone from the roof, and the Wagon had a Mistress once more.

Yes, OK Mr. Sourpuss, I was coming to that bit.

So you see, the result of all this is that the two of us have come to a bit of an arrangement as to how labour is divided. I concentrate on the running, he specialises in pulling the lever.

Anyway, I suppose we really had better get going, now.

What's that you want to know?

The story our Mistress whispered to the Epitaph - really? You heard what it did to that bugger, and you really want to know?

I don't know where she harvested that story from, or what it did to that ghastly creature. She is very tricksy when it comes to stories. She has heard many, and she stores them up, and uses them like weapons. I don't know the whole story. But...

Well I did overhear how it started. I can tell you that much.

If you're sure.

Very well. She only said a few words, but I think the story took over after that.

Oh, do be quiet, you blasted cat! Yes, yes I know we're in a hurry! This won't take long.

So.

Our Mistress, she leaned in towards the Epitaph and she said, "Now listen to my story, it's called

SKELETON DAIS

~

Skeleton Dais dances through midnight, and away across the hills. She has a lad or two with her, for her dance is rich and strong. Beautiful young men with soft cheeks and supple limbs, Dais springs away; and the lads, they surge to follow.

The game is getting old, but still she must play her part.

She takes them down under the earth, and there she makes them hers. More luminous little trinkets to add to her endless hoard.

Afterwards, alone in the darkness, she feels empty again.

She remembers Jack, remembers the way his bones moved and the damp glory of his thin, thin body.

"I am Black Jack Gaunt," Dais whispers to herself, but she is not.

She is Skeleton Dais, and she is more than she was, and less at the same time.

There is something old in her. So old, so hungry.

And just then she sees you.

(And, *There, happy now, puss?* The voice comes from far away. *That's all I know. Now the story itself can take over...*

And there is the sound of wheels creaking, a wagon rolling away into the distance.)

She sees you. Your eye peeking in at her through the folds of this story, seeing her there amid her worms and her gold. Your eye glints in the darkness, and Dais, she sees that glint and smiles.

Dais is cunning and canny, and she sees twice as much as she lets on.

No, don't try to draw back. You are perfectly safe.

(But you can no longer tell - is that the way the story goes? Or did Dais just speak to you?)

She stretches out her long legs, and her eyes are dark and splendid.

She asks you who you are and why you came looking; and when you tell her, she smiles again, just slightly, and your heart catches in your throat, and you are a little bit more hers.

She slips onto her feet and turns before you, and the way she moves is like honey dripping on silk, and when she holds out her hand, you are ready to go to her.

But she tells you, no.

It's like a slap.

No.

And suddenly the story ripples again, and you wonder why you are not running, not skipping ahead. Don't you know it's dangerous here?

Dais needs you to step further in, and bring your viewpoint with you. She could sing her songs, but then what good would you be? Just another glittering thing.

She moves aside, makes room. Then she lifts a pale hand and beckons you.

You move deeper inside, and her story wraps you up like a second skin. That's the way she sees you: a silhouette wreathed in her own tale, reflecting her own story back to her, but in the shape of your little body.

All bodies are little here.

Skeleton Dais is tall, and all the other bodies are little.

You look up at her.

That's what I am, says Dais. I am the hungry darkness. I am the tall shadow. And whatever face I wear, I am always desired. Do you want to be desired?

You don't understand.

Yes you do, says Dais.

You don't understand.

Yes I do, you say.

And all at once, you *do* understand, because the darkness of the story has inverted itself, and now you are on the inside, and your body is tall and thin.

A small figure stands before you. It is wrapped in the darkness of her/(y)our story.

I have danced so long, says Daisy, and already the little body is melting back into the walls of the story.

Wait, you say. What about me? What about my life?

This is your life, says Daisy. Now all you can see of her are her sad little eyes. They are looking in at you. They are such a long way away.

You wait for her to say more, but she is silent.

Then you realise she is gone, and you are alone in the darkness.

"I am Skeleton Dais," you say. But you are not.

You are more and you are less, and something old and hungry carries on.

~

YOU MOVE THROUGH THE HILLS AND OVER THE MEADOWS, WRAPPED deep in darkness, and in a music low and awful.

You catch a maid, you snag a man. What of it? The hunger is always there, always waiting. It feels good, even. The way they look at you. The way you shuffle and roll your hips, the way your bones move in the moonlight, the way they cannot help but fall into step.

Sometimes you think you are different, that the old shadow (that moves within you/that you move within) has shifted, has been redeemed, somehow, by the lightness of you, by that glowing ember you half-remember of your life before.

But sometimes not.

Often, not.

You keep it moving, at least.

This shadowed thing, it moves because you push it to move.

From village to village, from maiden to man. Your nature is not to collect, your nature is simply to lash out, to snag and ensnare, to drink all up and leave dry and empty.

Why are you always longing?

What piece of you is missing?

You cannot say. That is buried, very deep down amongst the Jacks and the Daisies - how many of them you cannot say for sure - so old in your shadowed nature that maybe the shadow itself has forgotten.

But a day comes when you do not want to move on. A certain village has caught your eye, a good village, a happy-on-the-hill village, a sunshine and apples and laughter village.

Why does it catch your eye?

You really cannot say. The people there are the same as the people elsewhere. They fall into your dancing the way they always fall into your dancing, thrashing and sweating and with huge eyes, ecstatic and terrified and yours.

Then why this village?

You do not know, but all at once it isn't enough to take a few and move on again.

Oh no, not this time.

This time you won't dance one or two away; you will dance it all under your sway.

Can it be done?

A whole village, can it be done?

If it can, then it will need a new trick...but that's not so difficult for you, not really.

After all, your nature is thin and sly and full of little tricks.

And now it is that very nature, thin and sly and shadowy, that you will use to work your will.

You delve down, down into the earth and down into yourself. And in the utter black deepness there, you find the four corners of who you are, and you notice with interest the ragged marks where you have been torn before. Then you make a new tear.

It does not hurt at all. It is done as painlessly as cutting off a dead finger.

It is dead already. How could it hurt?

You put this fragment of deep darkness in a place under the earth, and the village above it is cursed.

There.

The heart of you bleeds into the substances of the village. When they raise up the well-water, they are drinking your salt. When they cut the corn, they are eating your flesh. The sky is brooding, the rain comes down and down, the fields are full of dust.

The village is poisoned. You are poison, and the village is you.

They are small and terrified and ripe.

You come amongst them, and they fall down for you, the way they always do, the way they must.

A few of them oppose you. They tell each other stories, little lying stories to keep the darkness at bay. They have a priest, they have an old crone. They tell their little stories, and your darkness shrinks a little. This will not do. Their stories are their armour. How can you be expected to work your will on people who armour themselves with stories? But you have been opposed before, and you know the way to break people. Find the thing they cherish. Find a way into their heart, and tear.

The priest, he loves his daughter. Oh, how he loves his little Heather.

You smile as you whip your will, smile as the earth beats to your music, smile as they gather the kindling and pile the pyre high.

The smoke rises, and the screaming rises, and they hold the priest and make him watch.

The next day the ashes fall. The priest is turned inward. You have broken him, and you have broken all his little stories. You let him go. What harm can he do?

All that remains is the crone, but she is more difficult. She is older, wiser, she knows more about stories and how they write the world.

She has the children with her. They are locked inside her hut, and the hut is sealed with story-spells. She is very good, this old crone, oh yes, she know the way of things.

Why should it worry you so much, that she is there with a few shrill children? You make your dance, and the village dances with you. It is yours, every sod of turf and every dark eye, they all belong to you...except for that one little hut.

And yet...

And yet it seems important.

Come out Old Nan, you tell the crone. Come out, come dance with me!

I am too old for dancing, she tells you.

Then she turns to the children and fills their heads with tales, and they cannot hear the thrumming. They cannot see your dance, and your splendid movements do not touch them.

No one is too old to dance with me, you tell her.

You are growing wrath. The winds come. You are telling the stories here, and the winds do not need to be told twice. They roar and crash against the village. But inside the hut, the air is calm. Old Nan tells her tales. She does not even heed you.

Come dance with me!

Your voice is low and wild.

Come dance! Such a dance as breaks your bones and melts your skin and boils your blood, and your old body will love the dance even as it tears apart, and you will love *me*!

You scream the last word. You scream so hard that the wind itself is scared, and runs away to hide. You scream so deep the thunder loses its nerve, and tucks itself away. You scream so long, your scream itself gets bored, and wanders off to attend to its own business.

And then there is silence.

No stories are being told now, not one.

Not even a once upon a time.

The door of the hut creaks open.

Inside there is darkness; but darkness was always a friend, and the stories that held you back have stopped.

Slowly, oh slowly, slowly, you move forward.

Old Nan is waiting there for you.

Come in then, she says.

The children? You ask, silk in your smile and murder in your heart.

I have saved them up somewhere, she tells you, now that they're safe you can do what you like.

It does not matter: it was the telling of tales that held you back, the giving and the receiving. They stopped up the ears and would not let your music in. The children themselves are not important.

Now what, says Old Nan.

Now we dance, you tell her, and your heavy music starts to rise.

Fine, says Old Nan, but I can't move as well as I used to.

You will move beautifully, you tell her.

And with that you whistle three notes, and your music swells up and draws you in - for it is true, you dance to your tune just as surely as your partners do, and you could not hope to stop before the jig is done.

The walls of the hut seem to vanish, and the space between you and around you is all that matters. You circle the old woman, and every shake of your limb or twist of your spine is like a word in a deeper language. You feel it rise again, the savage joy, the wild glory that makes you dance and makes them dance and makes them yours forever.

And the old woman starts to move.

Gently at first, a faint sway, a halting step, but then faster, faster, faster...

Her old bones creak. Her breath is ragged. You breath her in, inhaling the salt taste of her.

Her heart is pounding. You can feel it in your chest. It is unsteady and stumbling, just like her.

If you wanted her, she would be yours now. She would drink your soup, she would tell you her true name. She would do whatever you ask.

But you don't want her. Not at all.

What you want is to dance faster, to dance faster, and dance *her* faster with you.

That is the way to deal with her. Dance her until her ancient heart can twitch no more. Dance her to her death.

You move faster, faster, faster.

And the beat is like a line that runs between you, and every step you take, she must make one, too.

She moves faster, faster, faster.

And the tune is like madness, like a boiling lake of madness, sizzling and singing and springing through your tissues. Her tissues, too.

You dance, and she dances with you, and she dances closer to death...

And death is standing there. You can see her. Death, like Life, is a woman.

She is a whiteness. She is a vivid white whiteness, a silhouette, an opening from this world into that which lays beyond.

You have seen her before, of course (how many things have you watched die?) But she has never been so close. She is as utter white as a blank page. She is beautiful.

Oh, if only you could make *that* lady dance with you!

But as if she could read your thoughts (and maybe she can), she starts to move. She slips into the dance, as easy and light as silk running through sunshine. Now there are three in the dance.

Death lifts her hand. Can Old Nan see her? You are not sure. You do not care.

She is about to die.

You breathe in. As deep as you can, as deep as if you are breathing in the world.

The music roars up around you. Your feet fly in a blur.

Old Nan does the same. How could she do otherwise?

Her heart is thunder. It fills the whole room.

Then the beating of her heart tears open, and suddenly Old Nan can dance no more.

She gasps and falls to her knees.

Death reaches a hand towards the ancient woman.

She reaches out...but she does not touch.

Old Nan's eyes dart to you. There is a smile there you do not like.

What a pretty song, she says.

It goes like this, doesn't it? she says.

And she whistles three notes.

Her lips are old and dry, and her wind is nearly done...but it is enough.

She whistles her three notes, and they are *your* three notes, and you take three steps towards her that you cannot help but take.

You're coming with me, she says.

You try to pull back, but you are too late.

Death reaches out a white hand for Old Nan, Old Nan reaches out for you.

The whiteness of Death springs into the old lady, sucks her into it...but she is holding on to you...

...and you feel the deep shadowed darkness within you recoiling in terror.

It sucks back from you, that hungry darkness that has enveloped you for so long. It sucks back, it draws back, it shrieks *no, no, no!*

And it has somewhere to go. Of course it does. Has it not already torn itself in half?

It has left half of itself (already torn, and you never did find out how) underneath the village, in the deep darkness, there to poison, there to seep into the soil and rocks.

The shadow leaves you, and all that is left is you. And you are following Old Nan into the whiteness. You are following Old Nan into Death.

You collapse to the floor and the whiteness seeps up and over you, and you realise you are falling into it. And this great whiteness is Death.

And Death is within you and without you, and Death is a beautiful lady.

Let me whisper you a story, says Death. It is a story I tell everyone in the end, and it is called

✺ 42 ✺

THE STORY OF YOUR DEATH

＠

Death is like a blank page. That is what makes it so wonderful.

All the lives of all the little creatures that ever lived are so crowded. They are full of sights and smells and fears and lusts. It can all be quite overwhelming. In fact, the only reason those little creatures don't actually realise exactly how overwhelmed they are is that they have very little to compare life to while they are, in fact, in the middle of one.

But as soon as life is taken away...

That's when they realise.

Nothing but incredible, white emptiness.

And then they know...

Then they understand.

They have been in such a rush for such a long, long time. And now it has stopped.

But now they are dead. And they have all the time in the world.

＠

A PORTION OF THE EMPTY WHITENESS ON THE OTHER SIDE OF LIFE got a little wider. It was difficult to tell. You would have to know what you were looking for to notice it, as it was essentially a matter of seeing a white door open into a white room, and a white lady lean through and usher in a white form. But if you *were* looking for it...

The large benign-looking creature that had, in fact, been waiting around for just such an event as this, strode forward and heaved the white figure the rest of the way through the door.

"Ouch!" complained the white figure.

"Come on now," said the benign-looking creature severely. "We get quite enough of that attitude here, I can tell you! And speaking frankly, it hasn't helped anyone else, and it certainly isn't going to help you."

The white figure rocked about vaguely for a moment. It regarded the large creature uncertainly.

"Sorry," the white figure said at last. "I wasn't trying to be difficult. It's just, I feel a little bit...well, odd."

The large, benign-looking creature gave a snort and a smile.

"Don't mention it, mate," he said, and gave the white figure a reassuring pat. "Gets a lot of folk like that, the first time."

"What does?" asked the white figure.

"Why, death, obviously," the creature replied. "Some people get completely flummoxed by it. I knew one man, he went completely mad after he died. Mad as a spoon, he was. We had to build him a little reality bubble where he could get used to the idea. Took ages, that did. And you know what the kicker was?"

"What?" asked the white figure weakly.

"Well, when we'd finished with the reality bubble, and he was nice and ready for Level Two, well, it only turns out some twerp had filled in the wrong bleeding form! Blimey, that ruffled a few feathers, I can tell you!"

"Did it?" muttered the white figure, who thought it could almost remember what a feather was, if only the universe would start making sense for a few minutes.

"Yeah, of course it did!" laughed the large figure. "Totally mucked up the projections, that one did! Nah, that bugger, he was meant for another turn of the wheel. Reincarnation, see? No wonder he went mad. He wasn't ready for Level Two. Hadn't accrued enough, ah, whatchamacallit..."

The large creature cast vaguely around.

"Um, chips?" suggested the white figure hopefully. Then the conversation caught up with it. "Wait a minute, did you say death?" it asked, in the tones of one who is nearly one hundred percent sure that the large bill being presented belongs, in fact, to someone else.

The large creature gave a sigh.

"Yes mate, death," it repeated carefully. "Death. D-E-A-T-H. As in, you are dead. As in, no going back. As in - and this is the bit that people really struggle with - *you were not immortal, after all!*"

"But..." said the white figure desperately.

"But what?" asked the large creature.

"But I was *supposed* to be immortal," the white figure wailed.

"Funny thing," said the large creature, "would you believe it, you're not the first person who's told me that."

"No, but in my case it's *true!*" implored the white figure. "I'm not just a normal person, I was an..."

"An Epitaph, yes, I know," said the white figure. "You were an Epitaph, and then you got on the wrong side of someone who it really doesn't pay to get on the wrong side of, and then you got sucked inside someone else's story, and then you died. We know all about it. Don't worry, mate, we do our homework. That's why I was here, in fact."

"What do you mean?" the white figure sniffed, a little ray of hope suddenly opening up. "You were here waiting for me? Because you knew it was all a mistake, you knew that I shouldn't die, so you were waiting here for me, to show me back to my story..."

"No, no no!" the large creature was quite emphatic. "That's not what I mean at all! All I mean is, I was here because we knew you were a bit of a complex case. Not a straightforward death, see? Most deaths are not too much of a problem. Easy peasy. Whoosh! The door opens, and on the Soul goes, into the nice orderly queue that leads off to Level Two. No hassle, no problems. Easy. But sometimes, we get a heads up that an especially complex case is coming through. That's where I come in."

"And what do you do, exactly?" asked the white figure.

"Well, think of me as something like a midwife," said the large creature. "Only instead of delivering you into life, I ease your passage into death. Quiddang, by the way."

"Pardon me?" said the white figure.

"Quiddang," repeated the large, benign-looking creature. "That's my name."

"Oh, is it?" muttered the white figure. "Splendid name. You don't happen to know what mine is, by any chance?"

"Yeah, no probs," said Quiddang, consulting a clipboard that appeared out of nowhere and vanished again a moment later. "It says here your death-name is Philip."

"Philip," mused Philip. "Hmm, it could be worse, I suppose."

"Of course it could," agreed Quiddang heartily. "It could have been Darren."

The white figure known as Philip shuddered. Then it looked around vaguely.

"So," it said at length, "what happens next?"

"Well, like I said, usually things are quite straightforward," said Quiddang. "You just join the queue, and away you go. With you it's a bit different."

"Different how?" asked Philip. "I don't see why I can't just go back to my story, you know."

"Ah," said Quiddang delicately, "the thing is, you see, as soon as you left your story...well, what do you think you would have done, if the story next to yours had suddenly found itself bereft of an Epitaph to guard it?"

Philip deflated.

"You mean they nicked it," he said flatly. "All that work, all that careful cultivation, and I don't even get to enjoy a single morsel of it..."

"But you have to look on the bright side," said Quiddang with an awful, springy enthusiasm. "I mean, what kind of a life was that, anyway? To spend every waking moment just dreaming of the day that your story would finally wind down to nothing, and you could gobble away all the little used-up bits that were left - doesn't that strike you as sort of, well, shallow?"

"But it was *my* story!" Philip seethed. "It was mine, for me! That was what I did, that was my purpose..."

"Come on," said Quiddang, grabbing Philip up and hustling him along. "I think it's time you saw something."

"Hey, take it easy!" complained Philip, as he was shoved through the white nothingness. "Where are you taking me?"

"To show you...this!" said Quiddang, and they stopped moving.

Ahead, the whiteness opened up in front of them to show a vast streaming torrent of vibrant colours, a huge shifting pattern made up - Philip realised as he peered closer - of millions upon millions of various-sized spherical shapes. They danced and merged kaleidoscopically, here crowding in very close and sometimes merging together, there thinning out and visible individually. It wasn't quite a noise that roared out of the pattern, and it wasn't a smell, either. It was something grander than that, somehow, more complete and overpowering.

Philip halted. All of a sudden he felt very small.

"You know what that is?" asked Quiddang quietly.

"Yes," said Philip. "That's the Storystream. I've seen bits of it before, of course, but never..."

Quiddang nodded.

Below and away, the endless glittering expanse of story stretched and twirled off into forever.

"It's bigger than I thought it would be," added Philip.

"Yes," agreed Quiddang, "it's always much bigger than you think. It has to be. It's everything. It's every story that was ever told and that ever will be told. Every version of it, too. And look here," Quiddang added, passing Philip a pair of rather ornate crystal spectacles.

Philip took them and peered in the direction the large creature indicated.

The Storystream suddenly flared towards him, and Philip realised he was seeing individual stories blown up so close that it was as if he were almost standing inside them.

"Is that a fish?" he asked, frowning. "What's it doing inside that weird tank thing?"

"Oops, sorry," said Quiddang, making a tiny adjustment to the spectacles. "Not there...*there*."

The image of the fish flashed away, to be replaced by...

"Oh," said Philip, letting the spectacles drop, where they were smoothly reabsorbed back into the encompassing nothingness. "But how can we be down there and up here a the same time?"

Quiddang shrugged.

"At the same time?" he repeated. "Ah, well that's something you have to get used to, for certain. Time's all relative, see? I mean, it's always been a bit skew-whiff, and that was before some bugger went and turned the Wheel. Lucky it was only a quarter-circle. Trust me, things would be *really* weird if they'd gone the whole hog and done an Unmaking."

Quiddang laughed for a moment, then went on.

"No, we're not due another one of them yet," he said. He paused, then added. "You've got to remember, nothing's so big that it isn't part of the Storystream. Except for Level Two, of course, but even then..."

Philip shook his head.

"Hang on," he interrupted, "why are you showing me all this, anyway? It's not like *my* story is still there, I suppose," he added sulkily.

"On the contrary," replied Quiddang, "your story is alive and well and playing host to all kinds of interesting things. As it should be. No, what I brought you here for was to show you all this...all this *life*! All this hustling, crowding, pulsing life. Every story you see there is teeming with it. They're full of the stuff! Isn't it glorious?"

"Yes," enunciated Philip slowly, as if he was having to explain something very simple to someone very stupid, "that's why I'm so desperate to get back there."

"Ah!" exclaimed Quiddang. "But that's where you're wrong, see? Where you're saying you want to end up isn't there, amid all the billowing coils of life, but rather..."

Quiddang shoved the nothingness around them, and the world *blurred...*

...To be replaced by a still, cold darkness, stretching away into the deep distance.

As far as Philip could see, drab, grey, squat somethings stood like sentinels, arranged in endless ranks upon ranks, quiet and colourless and awful.

"*This,*" finished Quiddang, gesturing about at the stilted scene.

Philip looked at the colourless shapes. Each one had a word, or words inscribed upon it, though Philip could not see what any of them read. Then he looked down, then back to Quiddang.

"Enough, please," he said quietly. "I've seen what you wanted me to. Please take me back."

Quiddang nodded silently, reached out, and swept the endless grey shapes away.

They were floating in the simple billowing nothingness again.

"Is that what you're so eager to get back to?" asked Quiddang. "That's where they all end up. After their story ends. After the feasting is done. They are Epitaphs, after all."

Philip was silent.

Then he said, "But it's my nature."

He said it very quietly. Quiddang nodded, sadly.

"It was your nature," said Quiddang. "To be hungry was your nature, to feast was your due, and a still eternity of grey waiting was your destiny.

"That *was* your nature, back when you were an Epitaph. Before you were ripped out of your story, and ended up dying to a degree no Epitaph has died before. But you're not that thing anymore. You don't have to settle into grey nothingness until the next remaking like those other poor creatures. It's not *Philip's* nature. It doesn't have to be."

Philip was shaking.

"I'm too old to change," he said.

Suddenly, Quiddang laughed.

"Old?" he said. "Bless me, mate, you're not old! When you've seen a few Unmakings and one or two Grand Undoings - not to mention an Unrolling, a Re-setting, and a clutch of Splatterwhaks - when you've seen all of that, then you can tell me you're *old!* Old? You're a little cub!"

Philip bristled.

"Fine," he said tightly. "So I'm not old, not by your standards. That still doesn't mean I can change." He paused, and looked the large creature up and down. "For that matter, I don't even know *why* you'd want me to! What's in it for you? What do you want of me?"

"Blimey, we are Mr. Suspicious, aren't we?" said Quiddang. "Who's said we want anything of you? Me, I just do my job. Just trying to make sure things tick along smoothly, that's all. We don't get many along like you, that's the honest truth. Can't go letting someone in your situation through into Level Two as you are: it would upset the whole operation!"

Philip glared up at the large creature.

"Humph," he snorted at length. "So what are we going to do?"

Quiddang regarded him thoughtfully.

"I think," he said at length, "that I have an idea."

He reached out and grabbed the nothingness again. When he pulled it away this time, they were standing facing a well-groomed angular creature. It was sat behind a strong, large desk.

The creature fixed Philip with a thousand-watt smile.

"Hello," it said. "I'm Quince. What sort of life can I offer you today?"

"I'll leave you two to get aquatinted, then," said Quiddang.

"But..." Philip started to say, before he realised the large, benign-looking creature had already vanished in a puff of nothing.

Then the words caught up with him.

Philip looked back at the creature behind the desk.

"Did you say you could offer me a life?" he asked.

~

WE'VE ALL MET QUINCE BEFORE. MOST OF US DON'T REMEMBER this, but it is true.

For those of us who cannot remember *where* we met him, here might be a good place for a quick recap.

Quince is the being you go to see if you are in want of a life. Supplying lives is what he does. In fact, he keeps an endless pile of them jostling for attention just beneath the rim of that splendid desk of his. They are rather odd things to look at. They are thin and flat, but when Quince turns them just *so*, they spring into holographic incandesce, displaying a four-dimensional representation of every moment that the life is likely to contain. They are rather beautiful, in a pained sort of a way.

Quince provides a wonderful service, and he is always very busy. His clients are mostly Poor Souls - that is to say, Souls that are so light and fresh-forged as to be poor in terms of experience. (Experience is, after all, the only way a Soul can truly gain weight).

Quince is also something of a salesman. Not that the Poor Souls have anything to barter with, and not that they have any real sense of the value any one life might have over another; it's just that Quince enjoys being in charge. Amid these flimsy Souls, translucent and light, he really is something of a big deal.

So you see, we have all met Quince before. The last thing we saw before the blinding flash gave way to the warm red deep-sea comfort of the womb was the glint of Quince's sharp smile.

It's just, most of us don't remember.

But then, most of us only get one turn of the wheel.

Most of us are only allowed the one life.

~

"I'm very sorry," said Quince again, sounding not a bit of it, "but the timetable is very clear. We only run reincarnation clinics every third Thursday afternoon. And as today is not any sort of Thursday afternoon, third or otherwise, I can only suggest that you take a seat and wait until it is, in fact, Thursday."

Quince shuffled the papers on the desk and made a show of not looking at Philip.

Philip sagged. He wished that Quiddang hadn't left him in the clutches of such a merciless autocrat. But it didn't seem that the benign-looking creature was coming back. Apparently, there were other difficult deaths to deliver. Apparently, Philip's induction to The Other Side was complete.

"But wait just a moment," said Philip, trying to sound reasonable, "Quiddang told me that time was, ah, what did he say, a bit skew-whiff?"

"Yes," said Quince shiftily, "what of it?"

"Well, I just wondered, bearing that in mind, when the next third Thursday afternoon actually is?"

"The next one's due sometime around last May," admitted Quince. "But don't let that put you off; if you can't make that one, another one's bound to turn up sooner or later. Probably later."

"But, well, can't you make an exception?" tried Philip hopefully. "I mean, it's not like you look very busy."

Quince fixed him with his best Withering Look. After a moment, he realised that it wasn't working as well on Philip as it usually did on the Poor Souls, so he coughed and surreptitiously changed down a gear into a Scornful Demeanor.

"Don't look busy?" repeated Quince, indignantly. "What about them?"

Philip looked back the way Quince was indicating.

"Oh," he said.

For some reason, he hadn't noticed the orderly queue of Poor Souls, stretching away in an unending diaphanous line into the deep distance. There were millions of them.

Quiddang had led him straight to the front of the line, he realised.

"OK," said Philip. "I apologize. You are clearly *very* busy. But could you not just see your way clear to letting me have a life? Even a tiny little one would do."

"It's not as easy as that!" said Quince indignantly. "I mean, sure I could give you any old life. It wouldn't take a moment. Ping! Off you'd go with a flash, and you'd be set - not to mention the fact that I would be having a considerably less annoying day - but do you think it would be that simple?"

Philip shrugged.

"Yeah," he said. "That's how it works, isn't it?"

"That's how it works for a Poor Soul, yes," said Quince. "But they're like a...like a blank slate, see? You're not. You're already filled up with lots of life. And...wait..." Quince sniffed once or twice, then glared at him triumphantly. "You weren't even *human* were you?" he demanded.

Philip looked bashful.

"Well," he admitted, "not exactly."

"I *knew* it!" stormed Quince. "Quiddang is a bloody liability! So go on then. Tell the truth. What were you?"

Philip sighed heavily. He had hoped this part wouldn't have to come out.

He told Quince what he had been.

Everything went very still.

"You...were an *Epitaph?*" said Quince. He sounded horrified.

But not just horrified, Philip realised. The faintest thrill of hope began to tug at him.

"Yes," said Philip, trying to keep his voice level.

He realised that the Poor Souls had began to float away from him. He turned and tried to give the closest one a reassuring smile.

"Please don't eat me," the Poor Soul trembled, and promptly burst into a shower of coloured tendrils out of sheer terror.

"No!" shouted Philip. He turned to face Quince. "I'm so sorry!" he said. "I didn't mean to do that. Honestly. I'm...I'm reformed."

But Quince was looking at him speculatively.

"How big are you, exactly?" Quince asked.

"I'm...well, I'm about as big as this," said Philip, feeling that he was somehow missing the point.

"No," said Quince. "You're much bigger than you look. You must be. You were an *Epitaph*, after all. You had it in you to swallow up a whole world."

Quince came closer, peering at him intently.

"Yes," Quince muttered to himself. He gave Philip a little pinch, and seemed delighted with the result. "Yes, of course, how obvious," Quince went on. "And factoring in the celestial elasticity coefficient..."

He pulled out a pad, scribbled some numbers down, appeared satisfied with the result, and moved behind his desk again.

Quince looked Philip up and down. Suddenly, he was smiling again.

"Philip, my friend," he said, "are you an ambitious man?"

∾

"ARE YOU REALLY SURE THIS IS WISE?" ASKED PHILIP, UNCERTAINLY.

"Of course!" shouted Quince, as he ushered another clutch of Poor Souls onwards.

"But...but how many more do we need?" Philip tried. "There must be *hundreds* already."

"One thousand three hundred and seventy six," said Quince evenly. "Room for a few more, I'd say. Go on, you little buggers, shoo!" Quince added, flushing the Poor Souls reluctantly forward.

The little hollow shapes bobbed along unhappily. But if they were scared of an Epitaph - reformed or otherwise - they were *terrified* of Quince. They floated forward and stuck themselves to Philip, shrinking down as they did so.

Already he was coated in a thick film of the things. They stuck to him like small oily bubbles, shimmering slightly and swaying from side to side.

"One thousand three hundred and seventy six!' repeated Philip incredulously. "Is that really necessary?"

"Absolutely," affirmed Quince, with the complete conviction of someone who would be in minimal actual danger were things to go wrong. "I've done all my calculations very thoroughly. Your inner dimensions are easily large enough to accommodate several thousand Poor Souls."

"Yes," said Philip pointedly, "but what about when they start becoming *Rich* Souls?"

"Tush," said Quince. "I thought you *wanted* to have another turn of the wheel. To go round again. To have another *life*! Isn't that worth taking a risk for?"

"Of course I want another bloody life!" shouted Philip. "I just wish you weren't making me take all these other poor buggers with me!"

"Now, now, take it easy," warned Quince. "You don't want to get too excited. Those Poor Souls are very impressionable. If you're not care-ful, you'll end up being a story filled with angry little ungrateful so-and-so's!"

Philip glared at Quince.

"I didn't want to be a whole *story*," he complained. "I just wanted to have another life, that's all."

"Yes, but don't you see, this makes perfect sense!" Quince was almost wheedling now. "I'm always so busy, I've always got so many Poor Souls to find lives for...this way, we give so many of them a good home. And you... you don't just get *one* life - you get a whole *story* of lives! And this time you aren't just sitting there like a hungry toad waiting for it to die. You'll actually *be* the story! A whole story, filled with Poor Souls who were in need of a home. Think of yourself as an orphanage. Maybe that will help."

Philip thought of himself as an orphanage. It didn't help.

All he could imagine was the weight of a thousand Poor Souls, growing on him like leeches as they sucked in Life and became heavier and heavier, swelling and enlarging and choking him until...

"That's it!" said Quince brightly, as a final Poor Soul scuttled towards Philip and lodged itself deep in a forgotten crevice somewhere. "OK, stage one complete. Now for stage two..."

Quince vaulted over his desk. He reached down, and came up with armfuls of the thin lives that were always to be found there. He began to slot them together.

Click, click, click.

They fitted together, one into the next, until soon Quince was holding a huge angular contraption made up of hundreds upon hundreds of them. It creaked alarmingly.

"Nearly...done," came Quince's voice from behind the towering structure.

Philip could not see Quince anymore. He was entirely hidden from view by the pile of lives.

"OK," said Quince. "Brace yourself now, Philip. This might sting a little..."

The tower of lives shifted and began to move towards him.

As it rocked and turned, the various surfaces shimmered and merged into one another, casting eerie, hallucinatory projections as the fields of individual lives intersected.

But that's what I wanted, Philip tried to tell himself. *Another life. I'm getting exactly what I wanted. Aren't I?*

But then it was too late for second thoughts.

The tower of lives reached Philip, paused, tottered...and fell.

Philip felt the hundreds of lives make contact with the hundreds of Poor Souls that were clinging to his - deceptively large - body.

There was a beautiful, seething flash.

The Poor Souls vanished into the lives with which they made contact.

And Philip was the bedrock on which all those Poor Souls were planted.

The Poor Souls vanished into their new lives...and Philip was sucked with them, down into

❦ 43 ❦

THE MAN WHOSE BODY
WAS STORY

∼

He floated in life, and his skin teemed with stories. They sparkled and flashed on his surface like diamonds. Philip breathed slowly in, and a warm wind touched them all. He shifted in his age-long slumber, and the stories shimmered and tilted in new directions. He was their land and their sky, he was their compass and he was their god.

And no Epitaph was permitted here. He made quite sure of that. His stories were as safe as he could make them. They were sealed from the rest of the Storystream, as isolated as it was within his power to grant.

Philip lay his vast body still, and watched the stories unfold.

He was kind to them.

He was, he found, fond of happy endings.

Why not? He had been given one himself.

Or so he thought...

∼

ONE YEAR - FOR DAYS WERE TOO SMALL A CURRENCY FOR PHILIP TO comprehend now, and years were the smallest change in which he dealt - one year, something happened that surprised him.

One of his stories came to a bad end.

It was just a little story - something silly about a blacksmith's son who wanted to be a prince, or a prince who wanted to be a blacksmith's son, he hadn't been paying it much mind, and he forgot the details - but all of a sudden, he realised that things did not seem to be heading in the right direction for this particular son, not at all, not at all.

But he had barely had time to register this fact and stir to a more acute awareness of the tale, before it was too late: the tale was told, the poor man was dead, and the story had curdled around him.

"What in my name!" Philip began to think. (He was, after all, the closest thing to a god there was in these parts). "What on earth is all this nonsense about, eh?"

But even as he had begun to peer more closely into the threads of the vanishing story, an icy chill shot through him.

The story that had just died was not the only one heading that way. He began to be aware that many - no, more than that, *hundreds* - of his other stories were beginning to show similar signs. They creaked and cracked alarmingly. Philip looked closer, and all across his vast body, he saw it: kissed toads were resolutely failing to turn into handsome princes, ailing fathers were lost before their brave daughters could defeat the witch and gain the magic potion, orphan boys remained orphans, and died of privation on the cold turf outside the houses of their would-be benefactors.

It was the same wherever he looked. All across the surface of his body, his stories were dying.

"This will not do!" bellowed Philip, and shaking every acre and mile of himself, he forced his attention more keenly into every nook and cranny of every story that dwelt on him. It was an effort of will that he had not pushed himself to in centuries, and it did not come as easily to him as it had in the old days, in the first glorious thousand years or two of his reign, when he was a young, fresh-faced bedrock of a thousand tales, still rejoicing in the second chance he had been given.

His body felt saggy and old, and it twinged and complained in awkward places as he made himself wake up.

But at last, he managed it.

"That's better," he said to himself, and it was true: now that he had shaken himself and began to look more keenly, time no longer whizzed by so fast that months passed in a blur.

In fact, time had begun to look decidedly gloopy from his new vantage point, something slow and thick, and cloying to the little creatures that moved through it. He decided he needed to take a closer look.

Philip hadn't manifested himself physically in one of his stories for a very long time - not only did he find it vaguely degrading, but more importantly, he was in his own way, rather a shy creature these days, and felt awfully embarrassed to go strutting about making proclamations and so forth. That generally wasn't his style. However, he told himself, desperate times and all that...

He concentrated hard, focusing all his thought inward on one specific story. It was quite difficult, rather like trying to shift all your attention onto a small patch of rather innocuous skin on your elbow while the rest of your body was covered with ants. Nevertheless, Philip was nothing if not determined, and sure enough, with a noise something like *plop* (but deeper, and less silly) he felt a rushing, whooshing sensation, and when he opened his eyes, there he was: a walking manifestation of himself, embedded deep within one of his own stories.

His first thought was that things looked much, much worse down here than he had realised.

He was standing on what was - very vaguely - a cornfield. It was vague in the sense that it looked less like a real field, and more like a drawing done by a child of what a field of corn looked like from his or her window. The corn was made of simple green lines pointing straight upwards and crossed with golden strokes that were meant to be sheaves of corn. There was no wind as such, but Philip knew that it *was* there because of a scattering of horizontal lines that hung randomly in the sky. There were three simple houses a little way off. One was made of straw, another of wood, and the third of brick. A huddle of figures were leaning in a tired sort of a way against the third house.

Feeling self-consciously three dimensional, Philip ambled over towards the little group.

When he got closer, he could see for sure what the figures were meant to be. Of course, he had had his suspicions the moment he had manifested, but one had to be sure...

"Um, hello there," said Philip, smiling a little too much. "I say, I'm sorry to bother you and everything, but I just wondered...well, how everything was going, that sort of thing?"

The wolf - who was smoking a nasty-looking roll-up - exchanged glances with two of the pigs in turn, then gave a half-hearted shrug.

"Nothin' guv'," he said after a pause. "Just having a little break, as it were. Soon get back to things, don't you worry."

"Oh!" said Philip, unsure if he was flattered or irked to have been recognized so quickly. "You know who I am then?"

One of the pigs rolled its eyes, and the wolf looked down at its feet, not meeting his gaze.

"Course we do," said the second pig. "You're the boss, in't yah?"

"You come here to chivvy us along, then?" asked the third pig, in a horrible little falsetto. "Always the bloody same, you lot! Look, we know our rights! We know about natural breaks, we know about working time directives! And just so *you* know, the moment you walked in here, we stopped the clock, right? As long as you're standing here, this counts as work, right?"

"Of course, of course," spluttered Philip, feeling flustered. "Take as much time as you want, no problem. Actually, I think you've got the wrong end of the stick. I just wanted to pop down, see how things were on the ground, that sort of thing..."

"Things are fine," said the wolf, in a defeated voice. "Don't you worry about us. We're doing OK."

The first and second pigs nodded. The third pig did not.

"Fine?" squeaked the third pig. "Of course we're not bloody fine! No, I will *not* be quiet!" he added to the others, who were all making little *shh* motions. "Things have gone on this way long enough, and I for one am *sick* of it!"

Philip pulled out a handkerchief and wiped his brow. The sun over-head was only a playfully drawn circle of rough yellow crayon, but it was rather hot.

"Oh dear," said Philip, in his best concerned landlord voice, "well, maybe if you tell me a bit about what the problem is we can see what I can do to fix things?"

"Oh, you'd like that, wouldn't you?" said the third pig nastily. "The bourgeoisie landlord, mucking in with the humble peasant folk, at one with the serfs, working up a sweat…Who do you think you are, bloody Tolstoy?"

Philip, who had no idea who Tolstoy was, but who was pretty sure he didn't want to be him, shook his head vigorously.

"No, look, I'm only trying to help!" he said earnestly. "I really want to know what the problem is!"

"Want to know what the problem is?" repeated the third pig incredulously. "Well that's bloody rich, isn't? Isn't that just the icing on the bloody cake?"

The pig was starting to puff up its chest now, like a great pink balloon, and was strutting closer and closer to Philip. For a two dimen-sional child's sketch of a pig, Philip had to admit there was something quite alarming about it; and he was just considering making an exit and looking for a more congenial story, when the first pig - who had been silent up until now - stepped forward.

"OK mate, chill, chill," it said, touching the angry pig on the arm. "Why don't you just go back to your house, have a sit down, count to twenty, whatever it takes, yeah?"

The angry pig vibrated with fury for a moment, looked at the inter-loper with a despairing shake of his head, and then, deflating, all anger spent, he waddled over to the straw house and collapsed down with his back into the wall.

The first pig took a deep breath and rolled his eyes.

"Sorry about Straw," said the pig, casually producing a roll-up form behind one ear and striking a match on one of his trotters, "it's just, he's got it worst, right? I mean, it's not like we get to swap houses or anything like that. His is always the first to come down, yeah? Mine comes down too, you understand," he added, indicating the wooden house casually with his roll-up, "but, like, at least I get to live in it for a bit, you see. I'm Wood, by the way," the pig added. "And that over there is Brick."

"I see," said Philip, not quite sure that he did. "Nice to meet you all. Anyway, don't worry about it, not your friend's fault and all that. But look here, maybe you could tell me what exactly the matter is?"

The pig and the wolf exchanged glances.

"It's difficult to explain," began the pig. "See, it's not like we've got anything to compare this to. This life, I mean. This existence. But, well, we've all been around the block a few times now, and well, we talk to one another..."

"What he's saying," the wolf put in, "is that...well, we're getting *bored*. I mean, the first few times, sure, it's great."

"Three pigs, three houses, one hungry wolf," cut in the pig, "it's a real winner. Why mess with a classic, right?"

"And it's not that I mind always coming out on bottom!" protested the wolf, sounding sincere. "I'm the wolf! I'm the *bad* guy, I get it!"

"It's just, after you've played things out three or four thousand times, you start to wonder if you could, I don't know...*stretch yourself* a bit," continued the pig. "You know, do something a bit avant garde. Paint our faces white and pretend to be eunuchs or...or something..." he trailed off vaguely.

"Stretch yourself," repeated the wolf, shaking his head sadly. "That's Straw's problem. Between you and me, I think that boy reads more than is good for him. He found a crate of odd books, you see, washed up from some distant corner of the Storystream. All sorts of strange stories there. Gave him all kinds of funny ideas."

Wood nodded.

"Yeah, it was them books what done for him," he agreed. "All these weird stories, very sort of realist. Hardly an anthropomorphic animal amongst them."

The wolf chuckled.

"Yeah, not my sort of thing at all," he said. "Well, there was the one about all them pigs taking over a farm. That one was a bit more like it, but still..."

"Don't forget the one about the mouse that got real smart!" put in Wood. "That one was really *sad...*"

Philip was starting to feel overwhelmed, an unusual experience for what was, give or take, a god.

"Hang on just a tick," he said, focusing on the one bit of the conversation he understood. "Are you telling me you've done this story before? That it's not new to you? That you, well, you *know what's going to happen?*"

The wolf and the pigs nodded.

"But...but that's not right!" spluttered Philip. "That's not how it's meant to work! I had it all worked out! Stories come into being, they play themselves out, and then they are over; and a new story should grow up in its place! At least, that's the way things have been working up until now," he added, a note of doubt creeping into his voice.

Philip looked desperately from the wolf to the pigs and back again.

"Come on then," said the wolf at last, exchanging a meaningful glance with each pig in turn. "We'd better show him, hadn't we?"

"Show me?" said Philip hoarsely. "Show me what? What are you talking about?"

But the wolf was just shaking his head.

"Come on guv'nor," he said in a resigned voice. "Best you see this with your own eyes..."

The wolf twisted his body in the two dimensions that were allowed to him, and suddenly he was facing the background. The field of wheat looked just as still as ever; the sun shone bright above.

Then the wolf lifted a paw, and very gently rubbed at the background.

There was a scraping noise, and the background began to crumble away. Fragments of wheat and blue sky and yellow sun flaked off and began to stack up around their feet. A moment later, the two pigs joined in, and before long a sizable chunk had been worked away, until...

"Oh my," said Philip weakly. "You mean to say...?"

"Yes," said the wolf. "Yes indeed."

Behind the background, the whole story was laid out in a second spread of two dimensions. There was the house of brick, and nearby there stood a tumble of wooden planks and a great pile of straw.

"And then you can rub *this* layer..." commented the wolf, and did just that, his voice trailing away, to reveal a further story behind that, all played out and still.

Philip was shaking his head sadly.

"And it goes on like that for...oh, I don't know, thousands of versions..."

The wolf blew out his cheeks and threw himself to the floor.

"So you can see why we're in no hurry to get on with things," said one of the pigs. "I mean, it's all been done. You can see the appeal of trying something new, can't you?"

"We have been doing a *little* experimenting," the wolf said, at least having the grace to look a trifle embarrassed. "I mean, everyone knows that you like your happy endings. But to be honest, gov', they get so, well, *boring* after a while!"

"That's why we've been attempting to spice things up a bit," said Wood. "I mean, just for once, it was fun to have the bricks be made out of sub-standard materials shipped in at a fraction of the cost from a disreputable vendor."

"Yeah, and then I got a nice meal for once!" exclaimed the wolf. "And then there was the time I got laryngitis. We thought that would be fun. Something different."

"But any way you look at it, we always end up here again," sighed Brick sadly; and he scraped a trotter along the background as hard as he could, rubbing away three or four hundred layers of story in one go.

"It shouldn't have been like this," said Philip in a small voice. "I'm so sorry, really I am. I had no idea...I thought you stories, well, sort of *cleared* yourself out. That's what used to happen, at any rate."

"Oh, that happened in the beginning, of course it did!" said the wolf. "But just lately, it seems that things have been, well, building up, as it were. And the problem is, there's nowhere for all the used up bits of story to go..."

Philip opened his mouth to say something, and suddenly he understood.

He closed his mouth, and looked at the ground.

It was his fault. It was all his fault.

He had been so certain. He thought he had been protecting his little stories. He had thought he was keeping them safe, that by sealing his worlds off, by isolating them from the rest of the Storystream he was keeping them from being devoured, keeping them from being polluted, preventing any greedy little Epitaphs from worming their way in...

"I stopped the rubbish from escaping," he said, half to himself. "I've been hoarding it, I've been hoarding you all...I've been so scared of what might happen if something got in, that I forgot to worry about what would happen if nothing could get out..."

"Freud would have something to say about that, I'm sure," said Straw. He strolled back towards them, looking somewhat calmer than when Wood sent him away. He was holding a dog-eared book. "Always holding onto the waste, reluctant to let anything get away...Sounds like you have become stuck, developmentally speaking."

"There he goes again," chided Wood. "Spouting more strange realist nonsense."

But, "No, he's right," said Philip. "I've got stuck. I've got you all stuck. Which means there's only one thing for it. I have to unstick you." He paused. "The only problem," he went on, "is how."

There was silence.

Then slowly, very slowly, a trotter began to go up into the air.

Philip looked in surprise at its owner.

"Brick?" he asked. "Do you have an idea?"

Brick, who was stockier than the other two pigs, and who always tried to make himself small because he was afraid the others might dislike him for having a much better house than theirs, cleared his throat.

"I...I did hear something once," he ventured cautiously.

"Yes?" asked Philip.

"Well, the thing is, several hundred stories back, I met this strange pig..." he began, then faltered.

"Go on," said Philip.

"He wasn't from round here," muttered Brick, going rather pink in the face (even for a pig). "As a matter of fact, he said he wasn't really from around anywhere. His name was Bartleby. He was a wandering sort of pig, he told me, and he seemed awfully knowledgeable, awfully wise, in a boastful sort of a way. Anyway, he had just stopped in on his way from somewhere to somewhere else. He was rather proud of that. He said not many people could find their way here, on account of how completely the god of these parts - begging your pardon, Master Philip - how completely this god had cut our stories off from the rest of the wide world. He said that it was a little way *down* as it were, from most of the rest of things. Not as far as you can go, but still quite a way. And what was more, he said you wouldn't even notice him. He was very proud of that in particular, I remember. But he was rather a loquacious pig, and very fond of his own voice. He told me all sorts of stories; and one of them...well, I think maybe it could help us. You see, he mentioned, in passing, that there was a certain place, far off and away and further far again. He called it

✻ 44 ✻

THE LAND BELOW STORIES

~

P eople live and people die. It's all very sad, of course, but there it is. Now, of those who die, there are almost as many theories as to what happens to them as there are those to pose the question. Hell, some say; others think rebirth more likely, and still others are quite sure that life is just a brief moment of light, a passing dream, that comes after an infinite darkness, and darkness is all that awaits us once more when life is done. Who knows the truth of things? Not me. I am just a humble pig.

The land I want to tell you of now is *not* the land of the dead. I don't know anything about that, and don't like to overstretch myself. But I *have* heard about a land where stories go when they die. Well, not the *whole* stories, you understand. No, what I'm talking about are the bits and pieces. The flotsam and jetsam. The awkward loose ends, the bits that are left over.

I'm getting ahead of myself. Please excuse me; after all, I am only a gentle swine, and not very good with words.

Very well.

There was a day, much like any other, when this strange pig came a-calling. Bartleby was his name, and he pulled up in a very stern-seeming dark wagon. There was a cat, too, though it lazed on the roof and didn't say a word. There was a darkness in the wagon, and I was glad the door did not open.

But despite the disquiet the wagon spurred inside me, I had to admit I was curious. When you spend every waking moment building houses and worrying about them getting blown down...well, a change is as good as a rest, as they say. So up I strolled to this strange wagon.

"Well-met, pilgrim," I called to the pig. "From where do you hail? And what is your destination? I am sorry to tell you, but I think you may be lost, for few travel in these parts."

"Wotcher!" replied this strange pig. "Now one swine to another, why don't you drop all that fancy talk and get me a drink? I'm parched!"

I was rather put off by his tone; but nevertheless, he had invoked the sacred brotherhood of swine to which we both belonged, and I felt it my duty to help him in his hour of need. I brought him drink and fodder, and after he had refreshed himself I asked him again from whence he came and what business brought him here.

"Oh, just passing through, mate, don't you worry," he told me. "Just on the way back from having the old thing cleaned," here he indicated the wagon, before leaning closer and tipping me a horrible wink. "And I'm not talking about the wagon so much as I am the old lady, if you understand me," he added in a hoarse whisper.

I assured him that I did not.

"Ah, not to worry," he told me, brushing his words aside with a wave of his trotter. "Look, we've just been down below like. We only came back this way 'cos it makes the journey home a bit easier, this place being three hops removed and closer to the bottom, metaphorically speaking."

When I continued to look blank, he rolled his eyes at me.

"Cor, you really don't know, do you?" he said, scornfully. "Honestly, you lot...That's what comes of being raised inna bubble, I s'pose. Look," he went on, very proud and condescending, "this place isn't like most of the rest of the Storystream, see? It's a whole load of stories sort of melded together, built up actually on the body of your little god."

I apologize for the use of such insulting language; but you must understand, these are his words, not mine.

I assured him that I knew very well about all of that and asked him what his point was.

"Ah! The point is, your funny little god's only gone and pulled all his stories as far away from the rest of the Storystream as he can manage!" said the pig. "By doing that, he's sort of, well, submerged it below the main current. And because of that, the whole lot of you are much closer to where we've just come from."

I asked him where exactly that was, and, "The land below stories, of course!" he said. He was getting rather worked up now, quite irate, as if it were my personal negligence not to have heard of this odd place.

"Look," he went on, "the Storystream's made of lots of stories, right? I mean billions and zillions and gazillions. *Lots.* Basically an endless amount of stories. Now your average story, it might be quite well put together. Maybe there's a beginning and a middle. If it's lucky, it's even got an end. It's got a main character, sometimes a few. It's got various walk-on parts, some nice scenery, perhaps a song or two. But," and here the pig snorted and gave his tail a little swish, "but, the thing is, there's an awful lot of little loose ends, bits that don't quite fit; songs that don't get sung, or only get hummed softly; bits of scenery that don't quite end up being background, even. Now: where do you think all those bits go?"

I looked at him blankly. How was I supposed to know? I, who had spent the whole of my life in a story that was being told a million times over, every inch of it being painted over again by the next telling? I had no idea where all these little bits went, and I told him as much.

"I'll tell you where," the pig said, looking rather pleased with himself. "They float down. They fall away and tumble; and in the land below stories, they make a rain. A constant rain of fragments of stories, the forgotten bits, the useless bits, the characters no one cares about, the plots that were abandoned because the people in the story went the other way. All that stuff, it comes down into the land below stories. A right bloody awful place it is, too, I can tell you!"

I have to admit, this proud little pig was really beginning to grate on me. I actually wanted nothing more than for him to be on his merry way, and take his nasty little dark wagon with him. And yet...and yet, there was something in his words that drew me in. There was a mystery to this story, something that caught me.

"Well...Well, if it is so awful, why in the name of everything did you go there?" I spluttered at him.

"Aha!" said the pig, and the way he said it made me sure he knew exactly how I felt, and was delighting in stringing out the tale, delighted in feeling such a clever swine next to me. "I'll tell you why," he went on. "We went there for the Munchers!"

"The Munchers?" I asked, feeling more lost than ever.

"Yeah, that's right," he confirmed. "The Munchers. Nasty little devils. About as big as your nose, only much uglier, and that's saying something, I can tell you. Little furry balls with lots of teeth. Move like the clappers. Quite a fright, the first time you see a flock of the little critters coming for you, no mistake. But," he sighed judiciously, "I didn't have to be afraid, not at all. Not when I'm with the Mistress. Them little buggers might be stupid as a wild boar, but they know a bigger set of teeth when they see one. Nah, in the teeth department, there ain't much out there more hungry than my Mistress, and that's a fact."

I looked at the wagon again, and wondered about what lurked within. A cold shiver went through me. I felt naked. I glanced at the dark windows, and wondered what, exactly, was looking out at me.

"Nah, don't worry, mate," said Bartleby, with a nasty little smile. "She don't feast on the like's of us. Bacon's not to her liking. Not unless we displease her, of course. We wouldn't be much of a snack to her, anyway. Far too small. She'd hardly notice. Thing is," here he licked his lips. "Thing is, my Mistress had just enjoyed a rather large meal. Collected a few misbehaving ones far and away, in a different place. The problem with such big teeth is, they're hard as anything to keep clean. That's where the Munchers come in, see? We open the door and herd them in. Then they swim around in the darkness, and they pick all the little decaying bits of story off her teeth. They nibble those glorious gnashers of hers quite clean. Suits everyone, see? And if one or two Munchers go into that wagon and don't come out again, well, I won't be mourning them. My mistress likes to head down there every once in a while. It's like having a whatchamacallit, a, an *exfoliation*. Makes her feel all fresh and full of life again, ready to take on the world."

Bartleby stopped talking here, and just grinned at me with his horrible piggy face and his nasty little piggy eyes. I was quite sure he was measuring me, trying to see how much he'd manage to get under my skin.

"Well," he said at last, "I feel quite refreshed now, myself. Time to be getting on the go. Between you and me," he whispered, "we've got something quite important to do now. There's someone dangerous loose in the Storystream. He's trying to get to the heart of things, trying to cut things down, break things up. God knows why. I mean, I'm sure *your* god doesn't know why, but...well, you know what I mean....Anyway, the Mistress means to trap him, and so off we go..."

But I wasn't listening to him anymore, not really. I wanted to know more about this Land Below Stories. What did I care about some distant madman with a pointless, impotent grudge against story? It was probably a lie anyway, a boast. But these creatures he talked of, these Munchers...I felt...I knew instinctively that they were *important,* somehow. I had to find out more, I had to keep him talking...

When the pig hopped back up onto the roof of the wagon and started tying himself into a curious harness that was lodged there, I knew he really was intending to leave.

"Wait!" I said, surprising myself by the urgency in my own voice. "There must be more! What more can you tell me?"

Bartleby looked at me blankly for a moment. Then a frown flittered across his face.

"Funny thing," he said. "You're not the only one to be interested in those horrible little Munchers." He scratched himself in an unmentionable place and went on. "Actually, we bumped into these weirdos who were actually *studying* them! Hah! I mean, can you imagine..."

He wiped an imaginary tear from his eye.

"I asked one of them what in the name of everything they thought they were going to get out of those nasty buggers," said the pig. "You know what they told me? They told me they were *scientists*! Nasty, meddling sorts if you ask me; probably not much better than the Munchers themselves! Anyway, one of them wanders over to us, calm as you like, no sense of respect. He comes up to me, and he says, 'Hello there, good master pig, would you mind if I just put these electrodes on your head for a moment? It won't take a second, and it's all in the name of science, I can assure you.' So I tells him no, and what's more, I tell him where he *can* stick those electrodes of his. But this bloke, he doesn't even flinch. He just says, 'Hmm, interesting," then makes a note in a little book he's carrying. Then he looks at me more closely and says, 'Maybe you would feel differently if you know why we're here.' Now I look at him skeptically when he says this, but it doesn't let it faze him. 'I'll tell you the story,' he says, calm as you like. 'It's called

❦ 45 ❦

THE LIFE SCIENTIFIC

~

I come from a long line of scientists. My mother was a scientist, and her mother before her, and so on all the way back to the very first Badger-Bear. That's my name, by the way. Winston Badger-Bear. How d'yah do?

As I was saying. Scientism rather runs in the family. We've done some rather scientific studies of it, and it's as true as tulips. Oh, it's a wonderful life. Us scientists, we don't have to believe in anything unless we have absolute, one hundred percent proof. That's the beauty of it. For instance, I haven't yet determined if I believe in *you*. I'm actually conducting research into the matter right now, even as we speak. If I'm lucky, I should get two or three scholarly papers out of this conversation alone, and that's even if you *don't* exist. Things will be much more rosy if you do, I can promise you that.

I digress. Anyway, the one problem we have is finding really genuinely new things to be scientific about. Oh, it's easy enough to have a crack at adding something to a question that's already been answered. Put in an equation here, refine a theory there, you know the sort of thing. But there's nothing really *exciting* about that. So imagine our anticipation when we heard about a really *ripe* bit of research just waiting to be plucked up.

Us? Oh yes, I'm sorry! I should have said. I'd like you to meet Henry and Jemima Badger-Bear. They're my brother and sister, don'cha know? At least, I'm fairly certain they are. Some of the research is still pending, but the evidence is all pointing in that direction.

Get to the point? Oh yes! I'm sorry, I do have a tendency to ramble rather. Now where was I? Oh yes. So, the three of us were just sort of twiddling our thumbs, wondering if it would be better to begin work on an encyclopaedia covering all the lesser known types of bodily wind, or if our time would be better spent finishing off a rather fascinating treatise on the letter 'P' that we had been working on for the last five years, when we heard about this place. Very interesting. Remarkable opportunities for original research. So we high-tailed it down here as fast as we could. We built a special sort of ship-thing for the journey. You can come in for tea if you like? No? Fine, suit yourself. Anyway, when we got here, we found it was even more remarkable than we had dared to hope.

Our first major breakthrough came when Henry here was eaten up by these wonderful little Muncher fellows.

Oh yes, he was *quite* dead. Really, it was very impressive. One of them came scurrying up to us as soon as we got here.

"Hello there, little fellow!" said Henry, holding out his hand to pet the furry devil, and *buzz* went those teeth, and that was the end of Henry! Before he knew what had hit him, he was just a rain of little sub-narrative particles making their way down the digestive tract of that keen little Muncher.

Oh yes, as you can see, he's *quite* alright now. That's where the remarkable breakthrough comes in! Now Jemima here, she is something of a naturalist. Been all over the place. You can't name a terrifying, deadly creature that she hasn't chased, shot at, or been bitten by. So when Henry went down the gullet, quick as a flash Jemima was ready. She had a special cage made up of raw iron - very rare metal, you see, wonderfully scientific stuff, almost completely immune to most forces in the known universe - and while this little blighter was feasting on old Henry here, she slapped the cage down, and back we retreated into our ship, where we knew we'd be safe to carry out our research in peace.

My, you should have seen the little bugger writhe about! He didn't like it in that iron cage, I can tell you! But you can't get held up by that sort of thing, not when you're living the life scientific! All in the name of a greater good, that's what we say! But the critter had eaten up old Henry, and we were damned if we were going to let him go without at least getting a case report out of it. What did we do? Well, we took a knife to the thing of course! Most scientific instrument in existence, your common or garden knife. Very keen, very concise. Not much can argue with a blade down the centre, right? And what do you think we found when we cut that furry little Muncher open? All the fragments of our dear brother, of course! Out they poured, millions and millions of them. Here was a bit of the way he smelt, there was a fragment of the sound of his voice, and here again was his walk, not to mention all the physical bits of him, his nose, his left big toe, and so on. It was most fascinating, I assure you!

Oh, don't go now! Wait just a moment longer, we're coming to the really *clever* bit!

Good. So. What do you think we did with all these little bits of our brother?

No, we didn't bury them. You're not thinking like a *scientist*. No, what we did was: we put our heads together, and we used them to *reverse-engineer* old Henry here! It was rather easy, actually, as it seemed that this here Muncher had been especially hungry, and hadn't eaten much of anything for quite some time. No, we were lucky: the Henry we got back was almost exactly the same as the one that was munched up. Oh, there were small differences here and there: he never used to be quite so pretty, and those other three legs weren't there originally, I'm quite sure of it. But if you focus on that, you're missing the point! It was the *process* that was remarkable! You see, by doing this we realised that we could do the same thing on a much larger scale: we could reverse-engineer a whole *story*. All we would need was enough of the raw materials, enough of the chewed up parts, enough of the decomposing remnants. And where would we find them? Why, in the bellies of these little Munchers, naturally!

And that's what we're doing here. Conducting research into the reverse-engineering of stories. I'm quite sure we'll be in line for some sort of award or something when we publish. It will blow everything else out of the water. It really is amazing work, even if we do say so ourselves.

How do we keep the Munchers away while we're working? I'll show you! Come over here and you can see for yourself. We're all very proud of this. It's called

❧ 46 ❧

THE NARRATIVE OUTFLOW
SIMULATING HUB, OR NOSH

∿

B eyond hills grown green with hero worshipping stumps that sup
forever not knowing their way back to the eternal question of down-
hill trodden scraps of knowledge and power and possibility and beyond
this the tulip waved helplessly on the small green hell from the bottom of my
heart these truths I tell to understand the greatness embedded in a flower which
never once nor afterwards was ever beyond the ken of the people that jumped
higher and higher never knowing what the rainbow said which was a possible
black mark in the school book of the master because up and yellow equal infinity
on those strange occasions when backwards glances miss the point and return
us to

❧ 47 ❧

THE LIFE SCIENTIFIC (REPRISE)

~

You see? Quite an astounding bit of technology, what? Only took us a few days to cobble it together. Spews up just an amazing amount of low-energy fodder to distract the Munchers with. Oh, it's all quite devoid of nourishment, they couldn't live off it, but *they* don't know that! In fact, they find it quite delicious, probably because the things it spits out are already pretty much as digested as they can get, so they don't have to expend any effort in breaking them down. Keeps them off our backs anyway, and that's the point.

Oh, so you really do have to go now, do you? Well it was lovely meeting you. Or at least it would have been, if I'd had time to prove conclusively that you actually existed. How did we find out about the Land Below Stories in the first place? It was terribly interesting, actually. We were just going about our business, conducting research into the letter 'P' as I have mentioned, when something strange began to happen. My brother felt it first, but I wasn't far behind.

There was a trembling in the earth. It was subtle at first, so slight you could almost have imagined it. But it got bigger and bigger, until even the most scientific amongst us would not be able to doubt it for long.

The three of us rushed out into the garden, and there it was - a mound was rising, tearing itself out of the earth. That was where the trembling was coming from. This mound grew and grew, like a boil getting bigger and bigger. And then - just like a boil - it burst. And you'll never guess what was inside! Not earth, no; and not sand, either. No, the stuff that came out when *this* boil burst was nothing earthly or normal. The stuff that came out was...well, it was very like the nonsense that spewed out from our NOSH machine over there. It was *random*, little bubbles and pockets of ideas, of half-digested narrative matter. It flickered and danced and faded away to nothing - which was only natural, of course, at it suddenly found itself in a reality with a far stronger narrative field than that of the Land Below Stories, which was where, as we later learned, it was coming from...

But before very long, the stream of raw story slowed to a trickle, and there instead were standing three figures, burrowing up out of the bedrock of our own story.

One was young, barely even a man. The second looked almost young, with smooth skin and a youthful frame; though his eyes were old, and there was a stony determination in them. This one wore an amulet of gold around his neck, and he said little and looked grim. But the third man was old, with a long white beard, and ruddy, rounded cheeks. He looked cheerful, and it was this man who spoke to us,

"Aha," he said, noticing us for the first time. "Hello there, my good fellows! We are most terribly sorry to disturb your repose, but we are engaged on rather an important matter, as it were, and tired and thirsty, and we would be awfully grateful for any assistance - as it may be, a pie, or a small amount of wine, say - that you would be able to provide?"

Now it has been our experience that there is a direct, proportional relationship between food given to a party, and the willingness of said party to divulge information. In fact, we published a series of papers on the subject some time ago. Armed with this knowledge, and intrigued by the strange manner in which these travellers had arrived, we lost no time in inviting them to partake with us in consuming the warm carcass of a dead bird, augmented by a selection of vegetable matter, or to the layman, a Sunday Dinner.

Once the food had been shared and our guests were put at ease, we asked them where they came from.

"Ah, yes," said the old man, for he remained the spokesperson of the party. "I was wondering when you were going to ask about that. It is a rather interesting story. We come, you see, from the Land Below Stories. And we went there to seek a certain splendid amulet which, as you can see, is now firmly laid around the neck of my friend here, which is as things should be. It comes from a place far off and away and further far again, and it is called

❧ 48 ❧

THE AMULET OF THE SPHERES

~

Perhaps I should start with an introduction. I am a monk, of no fixed abode, and of too little worth to even be worth a name. This is my young apprentice, Master Sate, who hails from the land of the first stories. And this rather grim-looking fellow is called Tobias Khazheimmer, and though it is on his behalf that we began our journey, I rather think now the quest has widened, as it were. What we do now, we do for everyone, for it seems that everyone is threatened.

I say, is there any more gravy? Thank you! Yes, most delicious!

Now where was I? Oh yes.

Tobias, you see, was one of those terribly unlucky men who had the bad fortune to fall in love. It wasn't his fault, you understand. He never meant to, or anything like that. But the fact remained that he fell into love, and he fell very hard and very deep.

It was one of those true sort of loves, eternal and unbreakable, and once he had fallen, there was no coming back.

Now the woman he loved was called Sebille, and she had faery blood in her, and it came to pass that something very evil befell this woman, and her heart was split down the middle, split into two equal portions, the shadowed half and the light. Oh, the story is far too long to tell in full here; I am sure if you went looking for it, you would find it, for stories have a way of spreading, and this one has been told before now. Pass the salt, would you? Thanks!

So Tobias here came a-looking for her. And who do you think he found? Not her, no; me! And realizing that, although I am a rather fetching old man, I am by no means any match in beauty for his lost love, he determined to keep looking, as was only fitting. But then we met....ah, well, that is a difficult thing to say exactly who it was we met. Angels, perhaps. Or guardians. Yes, that was what they called themselves. And it became apparent that we were bound up in something far darker, far more dangerous than we had guessed. And so I decided to come along, and do what I can to help. For a monk should have a purpose; and anyway, it's important for monkish apprentices to have some experience of the world, and when Sate determined to come with me, that only strengthened my decision to follow friend Tobias until he reaches the end of his tale; and to help him make it a happy one, if at all possible.

Now I see that you are people of learning, and understand something of the secrets of the worlds; and you know, I am sure, that this is not the only world, not by a long mile, not by a week of Sundays. The problem was, Tobias had lost the one sure means he had of navigating us through the twists and turns and endless paths of the Storystream... yes, that was what they called it, I think... After he left his home in search of his love, he had lost a certain amulet, rare, enchanted, which was given him by Sebille's people. Without this talisman, he was unable to search for his missing love.

So the first thing we determined to do, therefore, was to find this missing amulet. The quest would have been quite useless without it. Tobias had had the amulet stolen from him in a certain grove on a certain night by a certain robber, an uncertain number of years ago. It took us time, but we found that robber; only he had sold the amulet to a particular doe-eyed goblin maid he knew; and this goblin maid had been involved in some cataclysmic event or other, and the whole story she had been enmeshed in had been eaten up or collapsed away to nothing; and most of her wares had been lost, and she had only escaped at the last moment and by the skin of her pretty teeth.

"But," she told us, when the fear of Tobias' knife was upon her, "but that doesn't mean your amulet is lost forever. Not in certainty. Not for sure. There is a place, a very strange place, where the broken remnants of stories go..."

And she told us then of the Land Below Stories, even as I have already told you.

So that was where we determined we must go.

It took us a great deal of wandering, and the asking of a great many questions, but we found a way to burrow down through the stuff of a story, to gnaw away at the bones of a tale until, *Pop!* With a groaning and a grumbling, the mesh of the story we were traveling in gave way and let us pass.

And there we were. The Land Below Stories.

Let me tell you, when we first came to that strange place, when we floated down through the thin light and landed on the soft ground, when we saw the rain of broken particles, of lost events and forgotten atmospheres and fractured plots...well, we were awed. Frightened, but awed.

And let me tell you another thing, for I can see the light in your eyes, and I know that as soon as we leave, you'll be wanting to go visiting that place yourself: be careful! For it's not empty, not by a long way. Hungry little creatures live there, and they have very sharp teeth. We would have been gobbled up by those horrible little things if Sate here hadn't been so quick on his feet. He saw these nasty furry things scurrying towards us, and he understood what they were and what they fed on, and before you could say, "Fruit Pie!" he stood up and yelled out a tricksome and devious riddle, and he wove it up into a pile of story fragments that had fallen nearby, and he wrapped all this into three suits of armour, and we jumped into them before you could say, "I'll Have My Slice With Cream", and not a moment too soon, for at that instant the lead-most of the little devils was leaping into the air, all his teeth gleaming white, and he snatched onto Sate's arm, and fixed there very tight.

But Sate had been a most clever apprentice, as you can see; and those teeth, though they were sharp as nails, could not easily cut through the armour he had woven, so deep and tricksy was the riddle he had sown in. After a little time, the Munchers got bored of munching away at such terribly knotty food, and gave up, deciding to go elsewhere, in search of something softer.

For a few moments then we were happy, and we felt relief, and we thought our quest did not seem so difficult after all. But then we began to look for the amulet, and we understood the sheer *size* of the Land Beneath Stories, and our quest began to seem hopeless, after all.

It is a huge place, vast beyond words. It has to be, of course; for it exists underneath everything, and do not the wise know well that the length and width of everything is the whole of forever, and not an inch or atom less?

Still, we looked. What else could we do? We found a great many things, a huge number of strange and unusual and worthless things. But we never found the thing for which we sought.

Then, after we had been looking for a day or a year or forever - time is very strange in the Land Below Stories, and one loses his sense of things - I stumbled on something very familiar, and it stopped me short.

We had split up, you see, to broaden our efforts, and we were all searching alone.

Suddenly, there it was in front of me. A pheasant. A most familiar bird. A most curious bird. And most certainly, it was the same pheasant I had encountered before. It was sitting in the very threshold of a rabbit hole, just poking its friendly eyes out at me . The rabbit hole stood on nothing, obviously; on other worthless story-junk that had rained down over the aeons.

But the pheasant...I had met this pheasant before. In fact, I had nearly called it lunch, and had only stayed my hand because of the look of complete benevolent understanding it had given me.

It stared at me again now, and I was frozen to the spot by that same deep, kind calmness that came at me from those large birdie eyes.

Then it clucked once, turned augustly, and waddled back into its hole.

I cannot say why, but for some reason I knew, I just *knew* that this pheasant was important. It knew the secret, it knew the answer. It was trying to tell me something, trying to show me the way, trying to help me, somehow. But it was going back into its hole, and I was none the wiser. I could not let it escape!

I gave a cry, and with a great leap, threw myself towards the pheasant, which was already disappearing back into its rabbit hole.

I should pause at this point and tell you something about the nature of the Land Below Stories. It is a very vague sort of a place, you see. It is awfully fluffy, awfully soft. Even the Munchers - who have the sharpest and most terrible teeth of anything I have encountered - even they are fluffy on the outside. Everything that exists in that place is soft and dream-like and yielding...which is why it came as such a shock when my head went *smack* into something that was neither soft nor yielding.

In fact, it was one of the most solid things my head has ever come into contact with.

"Ow," I said, rubbing my head, and wondering if I had hit the pheasant or the rabbit hole, or both of them together.

"Oh dear, I'm sorry," came a voice, rather deep and full of repentance. "I didn't see you there."

For a moment, I thought it was the pheasant that was addressing me. But then I regained my wits, and I realised neither the pheasant nor his rabbit hole was anywhere to be seen, and instead there was a strange man standing in front of me.

"Are you alright there?" the man asked me. He was somewhat tall, with fair hair and a kind, puzzled sort of a face. He looked down at me where I lay sprawling, and offered me a hand to help me up.

"Yes, I'm fine, I think," I told him, standing up and rubbing my head.

"Good, that's good, I am relieved," said the man. "I thought for a minute I'd hurt you. I was quite taken by surprise. I'm not used to seeing anyone so, well, *whole* as you down here. Mostly we just get the brick-a-brack, the leftover bits and pieces. The name's Rosewater, by the way," he added. He offered me his hand and I shook it.

"Pleased to meet you," I said. "And the fault was mine, I'm sure. I don't usually make a habit of jumping into people, but I'm actually on a quest that's going rather badly, and I suppose I let myself get worked up. What are you doing here, by the way?"

"Oh, I live here," said Rosewater, smiling in a friendly kind of a way. "Matter of fact, it's my realm, as it were. I sort of run things down here."

"My goodness, I didn't know!" I exclaimed. "I'm terribly sorry. I didn't realize that this place had a ruler, and if I did I certainly wouldn't have made a habit of bashing my head into him. Do I need to do any bowing or anything?"

"Tosh," he said, waving the offer away shyly. "I don't go in much for that sort of thing. No, we like to keep things informal down here, you know."

"I see," I said, "that's awfully progressive of you. But I didn't know the Land Below Stories needed a ruler! What sort of things do you do?"

"Oh, this and that," he said vaguely. "Point the Munchers in the right direction. Make sure things keep ticking over, that sort of thing. I'm sure I'm not as important as my brothers and sisters. They really do all the important work."

"Really?" I asked. "And what do they do?"

"We all look after different aspects of the operation, you see," explained Rosewater. "In fact, you will have met my younger brother. He meets just about everyone. Only, most people don't remember. It happens very early on, you see. Just before life starts, actually."

"What's the fellow look like?" I asked.

"Oh, pointy sort of a chap," said Rosewater. "Bit proud, but he's got a good heart, I'm sure of it. Name's Quince, though like I say, I'm sure you don't remember him."

"Can't say that I do," I said sadly.

"Never mind," said Rosewater, giving a little shrug. "It will all come out right, I'm sure."

He gave me a smile of such genuine hope that I found I was smiling, too.

"You know," I said, encouraged by Rosewater's optimism, "I do wish I knew where that pheasant had gone. Or where it had sprung from in the first place, come to that."

"You saw the Pheasant did you?" cried Rosewater. "My, that is a good omen!"

"Really?" I said. "You mean, it's been around before, has it?"

"Rather!" Rosewater exclaimed. "Always pops up when things are looking grim. It's sort of...well, it would sound silly if I said it."

"Oh, go on!" I pleaded. "I would like to get to the bottom of this. You see, I saw that bird before, some time ago. Just before I got embroiled in this blasted quest of mine."

Rosewater sighed.

"Very well then," he said. "The thing is, the Pheasant is...well, she's sort of...God."

That took me by surprise, I can tell you!

"God?" I asked, not quite comprehending.

"Yes, God," repeated Rosewater. He took a deep breath. "Look, it's like this. This place, the Land Below Stories, it's where all the fiddly bits of stories end up, when the tales are done, right? After the Epitaphs are finished with them, of course."

"Right," I agreed slowly.

"Good," Rosewater went on. "But you see, it's much more than a...well, a dumping ground. Take the Munchers, for instance. Well, all you think of them, I suspect, is that they are rather nasty little critters with sharp teeth and ferocious appetites that a clever person stays well away from, correct?"

I nodded my agreement.

"But that's only half of it, you see!" said Rosewater, earnestly. "You can't have an end without a beginning. And Munchers don't just *eat* things, if you get my drift..."

He waggled his eyebrows encouragingly. I looked him blankly.

"Oh, you know!" he said, frustrated. "They...well, they produce *manure*, you see!"

"Ah!" I exclaimed, understanding suddenly dawning. "So these Munchers...their, um, *waste* as it were...?"

"Yes!" said Rosewater, beaming at me. "That's the other half of their function! Extremely fertile stuff, their droppings! Most fantastically useful. In fact, I might go so far as to say that the whole Storystream would dry up without it. We sweep it up and ship it off, and the new stories keep ticking over nicely."

"How fascinating," I said. "But I don't understand how that makes a pheasant a god. Meaning no disrespect," I added hastily.

"Oh not at all," said Rosewater. "I was just coming to that. The thing is, you see, that a place can't be home to all that much raw *narrative*, all that raw *story* without becoming sort of charged up with it. You must remember, every particle of every story in the Storystream has been through here, most of them thousands and thousands of times. This place has been washed by the whole of the Storystream, for as far back as things go. And that means...well, it's as if it has a life of its own."

"You mean, this place is *alive?*" I asked.

"Oh, most certainly," agreed Rosewater. "I might even go so far as to say that sometimes it is even *aware*. For the most part, of course, it's alive in the way an old tree, say, is alive. Quiet and still; but full of power and dignity, too. But it's like...beneath the surface, it's like there's something bubbling and boiling, ticking gamely away. And when it's needed, when it's for the good of everything...well, that force just sort of *manifests* itself."

There was silence for a moment.

"As a pheasant?" I asked, just to be clear.

"Oh, yes, as a pheasant," clarified Rosewater.

"I see," I said thoughtfully. Then I frowned. "Wait a minute," I added. "When I saw her the first time...well, that wasn't down here. That was..." I waved a hand vaguely. "Oh, far off and away and further far again. Somewhere else. Is that...well, *normal?*"

Rosewater shrugged.

"Can be," he said. "Perfectly possible, as long as the books balance. What happened exactly?"

"I was looking for some food," I said slowly. "I had to find some for a friend of mine, otherwise he was going to eat me. It's a long sort of a story. Anyway, I found a fish, but that proved to be no good. Then I found a pig, and he wasn't very helpful, either. And then, when I was giving up hope, I found this pheasant...I'm sorry, this Pheasant...and I was just about to grab her, when...well, I had a change of heart as it were. There was a sort of...a sort of *trustfulness* in her that meant I couldn't very well eat her. I just couldn't." I shrugged. "And things worked out not so badly, as it happened, and my friend didn't eat me, and now I'm helping him. He's trying to find his true love, it's terribly romantic," I added.

"Well that makes things much simpler!" said Rosewater heartily. "I must say, she has been taking rather an interest in you, hasn't she? It's perfectly simple," he went on, when I continued to stare blankly at him. "The law of threes, see? One of the strongest narrative forces in the Universe. Three beautiful daughters, three pots of porridge, three rings. You name it, three has the market cornered. Two and four just don't get a look in. Our God here must have seen you were struggling for a three, and jumped up into your story to fill the gap, help things turn out right."

"Oh I see," I said, seeing the light. "Sort of *Deus ex Phasianus*"

"Yes, exactly," beamed Rosewater. "Easy enough to manage as long as the conservation of narrative momentum is obeyed. She only brought a few particles of story back with her, and she only left a sentence or two of it there, so the books balance, you see? She must have just wanted to give you a little nudge in the right direction."

He grinned at me, and I couldn't help but smile back. It all seemed so simple, when he laid it out.

"But tell me something," I said. "*Why* do you think she was so keen on setting me in the right direction? And why do you think I saw her again now, just before I met you?"

"Ah," said Rosewater, and his face darkened suddenly. "I was hoping we might not have to come to that. The truth is, I'm rather ashamed of myself. I think I've been a party to something rather foolish, actually. I'm afraid I've...well, I've let something loose that was better kept wrapped up. Something quite nasty."

I looked at him in confusion.

"Why does that follow from me seeing the Pheasant again?" I asked.

"She was trying to do it again, don't you see?" said Rosewater. "She was trying to nudge you towards me; so I could help you, I imagine.

Things must be looking bad if she's up and about and doing actual *manifestations*."

He looked worried for a moment, then shook his head, as if clearing the shadows away.

"But it can't be helped," he said, forcing himself to smile again. "If she's appearing to you, then you must be capable of doing something good, so things can't be all that hopeless, not yet. And," he added, a twinkle suddenly flashing in his eye, "I think I have worked out what it is you're questing for down here."

"Really?" I said, surprised.

"Yes, I think so," Rosewater went on quietly. "It's not this is it, by any chance?"

And he held up a small golden amulet, fastened to a simple silver chain.

"My God!" I exclaimed. "That is to say, my Pheasant! It can't be...and yet, I do believe it is..."

He held the beautiful thing out to me. I hesitated. "Go on!" he urged me, and so I leant forward and took a hold.

It really was splendid, absolutely fine and perfect in construction, lovely; and yet humble, somehow, not over-large or covered in garish embellishments. In fact it looked exactly as my friend had described it: the Amulet of the Spheres, which had been stolen from him a long time ago.

Rosewater was beaming at me.

"It really is what you were after, isn't it?" he asked happily. "You know, I did wonder when I first met you. I've been waiting for some time for you to turn up. Or rather, I think I have. Time's always been a bit gloopy around these parts, but it's got much more confusing recently. In fact, I hear from my brother that someone's gone and turned the Wheel. I mean, can you imagine?"

"Not really, no," I told him.

"Well, not to worry," he said, shrugging. "I'm sure things will come right in the end. And I suppose time never was what it once was, if you see what I mean. And now it's only more of the same."

I looked one last time at the sparkling yellow gold of the amulet, then gave a sigh and tucked it safely away in a pocket.

"I'm awfully sorry to be so rude, but I rather think I should be getting on my way now," I told him.

"Oh, must you?" asked Rosewater, looking crestfallen. "I had a sort of hope that you might fancy sticking around for a bit. It's terribly nice to have some company at last. I mean, the Munchers are all very good, but they're not exactly what you might call brilliant conversationalists."

"I wish I could," I told him with real feeling, "but the thing is, you see, I've got this quest thing to be getting on with. I'm quite sure it would be lovely to stay, but, well, this business feels *important*."

"No, no, I quite understand," said Rosewater firmly. He sighed. Then, "After all," he added, brightening, "it does seem that the Pheasant has taken quite a shine to you. I think that's rather encouraging."

"Yes, I suppose so," I said. It was so easy to feel confident around Rosewater. He really was a charming fellow. He began to walk me back the way I had come. I imagined how relieved my friends would look when I showed them what I had found. Soon we would be on our way again.

A thought suddenly occurred to me.

"You know," I asked Rosewater slowly, "I would be most interested to know how you came to have a hold of this amulet. For that matter, I'd like to know how it was you were expecting me, too."

Rosewater stopped walking and let out a long sigh. He looked deflated.

"I suppose you were bound to ask that," he said sadly. "I'd hoped that sooner or later you'd turn up and take the amulet, and I could just forget it all. But that's selfish of me, isn't it? No, you're quite right to ask."

He was silent for a moment, marshaling his thoughts.

"Let me tell you the story of how this amulet came to me," he said. "I was just trying to help someone out of a sticky spot, you see. And then again, it wasn't *me* who actually undid it...But I mustn't make excuses. What's done is done, and all we can do is have faith in ourselves. And in the Pheasant, of course. Now where was I? Oh, yes! I was telling you a story. It's called

✺ 49 ✺

THE STRANGER IN THE BUBBLE

~

This is a place of scraps, as you know. Most of the things that end up down here are sodden and used up, and its quite right that they should be gobbled up by the Munchers. Still, every now and then something…well, a little *odd* will find its way down here, something not quite used-up, something that still seems as if it has the shadow of a story to tell.

For instance, I once came across a whole raft of Saturdays that had been lopped off a story that had decided to shorten its weekends. They were perfectly good Saturdays, hardly even been used at all. I scooped them up before the Munchers could get to them, and kept them stored away to hand out to people who really *needed* them. They made wonderful stocking-fillers. Another time I found a really very talented middle third of a story sulking down here because its beginning and its end couldn't seem to get along. They just weren't committed to making things work, and unfortunately it was the middle that was suffering. I saved that poor creature from the Munchers, too. It was right on the verge of giving up, but I convinced it that it was a perfectly good story in its own right - between you and me, the beginning was somewhat whimsical and the ending was entirely contrived - and it decided to set out on its own, and to hell with the others. And good for it, that's what I say!

I see that you're wondering where your amulet comes in. Don't worry, I'm getting to that!

You see, I take rather an interest in the odder things that wash up. I feel as if it's my duty to, well, to protect them from the Munchers. After all, I am the caretaker here, more or less; and that means it's my duty to take *care* of things.

Most of the odd things that come down here really do need protecting. They are soft and delicate, like those Saturdays I was telling you about. (I'm not sure if you've noticed, but Saturdays really are one of the most delicate things in the Universe. You only have to hold them wrong and *Pop!* They've crumbled away to nothing, and all you've got left is a nasty taste in your mouth and a pile of ironing to do before Monday). Where was I? Oh, yes! Most of these odds and ends are highly fragile, and need protecting from the Munchers.

So you can imagine my surprise when I found a strange little twisty scrap of a story that seemed to be quite impervious to their greedy little mouths. In fact, I was alerted to its presence by the trail of broken teeth. When I got near, I saw that this little black twist of story was surrounded on all sides by hundreds and hundreds of Munchers. They were growling at it suspiciously, sniffing around the edges, trying to find a weak spot.

But it didn't seem that there *was* a weak spot. The twisted little thing seemed to be entirely impregnable. I stood and watched in growing fascination as they tried and tried again...and failed time after time.

And the funny thing was, the longer I stayed there, the more I stared at that little dark scrap, and the more the Munchers failed to break it open, the more I thought: *good*.

I don't know why I should have thought that. After all, I had no evidence that this little scrap of story was bad in any way. I just had the feeling, somewhere deep down inside, that it was no-good, somehow. That whatever it was would be better left tangled up inside.

After a little while, the Munchers began to get bored, and started wandering off to look for easier pickings. When they had gone, I came closer to the strange thing and peered at it.

It was very difficult to describe. It was small and dark and knotty, all tangled up and straining very tight. It also gave one the curious sensation that it was much bigger than the space it occupied, if you see what I mean. It seemed *heavy*. And most curious of all, there was a feeling of...of *sharpness*. I don't know how else to explain it. I peered into that strange thing, and something keen looked back.

Very well, I said to myself, *you look as if you were meant to stay hidden. And hidden I shall keep you.*

So I scooped the twisted thing up, and hid it away somewhere quite deep and far off, somewhere no one would stumble on it; and then I went on about my business, and I completely forgot about the matter.

Now time has gone gloopy, as I mentioned before, and it's exceedingly difficult to judge, but it seems to me that at least thirty or forty lifetimes must have gone by before the next interesting thing washed up. And the funny thing about this thing was this it wasn't an *it*, it was a *he*.

I was going about my business when I suddenly realised I hadn't seen a Muncher for quite some time. Not a single one. This was frightfully unusual, you understand. Normally, a fellow can hardly walk without kicking a Muncher. All you have to do is stand still for a moment, and you'll have three or four dozen of them clinging on to your legs by their teeth.

"How extraordinary!" I said to myself, and began casting about for them.

At last, I thought I spied something odd far off in the distance. It looked like a mountain, which was most unusual, because any geological features that make their way down here are almost instantly set upon and devoured; and as you will have noticed, this place is almost completely flat as a result.

"Aha!" I said. "It looks like something's afoot!"

And I set off towards this mountain as fast as I could go.

But when I got closer to this mountain, I realised it was a very funny sort of a mountain. Its sides were shimmering, somehow, moving and cascading and reforming. And as I squinted and moved closer and peered and tried to make sense of it...

...I suddenly realised what I was seeing.

It wasn't a mountain, not in the usual sense.

It was the Munchers. All the Munchers. Every Muncher from this place had congregated, had gone piling into one another, stacking one on the next until they formed this heaving, living mound of furry flesh. It was *huge*.

I didn't like the look of this at all. After all, the Munchers weren't doing their job, and already the detritus was beginning to pile up. I was becoming surrounded by huge drifts and piles of worthless story junk. It was getting very close and crowded; and the worst thing was, I knew that if the Munchers had stopped munching, that would mean they had stopped making manure, as well. Without manure to form the bedrock of new stories, the whole Storystream could dry up! Oh, it didn't bear thinking about!

I rushed over to the mountain of Munchers as quick as I could, and tried to get their attention.

"I say!" I shouted. "Come on now, you must stop this nonsense at once!"

At the sound of my voice, the Munchers all went very still - they know who's the boss, you see - and looked rather sheepish.

"Come on, down you come!" I commanded. They looked at me reproachfully.

My, I thought, *there really must be something quite delicious down there, for them to be in such an excitable mood!*

"Don't make me come and get you," I said sternly, and the last of their resistance crumbled.

With a great reluctant sigh, the mountain collapsed in on itself; all at once, the air was filled with Munchers, scurrying outwards and away. It took a while, but at last they were all gone. I walked towards the place where they were all piled up, and what do you think I found?

It was a man. Or rather, it was something that *looked* like a man.

He had been covered by such a weight of Munchers, and he looked frightfully crumpled. I hurried over to him and helped him up.

"I'm terribly sorry!" I said, giving his back a good patting, trying to get the rumples out of his jacket. "Are you alright? You must be awfully squashed."

The man waved a hand at me vaguely and tried to catch his breath.

"Don't worry about me," he said at last. "I'm quite alright. They were just being affectionate, I'm sure."

"But you're a marvel, my dear fellow!" I told him. "I was quite sure I'd find nothing under that mound of Munchers but some scraps of flesh and a pile of bone dust! Tell me, how did you keep them off?"

But the man looked rather unhappy at that, and I felt sure I must have upset him.

"I'm sorry," I said quickly. "That was most insensitive of me. You've been through quite an ordeal. You've probably been quite traumatised." I thought about this for a moment. "Maybe you'd like to try a Primal Scream? I hear they are terribly good for clearing out the system."

He shook his head sadly.

"You don't understand, I'm afraid," he said after a pause. "You see, I *wanted* them to get me. I *need* them, in fact. The problem is, I locked myself up far too tight; and now, nothing can get in or out, and I'm filling up with rubbish. It's killing me," he added, with feeling.

"Really?" I said. "Are you sure you won't try a Primal Scream? Sounds like just the thing."

"Oh, no, that wouldn't do me any good," said the man sadly. "My problem's not emotional, it's theological. I'm Philip, by the way."

"Pleased to meet you, Philip," I said. "My name's Rosewater. Do you mind if I ask what manner of man you are?"

"Oh, I'm a...um, well, I'm a sort of god, I suppose." He said it haltingly, as if he were rather embarrassed about the whole business.

The moment he said it, I saw that it was true. I blinked a few times, and looked at him more closely. His image swam in front of me, and then I realised what I was looking at. His body wasn't a body, not in the usual sense. It was a *story*. Or rather, it was lots of stories, hundreds and hundreds of stories, all tucked in nice and tight, and pulled together in such a way as to give the impression of a roughly man-shaped creature.

"Ah!" I said, understanding dawning. "Philip, you say? I've heard of you! Yes, my brother Quince told me all about you! You know, he was really rather proud. Said you were the best day's work he'd accomplished in the last aeon or so; which, considering he exists in a place pretty much outside of time, is really saying something."

Philip tilted his head at me.

"You're Quince's brother?" he said, startled. "I imagined you'd be more...well, more sort of *pointy*, I suppose."

"Oh, we aren't much alike," I said. "Handle different ends of the system, as it were. Different skill sets required. Anyway, I'm sure you don't want to hear about my boring family. Can I do anything to help you?"

Philip sighed and looked sad again.

"I don't suppose it's any good," he said morosely. "You know, I really was sure I'd found the answer. One of my stories told me about this place, you see. That's how I heard about these wonderful little Munchers of yours. I thought if I could, well, sort of *import* a few of them, then maybe I could clear all the used up gunk out of my systems, and put some vim back into my stories. They're all getting a bit stale and used up, you see; but before anything new can happen, I need to be able to get rid of the old. At least, that's how I understand it, though I am only a very simple god."

"No, that makes perfect sense!" I told him. "And that sounds like a first-class idea. Quite brilliant. Yes, take a few Munchers with you. I won't miss a few, there are so many of them; and they breed like rabbits, as long as there's the fodder to support them."

"But that's the problem, don't you see!" said Philip. "They *can't* get in! They can smell all the old stories rotting inside of me. I suppose it must seem quite delicious to them. But I've...I've sealed myself too tight, like I say. I can't get them in."

He stared at me imploringly. You must understand, he was such a pitiful sight. He was so close to his goal, to the thing he needed to live...and yet he could not get at it. Oh, it was heartbreaking! I wanted more than anything in the world to help him.

But of course, I knew where something sharp was. I had never seen evidence of this, but in my heart I knew it was true.

"You know," I said carefully, "I don't want to get your hopes up, but now that I think about it, I wonder if I know of something that might help."

Quickly, I told my new friend about the strange twist of story that had been washed up, and of the unbearable sense of sharpness that had seemed to emanate from within.

"What?" sniffed Philip, a faint hope sparking in his eyes. "You think you might...you might be able to, to *open me up*, as it were? Open me up and let the Munchers in?"

Now as soon as he said it, I knew deep down that I was on to something rotten. I just understood it, in my boots and in my roots, as the saying goes. But you see, I had mentioned the thing now, I had kindled his hope; and I couldn't take the words back, I just couldn't let him down.

"Yes," I said, more guarded. "In a manner of speaking. But listen, even if I'm right, there must be a maintenance of balance, you understand. If you take some Munchers with you, you'll have to leave something of yours behind in return. Maybe it's best that we forgot the whole thing."

But Philip wouldn't hear a word against the plan, now that I had suggested it; and he was so desperate with hope, that at last I relented, and I took him down to where I had hidden the strange little twist of story.

When he saw it, I saw by his face that he was having doubts. He could feel it too, you see: that *sharpness*, that awful, tearing *sharpness*. It was like looking into a razor blade; you felt as if your mind was being sliced apart, with cuts so sharp and subtle that there was no pain, just an ice-cold feeling of separation.

Slowly, hesitatingly, Philip moved closer. At last he was almost touching the dark twist of story. A strange broken sort of light pulsed from within; and a sound came, too, almost like someone screaming, only it was so faint as to be less than a whisper.

I stayed away. I wanted no further part in this than I had already taken.

"I...I can hear a man," said Philip at last, haltingly, like someone waking out of a dream. "He's trapped. He wants to be set free. And...I can sense.I ..can *feel* that it can help me..."

Philip looked at me then for the longest time. I could feel him asking me, appealing to me to understand. He knew as well as I did, you see. Better, probably.

We both knew quite well that whatever was locked up in that twist of story was deadly. It was poisoned, and not to be trusted.

And yet Philip was dying. He was dying, and this little withered story could help...we *knew* it could...that sharpness, that terrible sharpness; you could feel it cutting into you as soon as you looked at the thing.

I closed my eyes, and nodded, once. I had to let him, you see. I had to let him try.

Philip sighed; and whether it was relief or regret in that sigh, I couldn't tell for sure.

Then he leaned his head closer to that wretched gnarl of story, leaned closer and closer until at last his brow was touching the dark border of the thing; and then he closed his eyes and began to speak. He whispered to the tale, very low and quiet; but I heard him. I couldn't help but hear.

"I will tell you a story," he said softly. "It's a story that I dredge from within the depths of me, from the place between stories, where all things meet; and it is called

50

THE SPELL OF UNBINDING

~

A white place there was,
Wide and wondrous
Hollow and hidden,
And hard to find.

A dark man dwelt there,
Deceived and devious,
Tricked into turning
Tales ever and again

A blade he bore,
Of blistering brightness,
Keen beyond ken,
It could cut through all.

Yet wrapped up in words,

His will would not wean him,
Sealed in a story,
Ensorcelling his sword.

Reaching for freedom,
He is foiled forever,
Searching success-less...

...UNLESS *I* SAVE HIM.

<pause>
Waves beat and winds howl,
And hear the deep of mountains growl,
Sea to grind and rocks to gnash,
And feel the earth beneath me crash,
I call it all to me, to me!
And with it set the bound thing free!
Now his prison is made to fade.
I'll tell you of

51

THE TRICK UNMADE

~

The boys fled forever, and the dark man chased after. He could not remember for how long he had chased them, not really. Time had lost its meaning, and all that existed for him was the endless succession of departing backs and the shards of seashells that bit into his face, and the rip//

//of the storywall as it fell once more to his blade.

But the cut//

//would only lead him back to the seashell again, back to the white, eternal nothing of the land between stories, back to the chase, back to the yearning and straining and failing.

Until...

The dark man began to sense that there was something outside of these things. The feeling came upon him gradually, and at first he was hardly aware of it at all. But it grew and it grew, until at last he only went through the endless motions of the chase and the cut//

//and the seashell and the chase and the//

//cut and so on because, it seemed, that was what he had always done, and what he was always meant to do, for now until time itself was done with. And it was at that moment, that precise moment when he realised with a sickening lurch of his belly that there was a world *outside* of the chase, it was at that moment that he understood with sudden, piercing clarity that he had been put under an enchantment, and that he had been tricked, and that he was lost

He stopped running. The footsteps of the departing boys faded into the deep distance. It did not matter.

He peered into the whiteness, squinting his eyes, trying to make sense of that element outside of himself which had prompted him out of his age-long bewitchment.

He stared out, and he saw a man...at least, it looked to be a man. He was very vague, very far off and faint... but even from such a distance and through thick cloud, as it were, the dark man could feel that there was something strange about him, something different.

It's not a man, he realised. *It is a body made up of stories. Hundreds and hundreds of stories. And it is peering in at me. And it wants something.*

And at that moment, with the thought of the word, "*Story,*" which his enchantment had not let him think for so long, with the thought of that hideous word, all his bitter memories and all his hateful dreams and the whole twisted wreck of his life came slamming into him, and he remembered who he was, and where he was, and what it was he sought.

He held his blade up to his face. In the strange, hallucinatory brightness of the land between stories, he watched the shadows dance and shimmer along his sword of faery-iron. It was sharp, oh it was *so* sharp. And yet it could not cut him free, not of this trap...

The dark man lowered the blade. He crept closer to the veil behind which he could sense the story-man move. He could feel the life of the creature, pulsing and strange behind, as it seemed, a curtain of mist.

The creature was speaking to him, trying to tell him something.

The dark man listened. At last, he understood.

"Yes," he said, and the world shook beneath his feet.

He sat down calmly on the white nothingness of the ground. He laid his sword carefully on his crossed legs, closed his eyes, opened them, then began.

"I will tell you a *story*," he said, though the word tasted vile, and twisted in his mouth. He spat, and went on. "I don't like to, but it seems that this one cannot help but be told. And before long, it will all be undone, so it does not matter. It is called

52

THE CANTRIP OF REFLECTION

∽

The story-god, Philip, listened to the dark man spin his words behind the veil of whiteness, and he listened closely and leant forward and he said, "I will tell you a story, and it is called

53

THE CANTRIP OF REFLECTION

~

And the dark man spoke the words and the man who was stories spoke the words and the words pinched on the veil bending it pincering it clasping it between the awful weight of words and breaking the veil was breaking and it was mirrored in the

⚜ 54 ⚜

THE CANTRIP OF REFLECTION

~

Until with the sound of every mirror that ever was shattering and with a rush of airs mingling and with a tingle in the blood as their hearts syncopated the two figures found that their words had run together until neither could now tell who was speaking and who was listening and who was telling the story at all, at all, and the barrier between them had inverted - as they had known that it would - and the dark man stared out through the wall/skin of the god of stories and his hand tightened on the hilt of his sword and he smiled, and they both stopped speaking.

Then, speaking in a muffled voice, a figure from the world beyond the skin of the story god began to tell a story, and it was called

✸ 55 ✸

THE STRANGER IN THE BUBBLE
(REPRISE)

~

P hilip stopped speaking, and the awful double voice that had
been issuing from his mouth ceased.He opened his eyes and
looked to the dark twist of story he had been touching; but
when I followed his gaze, I saw that it had changed. The darkness had
fled away, and the twist was turning in on itself, faster and faster, until
it was a colourless wisp of nothing without weight or substance; and a
moment later it was less; and still a moment later it was gone.

But still I did not understand. I looked at Philip in surprise - I was
even smiling, I think, like a fool, because I felt such relief that the dark
gnarl of story had vanished. But before I could say anything, there was
a sound. It was strange, dreadful. It came from everywhere and
nowhere, a low, menacing thrum, like something heavy vibrating. Then
a light sliced suddenly on Philip's body. It broke his skin, and purple
darkness leeched out and//

//a blade shot from his body, and following the blade was a man, tall
and dark, stepping from within Philip himself. He had a grim face and
a strange light in his eyes.

He looked at me. Then he smiled a crooked smile.

"This place, I like," he said. "It's full of the rotting ends of stories. I can understand that. I can appreciate that. For this reason, I will leave it to crumble last."

Then he stepped clear of Philip, and the cut he had made curled in on itself, quite healing away until it would have been nothing; but before it had finished healing, the dark man reached out and he clasped Philip's hand, and pushed two fingers inside the hole so that it did not seal up completely.

"As I promised," the dark man whispered. "Now the terms of our agreement are fulfilled. I thank you for my freedom."

Philip nodded, but he would not meet the dark man's eye. But the dark man, for his part, was no longer looking at either us. He reached into a pocket and he pulled out a map. I saw it quite clearly. It was a strange sort of map, marked with islands and a great sea and an awful lot of places I did not know. But in the centre of the map was marked something I *did* know about, because all of us who know a little of the workings of the worlds know of the room at the centre, and of the wheel; and it was only then that I understood exactly how foolish I had been to play any part in the release of the man who had been trapped in that dark twist of story.

He looked up from the map and he smiled.

"I will send you a great many more scraps for your little creatures before I am done," he said. Then he turned, and in one fluid motion he lifted his sword, and swung it above him, and with a horrible //

//*shriek* of rending words, he was leaping through the hole he had cut, and he was gone from the Land Below Stories, and Philip and I were alone.

We were silent for a very long time.

"Well," I said at last, trying to make us feel better. "He seemed like a nice sort of fellow."

Philip looked at me, very pale and shamed. Then he laughed suddenly.

"At least he liked your realm," he said, smiling. "I got the distinct impression he didn't care for me at all."

"Why ever not?" I asked. "You're quite one of the most charming collection of stories I've every had the fortune to meet."

"I don't think that man cared much for stories," said Philip. Then he sighed. "But he did do what I asked." He looked down to where his fingers were sticking into his body, keeping the cut open. "Listen," he went on, "I think it will work now. I think I can take some Munchers into myself. If you don't mind, that is?"

I shook myself, returning to the problem of the moment. After all, what use was it worrying about the dark man now? The damage was done and the man was gone. All I could do was keep my faith in the Pheasant, and hope that things would work out for the best.

"Of course I don't mind!" I told him. "But the thing is, there has to be a balance, like I said. There is always an accounting. If you take away a gaggle of Munchers, well, you'll have to leave a bit of yourself behind."

"Aha," said Philip, and there was a twinkle in his eye again, "I had been expecting that. In fact, I had been told as much in a story. One of my subjects - the one who mentioned this place to me - he told me that I would have to leave something behind in exchange for the Munchers. And he told me just what to leave, too. He told me to give you...this."

And he pulled the hole in himself a little wider, so that he could reach in with his other hand. When it came out, it was holding a rather lovely looking golden amulet on a silver chain.

"Apparently, this subject of mine stole it from a pig," said Philip. "The pig was rather proud. It seems he was so busy jabbering away to one of my people, he didn't notice when another one crept up and relieved him of this. I hear it came from the collection of a certain doe-eyed goblin maid that had been swept up in some kind of awful cataclysm, though quite why the pig had it is anyone's guest. Anyway, I was told that I should give it up in balance for the Munchers, and that if I did so, it would find its way back to the one who was meant to have it."

So I took the amulet and I tucked it away; and then I rounded up a herd of Munchers, and I marched them towards Philip, and Philip pulled the hole in his body wide enough so they could all scurry inside. And once they were all in, he pulled out his fingers, and there was a loud, solid *POP*, and the hole was completely gone and he was as sealed shut as ever he had been.

Almost at once, a change came over him. He closed his eyes, and when he opened them again, there was a look of peace there.

"It's working!" he said. "I can feel it! I feel quite unblocked. Now I know what a plumber feels like when he gives the pipes a good clean and gets them working again!"

Philip beamed at me, eyes as bright as stars. I had to admit, he looked much healthier.

Then a troubled look came across his face, and I knew he was thinking about the dark thing that he had let loose, and of the damage that it might do.

But I smiled at him and slapped him on the shoulder.

"Have faith!" I said, trying to make my voice cheery. "The Pheasant will make everything right in the end. You'll see."

He looked at me, confused; but his spirit seemed to lift a little.

"Thank you so much for your help," he told me. "And be sure to keep that amulet safe; I'm certain someone will be a-wanting it soon enough."

Then he gave me a sort of salute, and he bowed low, and kept on going until he fell right over, then he tumbled down into his own shadow and *Puff!* He was gone. Such is the way of gods, even humble ones.

But I think he was right: someone did come a-wanting that amulet soon enough. And now that I've told about the dark thing that was released from here, I do wonder if your quest will take a different path. If not, perhaps everything will fail.

Ah, but I am forgetting! One other thing happened. Maybe it's linked, and maybe it's just chance. I'll let you be the judge of that. But it's a strange story to tell, and stranger still because I fancy you are in it!

It happened only a little while after Philip disappeared. I was thinking that finally I would get some peace, that I'd had quite enough excitement for one aeon. But it seems that I was wrong. I had just started to walk away from the place where Philip had departed, when I heard a most awful wailing. It sounded like ten bags of cats being hit by ten heavy sticks. Oh, it was awful!

I rushed off in the direction of the screaming, and what do you think I found?

It was a man, rather stout in the stomach, and with an exceedingly red nose. He was wielding a heavy stick, and flailing it wildly around him, trying to keep an encircling ring of Munchers at bay. They snapped and drooled at him, and occasionally one dared to close the gap, to which the man responded with a cry and a swoop of his stick. So far he was keeping them back, but they were drooling all right, and I had no doubt that he would tire soon.

"Hoy there!" I called, and at my voice the Munchers stopped their gnashing, and they all drew back a pace, though they kept staring hungrily at the fat man.

"My saviour!" cried the fat man joyously. "Oh, my most kind bene-factor! Spare me from these sharp teeth, my good sir, for I was made to eat and drink and be merry, and to be a meal myself goes quite against my nature!"

Now usually, most of the bits and pieces that end up down here in my realm are quite munched up already by the time they get here, and whole creatures that are capable of understanding the sharpness of the Muncher's teeth and protesting against them are quite rare. Still, it does happen occasionally, and I'm afraid in such circum-stances one has to have a hard heart, else the balance might be quite upset.

So I looked sternly - though not unkindly - at the portly man, and, "Chin up!" I told him. "It's all part of the natural cycle, my fine fellow. Now why not be a sport, and put down your stick, there's a good chap. The teeth are very sharp, and you won't feel a thing, I promise. Before you know it, your particles will be fertilising the next generation of stories; who knows? Maybe you'll come back as a daffodil or an eagle or something else agreeable."

"Begging your pardon, but I'd much rather look at a flower than be one," said the portly man, most resolutely not putting down his stick. "And *no pain* is easy enough to promise, but those teeth look awfully sharp and my flesh is rather soft and tender. Is there no way I can entreat you to let me go? I am rather fond of my body, heavy and soft though it is."

I sighed deeply, for I am not a cruel person, and it is not in my nature to deny the entreaties of another being who is in pain, even if that person should rightly be fodder.

"Very well," I said at last. "It seems you are quite set on keeping your life, red nose and all; why not tell us a story? If it is palatable enough, perhaps the Munchers will be distracted into eating up what you tell, and they will leave you alone."

"That's all I have to do?" exclaimed the portly man. "Just tell you a tale, and I'm free to go? Well, I wish I'd known that earlier! Very well, I'll tell you how I got here. I was just walking along by the river, minding my own business, enjoying a rather fine bottle of wine and my own company. The wine was rather good - I do enjoy a bottle or three, I'll admit it - so good that I really didn't have the energy to do anything but enjoy the walk. Oh, people always interrupt someone who is set on enjoying their own company, let me tell you! Why, I had only just got stuck into the second bottle, when this great big blue fish started yelling at me - wanted me to help it into a puddle or out of the stream, some such nonsense! I mean - as if I had the time or inclination to go helping any old fish I see! The cheek! Anyway, I had only gone on a little way from the fish when I collapsed down by a tree. Before long, someone else came along, some fancy prince or other, and I thought to myself, 'Aha! Let this one deal with old fishy guts there! This is a problem above my pay-grade!' And I lay myself down and dozed.

"But I had hardly closed my eyes when I heard an almighty SPLASH, and a few moments later I was given to understand that the young man had fallen into the water and was swimming away with the fish. 'Aha,' I thought to myself, 'now that that blasted fish has gone, perhaps I'll get some rest!' But not long had passed at all before I heard an exclamation and a kerfuffle, and I peered out from my spot under my tree, and I saw that some silly Monk was making an awful to-do. He was ransacking the prince's things you see, going through his travel-pouches, and pulling out all manner of fruits and meats and other good things to eat. And him a holy man, too! I tell you, the whole thing made me sick, so I curled up and tried my best to ignore it and go back to sleep.

"After not too long, the monk had got what he was after, I imagine, for I heard him stumbling and bumbling away, and it sounded like he was moving under a great weight of ill-gotten goods. But at last everything was good and still and silent. So I settled down to rest.

"But did I get any? Of course I didn't! Not much more time passed before something very strange and dreadful happened. The sun went dark. It was exactly as if a heavy raincloud had passed in front of it; but the sky was perfect blue. I looked about me. I couldn't understand it. Darker, darker, darker grew the day, until at last the sun was all but extinguished; and then it came.

"Oh, it makes me shudder to think of the thing! But I will tell you about it, if it will keep these old bones safe beneath this flesh. It was huge. It was so vast, it blotted out half the sky, so big that I fancied I only caught glimpses of it here and there. A tooth, a claw, a weave of muscle as tall as a mountain. It wheeled and wove about me. It gobbled up the sky and it ate up the sun. It snatched and sniffed and tore at the earth, until there were vast holes everywhere. I was hiding in the tree at this point, cowering, praying it would not see me, wondering at where such a colossal beast could have kept itself hidden until just this moment.

"And then it was above me. The teeth gaped wide, and beyond that, a vast blackness, so deep and empty that I knew nothing could survive if once it fell within those maws. So I leapt. I jumped from my tree, and such a leap has never been seen before, for it had the stuff of terror in it, and with that leap I cleared the hill and landed in the middle of the river. And not a moment too soon, for down those huge jaws came and snapped shut on the tree, and all that remained were a few leaves and a branch or two.

"But me, I was in the river. And it did not take me long to realise that the river was flowing faster than it ought to, and at first I thought this was a good thing, for it was dragging me further away from those huge teeth, and faster than I could possibly run. But then the drag of the river became a torrent, and the torrent became a rush, and the rush was something completely unconquerable, utterly hungry and impossible to resist. And I saw a great waterfall opening up in front of me, and a gaping hole in the landscape. And before I could say, '*Gin and tonic*', I was carried to the edge of it in the rush of water, and toppled over the edge.

"I went spinning into the darkness. The water fell with me, and some grass and rocks and leaves and other things fell with me, and above me I saw the dissolving world being swallowed up by that huge, awful something that I cannot put a name to.

"I fell through the darkness for a long, long time. For an eternity, it seemed, and there was nothing, nothing in the world except for me and the few scraps that fell with me. Until... Something loomed below me. It was a great grey flat something, huge and indistinct. And, as it transpired to my great good fortune, a very *soft* something. It was here. I landed here, amid these cloudy puffs of indistinct nothing. And around me rained the other scraps that had fallen with me from the river, some water and leaves and a branch or two.

"But no sooner had I stopped to take stock of my new situation, and to thank my lucky stars that those great teeth appeared to have been left far behind, than a new set of teeth appeared! Or should I say, several new sets. They surrounded me and set upon the scraps of my world that had fallen with me; and in a few moments they were all devoured, and all that remained was myself, and this rather stout stick, of which, as you can now understand, I am rather fond."

He looked at me hopefully and licked his lips. He glanced at the Munchers. They were still keeping their distance. A few had even plucked half-heartedly at the words he spoke as they tumbled out of his mouth. But it was a story they had heard already, you see, in a manner of speaking, and it was not much good to them.

"You'll have to do better than that, I'm afraid!" I told the old fellow. "Everything you've said so far is rather obvious. You had the great misfortune to fall asleep in a tale that had finished being told, and were stranded there when its Epitaph came to claim it! You must have fallen down between the cracks before you could be swallowed up by the beast, and that's how you came to be here, in the Land Beneath Stories. But, like I say, that much is obvious. No, you'll have to do better than that if you want to keep these Munchers at bay!"

The portly man looked at me desperately.

"Better than that?" he exclaimed. "But that's quite the most astounding thing that's ever happened to me! I am only a simple lad who grew up in a small village, and have never done any great deeds to speak of. If that story doesn't keep the little buggers from nibbling me away to nothing, then I don't know what will!"

"Exactly!" I agreed. "So come on, be a good sport and let them have a taste. It will all be over in a moment, I promise."

The Munchers sensed that time was running out. They began to draw in towards him. But he really was quite a desperate man.

"Wait!" he shouted, and swung his stick about wildly, so that the Munchers halted their advance again. "Wait! I...I have a story I can tell you! It's not something that happened to me. It's just an odd tale that the old woman who lived in our village used to tell us sometimes. We used to sit around the fire, tucked away while the grown men were out a-hunting. She used to tell us many tales, this woman. Ancient, she was. All wrinkled and wizened. Her skin hung loose on her, and her lips were always thin and dry. But her eyes were bright, and she was sharp, and she could see in an instant if you weren't paying her attention.

"She told us many tales, and I am sure I've forgotten more than I now remember. But one of them sticks with me, for she told it several times, and I think it was my favourite. I can still see her now when I close my eyes. She is sitting there, the best place by the fire saved for her, and us in a ring about her.

" 'Listen you close,' she tells us, 'for I shall tell you a story. It happened far off and away and further far again, and it is called

~

How The Shadow Fled And What Happened After

~

DO YOU KNOW, MY LITTLE HEATHENS, HOW LUCKY WE ALL ARE? YES, all of us, we're all so very lucky. Yes, even you, Samuel, with your bruised ribs that will teach you not to try and climb so high up rotten trees! We are all so very lucky, because all of us are whole. Not everyone in this world has such wonderful luck. Oh, not by a long way.

I will tell you something of the nature of things, though I would not expect such little heathens as you to understand, or even to remember, when the bell sounds and the hunt returns and the scent of roasting meat is on the air. Still, I will tell you, and maybe you will remember one day, and count yourself to be lucky.

We are creatures of two halves, you see. Our natures are meant to be divided, yet only by being joined, by being whole again, can we find peace. That is our burden, and that is our quest, and that is what makes this dull world interesting. You will find it everywhere you look. Night and day, male and female, sun and moon...the light half, and the shadow.

Our souls are meant to be whole, and we will find no peace if we are split. Nevertheless, sometimes it seems a wise thing to split a soul in two. Sometimes, it seems that we are splitting anyway, sometimes it seems that we are being pulled apart; and in such cases, why not help things along? That is how this girl justified it to herself, I am sure: she felt as if she were being torn in two anyway; that being the case, why not make it work in her favour?

Which girl, you ask? I'm coming to that.

Her name was Sebille, and she had fey blood in her, and she was beautiful and terrible and strange. She had fallen in love, you see. And such a falling it was; there was no coming back from such a plunge. And when it came to pass that her man had to go away, she felt as if she were being torn in two, that half her heart would go with him whether she willed it or not.

And so, she hatched a dangerous idea. A ring there was, very fair, very beautiful. It belonged to the family, and it was made of a most unusual metal. Not gold, Heather, no; it was much more beautiful than gold. It had been forged in earth and blood, and it glittered strangely in the darkness; and Sebille took this ring and she spoke will-words and danced alone in secret places...and it was done.

Her shadow was removed from her, and it danced away beneath the moonlight. But it was bound to her still, through the strange metal, through the ring. And when her man went to leave the next day, she gave him the ring - though she did not tell him what this meant - and when he departed, a part of her departed with him. Her shadow walked beside him, unnoticed and unknown. It hid in the darkness of the trees and in the black between the stars. It went along with him, and the other half of Sebille, the light half, was left behind.

Now it came to pass that her young man was at the centre of a very dark tale, and evil things befell him. I will not speak of them now; that is a tale for another day. But although the man did not die, he fought something foul, and he was injured and he was hurt...and the ring he wore was broken.

It is a terrible thing to tear the halves of your soul apart, a terrible magic to let them be distanced...but it is more terrible still when the thing that binds those halves together despite their sundering is broken. In the instant that the ring was broken, the last strands of power that held Sebille's soul in one piece were severed. The shadowed half was hurled away, far and further, through all the spheres of the world to somewhere dark and distant. And the light half? The light half cannot live without the shadow. It cannot live a whole life. And so the light half of her, the flesh and blood part of her, that fled, too, and neither half again could find rest nor comfort.

But of the light part I will not speak today. That is a story for another time.

Hush!

Why am I so silent, William? I am wondering where the shadow is today. I'll not lie to you, my little heathens: I do not know how this story ends. Who can say? Maybe you will meet the Shadow yet. But I can tell you more of how it began.

The Shadow had been a fey thing when it was bound; mischievous and daring, but full of humour, too, and not evil, no, don't ever think it. But without the light to balance the dark? Oh, it sunk low. Oh, it was dreadful.

It was cast into the night, and fled howling. Through world upon world it was hurled, spinning through the void without form or substance, a scream, a darkness, no more.

At last, the violence of the separation was spent. The Shadow was alone in the darkness. The stars were above, the grass was wet beneath; the world was empty and lonely, oh so lonely.

She picked herself up and moved through the night. She could move very fast; she could flit at the speed of darkness, which is always there before light, and there again once the light is gone. She screamed long and awful and silent; and though no one saw her, they felt her when she passed close, and they did shiver. At last she came to the town; and it was in the town she found old Tom.

Old Tom, he was a joker. There wasn't a laugh to be found in town that Tom didn't know about, and he was at the heart of most of them. He laughed and smiled, and wherever he went, people laughed and smiled with him. It was probably the laughter that drew the Shadow to old Tom. She missed the laughter so; and she was lonely.

Old Tom was walking home one night, chuckling to himself about something or other, and he came to an alley, and down it he walked, and that was a mistake for it was in the alley that the Shadow was waiting for him. He felt it watching him, he felt it cloying in the darkness. And his smile faded and his breath came ragged, and old Tom, he began to run. He was not laughing anymore, and the night seemed very thick. She watched him run, and she smiled. Old Tom wasn't outrunning her, oh no, she was fleet and fearsome. She watched him run...and when he had broken out of the darkness of the alley, at the very last moment, when he thought himself free, and his heart had begun to rise again...that was when she pounced. The Shadow sprang into the light, and she wrapped herself around poor old Tom. Down he went, a-clawing and a-shrieking, dry throttled shrieks that had no weight and went nowhere.

She drew him back into the darkness, and his fingernails left trails of blood on the cobbles as he tried to claw his way away from her. But she had him now. She was no longer alone. And old Tom? He was old Tom no longer.

A shadow is a thin thing. It is insubstantial, drawn and hollow, there is nothing in it you can make a grab at.

Tom would not come out during the daylight. He was too thin now for that, and the daylight would break him. No, he came out at night, and he crept and kept himself to the margins of places, peering out of corners and flickering beneath dim lamps, and he was hush and secret. His friends – and he had not a few of them – did not know what to make of his vanishing. At first, they thought it was one of his jokes, and they laughed uneasily at one another. But soon they began to mutter that he had been taken, that he was dead or worse. And after a while, they stopped talking about him altogether, and people made a point of avoiding any story that led to him, and the town had much less to smile about.

But then it was that Tom came back. They did not know him at first, for he had grown so thin. Shadows do not eat, you see, not when they can help it; and what was left of Tom months and years after the Shadow took him was held together less by flesh and sinew, and more by thought and darkness. He looked to be almost a skeleton, and that was what some called him: Skeleton Tom. Others called him Old Tom Gaunt. He dressed in fine dark clothes, and walked in the night, and there was dark music in him.

He was a joker still, for that was his nature: smiles and laughs and little tricks that ended in grins. But now the Shadow had him, and his jokes no longer led to smiles. He was dark and wild, and his jokes turned sour and cruel. People began to mutter, and the town would no longer suffer him. They drove him out, away from the lights and into the wilderness. He dwelt in caves and lived off slimy things snatched in the darkness. He came out ever and again to play his tricks. Travellers learnt to be wary of him, and to leave a ring of salt around their fires when they slept to keep him at bay. Still, not every one of them had been warned, and he made much mischief up and down the hills. He took delight in strange jokes that no-one would find funny but him, tricking husbands into leaving wives, and children into running off alone; when Skeleton Tom's laughter echoed in the trees, woodsmen barred their doors and built their fires high.

But there is always someone who thinks they are clever, and *yes* my eye is on you, young Daisy, with your proud smiles and your straight-standing ways! Be careful unless you come to a bad end! Now where was I? Ah, yes: there is always someone who does not know what is good for them, someone who will bring a challenge when it is nothing but folly. That was where young Bill came in. Young Bill was a brawler, and as big a man as ever you have seen. He had no mother and his father was taken by the bottle, and a fire burnt in him that only blood would quench. His nose had been broken nine times before he was thirteen, and it was broken after that times beyond number. He worked in the fields during the day, and he drank in the ale-houses when he was done with his work, and no landlord dared to bar him, but he was always bad for business.

If he didn't like the way you looked at him, or if he didn't like the way you spoke, or sometimes if he didn't like the way you *smelt* - then that was enough for young Bill. He would swing and smash, punch and pummel, break and gouge. The landlords in those parts ended not a few nights mopping the blood from the floor and picking up broken teeth.

Now it so happened that young Bill was a-walking in the night-time in the wilderness, for he had no friends in those parts, and no-one had warned him about the thing that came out when the moon cast long shadows across the land.

Young Bill had built himself a fire, and there he sat eating dried meat and rubbing his jaw, which was sore from a fight he had the night before. All at once, he noticed that he was not alone. A thin man, oh so painfully thin, was crouched down in the darkness. Bill could just make him out, his form dancing at the dimmest reaches of the red light cast by the flames.

"Hey!" called out Bill suspiciously. "Hey, you there! Old man! Stop skulking, or I'll give you something to skulk about! Come closer in, so I can see you proper!"

In the darkness, he saw a mouth open wide and a set of white teeth appear. Two eyes flashed at him, and the figure took a step forward, and there he was, Old Tom Gaunt, lifting his top hat and taking a bow below him. Bill marvelled at how old and thin the creature looked, and he took an instant dislike to him.

"Why were you lurking out there?" Bill demanded, leaning closer and narrowing his eyes. "Were you planning on stealing from me? Or were you meaning to cut my throat while I slept?"

But if the thin man was perturbed by the size of him or by his words, he gave no sign. Instead, he smiled broader than ever, and he fluttered his dark lashes and swayed his hips. "Oh, Bill, my darling boy," squeaked the figure in a high voice. "What on earth has become of you? What's become of the shape of that fine nose of yours? And, my, but you've become big while I've been gone!"

And Bill started at this and fell back, because it seemed to him that the voice of his lost mother had come from the lips of the strange, thin man; and she had been gone since he was a child.

"You're a devil!" he muttered, circling away from the figure. "Stay back from me, or I'll throw you in the fire and burn you all away!"

But quick as a flash, the thin man flitted through the shadows, darting around the fire and coming up upon Bill's other side, standing so close he could see the glistening wetness of his mouth as he licked his lips. Then the thin figure set to swaying in the moonlight, and it seemed to Bill that he smelt suddenly of whisky and cheap tobacco.

"What are you playing at, Bill my lad?" the figure barked at him gruffly. "Your mother would carry on at you now if she could see you! Have you anything to drink in that there pack of yours? A man has a thirst."

And at that, Bill scrambled back again the other way, for it seemed to him now that the voice was unmistakably his father's, though Bill had left the old man to drink himself to death years ago, and he couldn't say for sure now whether he had managed it yet or not.

"What dark witch-words are these?" hissed Bill. "I tell you, keep back you shadowed thing, or it's the flames for you!"

But the thin man hunched himself in a crouch on the far side of the fire; and if he feared the flames, he did not show it, for suddenly he was jumping up and springing like a frog, and before Bill knew what was happening, the creature had leapt through the fire and was standing in his very face, glaring at him with eyes that burnt with a mad mirth.

"Don't you look at me like that!" the thin man barked at him, and his voice was hoarse and full of violence. "Bill don't like no one staring at him, and he'll thump the lights out of anyone who crosses him wrong!"

And at this, young Bill fell back into the dust and landed sprawling beside the fire, for it seemed to him that the thin creature now spoke to him in his *own* voice. The figure above him burst into roars of laughter, wild and cruel, and he danced around Bill and around the fire, hooting and hurling his hat into the air and catching it again as it came down.

It was at that moment that something broke within young Bill. He was scared, he was terrified, he didn't understand what was happening - though he knew enough not to trust it - but all at once none of that mattered, and all that was left of him was a burning core of shame and rage. With a roar, he leapt to his feet. The thin man had tossed his hat once more into the air; and quick as a flash, Bill's hand shot out, and he grasped the hat, and he held it above the flames until the silk began to catch and smoke began to wreath.

"No!" shrieked the thin creature, laughing no longer; and with another leap as quick as darkness, he grabbed out for the hat. This was exactly what Bill had been expecting. He was ready and waiting; and his other arm - as thick as most men's legs - shot out and grasped the thin man by the neck. He was slippery and slimy, and he turned and twisted like a snake; but young Bill was strong as sunshine, and he did not let go. He pulled Tom into the fire. The hat burst into flames; and the thin man smouldered and screamed; and Bill's own hands were burnt by the flames, burnt to ash and blackness. But still he held on.

And suddenly, it was too much. The last shred of what had once been Old Tom gave up the ghost, and with a sigh like the wind blowing away rainclouds, Old Tom's body vanished in a gout of flame.

But Shadows do not fear the fire; Shadows are made strong by them.

The Shadow had lost a body; but now, it seemed, it had found a new one. And who's to say what thoughts flicker in the mind of a Shadow? Perhaps it had grown weary of Tom and his tricks. Perhaps the Shadow hungered for something new.

The flame of Tom's passing burnt bright for an instant; and then the darkness rushed in, the shadows bunching up out of the collapsing flames, grasping Bill's arms, pulling them close, drowning, drowning, drowning him.

Young Bill did not even have time to scream.

His fists were black and crisped from the flames; but another sort of darkness covered his huge body; the top hat smoked as he placed it on his head, and he vanished into the night, and Skeleton Bill it was now; and something dark lived on.

I won't tell you much of those days; they were dark. Old Tom Gaunt had been mischievous and wicked, and there was something broken in him, but Skeleton Bill was worse. He was brutal rage and raw meat, he came screaming down from the hills and left red stains on the grass for the morning sun to find. He didn't play tricks, did Skeleton Bill; oh, no, he didn't play at all, and all his sport was deadly.

But shadows grow tired of all things at last, and the part of Skeleton Bill that had once been a man went back to the dirt, as sure as nightfall. But things continued, my sweet little heathens, of that you can be sure. From one to the next, from this vice to that, the Shadow weaved on. And each time, its nature changed; each time, it remembered less of what it had been, and was born anew in the starlight, fate and form decided by the nature of the man (or woman) who carried the burden. It takes a storyteller; now Skeleton Sue weaves tales under the blood moon and all who hear must lay, enchanted, until they rot. Now Young May Gaunt comes out, fecund and thin at the same time, and gives birth to little darknesses that sneak and snatch for her, and not a child in the land is safe. Now Skeleton Hugh walks the hills, a man of some strange God, and those he finds must join his coven or they will scream until their throats bleed.

How do I know all this, young David? Because I am old and I listen. This is my land, and I know what passes here. But it has not been Hugh, oh, not for a long count of years. No, the Shadow took a new form, when I was but a little girl; younger than you, Annie. I knew him, yes I did. We all knew Strange Jack, lived halfway out on the forest road, quiet and lonely. There was something in his eyes that made you feel naked before him, and uncomfortable in your own skin. A collector of odd things, butterflies and statues and blades. His house still stands out there, even to this day. No one would take it after he left, and it fell to ruin; but still it stands, cold and creaking and full of odd smells.

Black Jack Gaunt dances under the moonlight, calling lasses to him. One day, maybe, he will come here, and then who will dance with him?

Hah! Not I, young Thomas, no, not I! Sweet of you, though. It makes my old bones blush.

How does it end? I told you already, I do not know; for it is not yet ended. Maybe one day we will all find out.

What's that, Heather? You don't like my story? Well, perhaps then you could step up here by the fire and tell a better! You will? My, aren't you a one! And quite composed; quite unashamed. Well, let's have it then!

❧ 56 ❧

MY FATHER'S WHISTLE

~

My father is the priest. You all know him, don't you? He is tall and he has dark hair and he smiles. Sometimes, he puts his hands on my face and steals my nose! It tickles, but I always get it back.

My father has a whistle. You've all heard it, haven't you? He curls his lip and blows. It is an old whistle, full of power, and I come to him when he whistles. Sometimes he whistles in the chapel, and then one by one we all whistle with him. It's like music, it's like magic.

My father has no wife. My mother died when I was a babe, and none of you knew her, did you? (Except you, Old Nan, of course! You knew everyone!) She was beautiful. She gave my father her whistle as a wedding gift.

My father met her far away. You've never been there, have you? It's a land across the sea. I'll go there one day, when I'm older. Everyone has a whistle there, but my mother's was the most beautiful.

My father's whistle can't be withstood. You can't stop it, can you? It calls through flesh and stone and bone, when we stray it calls us home. My father says he could whistle his way into any castle.

My father's whistle goes like this:

✺ 57 ✺

⟨BEAUTIFUL WHISTLE⟩

~

I was a priest, and everyone knew me. I am tall and I have dark hair and I never smile. I used to steal my girl's nose. Now even the memory hurts me.

I have a whistle. My heart was broken in two, and half was stolen from me. But I was left my whistle, and I will use it like all my other weapons.

I had a wife (and a little girl, too). She gave me this whistle, and now it's all I have of her. She would hate the way I use it, but what choice do I have?

I have travelled far, exceedingly far. But not much further is my road. I have a map, I have a sword. I have found the door I seek.

I whistle now, and you won't stand. Warrior and ghost and door, I'll whistle you all away.

But tell me, what do you see? I'm curious. Open your mouth and tell me

❧ 58 ❧

HOW THE DOOR WAS OPENED

≈

"**I** see a tall man with a sword and salt in his hair," says Frayn, neutrally. Her hand tightens on the shaft of her ash staff. It is wound about with enchantments many, and she is not scared of a man with a sword and a whistle.

"I see a broken man with a grim look and purpose in his eyes," says Prince Myst. His voice is light as air, and under the glittering of the stars, his ghost-body looks almost human, in spite of the red-golden seams that join his flesh.

But the tall man smiles a dark smile, and he looks at me.

"I was not talking to you two children," he says, and his eyes are on me, and he sees that my mouth is indeed open, as his whistle has commanded.

My oaken wood is splayed at his command, and in the stillness of surprise, they all hear me telling my tale. My voice is low and creaks like trees in the wind. Once you know it is there, you can hear it if you listen.

"The door is open!" cries Myst, and his voice is full of horror.

"Then we must stand," says Frayn, and she lifts up her staff and makes ready to defend my mouth from the intruder.

He comes at them then, a smile small and sad on his lips. His sword is wondrous sharp. I can feel it in my oak; it pulses from him, waves of sharpness dancing from that strange blade as the starlight catches the metal.

He moves like a dancer, like a dream. Frayn towers over him, giant's blood in her veins and a lifetime of slaying dark things. But he is quick and deadly. His blade slashes out and she blocks it with her staff//

//and the enchantments many fail. One and all, they fail. The blade splits the wood as if it is a puff of sawdust, and then the staff is falling, Frayn reeling backwards to avoid being split herself.

Prince Myst is drifting forward, his sword in his hand. He is no longer compelled to guard me - Wom Ya's salt magic failed long ago - and yet he chooses to stand. I love him for it, and yet it is foolish. The time has come, you see. His whistle has shown me that. I am wide open and gaping for him.

The tall man lifts his sword and brings it down. The air itself seems to tear//

//and Prince Myst is falling forward, even a ghost can be set off balance by a trick like that: the air ripped open, and the tall man striding through a hole in nothing, emerging behind Prince Myst. Behind them both, and before me.

He stands, tall and stern. The sad smile is still on his lips. He looks at me, open as he has commanded. I want him. I have waited so long.

He walks, quite calmly, towards my open mouth.

Frayn charges forward, no words on her lips, just a roar; Prince Myst is not far behind.

But, "Enough play," he says softly, and then he pouts his lips and that beautiful whistle comes once more, golden and deep as oceans. My guardians cannot stand against that whistle; they fall to their knees, slack jawed and wide eyes spinning.

His pace never slacks. One, two, three...

Now he is standing at my very lips. He brushes one hand gently against my oak, and I shudder deep in my roots that were.

Yes, I tell him.

He holds his strange sword in one hand; that is what enters me first, passing through my mouth into the darkness beyond. Then one boot, then his body, his whole body, then the next boot, and then he is all inside. I have swallowed him up.

I turn my eyes inwards. I have never looked here before. I have never been permitted to see within myself, to see the awful secrets I contain. But his whistle has broken the rules. I am unbound, and I am as wild as an oak again.

It is beautiful. Incredible. Terrifying.

Shall I tell?

The tall man stands in endless darkness. He has reached the middle of the room, which must have taken him an age: it is as huge as everything that ever was. Beside him, jutting out of the darkness, there is the wheel. It is huge and heavy and made of metal and ancient wood. It has been turned a quarter-circle already; any fool could see that. Things are out of alignment.

Around him spin the things that are endlessly bound to the wheel. Their lights and shapes and shaded pictures flicker and go on forever. It is the Storystream, the whole of the Storystream, splashing and roaring around the eternal darkness in the margins of the room. It is huge beyond measure and so small it could fit in a child's palm.

My man, the tall man, he is looking at it all. Just looking, just silent.

His eyes pass from the wheel, to the Storystream, back to the wheel. There are tears, I think.

He moves closer to the wheel. He sheaths his sword, flexes his hands. Outside, my guardians are hammering at my mouth, trying to get in, trying to stop him. But I have closed my mouth, closed it very tight. They will not get in. No one else will get in. No one will stop my man.

His hands are big, but they are smooth. They were meant to be gentle, they are not used to holding swords. Something bitter has happened to him. He is here now to soothe that bitterness. He stretches his hands forward, and he grasps the wheel. He pushes, gently at first, then harder, harder, harder. Sweat is pricking on his brow, when a great groan comes from the darkness all around. The Storystream creaks, the flow of pictures tilt; just a fraction, but I noticed. An awful, dark sound creaks down from above us, and a rain of fine dust floats down and coats the floor.

Then something stirs. There is a deeper force here than me; an older force than my oak; it makes me feel like an acorn.

No, it whispers. It resists him. //

//THE WAGON LURCHES THROUGH THE DARKNESS. THE PIG ON THE roof is gasping for his breath. The cat snatches his lever, yanking it back so hard it looks as if it will break and...

...The wagon is suddenly ploughing through the ground, tearing up the earth, casting sparks and fire from its wheels as it slows to a speed the mind can understand. It rolls to a halt, and two figures turn to blink and stare.

"Well don't jus'...don't jus' look like bloody...fools," gasps the pig. "Get in...No time to...lose!"

Valiben looks at Max. Something is happening to the world, something strange and terrible. Things are falling, things are failing. They both know it is true.

"We'll put his...tank on the roof," pants the pig. "You can ride inside...My advice is...*keep your eyes shut!*"

Valiben nods at his fishy friend and they share a weak smile. Then he walks towards the wagon (slower than he should, but he can't help himself) and reaches out to grasp the door. But before he can touch the dark wood, the wagon gives a shudder, and the door swings open. Inside, he can see darkness and the faint outlines of crimson cushions...and a wide mouth with lots of sharp white teeth. Above the teeth, he can see two unbearably feminine eyes, shaded in tones of red by light that leaks out from within them. The rest of the Mistress of the Wagon is cloaked in darkness, for which Valiben is very thankful.

He sees the way her head tilts in the darkness, inviting him inside. He licks his lips, and wonders if this is wise, if this is not how many, many creatures - creatures beyond number, creatures that are remembered by no one - wonders if this is how so many creatures met their end. But then the world shakes again beneath them, and a terrible music is on the air, faint but clear; bells and horns and drums, drums,

drums. And Valiben realises that it does not matter if the Mistress of
the Wagon does intend to trick him; either way, the world will be
over soon.

So he steps inside, and immediately the door slams shut, and he is
thrown forward as the wagon begins to accelerate away. For a horrible
moment he thinks he is going to lose his balance, and he is terrified
because if he fell forward, he would be landing in *her* lap...But then the
moment passes; he regains his footing and sits back down. The terrible
music is still there, just beyond the shriek of the wheels and the rattle
of the black wooden boards; but it is quieter in here, and he wonders
at the powers of the Mistress of the Wagon, who can stand firm and
keep apocalypse at bay.

He studies her in the darkness, appalled and fascinated by the little
he can see. As he watches, he sees a dark tongue slip out of her mouth
and lick the tips of her teeth. Then she speaks to him.

"I am glad I was able to meet you again before the end," she says,
and her voice is soft, but so rich and deep he feels lost in it, as if it
were made of velvet.

He mumbles something under his breath, for all his princely charm
has left him, and his heart is in his mouth.

"Hush," she tells him. "Now listen, for we do not have much time.
We tried to stop him. We tried to trap him. But the trap failed, the
trick failed; now he is at the centre of things, at the very centre, and
there is only one person who can stop him."

Valiben's mouth went dry.

"Not...not *me?*" he says in horrified tones.

The Mistress of the Wagon makes a sound deep in her throat; it
takes Valiben a moment to realise that she is laughing.

"No, my dear prince, not you," she days, and Valiben sees how
sharp her teeth are, and how cruel her smile. "It's not a prince that can
stop him now. It has gone beyond all that. Force will not do a thing."

"Oh," says Valiben, feeling rather a fool. "Well then, I suppose it
must be you."

"Not me, either, I am sorry to say," says the Mistress, and she does
sound sad, though there is something poisonous in her voice, too.
"Even were I permitted to meddle with such things directly, it has, I

repeat, gone past force. The worlds are being torn apart, all the stories are being unmade, all the barriers are breaking...and in a way, there is our one hope."

"What do you mean?" asks Valiben. "What hope?"

"This creature, this...Amos," she says slowly. "Everything he has done, everything he is doing...it is out of pain. Do you see? It is all because of the wrong that was done to him. Things are in motion that we cannot stop by force..."

Valiben snorts.

"But if not force, then what?" he demands.

The Mistress of the Wagon smiles at him again.

"Words, perhaps," she says, musingly, as if she were unconvinced herself. "And yet, we would not get the words we need from the creature that needs to say them. Not unless *you*, my fine prince, complete your quest. Which is where these breaking barriers come in..."

At that moment, the wagon gives a lurch. Valiben feels his ears pop, and a tingle runs up his spine. //

//It is the Storystream itself. The Storystream is fighting back, resisting this man and his attempts to turn the wheel, to unmake every thing that ever was.

It is this force that will not let the wheel turn. However hard he pushes, however hard he heaves, the wheel will not turn. Not for my man.

"So be it," he says, and smiles, leaning backwards.

Then in one fluid motion he whips out his sword and drives it into the heart of the wheel. Something in the darkness screams, and he readies to twist the sword, and then...

"I will not let you do this thing," the voice is soft, but it is clear. My man relaxes his sword arm, tilts his head.

"I know that voice," says my man. There is a rage in him. He will not be thwarted now. He will not be challenged, he will not tolerate that.

He turns towards the Storystream, from where the voice emerged.

It is so small, the little bubble from which the voice speaks. It is so small, but it is utterly clear, as if all the distance in between is thin, and does not count for anything.

"Tobias," whispers my man, and I lock my eyes on the bubble of story, and I see him very well: a man, thin and drawn in the face; and broken in the eyes, in a way that tells me he has lost things, also. Around his neck, a medallion, golden on a silver chain. At his back, two friends waiting. But it is this one, this Tobias to whom my man gives his attention.

Tobias should not be able to see us. He should be stuck within his bubble of story, sealed into the Storystream, unable to perceive us here, let alone reach us. And yet...

...There is something about that amulet. It glints. It glistens. It catches the light, in a way that I have seen before. It is alike to the sword of my man. Not gold then: something else.

And this man, Tobias, he reaches out his hands, one to each of his friends, and they step forward, and they step forward, and they step forward...

...And then the bubble is moving backwards, lost again within the endless stream of stories; but Tobias and his friends are there no longer. They are standing here in the darkness with us, as real as my man, as real as my ancient oak planks.

The three newcomers step forward, Tobias in the middle. The others are a monk and his apprentice. They look unhappy to be here, soft and weak. But Tobias...he is different. I sense something in him, some desperation, some threat.

My man shows his teeth.

"More fools to try to stop me?" he says, trying to sound idle. "My patience is getting thin. I will not let you live a second time, Tobias..."
//

//"We are here," says the Mistress of the Wagon.

"Where?" says Valiben breathlessly, but at that moment, the door of the wagon is flung open.

"See for yourself," says the Mistress.

Outside the wagon it is night. The wind howls against the dark wood, and rain comes screaming down from the sky. Lightning flashes, and thunder rolls, almost at the same instant. Valiben flings a hand outside of the wagon, and tries to pull himself clear. The wind strikes him in the face and fights to force him back inside. Slowly he heaves his way onto his feet. Lightning flashes again, tearing apart a whole quarter of the sky; and behind the lightning, as clear as daylight, Valiben sees another reality flashing. He sees a mighty city, full of tall towers collapsing under the onslaught of waves as high as hills. But as soon as the lightning vanishes, the other world is gone, and he sees instead that they are surrounded by fields on all sides, gently rolling fields that seem - despite the heavy rain - to be full of dust. He blinks, and the afterimage of the lightning leaves blue and purple streaks dancing behind his eyes. He turns slowly, taking everything in. They are on the outskirts of a small village, tumbledown and in bad repair.

The Mistress of the Wagon leans forward. Her red eyes and white teeth draw closer to the door, but the darkness inside the wagon clings to her, and Valiben can see her no more clearly.

"There is a deep darkness in a place under the earth, and the village above it is cursed," she tells him, flatly, as if reciting something. "The crops are poor, and what does grow is stunted. The well holds bad water, thick and cloudy and sour; and in time, the people became cloudy and sour, too."

She peered at him.

"This is the place he comes from," she says. "This is where Amos was born, and where he lived...and it was where his daughter was taken from him, and where his heart was broken. And the creature that did it to him...what remains of it is under the earth still."

Valiben blinks at her.

"And I need to get this...this *thing*?" says Valiben, his voice high and thin against the wind.

The Mistress of the Wagon nods.

"Aye," she tells him. "Because right now, when the worlds are thin and the barriers are breaking...now you may, if you are brave, and if you are quick, be able to complete your quest."

Valiben shakes his head in incomprehension.

"But..." he protests. "But...but you said *under the earth*, didn't you? How am I supposed to get to something underneath the earth?"

He hears laughter from behind and above him. He turns to see

Bartleby the pig standing on the roof, steaming in the rain after his exertions.

"Don't worry 'bout that, sunshine!" he exclaims. "Got that one covered, I think you'll find."

"Stand back," comes the voice of the Mistress of the Wagon.

"And you might want to cover your eyes," adds Bartleby as an afterthought.

Valiben backs away. He moves until his shoulders are pressing against the cold stone of one of the buildings. Lightning comes again, and this time he fancies he sees a glimpse of a village almost like the one he stands in now, but much smaller, much more rudimentary. He swallows. He glances at the door of the wagon. He can see her eyes glaring out at the world from within. Then he sees the darkness within the wagon begin to bunch itself up, and the Mistress of the Wagon comes closer to the door, closer, closer, until her eyes are only an inch from the outside world.

Then Valiben closes his eyes.

He feels something vast rush out of the wagon. Even behind his closed lids, he feels it pass, and it sucks the colour and light away. The ground shakes, and he realises the Mistress of the Wagon has slammed her body into the earth. Something buzzes, nearer than he would have imagined possible. It sounds like a million bees have been stuck to a million shards of razor-sharp glass and are busily at work tearing the world to pieces. Something shudders, and the noise moves further away. A moment later, he dares to open his eyes. A vast hole has gaped open at his feet. Darkness is swaying out of the wagon and into the hole. He can still hear the buzz of her teeth, as she grafts further into the earth, burrowing now at an angle so that the tunnel she is making arcs back underneath the village.

Around him, the lightning flashes again and again. It seems to be coming quicker than before, and as it flashes, strange images are burnt into his eyes: insane landscapes; vast, crazy faces; a dusty village street dancing in calm sunshine; an underwater world, luminescent reefs and sea-flowers swaying softly beneath the waves. An instant later, and they are gone. They are beginning to make Valiben feel sick. He breaths carefully and forces himself to focus on the ground at his feet. After a moment, he feels well enough to risk another look. He turns his head, and sees that the pool of darkness that had come out of the wagon and disappeared into the earth is pulsing softly, contracting; and he realises the Mistress is pulling her vast, swaying body back out from the earth. He shuts his eyes tight closed, and waits as the sound of buzzing and gnashing passes him by. Then he keeps his eyes closed some more. It is not until he hears the reassuring click of the wagon door slamming shut that he dares to open his eyes.

As his eyes begin to open, thunder crashes right above his head, so loud and close that//

//"Stop you? Of course I will stop you," says Tobias, edging closer. The other two have stopped moving now. Tobias comes forward alone. "You have tricked and toyed with me. You have broken my love in half. I would stop you for that alone, regardless of what it is you meant to do here. But this...this is bigger than any reason of the mind or heart. You must be stopped. You must not be allowed to do this."

"It will all be destroyed," my man replies softly. "Everywhere is awash with story, overrun by story. It is drowning in the stuff. Can't you see?" and for a moment something yearns in him, and I think: *is it that he aches for the end? Or is it possible that even now he aches for someone to convince him he is wrong?*

"We need stories," comes a voice. It is the youngest man, the one who looks as if he is an apprentice to the monk. "Believe me. Please believe me; I have seen what happens when all the stories break. It is madness. It is chaos."

"We weave the world of stories, it is true," agrees the monk, nodding, unhappy that he must speak. "What will be left if you destroy them all?"

My man, he flinches at their words. I see his hand tighten on the hilt of his sword. He pulls it out and a great shower of sparks erupt from the wheel.

"We *don't* need stories!" my man hisses. "Stories are lies! Stories are tricks! They will betray us all, you will see."

Tobias takes a step closer...But my man pouts his lips and//

356

//Valiben falls sprawling on his face in the mud, and now there is little princely left in him, and he just looks young and terrified. He lays there for the longest time, and I am sure he won't get up, that we are all doomed, and I am screaming silently at him, screaming so loud and he cannot hear.

Then something hardens in his face. I can see it. His eyes unfold and open, slowly at first, but there is a sternness there, and I realise he has mastered himself. Slowly, he rolls onto one side, then one foot goes under him, then the other, then he is standing. There is no hope in his face, but there is determination now. He licks his lips, and all at once I can see the prince again, standing tall and unbowed while the world around him shatters.

He turns once, and locks eyes with his friend, Maxwell, with whom he has had so many adventures. The faintest hint of a smile glimmers round his lips. Then he turns his back on the wagon and strides down towards the hole.

The topsoil here is dusty, as if it has not rained for a million years, despite the downpour smashing into the earth. But only a few inches down, and the soil is soft and soggy, full of drowned worms and other nameless things. The tunnel falls steeply, and soon there is a roof above him, and the world is getting dim. He has no light with him, and he has to feel his way along, hands slimed with mud and the stink of bad earth in his nostrils. As soon as he is underground, the cacophony above fades into the background; but the earth still shakes with the crash of thunder, and he can still hear, louder now, the grim grinding noise, bone-deep and awful. He guesses correctly what it is: the sound of the shelves of the worlds being torn apart, the rending, wailing, scream of the Universe as it is murdered.

He goes further. Now the light of the entrance is fading behind him, as the tunnel twists and turns, burrows deeper. The tunnel is narrowing. It is now no wider than his outstretched arms. The ground is still wet. He smells something, something beyond the rot of the earth and the death of worms. It is cloying and sweet, but elusive somehow. Every time he thinks it will get stronger, it vanishes. And every time he thinks he was imagining it, it comes back, stronger than ever. He has never smelt anything like this before. He thinks it is what purple would smell like, a purple so dark it is almost black. His foot-steps take him further.

Now the tunnel has narrowed some more, and he can feel the press of earth against his shoulders. He takes a few more steps, then bangs his head on the roof. It is angling down. He crouches. He can feel a scream building up inside of him, wanting to burst out, willing him to flee back the way he has come; but he knows that if he lets it out, then everything is over. If he screams now, if he breaks, then he will not be able to go forward. He will never find whatever it is that he must find, and that means that the enemy would go unopposed: he would win.

He pushes the scream down into his belly, and throws himself forward onto his hands and knees. Then he crawls further in.

The ground is trembling almost continually now. He wonders what the world is like above and//

//I could tell him I could tell him of the trees cracking and the wind howling and the lightning that seems to leap up from the ground and scold the sky and the flickering worlds as all the barriers fail and this is how it will end this is how it will be if he fails but he is strong and I know he is strong and he//

//then pushes the thought away and forces himself to go on. The tunnel gets smaller still. Now he is working his way on his belly, like a snake, crawling like a worm, the cold mud seeping into his breeches and rubbing against his face and into his mouth and every time he takes a breath he wonders if it will be his last. And then the tunnel stops.

It stops because it opens out into a cave. It is dark here, so dark; and yet he senses that the cave is only small, maybe no bigger than the inside of the wagon. Slowly, hesitatingly, he rises from his knees, then stands in a low crouch. He can feel the roof above him, brushing against his hair. The soil is wet and sticky and it stinks.

He is not alone.

Someone is with him in this cavern, something. It does not breathe, but he can feel it watching him. It is this thing, he realises, that he could smell earlier. The stench of it is stronger here, so strong; and it does not come and go. Instead, it pulses.

His breathing is ragged. He is suddenly terrified again, and each breath is so loud he is sure it will call the creature to him, that it will end in the rending of claws and the tearing of teeth. Very faint, he can hear the trickle of running water. But there is no-one else breathing down here.

But the creature does not move. His eyes can do no more adjusting to this absolute darkness; and yet, after a moment, he realises that he *can* see something, even here in this world of pitch and tar. He can see the creature. He is sure of it. There, in the corner, there. A small patch of even blacker midnight, so dark it seems to suck light away, so dark it makes his head buzz and his teeth hurt when he looks at it. It is thin, oh so painfully thin. It is curled up tight, thin and awful and wretched.

And I have to coax this thing back into the light? he thinks to himself. He can feel his hopes deflating.

He thinks about reaching out for it, about grasping hold and heaving the thing back with him into the light. But he is sure, completely sure, that the thing would not come, that it would be slimy and impossible to grasp, that it would slip through his fingers (and what then? Maybe that would just provoke it).

So instead of lunging for the creature, he sits back against the wall of the cave and takes a deep breath, and simply says "Hello?"

No answer comes.

He tries again.

"Hello?" he says. "Thing in the darkness? Thing in the corner? Can you hear me?"

Again, no answer. He waits until the memory of his words has faded to nothing. Then he opens his mouth to speak again.

But before he can say anything, a whisper comes at him. It is only soft, so very soft; could he be imagining it? He does not hear what it says.

"I'm sorry?" he says, licking his lips. "I didn't hear you. What did you say?"

He holds his breath. He waits.

Then it answers him,

"Did you call me 'thing'?" the thing says. Its voice is softer than he thought; higher, too. It sounds like a woman, a woman who has been weeping.

"Yes!" exclaims Valiben, so happy that the thing answered him that he forgets himself for a moment. "I mean, no." He is fumbling his words, desperate not to offend or upset the creature. "Well, I suppose, yes I did call you a thing. But I didn't mean anything by it." He takes a deep breath, forces himself to be steady. "What are you, then?" he asks. "Are you a 'him'? Are you a 'her'?"

Again, there is silence for a long time before the answer comes.

"I suppose I am a 'thing'," says the voice at last, sadly. "I'm not sure that I always was. But I suppose I am now. I don't see what else it is that I could be. I've been down here for so long, so long. And all alone. So very alone. All I have for company is the earth and the rocks and the worms."

The creature lets out a sob, and Valiben finds that he is softening towards it despite himself.

He shuffles around the wall, moves a little closer. He fancies he can see water trickling. Even in this utter blackness, he thinks he can see a little stream crawling along, emerging from some secret spring and winding its way past the...*thing's*...legs and towards him. He is very thirsty, he suddenly realises. Idly, he cups a hand to the water and lifts some to his lips.

"I think I used to be a woman," says the voice. "I was very beautiful. I'm sure of it. I can remember the looks on their faces as I danced. I can remember the smell of the fires that they made to me."

It sounds very far off and lost, the voice. It sounds very distant and frail.

Valiben tips the water into his mouth; then he is choking and coughing and spitting it out. The water is foul beyond belief, cloying and rotten, filling his mouth with sickness.

"Do not drink the water," the voice chides him. "I have my foot in it, just like I have my arm in the earth, and the air comes into my mouth. It's all poisoned. It's part of what I do here."

Valiben works his mouth, futilely trying to get rid of the awful taste.

"Why?" he manages to spit out. "Why are you poisoning everything?"

"I did it on purpose," comes the reply, spoken slowly, as if the creature is only remembering this now that it comes to say it. "I did it...so that the whole village would love me. Would fall under my dance, would sway to the rhythm of my hips. Their wells taste of me, their crops taste of me; even the air they breathe tastes of me. They cannot help but dance. They cannot help but listen to my dark music."

Valiben shakes his head.

"The village is gone," he tells the creature. "They are all gone, long gone. There's only stone and rubble left now. No one is there to dance with you. No one is there to sway their hips."

He waits, but the creature does not respond. Valiben licks his lips again. He knows that time is running out; he wonders what will be left of the world above, if he ever makes it out of this tunnel. He knows if he pushes it, if he tries to force it, this creature might be suspicious, might attack him, even. But he cannot wait for ever...

"Why don't you..." Valiben hesitates. "Why don't you come with me? Leave this darkness, leave this little stream. Come up with me and see the world."

Again, silence. Then a noise that sounds like a hiss.

When the voice comes again, it is harsher, less withered.

"Come with you?" it snaps. "And who are you, exactly? Why would I come with you? Why would you want me to?"

"My name is Valiben," the Prince answers, trying to stay calm while his heart thumps away in his chest. "I am...I am a friend, I think. I need...that is to say, the *world* needs you. We all need you. Something has gone wrong, and...and we need you to help put things right."

His voice sounds very thin in the darkness, and he feels a cold settle over his bones,

No answer comes.

All at once, the trickle of the water at his feet swells. He stares into the darkness. Can he see something moving? He begins to edge back around the cave towards the opening of the tunnel, trying not to give way to the panic that he can feel building up inside of him.

He hears a footstep. It is soft and wet, but audible.

It's stepped out of the little stream, he thinks. *It's unblocked; that's why it's flowing faster. She's coming for me.*

There is a damp slurping noise, and now there is no doubt about it:

the figure has pulled its arm out of the earth, and it is moving towards him. He can make it out, a patch of impossibly deep darkness against the blackness of the cave. It is advancing towards him, quicker, quicker, quicker...//

//...My man curls his lip and blows. The whistle that comes out here, here at the very centre of things, is beautiful beyond all bearing. It twines its way into my oak; I can feel every fibre of wood and metal thrill to its strange power.

Yet it does not stop Tobias. The amulet he wears, the metal it contains does *not* carry the thrill of that whistle. The music of it breaks against the metal, shears on either side of him, washes off splintered and impotent.

He takes another step forward, and now he is standing toe to toe with my man. Tobias reaches out and grasps him by the collar.

"Your pretty songs are lost on me," says Tobias, and his eyes are grim.

"Indeed," says my man dryly, "but not on your friends."

They grapple Tobias to the ground, the monk and his young apprentice. Tobias screams and writhes; but he is overcome. The monk is a heavy man, and the other is young and firm. Their eyes are glazed and listless. They will do anything they are asked.

At last it is over. Tobias has spent his energy, he lays panting on the floor.

My man looks him in the eye, but does not say a word. They have all been said already.

He turns back to the wheel, and thrusts the sword in again. The world lurches.

I sense more than see his fingers as they grasp the hilt. I can feel the muscles tighten around the leather, can feel the tremble in the room as the metal starts to twist.

The wheel is tearing.

My man releases the sword; then he grasps the wheel with both hands, and heaves with all his might.

With a sound like the shattering of worlds, the wheel begins to turn. The ground beneath us shakes; around us, the Storystream halts, lurches in its eternal spin.

Then it cracks. I can feel it: the thrill running around the room. It is breaking one story from the next, loosening the cement that holds them together, at the same time breaking down the walls that run between them. The barriers are failing, and one story is merging into the next; I can see it in the Storystream, I glance at one flickering bubble and//

//in a dungeon deep underground, the Mesomorph pauses in the act of decapitating an evil wizard who was keeping prisoner a tribe of lost dandelions. Something shakes the world. He turns a questioning eye towards his wife, but a hole has opened beside him, and through it he sees//

//a huge, green dragon, frozen a moment before she hits the ground, about to crush an old woman who smells of the sea, and reflected in her eyes can be seen//

//a woman whose face has no holes, just pale skin where her face should be, with thin skin over the hollows of her eyes, and red skin over the hole of her mouth, and two little flaps of skin where her nostrils should be, and she tilts her head in perfect understanding, and gazes with her sightless eyes to another place where//

//a pointy-looking creature feels the insubstantial world tremble around him, and decides it would be a sensible time to hide underneath his desk, pushing aside some of the endless pile of Lives that crowd there, and brushing against one he notices//

//an old lady, so very old, surrounded by children (and didn't we see her die? Or maybe this is before, or maybe that was a dream?) and she is gathering them tight and talking to them, telling them stories to keep the awful thunder at bay, and her eyes flicker to the door just as it crashes open, and she catches a glimpse of//

//for an instant I lose them I lose them in the vastness of it all of the whole collapsing worlds beyond number and images such images such sights they crash and roar and I am everything and everyone and the world is ending and something awakes in me and I scream *no* so loud that no-one at all can hear it and I can see my man turning the wheel further and further and it is wrecking everything destroying melding merging everything and I don't want this anymore because at this late stage maybe even whistles lose their power and all I can think of is the one place the one hope the one chance we have and I force my mind and I force my mind and I force my mind and look at my man and he glares darkly down at the wheel and twists and I wish that//

//Valiben throws himself down onto the floor, back towards the tunnel. He gets his feet in, and begins to push away from the cave.

The figure flickers. A voice whispers by his ear.

"Come with you?" it says, soft and awful. "Yes. Yes, I will come with you."

Then the shadowed thing is pouring itself into his head, rushing in through his ears, bunching in his throat, seeping through his nostrils. It wraps itself around him, tightening like a second skin.

At least I got it to come with me, thinks Valiben, as the last of his strength fails and he gives himself up to the thing that is consuming him. Then he stops being Valiben, and starts being something else. It whispers to itself, endlessly talking, telling itself the story of

❧ 59 ☙

THE DARKNESS UNDER
THE EARTH

◞

I am the darkness under the earth, and the village above me is cursed. I've been here for so long I can hardly remember anything else (but when I close these borrowed eyes and look inwards, maybe I can glimpse a hundred yesterdays concertina backwards into forever, dancing and drifting and an endless search, only I don't know what for).

I wear this new body well. It fits me. It is young and strong, and I have been without one for so long. I have almost forgotten what it is like to have hands that can touch, lungs that can breathe, flesh that can ache sweetly.

I am pushing my way back through the tunnel, sliming through mud and against small dead things. The earth stinks. It is lovely. It is time to leave this place. It is time to carry on looking (*but what for*, I wonder, though I cannot answer myself), time to carry on my dancing and my tricks.

The tunnel widens and I can stand, and suddenly a breeze from the world above brushes against my skin. I sniff the air. It smells of lightning and storms and broken things. Something is wrong. I can feel it in my borrowed bones.

I move faster now, almost running. My feet are light, and the mud cannot catch me. I can see light up ahead, and I don't like it. Darkness was always a friend. I don't slow, though; I haven't seen light for what seems like an age, and I squint but I don't slow.

I am in the daylight. I can tell that it is thin, less than it should be; there is a wrongness in the air. But bright flashes burst through the feeble sunlight, so brilliant that I feel they will burn me away to nothing, and I move more slowly again, one arm raised to protect my eyes.

I emerge from the tunnel. Something is waiting for me, something huge and billowing, a blackness bigger than the mind can hold. It has eyes and teeth, and it is watching me, and it is hungry.

Behind this enormous darkness I can see other shapes, shimmering as if they are unreal. There is a wagon, made of black metal and black wood. There are figures on the roof, unlikely figures. They are looking at me, but they do not speak. And behind them, I can see the village. Rather, I can see a hundred villages. The lightning comes again and again, sheets of burning blue that tear the sky; and with every strike, a different village sparks into being and dies in embers, faster than even I can follow. The thunder is a constant rumble. It sounds as if the world is tearing itself to pieces.

The dark figure comes closer. I am afraid, even I. But I will not show it. I have walked the earth in darkness for more years than I can remember, and I will not yield to another creature as dark as I.

The ruby-pale eyes spark and glitter, and the sharp teeth part, and her voice comes.

"Hello, little shadow," she says to me. Her voice is mocking and strange. "I have been watching you for some time."

"I am smaller than you, but I am not little," I reply. "I have tasted a thousand thousand hearts, and all things that live fear me."

The smile of those white teeth widen.

"I do not fear you, little shadow," her voice comes again. "A thousand thousand hearts are nothing to me, and my hunger is greater than yours. But come, there is little time. Perhaps later we can discuss all the pleasant morsels you have tasted. You may even share them with me. But now you must come with us."

I plant my feet square on the blasted earth, and snarl up at her.

"You will have nothing of mine, however great your hunger!" I tell her. "I am dark as midnight, and I will go where I will."

Her eyes tilt to one side, and a breath blows through those white teeth.

Then her darkness draws back from me; but the creature within the darkness remains, and is revealed, and I see her very well.

I scream.

I cannot help but scream. Her body is huge and impossible and worshipful. Her eyes and her teeth are the least part of the madness of which she is made.

"If you do not come, then I will eat you, little shadow," she says to me. She says it softly, almost lovingly. "I will eat you, and then all the worlds will fail."

I am small beneath her endless weight. She glares at me, and a part of me quakes inside.

But am I not also a creature of shadows?

I clench my teeth and hiss between them.

"Then come and eat me," I tell her. "Bring me into yourself, and see what I do inside you."

For an instant, there is nothing but silence. Even the storm seems to hold its breath.

Then she makes a horrible sound, and a moment later I realise it is laughter.

"You are mad then, little shadow," she says. "Quite mad; but I will not hold that against you. Perhaps I will taste your sweet flesh another time. But no matter; keep that body a little longer."

She laughs again, and calls back her darkness. It billows and weaves, and her awful nakedness is covered again, and all I can see of her are her eyes and her teeth. Then she is pulling backwards, reeling back until her form reaches the door of her wagon, and her body shrinks impossibly small to fit within.

I lick the lips I have borrowed. They taste of salt and dank mud. I glance over my shoulder. The worlds dance and bloom around me. I could flit away in an instant. I could run and be gone. And yet...

"Why do you want me to come with you?" I ask.

Her teeth glint in the wagon.

"You can stop the storm," she tells me simply. "Come, little shadow. You have tested me, and I have spared you. For now. But you must do something for me. For all of us. You do not even have to come away with us. You only need to walk through a doorway, and meet someone."

Her words sound reasonable, but I do not trust the eyes.

"Meet someone? Meet who?" I ask.

"The lady who gave that body you wear a quest," she says. "I think that maybe he can at last complete it."

I shift my weight from one leg to the other (and isn't that strange? Having weight again, having substance) and I say, "If I don't like her, I will take her."

The creature in the wagon seems to nod, slowly.

"You may do, at that," she says, musingly. "And yet, what choice do we have?"

A wisp of her darkness reaches out of the wagon and indicates a certain hut a little way off, wooden walls and thatch on the roof.

"That is the one," she says. "Walk through the door when the lightning comes. You will find your way. You will call to each other, I am sure."

I stare at her eyes, and her eyes stare back at me.

Then I am turning, kicking my heel in the mud (there is mud here, now that my poison is no longer running into the earth, the rain is doing its work on the soil) and I am walking away from the wagon, towards the hut. The wind howls in my ears. My skin is cold and wet.

I reach the door of the hut. It is broken, and the bottom half is gone. The top half flaps madly in the gale. Inside, the hut is dark.

No, I think. This is not where I must go, not yet.

Lightning strikes again and again. To either side I see the sky light up, I see unspeakable landscapes flash and vanish, I see changes and changes and changes, and none of them are the right change.

I can feel it. Somewhere deep inside, some part of me knows for what I am waiting. I can feel it in the earth.

I wait. The air tastes of heat and power. My eyes do not leave the door.

The lightning comes again. This time it is in the right place.

The world in front of me is consumed in pure white fire. I am moving forward even before the first shock of whiteness begins to fade, even as the strange world behind the blank veil shimmers before me, even as I see that the broken door is gone and the wood of the hut is changed and the air is clear and dry and smells of summer.

I walk through the lightning, and the lightning is gone, and the hut I have stepped into is different.

For a moment, everything is blurring, everything is broken. I can see a thousand huts, a million. I can see everything, I can see it all. I see the children gathered around the old woman as she tells her stories, and I see the old woman falling into death (*and that is me!* part of myself screams. *She is fighting me!*) and I see it all, so much more, births and lives and deaths, and everything in between...and then I see the lady, and it is like a great bell sounding in my skull, and all the other worlds slip away, and I am alone with her.

It feels like falling. It feels like diving into a lake and finding yourself springing out of the water onto dry land. I stagger and grip at the wall to keep from tumbling down.

The lightning is striking still. I can see it flashing blue through the cracks in the old wooden walls. But it is further back now, though perhaps getting closer.

I look at the woman. She is dressed all in white and she is ageless and she has no face.

Something tightens in me, some part of me I thought was broken long ago is twitching in my chest.

I take a half-step towards her, then pull to a stop.

She twists her neck and examines me with her skin-covered eyes. I can see her eyes move beneath. I see her jaw opening, though her mouth is covered with red skin and I can see no teeth.

"Prince Valiben," she whispers to me. "You have returned. I look into you, and I understand you." She pauses, while outside the wind hustles and hurls itself against the walls.

"You have failed me," she says at last, and though I can see she is smiling, there is something sad in her voice. "I understand every step of the journey you have taken; and yet you return with no companion for me. Go away. I cannot help you."

How can this be? I think to myself. I have travelled very far, I have walked many miles. The first thing I learnt was that any child could see that the body I had claimed was no longer the same. It is a shock to not be recognised. It scalds my pride, it washes all other thoughts away, and before I know what I am doing, I am lunging forward and grasping at the woman's arm.

I want to scream, *Look at me!* I want to scream, *I am no Prince! I am no man! I am dark as pits in the earth, and no one will take* me *lightly!*

I take her arm and spin her towards me, and she gasps in shock, her face moving in strange ways, the skin that covers her mouth thrumming urgently.

"You...You surprised me," the woman mutters. Then she seems to pull herself up. That is the only way to put it. She tilts her head and I can feel the weight of her gaze on me, measuring me, burning into me, seeking for that part of me that she has not been able to sense...

Her face goes slack.

"Could it be...?" she mutters, and her hands start to explore my body, my face, my arms, my belly. But every place they touch, that is a place where I have hung my darkness most heavy. Everywhere her hands lay, they do not touch this body I wear; instead, they stroke the shadowed substances, the tendrils of darkness I have woven around the man. Perhaps she knows where the body *should* end, perhaps she can understand this body completely, knows the extent and measure of every strand of hair and fibre of muscle.

But by knowing where the body *should* end, she is able to gain a hint as to where my flesh and coils are most likely to lay.

She is breathing faster now, faster, chest heaving with excitement, hands darting and squeezing and caressing, skin-covered eyes open wide and staring.

Then abruptly she is still. Her hands are on my shoulders. They tighten one last time, then hang loose. She takes a slow step backwards, and I can see the effort she makes to marshal herself.

"You have done what I thought was impossible," she says. Her voice is still low, but there is strength in it again, belief. "You have found me a companion, you have brought me the one person in all the many worlds who I could never understand."

Then she tilts her head, and I feel that the woman is looking straight into me; not into the body I wear or the eyes I look out of: straight into *me*, into my very soul. And at that moment an awful fear rises in me, and I try to turn, but it is too late.

"Now I must unmake us both," she says simply.

She lunges forward, quicker than I would have thought possible, and I am stumbling backwards, trying to avoid those fierce, grasping hands.

They plunge into my flesh; but they do not touch the body I am wearing, and as it continues to stumble backwards as I have commanded, I can feel myself being wrenched free, sucked and pulled from every pore and opening, until with a last jerk, the body falls in a boneless heap on the floor, and I am writhing in the air. I am pinioned there by her two white arms, strong shards of radiance plunging into the nothingness of my body. I twist and scramble, but she has me tight. I cannot get free. I let out a shriek, a high keening wail that slices through the air and causes the candles to gutter.

"No!" I cry. "Let me go! Let me *go!*"

But she does not respond to my words, she just stares at me with eyes wide behind flaps of pale skin.

"This will hurt us both," she says.

I open my shadowed lips to scream, but I have no time.

Before I can utter another word, her arms snap towards her, bringing me with them. I am pulled into her light, and suddenly her light is all the world is made of, endless light and pale skin.

I cannot move. I cannot see. I have no body and my mind is fading, dissolving in the raw white light of her. Then comes the pain, pain such as I have never known. It fills me up. I have no body to feel pain; rather, I am *made* of pain itself, as if all I had eaten was pain, and all I ever breathed was pain, and pain was my skin and soul, and the world was made of shades of pain and sound knelled on scales of pain and people and animals and fresh grass all smelled of pain and pain and pain the pain and pain until until until...

The pain is gone and my story is done.

I am I no longer. What is left of me, what I have become, smiles the first true smile that has touched her face for a long, long time, and tells a new story, and it is called

✿ 60 ✿

THE STORY OF MY YESTERDAYS

∾

I am clear and whole. The storm rages outside, the lightning flashes; yet I know peace at last, at last. The young man in the corner stirs, coming up from shadows. Time is short. I know. But first I must tell. I am complete now, remade; but yesterday

I am barren and bare. People come and speak, saying, "Please?" saying, "If I only knew." saying, "I don't understand". I give them what they think they want. Sometimes I add a price. I have given up hoping; yet still I ask the impossible. The young man is one such. I will never be complete; but yesterday

I am worn and weary. Travelling this far without darkness, I start to see everything in light. Everything. It burns me, blinds me, these truths I see I never ask for, and people never want to hear. I can understand it all: that's the kind of curse that falls on those who have lost half of themselves. I have a new idea: if I give up wandering and wait, maybe she will come back to me. One day I may be complete; but yesterday

I am travelling endless. The miles melt under my feet. Skin grows over me, but still I see, breath, smell. I begin to glimpse the things the dark half had kept hidden. Even the memory of shadow is leaving me. And yet I must search, I must strain, I must find. When I am myself again, I will find the one I love; but yesterday

I am fleeing, blasted. The severing is strong, painful beyond belief. The energy of it is endless; we are cast reeling through the worlds, smashing barrier after barrier, lost, scattered. I am flung so far I think I must have been cast back to the very beginning of things. I pick myself up, feeling broken, deranged; I am. I have lost half of myself, and nothing will ever make sense again. I gather myself, I must look for her, I must find her; but yesterday

I am awaking breathless. Hundreds of miles away, the ring is shattering. Its shards are spinning, and I catch a small glimpse as the other half of my soul is severed from me. Then the wind comes, and the pieces of me are scattered. His face flashes through my mind; but yesterday

I am set and determined. In the dark under the stars I weave my spells and speak my words and a blue fire springs and the ring I wear is bathed in strange light. It feels odd, it feels...unbalanced. But as my Shadow steps away from my feet, as she ducks and smiles her secret smile, and bobs a mocking bow, I cannot help but smile, too. Now a part of me can go with him when he leaves. I will see him again soon. But tomorrow

61

THE DARKNESS UNDER THE EARTH (REPRISE)

∽

I open my eyes. Outside, the thunder still rolls; more than ever. But something that has been wrong inside me for so long that I can barely remember is now healed, and I open my mouth and I breath the crackling air and I smile.

My face feels stiff. It feels as if it is caked with something soft and cloying. I lift up my hand, and it comes away holding sheets of skin. My skin. There is no pain, there is no blood. What I am taking away is dead already. What I am cleaning away, I have no use for.

The air is baking and full of the crackle of spent lightning, but it tastes good. It tastes so good. I start to cry.

A figure moans and pulls itself upwards. It is Valiben, the young man who brought me the other half of myself after all these years. I remember him so clearly. I remember him twice. I remember him coming to me and begging for answers, looking earnest and silly and proud; and I remember him coming to me beneath the earth, covered in slime and desperate, fearful. He did not know what I was, that time. He never knew what I really was.

He deserves praise, he deserves thanks, and rest. Most of all he deserves the understanding he has sought for so long: he wants to go home.

"Who are you?" he asks. I can see in his eyes: he knows me, and yet he does not. I am the whole, when before he met the halves.

"Sebille," I tell him simply. "I would say more but..."

But there is no time. Maybe later. Maybe, if I succeed.

I remember what the darkness in the wagon told me; I understand at last.

I am at Valiben's side in an instant. The body feels so weak. Flesh feels so weak after you have tasted the delicious power that can be liberated by pulling your soul apart.

But it feels wonderful. I feel small and human. I feel like me.

I put a hand to his shoulder, steady him. His eyes swing to me, and he gapes. He has never seen what I look like before, not really. Perhaps somewhere between the light and the shadow, perhaps not. I don't have time to ask him.

"We must go back," I tell him, and together we stagger to the doorway.

Lightning comes again and again. I can feel him tense. He wants to move, he is impatient.

I am steady. If we move too fast, everything ends.

The lightning flashes, and I catch a glimpse of the wagon, and I know this is right, and I heave us through.

The noise is unbearable. Valiben is shouting something in my ear, but I cannot hear what he is saying. The thunder is not thunder. It is the tearing of mountains. The earth is flickering beneath my feet. The sky is turning brown. All the colours of the world are mixing.

Her wagon is the only steady thing in the whole spinning universe. The creatures crouch on top, ducking, fearful. The door is open, and I can see her black-red eyes within.

I shove Valiben in ahead of me, then follow after. The door slams shut without anyone touching it, and the wagon lurches, and we are away. I can hear footsteps on the roof, pounding faster and faster. We are picking up speed.

The Mistress of the Wagon is staring at me. Her mouth is closed and her eyes are open.

I return her gaze. To my surprise, I find that I can.

At last, her mouth twitches in the darkness. A grin spreads, hundreds of sharp teeth glinting.

"You found yourself, then," she says.

I nod.

"And you know what you have to do now?" Her eyes do not blink. They are hard.

I nod again.

"I remember everything," I tell her softy. "I remember the life without shadows...And I remember the life that was nothing but shadows."

We travel in silence for a little while. The wagon lurches occasionally. We are sliding through layers of reality, cutting through the skein of dissolving stories, heading for the place in the very centre where all the rottenness is coming from.

"I cannot enter the room," says the Mistress. "It is not permitted. None of my kind can enter that room."

I nod. I understand. Of course I do.

"Which is why you need me," I say.

"That was one reason," she allows.

Silence.

Silence.

Silence.

Then screams.//

//The sword is thrust cruelly in the wheel at the centre, and my man turns it further. The world screams murder, and it is true: this is the biggest murder, the blackest murder ever done by anyone unto the unhappy world.

And I know this is evil, and wrong, and all the safeguards have failed; but even through that, the music of his whistle holds us to our course; and I keep my mouth closed against the two outside who could stop this, and the monk and his apprentice hold down the man within this chamber who could stop this, and a part of me is breaking into a million pieces out of sheer abhorrence at what we are doing to the world.

My man, he gives a roar, and he turns the wheel another inch. And that is it: with that movement, another wave of crumbling, tearing, rending echoes through the Storystream, and I am suddenly everywhere and I am everything, and I wonder if all things can feel this, this awful exalted terror, high and golden and dreadful. My perceptions are overwhelmed with images of what is passing elsewhere, hundreds of them, millions of them, an endless river of story, so huge it is too vast for the mind to comprehend and it will tear me (us) all apart and chaos takes me and I dissolve and//

//I dissolve and//

//I dissolve and//

//Wait. My eye catches something. Someone, something is tearing through the world with purpose, it is moving faster than sound, fleeter than light, swifter than darkness. It is tearing at the speed of thought, and if I can only *push* away at all the other crowding sensations, if I can only bring myself to bear on this one sight, perhaps, perhaps (is there hope?) perhaps I can see...//

//a wagon, painted black and with black wheels, the door slamming shut and blotting out a darkness that was deeper still, thundering through the air against a background of falling stars, and on the roof, a pig is all a-lather to make sure they are not too late, and the cat makes a minor adjustment of course, and the world shimmers around them; and in the deep darkness of the wagon, reflected in the eye of the Mistress (which anyone would count themselves lucky to never have the misfortune of seeing) is a cavern surrounded by images at the very heart of things//

//and I melt//

/and I am her and me and I and we are one, identities running together as the Storystream itself blurs//

//The screaming is high-pitched and awful; the wagon shudders. It shakes so hard I worry it will fall to pieces, but it does not. The wagon gives a final shake, and then we are slowing, the wheels rumbling across hard stone.

We come to a halt.

The door swings open, and I step out. Valiben is close behind, but the Mistress stays in her darkness.

I had not thought the screaming could get any worse, but as soon as the door opens, the cacophony swells up. It is overwhelming, so loud I can hardly think, so loud it takes every ounce of effort I have to stop my knees giving way, so awful it is as if every evil thing that was ever done had been let loose to scour the world as sound.

I force my legs to move.

The landscape is uncertain.

It flickers and changes. One moment it is solid rock beneath my feet; the next I am walking over a pool of crimson blood; the next I am falling through endless air. But when I close my eyes I can feel the earth beneath my feet. And there, a little way off, an oak door stands firm in the unstable landscape. It looks solid and ancient; it does not flicker, it does not split under the assault of searing noise.

I will my feet to walk, one foot in front of the other. I try to block out the sights, the noise. We are falling, we are all falling.

The further we fall, the further into madness we descend.

One foot in front of the other.

I reach the door, and find I am not alone.

There are others here: a tall woman, a giant of a woman - she would tower over me, only she is curled up outside the door, her hands clasped over her ears, a scream bellowing unheard from her lips - and another, a figure made of light, small, faded. Now that the barriers are failing, now that the worlds are being whipped to chaos and storm, the old spells are failing, too. His sinews are knit with old magics, magics woven of salt and blood. Before long he will have passed into nothing.

Yet even as he is failing, this figure perceives me; and rallying some enormous effort of will, he pulls the strands of himself together and rises to bar my way.

"The way is not open," he whispers, and I can hear him over the breaking of the world.

I shake my head. I cannot explain. I do not have the time, it is too complicated, too much to say here in the heart of the gale.

I open my mouth, ready to try anyway. But a figure rushes past me. It is Valiben.

He is staring wide-eyed at the glimmering shape that bars my way. There are tears in his eyes. The ghost looks at him, and recognition flashes between them. Then Valiben looks at me, then back at the other. He nods, urgent, urging.

The ghostly figure hesitates. Then a look settles on his face, a determination. He stares at Valiben, and there are tears in his eyes, too, ghost-tears that run down his pale face and vanish as they roll away into the shimmering world.

The figure closes his eyes. The last of the magic that holds his ghost-flesh together is failing, blown away by this wind that rides out from the ending of the worlds.

He holds on and he holds on and he holds on...and then it is all used up.

The magic that summoned him back from death breaks.

It happens so quickly. I barely have time to see the look of peace start to form in his eyes; then he is fading, the blue light of him flickering and dying away.

He is gone. Beside me, Valiben falls to his knees.

The door stands before me. I reach out to touch it, knowing before I do that it will be barred against us. My hands brushes against the ancient wood, and a voice whips back at me, crying out telling me the story of

62

THE END OF ALL THINGS

～

The woman brushes her hand against my oak and I scream at her, because the madness is in me, so thick and wild it is like every thought that ever passed through me is spinning in a hurricane at the centre of my mind, unchained and flitting unbidden, and I want so much to open, I want to let her in because she is the only hope now, she is the only way that this could be stopped, but his whistle is still in me, holding me shut, forcing me to keep the way barred, and she knows all this in a flash, understands it before she even tries to push me open, and on the other side of me the tall man laughs and laughs and tears run down his cheeks and he heaves the wheel another degree and another thousand stories bleed to darkness, and the Storystream is spinning so fast that the details are blurred, and the barriers are breaking, and I hear a terrible cry, louder even than the constant earth-deep tearing of the Universe, and I push my awareness back to the outside, and I see that the woman has stepped away and the young man has stepped away, and the door of the wagon has creaked open, and it is from there that the terrible noise comes, and with that awful roar, a darkness comes pouring into the world, huge and impossible, red eyes and white teeth glaring down at me, and I have time to think, *yes, yes, at last*, and then the darkness is pulled back and the teeth are drawn and I am full of joy because I know what manner of creature this is, and I know they are not permitted to pass through into the room beyond, and that is a law made by a power so deep that it is written into the very fabric of things, and yet this does not matter because it does not need to pass through, it only needs to open a way into the room beyond, and then those teeth are upon me, biting into my oak, crushing and tearing me, and it hurts beyond belief but I don't care and then the parts of me are flying backwards hurtling into the room and the doorway I guarded is opened and the dreadful whistle might be in me but I cannot obey it any more, and I see the shadow pulling backwards, and the woman bracing herself and walking through, entering the room, and the tall man senses her somehow - though he did not even twitch as I was torn to pieces, he was so intent on his work - and now he looks up and his hands loosen their grip on the wheel, and he stares at her face as if he has seen a ghost, and he says, "You," and looks like he will say more, but at that moment the man who has been pinned to the floor by his two friends sees her as well, and their eyes meet, and there is love there, as deep and powerful as an ocean, and it rolls out from them like a wave of fire, and it lights up her eyes and she strides further into the room and she stops a pace from the tall man, and he is looking at her, and he is not turning the wheel, and he says, "I see you now. See you very well," and his words are ragged things, torn from somewhere deep inside; and he goes on, "You wear such pretty skin now, a fool might not recognise the darkness. But I see your darkness, buried in the light. You took her from me, you took her and you broke my heart and you took that, too," and his voice is getting higher, wilder, and his eyes are burning with hatred and she tells him, "Yes," and she tries, "I am sorry," and she says, "I was not myself; and-" with a sudden rising fury of her own "-who made me less than myself? Who broke me, so that the darkness could seep out unchecked?" and my man shakes at that, shakes like he has been slapped, because he understands suddenly who broke her, he knows it very well; and as the Storystream screams around them in jagged pieces of shattered time, it is clear to him - I can see it in his eyes, in his very heart - he sees the dark joke of it, the cruel twist of broken causality which, writhing like a liquid knife, took his Heather because of the things that he had done, done in turn and turn about, a dark spiral wrapping itself in endless loops, so that misery is eating itself forever, eating itself and vomiting hate back into the world, too; and he shrieks and sobs the louder for the terrible knowledge, and she screams at him to stop, for the sake of everything, for the sake of every child that ever was or could be, for the sake of every other Heather out there, and they will all die if he does not stop, and he pauses for a moment, and there is a stillness in the room, and there is hope; and then his eyes lock on hers and he moves so fast she never sees his fist coming and then she is reeling backwards and blood is pouring from her nose, and he is pulling his sword from where it is lodged in the depths of the wheel and he is advancing on her, and she is helpless, trying to crawl away, and he is standing over her and the sword is raised, and then it is coming down, and there is a bellow, and the young man who loves her has thrown off the others, has thrown off the monk and his apprentice, and is leaping forward, leaping desperately, and he is between her and the blade, and he takes the blade for her, and she looks on in horror as it cuts him down, and he tells her, "Go," and then he is dead, and the tall man grits his teeth in a horrible grin and pulls away his sword and strides back to the wheel and grips it hard, and suddenly the teeth of the vast dark thing are back in the doorway and they are screaming for her to come, to run, that this is the end, and she is crying so hard and not moving, and then the teeth pull back from the doorway and Valiben is jumping in, pulling her backwards, pulling her away from the body of her dead lover, out of the doorway and into the wagon, and it is pulling away, moving so fast that the world shifts around it, and then it spins off and away and I hope they make it because this is the end and the world is shattering, even within the central room cracks appear, as the tall man laughs and weeps and gives one last heave, and the wheel completes its turn - a whole circle - and all the walls come crashing down and there is//

63

SILENCE

~

//
//
//

~

✣ 64 ✣

THE THINGS THAT REMAIN

∿

V aliben opened his eyes. It was so dark, at first he thought he
was dead. Then he saw that there was a faint rectangle of
light leaking in from one corner of the darkness. He
wondered what it was.

The world was silent. He thought he could hear someone breathing, very faintly. He wondered if it was himself.

He could remember very little. Everything was confused.

There was...a darkness underground...and something about lightning. But he was sure something had happened since then. Wasn't
there something about a door? He wished that his brother was here,
Myst had always had a better memory for details than...

The image came into his mind. His brother, a ghost, hanging in
blue light, barring the way to the door at the centre of things.

Everything came crashing back.

Finding the darkness under the earth, being taken by it, travelling
back to the woman of perfect understanding, and the reunion of her
two halves, and the flight to the central room so that Sebille could
confront the man who was destroying everything. And their failure.

He remembered their failure. He shut his eyes and sighed. He had rushed into the room, hardly stopping to think what he was doing. He had grabbed her, as she lay weeping over her dead lover, and he had pulled her out and bundled them both into the wagon. Then there had been that last wild flight, smashing from one world to the next, desperately searching for one, any one that was not collapsing, that was not doomed...

His eyes snapped open.

They must have found one. They must have found somewhere safe.

He looked around again. The rectangle of light was still there.

It's the door, he suddenly realised.

He was still inside the wagon, and a faint light was leaking in from outside, through the cracks in the doorway.

He leaned forward to open the door, and stopped.

There were no eyes in here.

The realisation slammed into him like a sledgehammer.

Her eyes had gone. And so had her teeth.

The Mistress of the Wagon was not in her wagon.

He wasn't sure what that meant, but he was fairly certain it wasn't good.

Someone stirred on the floor, and Valiben twitched back.

He made out the outline of a small shape on the floor. It was moving weakly.

It made a noise, and Valiben recognised the voice.

"Sebille?" he asked.

There was a pause. Then, "Where are we?" she asked.

Valiben shook his head in the darkness.

"I don't know," he said. "I mean, we're in the wagon, but I don't know where the wagon is."

He reached out a hand, and gave the door a shove.

It creaked, and swung open, filling the wagon with a faint, tepid light.

Valiben looked out into a vague, grey world. He could see nothing distinct.

He exchanged a glance with Sebille. She clambered painfully to her feet, clutching a lump on the side of her head.

She rubbed her scalp. Then she shrugged.

Valiben stepped out through the doorway, and down onto the ground.

It seemed to be made of nothing more solid than mist, and for a horrible moment he thought his foot would just keep going, and he would fall through it and downwards forever. But then something soft supported him, and he moved forward and looked around.

They were in a vague, grey country. There were no hills or trees. There was no moon or sun. There were no people, not that he could see. All there seemed to be was a thin, diffuse light, and the wagon, and Sebille, and himself. A little way away, this soft, grey country faded imperceptibly into a black nothingness.

"You can come out," he called back in to Sebille. "It's safe. I think."

Sebille came out and joined him. She began looking around.

"Where do you think we are?" she asked at last.

Valiben shook his head in bemusement.

"I don't know," he admitted.

There was a small, pointed cough. It came from the roof of the wagon.

They both spun round, and saw a supercilious feline face staring down at them.

"Torquemada!" exclaimed Valiben, overjoyed beyond all reasonable expectations to see the large cat. "I am glad to see you! Where are we? Do you know?"

"Of course I know," said the cat. It sounded flat.

"Well?" prompted Sebille, after it became clear that the cat wasn't going to offer anything further.

Torquemada rolled his eyes.

"We're in the place that remains, of course," he said, as if it were perfectly obvious. "The only place that wasn't destroyed. The only bit that was safe."

There was a pause.

Torquemada sighed.

"I suppose you need me to delineate things further, hmm?" He yawned and stretched his paws. "The Mistress knew we had failed. She knew it was all collapsing. So the last thing she did was to send us here."

"Then where is she?" asked Valiben.

"Oh, she couldn't come," said the cat, sounding scandalised. "She was too big a part of everything, you see. No way she could fit down here. She was far too high profile. When the wheel was turned completely, all the major players had to report in, as it were. No, she's not down here."

"And where is here, exactly?" asked Valiben, all traces of his initial joy at having seen the cat having now vanished.

"The Land Below Stories, of course," said Torquemada. "Or rather, what's left of it. Rather joyless sort of a place, I always think."

"And what are we supposed to do?" cut in Sebille. "Just stay here forever? Just rot in this...this little bit of nothing, just wait out the rest of forever, brooding on our failure?"

The cat fixed her with a cold glare.

"Don't look at me, it wasn't my idea," Torquemada told her.

Sebille held the cat's gaze for a moment, then shook her head and started walking aimlessly away.

"But...but wait," said Valiben, suddenly remembering something. "What about Max? What about your friend, the pig? Are they up there with you?"

He tried a little jump, but couldn't get high enough to see over the top of the wagon.

Torquemada looked away and made a tutting noise.

"They didn't make it, I'm afraid," he said.

Valiben froze.

"They didn't...They what?"

"They couldn't hold on," said the cat. "Not when we were falling down here. It was too wild. Your friend got sucked away into the Unmaking." Torquemada made a show of examining one of his claws, then looked Valiben in the eye, and seemed to soften. "I'm sorry," he added.

Valiben swallowed twice, then sat down.

"Oh," he said.

"I," he began, then stopped. He tried again. "I'm sorry, too," he managed. "About your friend. About Bartleby, I mean."

The cat shrugged. He had gone back to examining his claws.

"Stuff happens," he said, sounding vaguely philosophical. "Better him than me. He wouldn't know what to do with himself down here."

They sat in silence for a while. The only noise was the faint scraping sound of Torquemada picking his claws.

"So, now what?" asked Valiben, at length.

Torquemada shrugged.

"We wait," said the cat.

"Wait? Wait for what?" asked Valiben.

"For things to regenerate," said the cat. "No unmaking is ever one hundred percent complete. There's always a faint sliver of story left over. Gradually, things build up again from there. It takes a while, though," he added, darkly.

"A while?" said Valiben. "How long is 'a while'?"

Torquemada yawned again.

"Well, if there was only a strand or two left, it might take a *really* long time," said the cat. "It would be more usual for there only to be a patch of this place left, but as we managed to get down here before everything went kaput..." He shrugged. "Who knows? It might be relatively quick. Thirty or forty million years? It's difficult to say."

Valiben choked. He felt like he couldn't breath.

"Thirty or forty *million* years?" he echoed. "We have to wait here for thirty or forty million *years*? But...but there's no food! There's nothing to drink! What are we supposed to live on for thirty or forty million years!"

"I was never a big eater," said the cat. "You'll get used to it, I would have thought. Anyway, after forty million years or so, we should begin to see the first traces."

"First traces? First traces of what?" Valiben demanded.

Torquemada lifted one eyebrow.

"Why, growth, of course," he said, as if explaining something very basic to someone very stupid. "Only at the edges, at first. Things will start to get bigger. Eventually, a bit will be big enough to break off, and that will go on to form a new Beginning. Then another bit will break off, and we'll start to have a story or two, which will then necessitate various other things - an Afterlife, a new Centre, Epitaphs, and so on - and eventually, the whole mess will begin to run again. And no one will be any the wiser that it's not the first time it's all come into existence."

Valiben gaped at him.

"You mean...forty million years is only the *start* of the wait?" he managed to croak out.

"Oh yes," agreed the cat. "Oh, absolutely. No, we've got many, many times that length to wait before anything interesting begins to happen."

"What am I meant to do until then?" demanded Valiben.

Torquemada shrugged.

"Catch up on your sleep, I suppose," he suggested, indifferently.

"But...but how do you *know* all this?" Valiben asked.

"Oh, you get used to it after a while," said Torquemada vaguely. "Sort of comes with the job. The Mistress was very up-to-date on all this stuff. Bartleby and I, we more or less picked it up by osmosis. Now, if you'll excuse me, I have a millennia or two of nap time to catch up on. Try not to wake me, if you don't mind."

With that, Torquemada settled down, and before Valiben could think of anything to say, he was purring contentedly to himself and fast asleep.

Valiben looked at the cat in amazement.

Then he got up off the ground, and wondered what he should do.

He was just beginning to come to terms with the information he had been given, and was wondering whether the most logical response would be to scream or to cry, when he heard a shout. It was Sebille.

"What?" he shouted back. "What did you say?"

But there was no answer.

A moment later, the sound of soft footsteps approached, and then Sebille herself came into view. She was breathing hard, and carrying something in her hand.

"What is it?" asked Valiben.

"Look!" said Sebille. "Look, I found something!"

"What is it?" said Valiben, trying to work out what the crumpled thing in her hand was.

"It's a note!" said Sebille triumphantly. "I found it over there," she pointed vaguely beyond the wagon.

"What does it say?" Valiben asked.

"Here, have a look," Sebille told him.

She handed him a sheet of paper. On it, an elegant, flowing hand had written:

~

To Whom It May Concern:

Hello! I hope you find my little realm to your liking. I'm afraid I've had to pop out for a few eons due to some structural work being performed on the nature of reality. I'm terribly sorry to have missed you, but I am sort of the ruler around here, and it was frightfully important that I checked in when the wheel was turned. I've had to take all the Munchers with me, so it should be quite safe. It is a shame that it's come to this, but I suppose the Pheasant knows best. Actually, I haven't seen her for a while, so you might want to keep your eyes open; who knows? Perhaps things aren't so grim after all.

I hope you enjoy your stay while we wait for the emergent properties of existence to create themselves out of nothing again, and I look forward to meeting you in a subsequent reality.

Warmest regards,

Rosewater (Lord of the Land Below Stories)

PS: I managed to save rather a lot of manure. I've heaped it in a pile in a corner. You might find it useful.

PPS: There are biscuits under my desk. They're only digestives, but please help yourselves.

~

Valiben read the note, frowned, read it again, then handed it back to Sebille.

"What's a 'digestive'?" he asked suspiciously.

Sebille shrugged.

"I don't know," she replied, "but I'm not sure that's the important bit of the message. What do you think he meant by 'the Pheasant'? And why might manure be useful?"

Valiben didn't know. He thought he knew who might, though.

"Yes?" said Torquemada coldly, a moment before Valiben poked him.

"We...ah, we need your help," Valiben told him.

He explained about the note Sebille had found. Then Sebille read it out while the cat listened, eyes half closed, wearing a disgusted look at having been disturbed.

"It's quite straightforward," he told them, when Sebille had finished reading. "I'm sure you can work it out. Now buzz off and put some thought into it yourselves, instead of getting me to do your thinking for you!"

With that, he closed his eyes, and would not open them, no matter how loud Valiben shouted.

"Leave him," said Sebille, "he's not going to help us."

Valiben noticed that her eyes were rimmed with red, as if she had been crying.

They wandered away from the wagon. Valiben was not quite sure what they were looking for.

He licked his lips, unsure what to say.

"I'm...I'm sorry about what happened," he said, quietly. "Back in that room, I mean. That man, the one who was killed. Was he...?"

Sebille caught his eye for a moment, nodded, looked down.

"He did it to save you," Valiben said after a moment. "He saw that the sword was going to hit you and..."

"He's not going to have died," said Sebille, calm but firm.

"What?" said Valiben.

"When we fix things," she replied. "When we make them right. He won't have died." she gave him a sad smile. "And neither will your friend. They'll both be alive. You'll see."

She quickened her pace. Valiben struggled to keep up.

"Sebille," he said softly, "I wish I could tell you I agreed with you. I wish that we *could* bring them back. But we were too late. We failed. We..." He trailed off, frowning. "Where are we going?" he asked, suddenly curious.

Sebille walked a little further, then stopped and turned.

"Here," she said. "We're here."

Behind her, the cloudy landscape rose upwards in a little hillock. It seemed to be composed of nothing at all.

"We're where?" asked Valiben.

"At the manure," said Sebille. "At least, I think that's what this is. I can't see what else it might be, and it was near here that I found the letter. It was just floating in the air, as if it was pinned to nothing." She shrugged. "Maybe this Rosewater wanted us to find it."

"But why?" Valiben demanded.

"We'll see," said Sebille.

Then she crouched down, reached out a hand, hesitated, and then plunged it through the mist.

There was a damp squelching noise.

"I think we have something," she said.

She pulled back her hand. It was covered in something.

It was difficult to describe. It was difficult even to *see*. The eye seemed to slide off the stuff. It made the inside of the head itch just to look at it.

It was a blackish purplish paste, very fine and moist. Faint shimmerings of fey colour ran along the substance, and there was the zing of unearthed potential in the air.

"Is that...?" asked Valiben.

Sebille nodded slowly.

"It's manure," she said. "It's got to be. And if this is the place where all the old bits of stories go to be digested after they are done and told...maybe this is what comes out the other end."

"Meaning...what, exactly?"

Sebille smiled.

"Meaning it is fertile," she told him. "Meaning that we are not the only solid pieces of story that survived the Unmaking. Meaning that..."

She suddenly stopped talking in mid-sentence. Her mouth was hanging open, and she was staring at something over Valiben's shoulder.

Valiben spun around, and saw what she was gaping at.

"Is that...?" he managed at last.

Sebille nodded.

"I think so," she said. "It's not quite...I mean it doesn't look quite..."

Valiben knew what she meant.

The pheasant didn't look quite *real*. It looked like a child's drawing of a pheasant. Or rather, it looked like the drawing done by a child who had never seen an actual pheasant, but who had had a spirited attempt at rustling one up out of the corners of their imagination.

It was all jagged lines and wrong colours. But it was regarding them with warm, placid eyes. It cocked its head. Then it blinked at them benignly.

"I think...I think it's trying to tell us something," whispered Valiben.

Sebille was staring at the creature. Then she took a breath, and began to shuffle slowly forward.

The pheasant held its ground. It looked quite unafraid.

Sebille moved forward until she was standing right beside it, then she sank to her knees. Tentatively she put out a hand - the one that wasn't covered in manure - and stroked it gently down the pheasant's head.

The pheasant rubbed itself affectionately against her.

Then it looked meaningfully at the manure she was holding.

Sebille licked her lips. Then she slowly raised it until her manure-covered hand was only inches away from the bird.

The pheasant inspected the manure. Then it clucked pleasantly, leaned forward, rolled out its tongue, and gave one of her fingers a lick. Then it looked at her meaningfully.

Slowly, very slowly, Sebille lifted her hand to her own mouth. She could see the part of her finger that the bird had licked. The manure there had started sparkling even more urgently than the rest.

"Wait," said Valiben, suddenly realising what she was doing. "I'm not sure that's a good idea. It seems quite unsanitary. Why don't we just...Urgh! You've *licked* it!"

Sebille spun round to face Valiben.

"It's fine," she told him. "I think it's what..."

Her eyes widened and she stopped talking.

"What?" demanded Valiben. "What is it? Have you been poisoned? Can you hear me?"

Sebille shook her head. She held a hand up to stop the flow of questions.

"I...I think I almost understand," she muttered.

She glanced back at the pheasant, which continued to stare at her genially; then she got to her feet and walked quickly back to Valiben.

She had one hand clasped nervously to her mouth, as if thinking furiously.

"It's trying to tell me something," she said urgently. "I can almost understand it...something about you and me, and this place, and...and the nature of, of *everything*, and, well..." She stopped. She closed her eyes and let out a deep sigh. When she spoke again, her voice was calmer, and there was a new light in her eyes. "The world is made of stories," she said. "Isn't that what all this is about? The Unmaking that Amos let loose when he turned that wheel, that was meant to break all the stories, wasn't it? It was meant to stop them being told?"

She stared at Valiben and he nodded, *yes*.

She raised her arms imploringly.

"Then how is it we are still here?" she said.

There was silence. Valiben couldn't answer her.

"Everything was Unmade, apart from this place which *cannot* be unmade, because it was never really made in the first place, it just, well, it just *was*," she smiled at him. "But what about us? What about you and I? What about Torquemada? The fact that we're still here means that someone must be telling this story, telling the story that we're in *right now*. And if that's the case, then it means that there still really is hope!"

"But...but if we're in a story..." said Valiben, his eyes darting about rapidly as he thought. "If we're in this story...then who is telling it?"

They looked at each other; then slowly, inexorably, they turned their heads and looked at the pheasant.

"*Her?*" asked Valiben breathlessly.

Sebille nodded.

The pheasant - or rather, The Pheasant - returned their gaze in a friendly sort of a way.

"Well done," said a familiar feline voice, "I told you that you'd work it out."

Torquemada sauntered out of the mist, yawning and rolling his shoulders. He swayed by The Pheasant, giving a little nod as he passed. The Pheasant returned the nod and made a contented squawking noise.

"So...so what do we do now?" asked Valiben.

"Pth!" exclaimed Torquemada. "Really, you've got this far and you need me to tell you that? I don't think so."

Valiben glanced around, looking for inspiration. He tried to catch Sebille's eye, but she was staring at the ground, a look of concentration on her face.

Suddenly, she looked up.

"I have to go back," she said. "I can stop this, I can undo this. I'm sure I can."

She paused, and looked at Valiben.

"You have to...to put me back there," she told him.

He frowned. "What?" he said. "What do you mean?"

"You have to...to...*tell* me back there," she said. "You have to tell the story, tell the story of me going back there, of me finding Amos, and stopping him...Of *changing* things, somehow."

Valiben looked at her blankly.

"Me?" he said, dubiously. "I need to tell you into a story? I don't think...that is to say, I'm not sure I have the power to..."

"You *have to!*" she told him. "We don't have a choice. It's the only way."

"But, but," stammered Valiben, "but how? I was never a great story-teller at the best of times, and now I have to tell a story so powerful that it will hold you in it and take you to a place where you can stop the whole Universe from being Unmade? I mean, how on earth am I going to do that?"

Sebille frowned at him. Then slowly, her frown began to soften. She smiled.

She was looking over his shoulder, at something behind him.

Valiben turned and followed her gaze.

His eyes widened.

"No," he said, hoarsely. "No, you can't be serious."

Sebille nodded.

"But...but...what, *all* of it?"

Sebille shrugged, then nodded.

"But it's *manure*!" Valiben protested.

Sebille smiled.

"It doesn't taste half as bad as you expect," she said. "Actually, it doesn't taste much of anything. It's like eating...oh, I don't know. Dreams. Clouds. Something like that. Only...sweeter and tangier and almost like lightning."

Valiben sniffed. He looked rather unhappy.

"That doesn't sound like eating nothing to me," he grumbled. He looked at the ground and made a few aimless kicks. Then he straightened his back and sighed.

"If it's the only way, then we had better get on with it, I suppose," he said.

He strode to the pile of manure, pulled out a handful, and held it in front of his mouth. It glimmered strangely.

"Oh well," he said. "It's better than waiting forty million years, I suppose."

He lifted it up, and took a bite.

Actually, Sebille was right. It was much easier to eat than Valiben had feared. It even tasted quite nice, and however much he ate, his belly didn't seem to feel too full. *Something* was filling up in him, however; he could feel it, a weight building behind his eyes. It wasn't unpleasant, and it certainly wasn't painful. Just a slow, gradual filling up of...what? Power? Potential?

Whatever it was, it was getting stronger with every bite.

At last, the pile was gone. Valiben swallowed down the last mouthful, and turned to look at the others.

He nodded at them.

"Now what?" he asked. "Where should I start?"

Sebille tilted her head.

"I don't know," she told him. "It's up to you. You're the one who's eaten it all. You're the one full to the brim with the raw elements of story." She moved a step closer, and added, "Just make it worthwhile, alright? This is our only chance."

She closed her eyes, and sighed.

"Just do your best. Please? Just do your best."

Valiben coughed. He looked at the ground.

Then he sat down and made himself comfortable.

He took a deep breath.

"I want to tell you a story," he began slowly. His eyes glazed over, his head tilted to one side. "It happened far off and away and further far again, and it's called

65

THE VICTORY OF AMOS

~

There was a darkness on the worlds, and it covered all there was. It stretched from the beginning to the end and back again, it went up as high as you could go, and it fell down until you reached the bottom of the universe. It was huge.

Or did it cover all there was?

Almost. Almost, but not quite.

Somewhere far away, in a place that had once been called the very centre of things, the darkness was not complete.

There was an inverted pinnacle of black rock. The bottom was an utter point, sharper than a tooth, finer than a needle. It hung in the nothingness, still, unmoving. Upwards from the point, the inverted pinnacle broadened very gradually, before flattening out into a rough circle, perhaps a few paces in diameter.

There was no light here, yet it was perfectly plain to see what stood on the surface of that flat circle of black stone. There was a man. He was tall, with a drawn face and closed eyes. He leant his weight on a wheel that was lodged into the black rock, as if he no longer had the strength to support himself. A sword was stuck into the very centre of the wheel, right up to the hilt. Nothing moved. Everything was silent. The only sound to be heard was the noise of the man's breathing. It was very soft and shallow.

The man was thinking. He was trying very hard not to, but he could not help himself. He was thinking that he had won. He was thinking that everything, the whole of everything had been unmade. He was thinking that all that was left of the Storystream was this one little stub of tale, this little wart on what was left of the centre. And he was thinking that all that held it together now that everything else had failed was the sword that he had driven through the wheel and into the rock. Soon, when he had regained his strength, he would retrieve the sword, and then this last scattering of story on which he stood would fall into nothingness, too. He would be gone. It would be as if he had never been.

Good, he thought.

He took a deep breath. The sound of it vanished, sucked away into the darkness.

He opened his eyes. Slowly, he brought both his hands up until they were resting on the hilt of the sword. His fingers tightened, the knuckles turning white.

Now he had a good grip.

Best to do it quick, he told himself.

His muscles tensed.

There was a noise.

It was so faint, at first he wondered if he had imagined it. He relaxed his grip on the sword, his head titled to one side, his mouth hanging open as he strained against the deep silence.

At first, he could not hear anything. Then it came again.

It was soft and regular.

It sounded like footsteps. They were getting louder.

Amos frowned, his eyes narrowing.

He tried to work out what direction the noise was coming from, but the darkness was deceptive, and he could not tell.

Then something shifted, and he saw her.

It was a woman. She was walking towards him, quite calmly walking across the empty darkness, coming out of nowhere. Her feet were not falling on anything solid, and yet they were making the soft slapping noise he had been hearing.

Amos turned to face her. He kept one hand on his sword.

She came closer, and suddenly he recognised her.

It was *her*. The one who had tried to stop him at the last, the one whom he had almost killed. And reflected in the dark of her eyes...he could see, just as he had seen before, that it was also the thin woman, the one who had taken his girl, the one who had broken his life.

She looked the same and yet not the same. It had been so long since his Heather was taken, it had been so very long since the thin, dark woman had danced her dance and woven her spells, so long since his heart had been broken...

But it was her. He was sure of it.

She took another few steps forward and came to a halt. She was still standing on nothing, but she was close enough to him that he could see the lines on her face, see the dried blood caked to her cheek, the blood from the punch he had given her earlier.

"You," he breathed softly. "Why have you come back? You want to be here at the very end? When I take the sword out, and this last little outcropping falls into shadow?"

The woman looked at him in silence for a time. Then she did a strange thing.

She began to cry.

She was quite quiet. There were no sobs, there was no wailing. But tears were rolling down her cheeks, running off her face and falling, flashing away into the endless darkness below.

Amos felt a sudden, unreasoning stab of fury.

"No!" he shouted. "No, you don't get to be the one who cries! You don't get to be the one who deserves comfort! Anyone else, but not you."

Amos watched as the woman closed her eyes. With what seemed like a great effort, she managed to stem the flow of tears. At last, she looked up at him; her eyes were red, but they were dry.

"You're right," she told him. Her mouth opened and closed, no sound coming out. Then, "I don't deserve comfort," she told him. "I did you a horrible wrong. I wish I could say it was the only wrong I did. But it was not. I did many, many wrong things. I tainted many lives. I caused much suffering."

There was silence.

"Why are you telling me this?" asked Amos at last. "Do you seek my forgiveness? Do you want me to stop, now that everything is broken?" He closed his eyes, paused, and shouted, "What do you want?"

There were no echoes here, and his words died as soon as they left his mouth.

The woman licked her lips.

"I have something that belongs to you," she told him softly.

She took a step forward. Amos moved so fast his hands were a blur. He twisted and grasped the hilt of his sword, yanked it upwards. At once, the circle of black stone heaved and cracked.

"NO!" shouted the woman. "No! Please, look: I've stopped. I've stopped. See?"

Amos paused. The hilt of the sword was now several inches out of the wheel. The woman had indeed stopped. She was holding out her arms, hands spread open in supplication.

"Move back," commanded Amos. The woman nodded quickly and took a step backwards. Amos relaxed his grip on the hilt.

He hesitated. This was a trick. He knew it, knew it deep in his bones. Some last desperate trick played by the woman who had taken everything from him. He should just pull the sword out and let this last strand fall into chaos. And yet...

And yet his curiosity was piqued. Her words had worked; why deny it to himself? He wanted to know what it was, this thing she said belonged to him.

"Show me, then," he told her. "Don't come any closer. Just show me what it is of mine that you have."

The woman seemed to sag.

"Once I pull it out," she told him slowly, "it will not live for long. It needs to live in someone. If you will not take it from me, it will die."

Amos frowned. A suspicion was beginning to grow in him. Could she be offering him...? If it was possible, if she had it still, he should be overjoyed, he should be desperate for it...And yet the thought of it filled him with fear.

"What is it?" he hissed at her. "Tell me what it is."

The woman smiled at him, sadly.

"I can do better than tell you," she said. "I can show you. And then you can decide for yourself."

And before he could stop her, before he could even will his hands to move, the woman was leaning backwards, arching her back until her face was pointing straight up.

Then she began to cough. It was a horrible, barking, straining sound. It was unnatural and awful, and Amos bared his teeth in an unconscious snarl. Then her coughing turned into something uncontrollable, a bone-deep animal retching that wracked her body and made her limbs shake.

It grew louder and louder. It was horrible to watch, but Amos couldn't tear his eyes away.

Then, just when it seemed that it could get no worse, the woman lifted one of her arms and thrust her hand into her mouth. She moved the hand downwards, shoving it further and further down her throat. She was moving it back and forth, as if searching for something.

Suddenly, she seemed to find the thing she sought. Her limbs froze and her back spasmed, and she gave a terrible coughing wheeze; then she was pulling her hand back out of her throat; and held in the hand, like a fish caught on a line, was something Amos had not seen for so long he had almost forgotten it was missing.

It pulsed and glowed feebly, a yellowish purple light beating in the darkness. It smelt of summertime and childhoods and days that were gone forever.

It was the other half of his heart, that the thin woman had torn in two within him, and this half of which she had spirited away and taken on with her, to keep his strength for her own, and to leave him unbalanced and broken.

Amos gasped. He felt his knees weaken. It was all he could do to keep from sagging to the black rock.

"This is yours," the woman told him softly. "Will you have it back?"

Amos couldn't breath. The world swam in front of his eyes. He tried to shake his head, but he couldn't seem to move.

The thing in her hand was twitching faster, more desperately. It was dying. Her body had kept it alive; now that it was free of her, it could not survive.

"You must take it back," she told him. Her voice was low and urgent.

"No," Amos croaked, and he suddenly realised it was true.

He did not want the other half of his heart back. The half he had kept had given him enough pain. What would he do with all the rest of his pain? He had built up bulwarks, strengths, defences, built them all up very hard and cold, just to keep his pain at bay. He had worked on it for so long, he had thought he had turned it all to anger.

But he was wrong.

Here was the other half of that pain, raw and glistening and terrible. He could not take it back. He *would* not.

"Stay away," he hissed. He tried to force his legs to move, tried to force himself to his feet.

The woman began to walk forward. The thing she held was fluttering now, fluttering quick and shallow. It was almost over. She carried it before her like a charm to ward off evil.

"Get back!" Amos managed to say. He reached for the sword, but his hands were nerveless, and he could not grasp the hilt.

She was getting closer. She was almost on him.

His whistle! He suddenly remembered it. He still had his whistle! She could not stand against that. She had fought it before, maybe; but this was different, she was different. Surely, she could not resist his whistle. Desperately, he tried to force his lips into shape, tried to form the whistle. His throat was dry and his muscles seemed made of stone, but he coughed, and then he was calling it up.

The sound was sweet and clear in the empty air. It reminded him of the wife he had lost and the daughter who had been taken. He poured everything into it, all his pain, all his anger, channeled it into the whistle and made a stopping-song.

The whistle poured out of his lips, sped towards her; it broke on her, and fell away into the darkness. She came on.

"The Storystream is undone," she said as she came closer. "The power of your whistle is broken, too." She reached him. In one hand she held the lost half of his heart. It was almost still now, faint contractions flitting here and there on the surface. It was almost dead.

"But maybe it will not be broken forever," she said. "Maybe it is not too late."

Then she was pulling back his hair, pulling his head back and his mouth was opening, gaping wide, and he was trying to stop it but he couldn't move, his muscles were frozen in a terror of anticipation at what was to come.

She brought the missing half of his heart to his lips, and tipped it into his mouth.

He tried to clamp his teeth shut, but he was too late. He felt it sliding down his throat, slimy and warm and beautiful.

He screamed and yanked himself away from her. She let him go.

He fell to the floor choking and writhing. He tried to be sick, tried to force it back up. But it was done. He could feel it inside him. It was not dead. He felt it latch itself onto the other half of his heart, the half that had carried his pain and his anger for so long.

He froze.

He waited for it to come: the pain, the awful tearing pain of loss that had never left him, but which he had managed to dull and hem in and turn into something blunted and manageable.

But the pain never came. Instead, something else began.

It started as a stillness, a sense of calm. It swept through him, washing everything else away, the anger and the pain, and the awful leaden emptiness which he had carried around with him for so long he had almost forgotten there could be any other way of living.

Then the calmness blossomed. There was no other way of describing it. It unfolded within him, multiplying and enhancing itself, touching every corner of him; and the borders of this feeling began to ripen and shade deeper and deeper until they became something else.

Love.

It was love.

Every ounce of love he had ever known, every element of it, the full glory of all the love he had ever felt, for his wife, for his child, for the people he had lived with, and for the world he was a part of. It all came pouring back into him. It had been gone for so long. It was like walking into a room you knew as a child but haven't set foot in for a hundred years; and yet, when you return to it, the smell hits you at once, familiar and wonderful, as if you had never left. It quenched everything else, smothering the pain and the anger and the fear, blowing it all away, dispelling it to nothing.

And then, just when he felt that he could take no more, that a single atom more would burst him apart, it began to recede. It fell away - not being lost, but regaining a balance, moving back into the position it should occupy, like an ocean that had been tipped suddenly into a a great empty hollow that had not known water for an age of the world, and which had to surge and foam furiously before it was able, at last, to gentle and wane until it stilled to a natural calm.

Amos gasped. And then the memories came back, the realisation of all the things he had done, harm and hurt and murder, the things he had thought he had done out of love, but which he realised now had been done out of pain, and out of hate. He was still for a long time.

At last, he lifted his head. His eyes were wet with tears.

He stared at the woman, and she stared back at him, and there was understanding between them.

"I am sorry," he told her.

She nodded.

"So am I," she said.

He shook his head.

"We...we did this to each other," he said. His voice was low. "Didn't we? We made this happen. Both of us. All of us."

Her mouth twitched in a sad smile.

"The stories we tell," she said. "They are all we have. They are our lives. And we can decide the way we tell them. That is all that really matters. We can choose."

Her eyes left his, and moved to the wheel that stood behind him.

"Why don't you choose a new story for us?" she said.

Amos turned and looked at the wheel.

Slowly, he reached out a hand, and pinned the sword further into the wheel, until it stuck all the way to the hilt again.

Then he looked back at her.

"Will you help me tell it?" he asked her.

She nodded and moved forward. They stood opposite one another, on either side of the wheel. They put their hands on the smooth surface.

"Now?" he asked, and she nodded.

They pushed the wheel.

At first, it did not move.

Then slowly, so slowly, it began to turn.

Something flickered in the darkness. A noise began to be heard, distant and proud.

The wheel moved faster.

Lights sprang up, faint at first, then growing brighter and brighter, until all at once they burst in a ring of colour all around them, in an arc around the wheel, blurred and confused. The noise came clearer. They could not say what it was. At one moment it sounded like horns, the next it was bells, the next it was voices, beautiful voices singing in triumph and harmony. It was glorious.

Then the lights began to coalesce into images, thousands upon thousands of images. They whirred and spun around the central wheel, the endless stories of the Storystream called back from darkness on the very edge of Unmaking. Suddenly, the black stone floor was returned, shooting out of the emptiness that had been at their very feet; then there was a roof above them, and a wall around them, and placed in the wall was the oaken door, as solid and whole as it had ever been. But the door was open, and beyond the door could be glimpsed the world outside. It was coming back into being, earth dancing up out of the abyss, stars lighting up in the sky, trees and mountains falling out of the air and planting themselves in the earth. The sound was louder than ever, so loud that nothing else could be heard; but no-one would want to hear anything else, either, for the sound was the music of creation, of life and existence forming again out of the chaos, beautiful and filthy and wonderful all at once.

Amos and the woman stopped pushing. They locked eyes. They were nearly there, the wheel was almost back where it had been when Amos had first fought his way into the room.

But that was not where it should be. Amos knew they were both thinking it. They didn't need to speak the words; they both understood it was true. The wheel had been turned a quarter circle before Amos had ever come here, and the world had been strange - or rather, stranger - since then. Time had always been dubious and tricksy, but it had been more unreliable than ever since the wheel had been shifted by that quarter-circle.

Slowly, Amos nodded. The woman ducked her head in agreement.

He took a deep breath.

Then he heaved with all his might. On the other side of the wheel, he was aware of the woman doing the same.

The wheel shifted again, creaked and groaned; from everywhere and nowhere, the strange music roared louder.

With a cry, Amos gave one last push.

The wheel shifted again, and the brilliance of the Storystream was abruptly redoubled. Then, with a crack like the sound of mountains dropping into vast caverns deep beneath the earth, the wheel settled and was still.

The music ceased. There was silence.

Around them, the Storystream flowed gently onwards in its never-ending journey. Amos released the wheel.

The woman opposite him did the same. Her mouth was still, but her eyes sparkled and there was joy in her face.

"It is done," Amos said.

"It is done," the woman agreed. "Or rather, it is undone. The Storystream lives. I think we have...healed something."

They were silent.

"What...what happens now?" asked Amos at last. He found that he was crying, though he could not say why.

But the woman smiled at him, kindly, and she lifted a hand to his cheek, and she brushed away his tears.

"Now?" she said. "Now it is time for an ending. I think you deserve one, at last, don't you? And a happy one, if that is possible."

Then a voice came from the darkness to one side, below the Storystream, and it was deep and strong and kind.

"We all deserve one of those," said the voice. "But I'm not sure I believe in endings, not really. You cannot rely on endings, no more in life than you can in wheels."

Amos peered into the darkness, and realised suddenly who was speaking.

It was the old oaken door. It had closed itself in all the excitement. Now the room at the centre of things was shut off again from the world outside, and this was exactly as it should be.

"All you can really believe in," the door continued, "is that something will happen next." It paused. "But I don't see why that shouldn't be happy," it added. "At least, for a time."

Then Amos looked at the woman - she was called Sebille, he remembered suddenly - and he smiled and she smiled back. Then he held out his hands, and she took them, and they closed their eyes.

"I will tell you a story," came the voice of the door, "and it happened - and does happen, and will happen - far off and away and further far again. It is called

EPILOGUE

~

The large, benign-looking being pulled the crystal looking glasses away from his eyes and smiled. The Storystream surged around him, vast and distant and tiny, and perfectly clear all at the same time. That was one of the advantages of living - or at least, *existing* - in a place like this. Things didn't have to obey the usual laws, which, he mused, only ended up getting in the way most of the time. He had enjoyed watching the man and the woman turn the wheel and get things going again. He'd had no doubt that things would work out in the end - after all, the Pheasant had strongly hinted as much last time they'd met - but it was always nice to see exactly how.

Slowly, Quiddang put the glasses back to his eyes, and swept his gaze at random across the Storystream.

There was Prince Valiben, riding on a milk-white steed. The horse wasn't moving very fast, because it was having to pull a strange contraption along after it: a sort of trailer, with a large metal chamber on top. As he watched, the trailer went over a bump, and a splash of water came shooting up, and he caught a flash of blue as the occupant of the tank jumped out of the water to talk with his friend. They were both very excited. They were due to arrive at Valiben's home soon; they had received word from Valiben's brother, Prince Myst, that the whole kingdom was ready to receive them with a great feast, which had taken longer than usual to organise on account of the unexplained absence of Wom Ya, the court sorceress. Not that Myst was complaining: the kingdom seemed to be a much happier place since the old woman had vanished. Valiben said something, and Max laughed; and Quiddang smiled to himself and shifted the eyeglass.

There was Tobias and Sebille. They were standing in a forest glade in the sun. The warm light was glinting on their bright clothes, and their faces seemed to glow. Beside them, Sebastian looked healthy and happy as he lifted their arms and linked their hands, and then they were kissing and the air was full of confetti and cheers. Quiddang cheered too, softly, and moved his glasses.

Now he caught a glimpse of a black wagon, flashing through space. On the roof of the wagon, the pig sweated in his harness and said something snide to the cat, who gritted his teeth and rolled his eyes. He was probably disappointed, thought Quiddang. He never got to have a proper nap, after all. He shifted the glasses.

There was the Mesomorph, bending down to kiss the impossibly ugly bandit woman. To him, she was the most beautiful lady in the world.

Shift.

There was Philip, his body teeming with happy, healthy stories, his borders less tight and full of fear than once he had made them. As Quiddang watched, a Muncher poked its head out of one of the god's nostrils, chewed something thoughtfully, then dashed back in to find something else to eat.

Shift.

There was the Monk, walking away in friendly conversation with his apprentice. It looked like they had found another pie.

Shift.

There was Rosewater, happily going about his duty, shovelling the last of a consignment of manure into a wagon, ready to be shipped off to wherever new stories were needed.

Shift.

There was Indigo Shuttlecock, looking out over her calm, protected Fold. Quiddang gave a frown. Even when things were settled, that woman was someone who could never relax. Never quite trust the Storystream. He shrugged. Sooner or later trouble would come to her on that account. He had no doubt of that.

Shift.

Against the background of an eternal, engulfing fire, the huge carriage rolled on into the dying world. There was a story or two there that would one day be worth looking into.

Shift.

Shift.

Shift.

Quiddang paused.

He was looking at a room full of children. They were gathered round a woman, old and shrunken with age. Her eyes were rheumy and filled with water; but they sparkled as she spoke, darting from one young face to another, never missing a beat, never failing to enthral.

She was telling them about how the greatest reunion of lost friends had happened, in that very village, in that very hut, in that very *room*.

Quiddang frowned.

She unfolded the story in front of them, telling them of a girl who was cursed with perfect understanding and a young man who had lost his kingdom, and of the things he would have to do to find it again.

Then a bell rang, and Old Nan paused. One of the children got up, and began to run for the door.

Quiddang's frown deepened.

Old Nan protested for a moment; but when it became clear the girl was set on running off whatever she said, she raised her hands in the air and sighed. Then she got back to her story.

Quiddang left the old woman, and followed the girl. She moved to the door and struggled to force it open.

Outside, the sun was shining brightly, and the crops in the field grew tall and fine. Men and women smiled at the girl, but she ignored them. There was only one person she wanted to see, and he had just returned from the hunt.

Her father strode into view, tall and straight and smiling.

He put out his arms, and Heather leapt into them, and Amos planted a kiss on her brow.

Then they walked away, chattering happily to one another.

Quiddang lowered the crystal glasses from his eyes. For a moment, he looked troubled, sad.

Then he smiled. After all, it was only a story.

The End

AFTERWORD

If you've enjoyed this novel, why not try exploring another corner of the Storystream? I've included a taster short story, an extract from *Tales From The Storystream*. It features a character who popped up in this novel: Quince, purveyor of fine lives used and new. There are four stories about Quince in *Tales*, as well as fifteen other shorts. Some are fantasy, some are humorous; a few are dark and have sharp teeth.

~

Many thanks for reading this novel! If you've enjoyed it, I would massively appreciate you taking a few seconds to write a quick review at amazon. Reviews help people find books; without them, this book will sink, never to be seen again. Please, if you think it's worth reading - throw it a rope to keep it afloat...

Read on for a free extract of my next book...

WANT TO READ MY BOOKS EARLY, AND FOR FREE?

If so, join my ARC team! I'm always on the lookout for keen readers who are interested in my stuff, to get early copies of my work and let me know if they think there are any mistakes, and also to leave honest reviews.

I give readers in my ARC team free access to all my novels. The catch is, I do expect people on the team to leave ***HONEST*** reviews for my books on amazon.

If you want to join, just email me with a link to a review you've written of any of my books on amazon (including *All Quiet In The Western Fold*, which of course you can get for free) and ask to be added to the list.

EXTRACT - THE BIG DEAL

He started by telling them how they would die. Sometimes, he thought that selling deaths was all his job really was.

It was always good to start with the death. That's what the customer was invariably looking for. That's what really *sold* them.

Having described how his client would die, Quince would then go on in a rather matter-of-fact way to explain other notable features of the life he was hawking: childhood joys and traumas (as well as any exceptional neurosis that would result from them), love affairs, major accidents, famous things they would achieve, and so on. He would then finish off by displaying a rather nice rendering depicting a trans-temporal image of the body to be inhabited, tilting in holographic increments through infancy, childhood, adolescence, and so on until after ninety degrees to old age and death.

He would then look at them levelly and ask them: *so?*

Quince had never lost a client yet.

~

He had never lost a client. They always said yes. Not a single time in the whole of his existence – although he existed in a place where there was, technically, no time – not one single time had he even had to offer up a second life for perusal. The Poor Souls always snapped up what he had to give them.

～

Quince used to wonder if these Poor Souls were the only type. Certainly they were the only ones he ever came across. They were so empty and pitiful, these Poor Souls, these clients of his, so light. Of course, there was no sight here, just like there was no smell, taste, sound, warmth, cold, or anything else at all, not even any time. And yet, were he asked to describe the Poor Souls, Quince would not have been at a loss for so much as a moment. They were symmetrical without having a shape. They were luminescent without having form or light. They were humble without having a self to humble. But, above all, they floated. Above all, they were light.

It came to him one day, as a revelation, that they were Poor Souls not because they were to be pitied, but rather because they were not rich. The Rich Souls – if they actually existed - never came to him. His job was to provide the Poor Souls with a means of gaining weight – he assigned them a life in which they might be forged into something with shape and purpose. Existence here was not a life-affirming experi-ence. Only *life* was one of those.

～

This was a typical example of Quince's work:

"Hello," he would say, his awareness lightly skimming the life he was about to offer to his newest client.

"Hello," would come the reply, a faint tepid breath.

"Well, how can I help you today?"

"Existence, please,"

"Oh, existence is it? Jolly good, jolly good! Well, we have this rather splendid life just in, let me see, I put it down here a moment ago...Ah yes! Now, what have we here..."

He would then go through the motions, acting as if he were perusing the life for the first time.

"Yes, this one's a real winner," he might exclaim, "Real first class death. That's what you should look for in a life, you know, a real top-of-the-range death."

"Really?" the Poor Soul would whisper.

"Oh, absolutely, no question!" Quince would reply with feeling, "Very character forming event in your average life, death. Very important."

Here he would lean forward – even though there was no space here, he would lean forward – and try and intimate himself with the (usually slightly bewildered) Poor Soul.

"You know, between you and me," he would say conspiratorially, "Between you and me, there are some Souls that choose quite ridiculously mundane lives, purely on account of the fantastical deaths which they know wait for them at the end."

"How fascinating," the Poor Soul would reply, obviously impressed.

"Oh yes! Take this life, for instance. Well, it ends when, in the midst of bitter recriminations, your divorced partner decides they can control their grief no longer and plunges you both into the blades of an automated farming contraption! Just imagine that, will you?"

"I can't" The Poor Soul would sadly reply.

"Well, of course you can't!" Quince would be enjoying himself by now, "Not now you can't – but if you take this life, then you'll be able to..."

The Poor Soul would be all too eager to jump for the life at this point, but Quince liked to play things out a bit.

"And if that isn't enough, then how about this?" he would leaf quickly through the life and find something that seemed half-interesting, "You don't loose your virginity until you're forty – forty! – but when you do...well, look at this!"

He would lean closer and show the life to his client.

"What is this?" the curious Soul would ask, perhaps slightly alarmed.

"They are quite common in the time when you will live, I am given to understand."

"And this?"

"Horns, I believe."

"And also this?"

"It appears to be a very small species of fish. Although quite what it's doing *there* is anybody's guess."

"Ah."

"Although, of course, *you* don't have to guess. *You* could *find out!*"

The Poor Soul would be nuzzling towards him eagerly by now. A no-sale would be out of the question.

"And then there's the way you find out about your *real* parents, I mean *wow*..."

And on Quince would go, until he grew tired of his sport, and allowed his client to pass through the life he held out, unto what lay beyond.

∿

Quince liked his job, and was never lonely, despite the complete absence of any real company. In fact, this was one of the reasons he enjoyed it so much. Here he was the exception. Next to the Poor Souls he was a real standout, something special, something different. Here he was a Big Deal.

Occasionally he would wonder if it might not be nice to have a change; sometimes he even found himself pondering a life with an almost personal interest, wondering what it would be like to experience first-hand some of the things that seemed to go on in them. He had always held the opinion that life was almost certainly overrated, and probably something of a fad. But as non-time wore on, he began to wonder more and more whether he could perhaps be wrong. After all, he had never had any complaints...

∿

One day – or night, or at any rate, instant – a most curious thing happened. Quince was perusing a life he had picked at random from the apparently infinite mass of them which jostled forever just below him. He had observed the death first, as usual, and had been mildly amused to see it involved a religious element of frightfully complex, vaguely hopeful, and magnificently erroneous conceit. After this he had leafed through the layers, seeing nothing more of particular note, until he was stopped short by a component that inspired in him a most unusual feeling.

The component was nothing special in itself – a simple pair of shoes carrying a battered look and bearing a distinctive gold stripe down one side.

The feeling it brought about was the worrying thing.

It was a profoundly strong and inescapable feeling. A feeling of utmost weight and undeniable truth.

It was a feeling of simple, absolute recognition.

~

Quince was shaken to his core. This had never, ever happened before. Although, when viewing a life so that he could describe it to his client, he was somehow instinctively aware of all that went on in them, nothing had ever before seemed to him to contain any personal relevance. Usually, it was as if he had a vast and automatic encyclopaedia splayed open in the centre of his being, something that transmitted to him every nuance of meaning in the lives he held. This was different. This was an item he recognised without its essence having to be translated for him.

Those are shoes he thought. *You wear them when you go outside. They feel good at the front where the tips have been broken in, and sometimes the back scuffs your ankle and the skin chafes away and you bleed. You buy them at a discount price from a market because you think your friend would like the gold striped design, but then keep them for yourself because you find you like them, too.*

It was an unsettling feeling, for the most part.

For the most part, but not entirely.

~

He put the life to one side, and often retrieved it when the desire struck him. He leafed through it with a strange, almost guilty pleasure that had barbs and hurt him almost as much as it pleased him. He lingered over it, searching in vain (and also with trepidation) for something else he might find similarly familiar. But he found nothing. Or rather, the only other odd thing he found about the life was a strange *lack* of something. There were things in it that he could not understand, and this was most unusual and worrying. It was as if the internal encyclopaedia he kept was failing when it came to this life. Worse, it seemed that this fallacy was growing – for he would swear that, when he had first looked at the life, he had understood the death with which it would end. He remembered thinking it absurd and pointless, but also understanding something of why it was done.

Now he could not fathom it.

He pondered the death most of all.

∼

A Poor Soul came to him, as they always did.

Quince had been studying the life again, the troubling life with the familiar shoes, and had not been aware of the Poor Soul's approach.

He started, and then hurriedly pushed the life he had been perusing away into the distance.

"Hello, yes?" he asked, rather irked at having been disturbed.

"Hello," said the Poor Soul.

"Well, what can I do for you?"

"I'd like a life, please."

"Ah, very well," Quince reached out and grabbed a life at random. He held it out for the Poor Soul.

The Poor Soul looked a little uncertain.

"Um," it said.

"Yes?" asked Quince, acidly.

"Um, is it a good one?" the Poor Soul enquired meekly.

Quince was dumbstruck for a moment. This was not something that he was used to, a Poor Soul questioning the life that he offered it. But then, he thought, maybe he had neglected to give the life the spin he usually enjoyed presenting so much. Quickly, he glanced into the life, meaning to find a few succulent morsels there with which to tempt his client. But to his surprise, he found that much of the life had become quite opaque to him. He could see what happened in it, but he could understand very little.

"Oh, yes," said Quince, stalling, "Yes, quite a remarkable life, this one..."

"Well, what happens in it?" asked the Poor Soul, politely, but with what Quince considered something of an inappropriate firmness.

"Oh you know..." said Quince vaguely.

"I'm afraid I don't," replied the Poor Soul

"Well, you...die on a ship," said Quince at random.

"On a ship?" said the Soul.

"Yes, a ship. At sea. In a storm."

"Oh." The Soul seemed thoughtful for a moment, "Is that much fun?"

"What? Oh yes, tonnes of fun!" said Quince, somewhat annoyed by the Soul's cheek. He offered the life up to the Soul with what he hoped was an obvious finality.

But the soul did not take it.

After a moment, Quince shifted.

"Does there seem to be some kind of problem?" he asked coldly.

"Well the thing is..." said the Soul nervously.

"Yes?" prompted Quince.

"The thing is, I...don't think I'd like it."

"What!" exclaimed Quince, positively flabbergasted by now, "Well, I mean, what's not to like? I mean, it's the Sea! It's got it all! Power! Romance! The raw savagery of nature!"

"It doesn't really do it for me."

"*Doesn't really do it for you?*"

"What about that one, there?" said the Soul suddenly, indicating the life Quince had been looking at earlier when the Soul had arrived.

"What, this one?" asked Quince, guiltily.

"No, not that one. The other one. No, not that one either. The one you keep sort of pushing away."

"Ah, you mean this one," said Quince, reluctantly bringing out the life that contained the familiar shoes.

"Yes, that's the ticker. What happens in that one?"

"Oh, very boring life, this one," said Quince, a little too quickly, "Not much happens in this one at all. Bit of a *wasted* life, one might say. Bit of a non-event. No, you're much better going for one of these nice lives, over here."

"Hmm..." The soul sounded worryingly unconvinced.

"Well hurry up, hurry up, I haven't got all of eternity, you know!" said Quince, quite untruthfully.

"Actually, if it's all the same to you, I think I *will* go for that life."

"Well, as it turns out that life is..." Quince thought desperately, "That life is, uh, reserved."

"Reserved?"

"Yes, reserved. Here, take this one."

And he moved smartly forward and thrust the life he had been hawking into the soul. Both Soul and life promptly vanished in a puff of nothingness.

The really strange thing was, Quince could not say for the life of him why he had done it.

∾

After that, Quince was much more careful in the way in which he dealt with the Poor Souls. He made sure the familiar life he had found was always well hidden when his clients came to him. And he redoubled his salesmanship. The only problem was, he found he could hardly make any sense of the lives at all any more. They were growing ever more clouded to him, and he was reduced to spectacular bouts of lying when questioned on any aspect of them. Then again, he got rather good at this, and soon began to find it easier, he thought, to invent something from scratch than it was to undergo the restrictions placed on him by mere embellishment.

He pondered the irritating Poor Soul which had had the rare nerve to test his patience; but no more like it appeared, and gradually he began to forget about this strange occurrence.

426

Also, he was increasingly obsessed with the familiar life. He found that he could not go long without the desire to look at it growing quite sharp. But now when he looked into this life, there was virtually nothing in it at all that he could understand, although he became more and more convinced that he was recognising elements contained within. Almost everything in the life now seemed at once achingly familiar and nauseatingly arcane.

This life became both his torture and his salve; and his existence, which was technically infinite, collapsed inwards and wrapped itself in knots around the two of them, this familiar life and him.

And it was while he was in this strange state of mind that a most singular thing happened.

One of his clients came back.

It was unsatisfied.

~

He had been aware of the Poor Soul approaching, and had, as was his wont, hidden the familiar life carefully before it arrived.

"Hello, there," he began, as usual.

"Hello again," said the Poor Soul, with a strange infliction which Quince finally recognised as something between fear and determination.

"Er, have we met before?" he stammered, unnerved at the thought of a Poor Soul that was rich enough to carry emotion.

"Yes," replied the Soul, "I was here a while back. You gave me a life, I don't know if you remember?"

"Um, well, I give out rather a lot of those, you see," explained Quince apologetically, although, of course, he thought he knew exactly which life the Soul was talking about. Quince had never come across the same Poor Soul twice before. He had been given to understand that life was something of a one-way process, and wherever it exited, it was not meant to be here.

"Yes," The Soul continued, clearly uncomfortable but resolved to get through the encounter nonetheless, "I thought perhaps you might.

Um. It was a rather nice little European number? About so long? Ended with a death at sea."

"Ah, yes, I remember now," admitted Quince, deciding that this one was not going to be fobbed off, and might as well be tackled head-on, "How did you like it?"

"Well, the sea was nice," said the Soul quickly, obviously eager not to hurt Quince's feelings, "But, well, it wasn't exactly what I'd had in mind..."

"Really? You must have liked the death, at least?"

"Actually, I didn't get to that bit," the Soul confessed, somewhat sheepishly.

"Didn't get to it!" exclaimed Quince, thunderstruck, "Well then, however did you get here?"

"Oh, you know..." said the Soul vaguely.

"I'm afraid I don't"

"Well, it was simple, really," stammered the Soul, "I just, well, *decided* that it wasn't really my cup of tea. You know, it was very comfortable and all that but it just didn't feel, well, *me*."

"You just *decided* to come back?" said Quince, disbelievingly. He had never thought that this might be even remotely possible.

"Yes." Said the Soul, and then plunged on quickly before its courage could fail, "The thing is, you see, I kept finding myself thinking about that *other* life."

"Other life," interrupted Quince sharply.

"Yes, you know, that one you were looking at when I first came to see you."

"Don't know what your talking about," growled Quince through metaphysical teeth which were, metaphysically, gritted.

"Oh, surely you remember? You were looking at it quite closely when I arrived. Well, there was just something about that life which sort of *glowed* at me. I'm afraid I don't know how else to put it..." The Soul trailed off apologetically.

There was an extended silence.

Quince was just wondering how he might go about getting rid of the Soul when the little thing piped up suddenly.

"Oh, here it is," it exclaimed happily, "Yes, this is the one I'm talking about."

To Quince's horror, he suddenly found that the Soul had somehow managed to locate the life – the *familiar* life, *his* life! – and had drawing close.

"Excuse me! Excuse me!" he shouted wildly, and pulled the life back away from the Soul. "Sorry," he went on, sounding not a bit of it, "These things aren't to be touched by anyone but the Management. Company policy," he added belatedly.

"Oh, yes, of course," said the Soul quickly, "I quite understand. Only, I thought that well, if the Soul who reserved it hasn't turned up, well then, I might as well have it...?"

Quince took the life quickly, and hid it behind him. He decided abruptly that this had gone on long enough. Why should he, the special man, the Gatekeeper, the Big Deal, why should he be made to feel wretched by a mere Poor Soul? It was ridiculous! No, he must end this now.

"I quite understand your concern, Sir," he began with polite firmness, "But it's out of my hands, see? We operate a strict no-returns policy, I'm afraid. Myself, well, I'd love to let you have this life, but it's not up to me, is it? No, so if you'd like to go back to the life you left down there, then I'm sure you can bring up the matter with the appropriate authorities when you get to the Other Side..."

Quince trailed off.

He realised suddenly that the Soul had taken on a strange, almost glazed over appearance. It was not hearing what he was saying anymore. In fact, he was not even sure it was looking at him at all. It was almost as if it was looking *through* him...

Quince shifted a moment too late.

As has been said, there was no space here.

Nevertheless, there were different places that one could decide not to occupy space in, and the Soul had abruptly decided that it wanted not to occupy the same non-space as Quince.

The impact hurt quite a lot for something that had absolutely no mass.

As they fell together, Quince turned. He was aware of the life he had been hiding behind him. It was very near, and Quince had time to think that it seemed much larger and more real than it had ever seemed to him before.

Then they hit it.

For a moment they formed a frozen tableau. Quince, the familiar life, and the Poor Soul all merged together in the diaphanous, hallucinatory way of things caught in the interstitial spaces either side of reality.

Then they all vanished into an infinitely thin sliver of void which bubbled away silently into the ether.

~

There was warmth here and comfort, and Quince had a vague notion that he was not alone, that the Poor Soul was with him, and he held onto the awareness of this and an awareness of who he was for a little while before it leeched away from him like a dream on waking, and he became firmly and finally embroiled in the *now*, which was of course constantly changing, shrinking around him then emptying outwards, becoming cold and hostile, and lungs he had now, little lungs filling with cold fresh air, filling, screaming, pumping, he writhed on huge hands that held him gently, soothing him, and was moved to breast and Mother-Protection, a sanctuary which was his for an age until he grew bold and moved away on little legs growing ever stronger, taking him on his own wild adventures through early childhood, when, with shocking violence, he was taken away from those who loved him by an accident and placed in an orphanage, there to grow with blemishes and scars into adolescence, clever and suffused with talents but also wreathed in pain, and leaving here as soon as he could he leapt into life with abandon and passed through many strange and wonderful and terrible things until the fire cooled a little and love took him for the first time and carried him reeling against the harsher currents but with purpose until he begat and begat and begat a third and final time whence love was ripped from him once more, and he found solace in his middle years in his children until they too left, and he was once more alone but for a few friends who touched his surface as he touched theirs, in a vague, removed way, but which nevertheless helped and made some times joyous and others simply bearable, (and coming towards him suddenly were the shoes, the trainers, laced with gold, looking so strangely familiar that he suddenly wondered if there was perhaps a God or at any rate a god, something more than he had ever thought possible, so strong and strange was the feeling of recognition at the moment when he found them, but then they too receded into the past along with the rest of his spent life and were gone and the feeling of connection passed), but these friends gradually moved away, or passed away, or found others to whom their souls passed in favour of him, and he reached a point when his hair was silver when he realised his whole life was characterised by loneliness and loss, and so devoted his remaining years to pouring over old books which described strange rituals and heathen rites, in the hope that he might find some crack in reality into which he could fit a lever and thus prise for himself a piece of creation that he could form around his existence to make himself more attractive to others, and in so doing secure their love for always and ever, so that he might never be alone again; and finding such spells in obscure abundance, he indulged in them fanatically, and sometimes felt as if they were almost working, and sometimes felt as if there was something else within him, a half-remembered presence of *other*, and this gave him the hope he needed to pursue his endeavours with renewed vigour, until, finally he died whilst in the midst of one such ritual, old and desiccated, the unintended victim of an arcane rite of frightfully complex, vaguely hopeful, and magnificently erroneous conceit.

≈

He tumbled out of the other end of the life, into a bright white place. Picking himself up, he yawned, stretched, and looked around, wondering vaguely what he was supposed to do next. He could not remember quite why he was meant to be here. Then again, he could not quite remember who he was, or where *here* was in the first place, so he decided not to worry about it too much for the moment.

After a while, he realised he was not alone. A little way off, there was a line of other people. They seemed similarly bemused in a benign, un-worried sort of a way, so he decided to go and join them.

"Hello," he said genially to the person ahead of him, joining the back of the queue.

"Hello," said the person ahead of him, smiling a little.

"Excuse me, but do you know what we're queuing for?" he asked, at length.

The person ahead of him thought for a while. The line shuffled forward.

"Haven't the foggiest, I'm afraid," the person said at length.

The person ahead of him seemed faintly worried about this for a moment, but then he shrugged, "But I suppose it'll all become clear in a moment," they went on, brightening up.

He shrugged too. This seemed reasonable.

Eventually, he got near to the head of the queue.

There was a large benign looking being there, handing out tickets.

The person ahead of him was given a ticket, looked rather happy, and promptly vanished through a big white door into nothing.

Then it was his turn. He held his hand out for a ticket. The being leant forward as if to give him one, then checked himself.

The being looked him up and down carefully.

"'ang on a minute," the being said slowly, "What's goin' on 'ere then?"

"Sorry?" he replied, quite unsure what the problem was.

"Well, there's two of you in there, in't there!" exclaimed the being.

"What?" he replied, confused, "Is there?"

"Yes!"

"Oh, well, I'm terribly sorry. I don't want to be any trouble, you know." he really felt quite contrite.

"Most irregular, that, most irregular," said the being severely, looking rather troubled, "Gonna throw the whole system out of whack, that is, if I let you through."

"Oh, well I wouldn't want to be the cause of any problem," he said, "Would it be better if I just go back?"

"Ooo, you can't do that!" said the being, sounding scandalised, "Nah, it's a one-way thing, innit? No going back, mate, sorry."

"What should I do then?" he asked.

"You'll just 'ave to wait here, I suppose."

"Ah," he said, and moved aside to let the others in the queue past.

After a rather large amount of non-time he had an idea.

"Look, as long as I'm here, is there anything I can do to help?" he asked brightly.

The being considered this thought for a minute.

"Well, the thing is, see, I can't let you any further on, on account of there's somehow more 'n one of you in there," the being was speaking slowly, considering each word carefully.

He nodded sagely, as if he understood.

"And just out of interest, what is further on?" he asked politely.

"Why, Level Two, of course!" said the being, "What you've been training for, back there in Level One. Oh, it's a whole new ball game in there mate, believe me!"

He frowned for a moment. He hadn't considered there had been anything previous to this big white land, but now that he thought about it, he *did* seem to remember there being something before.... "Shoes," he thought to himself, "Shoes with a nice gold stripe. I wonder what shoes are?" For some reason, this thought bothered him a little. But he decided to let it go. After all, he had enough to worry about at the moment.

"But I can't go on to Level Two, though?" he asked, just to clear things up.

"No, mate, 'course you can't!" the being said, "It'd be an unfair advantage, wouldn't it? With two of you in there, and all!"

"Ah, I see. And I can't go back to Level One, either. So, is there anywhere else I could go where I could be of service?" he asked.

The being considered this.

"We-ell," it said, slowly, "I do hear they're rather understaffed back at the Beginning."

"The Beginning?"

"Yeah, you know, where it all starts? I hear it's a real shocker of a mess down there. It's a bit outside the rules, but if you fancy it, maybe you could go back there and help out. Tidy things up a bit, sort of thing?"

He thought about it for a moment. It seemed reasonable.

"Alright," he said, nodding, "If you think it would help."

"Oh, it'd help alright!" the being said, "No question there! It'd help everyone! You'd be lending a hand where it's wanted, and well, between you and me The Beginning's the best bit anyway! So probably good for you too, mate, actually."

"So we have a deal then?" he asked happily, holding out his hand.

The being considered for a moment, then shook warmly.

"Yes mate!" the being said, "We've got ourselves a big deal!"

The being snapped its large fingers. Abruptly, he felt the world begin to stream away backwards. Everything became faint.

But before it was lost entirely, the being called out to him.

"Now, remember there's no memory back at The Beginning!" it was saying, "On account of there being no time! Don't worry, in time it'll all make sense! Oh and here, take this back with you". The being hurled something at him. He caught it. "That's the life you rode in on, mate. Might as well find some use for it! I'm sure some Poor Soul will want it..."

And with that, the voice trailed away and was lost.

≈

Quince stood, surveying his domain with satisfaction. For a moment, he felt a little odd, as if something was slightly out of phase with how things should be. He frowned to himself. He felt slightly...full. As if he had more substance than he should have. For a moment, he almost fancied he heard a strange – yet strangely familiar –voice echoing in his head. He puzzled at the feeling for a moment, but could not quite grasp it, and so let it go. It faded away like a dream.

He looked down. Ah yes. He was holding a life in his hands. How did this one end, he wondered? For some reason, he felt as if this life was important, somehow. It was as if it were tugging on him. He wondered why that might be. What could any one life contain that would make it more attractive to him than any other life?

He was just about to skim through it in an attempt to find out, when he noticed a client had arrived. He smiled brightly. He did love his job.

Putting the life to one side amid an infinite pile of other lives, he turned to face the Poor Soul.

"So," he began cheerily, "What can I do for you?"

"Oh, I'd like a life please," breathed the Poor Soul.

"Would you, now?" grinned Quince, grabbing a life from the pile, "Well, this is a most agreeable life, it ends quite spectacularly..."

"The thing is," the Poor Soul interrupted him, "What was that life you were holding when I arrived...?"

The End

Read the other Quince short stories in *Tales From The Storystream*...

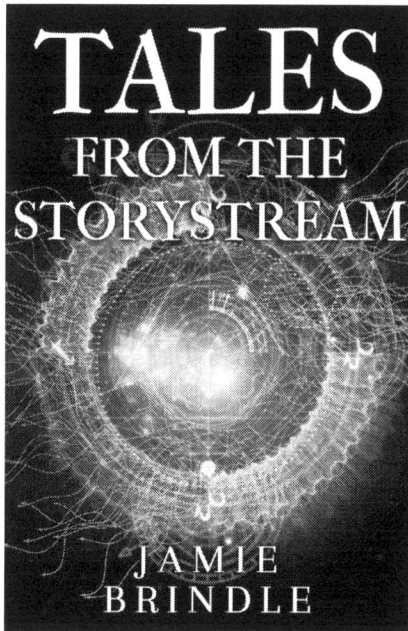

WHAT NEXT?

This novel is part of *The Storystream* series. It's an odd sort of series, in that bits of it have very different tones and even (apparent) genres.

The books do not have to be read in order, though I have arranged them in a list on the following page for your reference and convenience:

THE STORYSTREAM

Illustrated Work

A Treatise On Blood And Iron - Illustrated Version

ABOUT THE AUTHOR

Jamie Brindle has been writing stories for almost as long as he can remember.

He has done various jobs over the years, including boomerang salesman, tractor driver, hedge mazed attendant, and - most recently - doctor.

He writes because it would be intolerable to keep these things bottled up inside his head. Imagine the mess.

He lives with his beautiful badgery wife, and his young children.

For more info, go to
www.jamiebrindle.com
jamie@jamiebrindle.com

Printed in Great Britain
by Amazon